"HURT HIM!
HURT HIM!
HURT HIM!"

Bucky's head screamed at his body, and he charged, snarling and spitting, driving his head into the big man's breastbone, cursing him, tearing, punching, kicking.

Olsen stepped back in surprise, stumbled over the ax, but managed to grab Bucky in a bear hug before they both fell on the dock. "Kill! Kill! Kill!" Bucky screamed, and clamped his hands around the old man's neck. He could feel the slow chug of the dark arterial blood coming to a strangling stop. Bucky Foster was poised on the tip of ecstasy....

DENNIS J. HIGMAN

PRANKS

LEISURE BOOKS NEW YORK CITY

A LEISURE BOOK®

October 1993

Published by

Dorchester Publishing Co., Inc.
276 Fifth Avenue
New York, NY 10001

Printed in the United States of America.

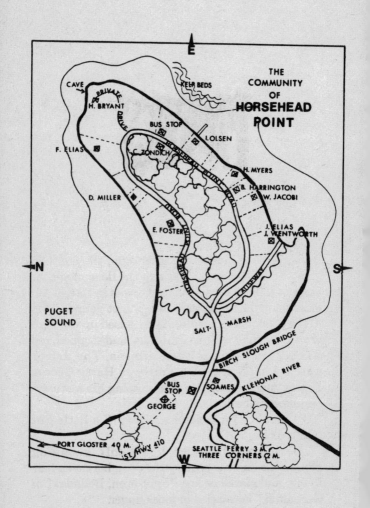

CHAPTER 1

By three that Halloween afternoon, the sun had
given up trying to get through the dense fog that
hung over Horsehead Point and was in retreat, an
indistinct white disc, high over Puget Sound.

The school bus, headlights on, eased up the high
gravel shoulder next to the bridge and stopped, red
flashers clicking in the stillness. The driver
watched in his rear-view mirror as Harry George
Junior lumbered up the aisle, zipping his motorcycle jacket as he came.

"Where's your costume, Harry?" a little girl
taunted him.

The Indian boy turned suddenly, swinging
around the chrome post by the door, his raven hair
flying, and glared at her. "I got it on, Belinda. I'm
Geronimo," he snarled in mock anger.

This performance was rewarded by a titter of

7

alarm from several little girls, including Belinda Myers, who was sitting directly behind the driver in her all-white Princess Leia costume.

"Get on or get off," the driver told Harry. He had no time for a smartass fifteen-year-old who was still in the seventh grade. In fact, the whole busload of kids, overflowing with Halloween excitement, was trying his patience.

Harry stuck out his jaw, gave his pals a jaunty thumbs up sign and vaulted the three steps onto the shoulder.

"What a weirdo," Belinda said as the driver checked his mirrors before pulling out. A blond boy was leaning out a window.

"See you at the secret cave," he shouted to Harry George.

"Foster, get your head in and shut the window," the driver barked.

Bucky Foster did as he was told but muttered something that could have been a "fuck you." The driver decided to ignore that possibility. He had only three months to retirement and couldn't live without a pension.

Instead, he wrapped his hands, seven fingers and three stubs from a logging accident, tightly around the steering wheel and drove the yellow-and-black bus carefully out onto the wooden one-lane bridge separating Horsehead Point from the mainland.

The fog was even thicker over the muddy salt marsh. Back when he had all his fingers, there had been no bridge and the Point was called Horsehead Island. After they had logged it to the ground it was nothing but a mess of blackberries and nettles. He could have bought the whole place for a nickel.

The heavy dual rear wheels clattered across the worn bridge planking and down onto the narrow asphalt lane that wound around the perimeter of the Point.

"That Bucky's a creep," the girl next to Belinda was saying. Her name was Carrie Miller, and she was dressed as Paddington Bear. Both girls were in the third grade.

Although he seldom talked to any of them beyond normal greetings, the driver knew all the children just from listening to their conversations twice a day, five days a week. They, in turn, called him Three-Fingered Jack, but never to his face.

"All boys are creeps," Belinda informed her friend.

"Bucky scares me," Carrie whispered.

"Well, he doesn't scare me," Belinda replied forcefully, a stern little princess. "He's nothing but a creepy bigmouth bully."

"Like Billy Jacobi?" Carrie tittered.

"Oh, I think Billy's re-ea-lly cute," Belinda announced loudly.

"Cuter than an icky old frog?" Carrie prodded. Then the little girls dissolved into hysterical laughter.

In the seat directly across the aisle, their classmate Billy Jacobi, his face hidden behind a Kermit the Frog mask, turned away in embarrassment.

The driver smiled to himself. Some were nice, some weren't. The kids hadn't changed much over the years, although very few used to live on the Point. Now he let off half a busload there every day. The place even had its own sign, a huge, carved cedar plank mounted by the side of the road just

9

down from the bridge. "Welcome to the Community of Horsehead Point," it read, "a planned residential development."

Very few residences were visible from the road. Clusters of mailboxes marked long driveways that cut down to waterfront homes. The interior of the Point was tightly packed with second-growth Douglas fir.

They called it a green belt. The bus driver called it a waste of good timber that should have been thinned out ten years ago. He sighed and listened to the tires hiss over the carpet of brown leaves covering the road. But what did he know?

If he'd bought the whole damn place for a nickel in the Thirties, he'd be a millionaire today instead of taking a lot of horseshit just to get a little pissant pension. It all made him feel old and stupid.

"I can hardly wait for the party," Belinda told Carrie Miller, bouncing up and down in her seat. The Millers' Halloween party was the talk of the bus. Everybody was going, as far as the driver could determine. It seemed like a bigger deal to the kids than Christmas.

"Come early," Carrie squealed.

"Can I come early too?" Bucky Foster asked, leaning over the seat.

"You can't come if you don't have a costume, and you don't have a costume on so too bad," Belinda snapped.

"I got a costume," Bucky told the little girl contemptuously. "Just wait till you see it." He pushed the blond hair out of his eyes and slumped back in the seat, a self-satisfied smile on his pimply face.

"Oh yeah, what kind of costume is it?" Belinda

10

challenged him.

Bucky Foster folded his tall, thin body until he was sitting comfortably on his spine, knees braced against the seat in front of him. "You'll see. It's going to be a big surprise," he replied smugly.

"Oh sure," the little girls chorused.

The driver took this all in as he squinted into the mist, occasionally glancing back in his rear-view mirror. Kids like Bucky Foster gave him a royal pain in the ass. In the old days you could just throw them off the bus. Now you handed out "warning tickets." What a comedown for a man who had set chokers on the world's biggest trees, he thought bitterly.

"And then again, we might not even come to your party at all," Bucky informed Carrie Miller in a superior tone. "Jeff and Harry and I, we got important things to do. Right, Jeff?" Bucky punched his seatmate Jeff Myers in the shoulder. Jeff was short, with red hair and freckles; he was also Belinda's older brother.

"Right," Jeff agreed.

"Things like what?" Belinda asked her big brother.

"Stuff," he replied vaguely. "Stuff you wouldn't understand, stuff at our secret cave, stuff we do on our motorcycles. We might even paint the bridge. Right, Buck?"

Bucky Foster nodded.

The driver braked lightly as the bus rounded the end of the Point. The land had been cleared here and was studded with maples and alders, their dying red and gold leaves hanging limp in the thick mist. He pulled the bus into the turnout and

11

stopped for the children to unload.

"You can't go anywhere, Jeffrey," Belinda reminded her brother officiously. "You're supposed to take care of me until Mom and Dad get home. Besides, you can't ride your motorcycle off the property, Daddy said."

Bucky Foster turned on her. "Hey, why don't you just kiss off, Belinda? Why don't you keep out of other people's business?"

"Because I don't have to, Mr. Bucky Foster," she said evenly, standing up to get off the bus.

"Come on, just shut up, Belinda," Jeff told his sister in a worried voice.

The driver swung around in his seat. Two thirteen-year-old boys ganging up on such a sweet little girl was too much for him. "Goodby, boys," he told them, barely restraining his anger. "It's time to get off. Now!"

Jeff hurriedly gathered up his coat and lunchbox. He was already on his way. "See you at the cave," he mumbled over his shoulder.

"Yeah, and don't be late, Jeffrey," Bucky reminded him.

The driver watched the children pour off the bus and cross the fog-shrouded road. He waved at old Clara Zondich, sitting in her front window, the green light burning behind her as always. She was guarding her lawn against any child who might be tempted to cross it on the way home.

He'd never met the lady personally, and Clara never waved back, just nodded politely. But she was there every morning and afternoon. They'd been saying hello like this for years now.

"Clara the Cow, Clara the Cow, can't catch me," some of the children cried over their shoulders as they ran off, but not one of them crossed the immaculate green lawn.

Clara Zondich was one of the oldtimers on the Point. There were only a few left: Hilda Bryant who owned the sheep farm across the road, Fred Elias and his wife Sonia over on the north side, and Ivan Olsen, a sour old Norwegian halibut fisherman. Everybody else was new. They came from all over the country—bankers, lawyers, corporate big shots. The names on the mailboxes were constantly changing.

It was the end of a long day, and the driver leaned on the wheel and let the bus idle while he rubbed his eyes. Out on the bay he could hear the foghorns braying. The damp air smelled of burning leaves.

He yawned and stretched. It was hard to believe that only forty years ago he'd been skidding virgin timber down into big log rafts up by the bridge. He sat up and checked his mirrors. He didn't want to ruin a perfect safety record by having an accident in the last few months on the job. Of course, that record wouldn't buy him a thing; it wouldn't add one dime to his pension.

He checked again, just to make sure. The road was deserted. He closed the doors with a hiss of compressed air and had started to pull out, just as the hand fell on his shoulder. He jammed on the brakes in surprise; the ten-ton bus lurched to a stop.

"What the hell are you doing?" he shouted at Bucky Foster.

"Waiting to get off, Mr. Bus Driver," the boy said

innocently.

"Son-of-a-goddamn bitch, you goddamn near gave me a heart attack. Why didn't you get off with the other kids?"

"You closed the door too soon, Mr. Bus Driver," Bucky pointed out.

"Well, get the hell off now," the driver told him, opening the doors.

"Goodby." Bucky Foster waved as he stepped down. "Have a happy Halloween."

Ashen faced, the driver turned out again. In thirty-two years of bus driving nobody had ever pulled a stunt like that on him before. Those little girls were a hundred percent right: Bucky Foster was a first-class creep.

CHAPTER 2

When Belinda Myers saw him in his costume, it would wipe that little good-girl, smartass smile off her face. Bucky Foster, stripped to his jockey shorts, began easing the black neoprene costume over his milk-white skin. The arms and legs had to be bunched carefully and rolled on like a diver's wet suit.

It was a genuine authorized Captain Terror uniform, authentic right down to the secret pockets where the Lone Hero kept the tricks of his trade. There were pockets for mini-napalm bombs, blinding acid pistols, medium-range nerve-gas grenades and, of course, the deadly Black Downfall poison syringes.

A chrome zipper ran from crotch to neck, a faint silver stripe graced each leg, and a yellow death's head insignia, guaranteed to glow in the dark, grinned on the right breast. Bucky pulled the zipper shut and took several experimental steps around his silent bedroom. The suit molded to each subtle movement, giving grace and form to his adolescent body.

His shoulders squared, his arms rippled, his crotch bulged. Bucky Foster struck a Captain Terror pose in the floor-to-ceiling mirror. He was awesome! He was fearsome! He was Captain Terror!

He spun around, dodged and feinted, his long blond hair whirling. They would tremble when he appeared, just as they did when the comic-book hero rose from his base beneath the ocean, riding his famous SeaBike through the fog. The shadowy champion of truth and justice, out to destroy all who dared oppose him!

From his desk he withdrew twelve pencil-size tubes of Everlast Red Spray Enamel—one for each secret pocket—and a razor-sharp fillet knife that went in the leg holster where Captain Terror kept his laser stiletto.

Gliding noiselessly across the wall-to-wall carpet to the closet, Bucky withdrew his gold-flecked motorcycle helmet. He placed it carefully, reverently, on his head, adjusted the chin strap, pulled down the silver-glazed one-way face shield and stalked into the hall. The bronze knight was ready for battle.

He would astound them at the Millers' party, and the first one he intended to astound was little Belinda Myers. He would hide. She would come in. He would appear out of nowhere, without warning, and his hand would move silently toward her. She would scream, and he would leap.

Surprise! Surprise!

But what was this? An infinitesimal movement at the end of the hall, invisible to ordinary human eyes? A noise? His mother was at the club. His stepfather was at the office.

His fine-tuned supersensitive ears heard something. Sensors flashed immediate action. Bucky dropped into a defensive crouch, whipping out his knife in one lightning-quick motion. He cocked the weapon behind his ear. He was fast, faster than anyone in the world. The silver blade gleamed. Nothing moved. He waited. They were always testing him to see if he were ready. They wouldn't try again for awhile.

He replaced the knife and then, keeping close to the wall and alert for additional ambushes, sprinted for the garage.

The 450cc Japanese scrambler gleamed under the naked lights, a chrome and gold-flecked charger, smelling faintly of gasoline and new rubber. Bucky climbed aboard, adjusted his helmet one last time and stomped down on the kick starter.

With a shattering roar, the unmuffled, high torque two-cycle engine exploded into life, belching blue exhaust. The machine shook violently as he twisted the throttle. It quivered and jumped under his hand. The fluorescent pink rpm indicator surged.

As the automatic door slowly wound back, the thick fog crept in, drifting under the yellow lights in tattered wisps. Crouching over the handlebars, Bucky gunned the engine, popped the clutch and stood the scrambler on its rear tire. The gold bike leaped forward with a screech of burning rubber.

Boy and machine hurtled down the wide cement drive in front of the Fosters' two-story colonial and out onto the main road, engine howling. He was off to the secret cave. The foggy world raced at him. Bucky hugged the SeaBike between his knees, feeling each throbbing revolution. He leaned hard into the corners, checking centrifugal drift with superhuman strength, his superior, radar-programed intelligence unit scanning the road ahead for hidden dangers.

Bucky Foster! Bucky Foster! Bucky Foster! he screamed inside his head, slamming through the gears. Watch out! Watch out! Watch out! Here he comes! Here he comes! *Here he comes!*

CHAPTER 3

The high-pitched scream of the motorcycle engine
sent old Clara Zondich hobbling for the telephone,
her mouth pulled into a wrinkled, tense grimace of
extreme disapproval. Really! This could not be allowed to continue. The little savages were already
running wild out in the fog. There was no telling
what malicious Halloween tricks they would think
of by tonight.

As she dialed the Sealth County sheriff's office,
Clara glanced fearfully at the front door, checking
to make sure each one of the three locks was engaged. Her elderly miniature poodle, Milly, whined
and whimpered at her feet.

"That's all right, darling, baddy boy go by-by,"
Clara assured the dog in baby talk as the motorcycle faded in the distance.

The phone rang and rang. The old lady tapped

19

her crooked arthritic fingers impatiently on the black plastic receiver. This was an emergency! Back when Horsehead Point was a nice neighborhood of retirees, the sheriff's office answered right away. Now everything had changed.

A doctor on television was explaining to the host of the *Northwest Afternoon Show* the various health benefits of consuming live chicken embryos. Clara had never heard of such a thing in all her born days. Of all the trash! She must write and tell them. She hadn't sent a letter to anybody all week. What was next—cannibalism?

Clara Zondich had many opinions she wanted to share, many important points to make, but there was nobody to listen.

Finally the county answered. It was about time! "This," she told the deputy sheriff, "is Mrs. Clara Zondich of Horsehead Point." She came down hard on the "Mrs."

"Yes, ma'am?"

She knew what he was thinking. But she was only doing her duty as a good citizen, nobody else seemed to care. "Just a few moments ago, Deputy," Clara recited formally as she consulted her orange spiral notebook, "at exactly, let's see, exactly three o'clock, a certain juvenile person was speeding down my road on a motorcycle. This person does not have a license."

It was all in the notebook; they had to accept it. She had a daily, written record of every infraction of the law, each violation of private property. In fact, just to make sure that not one piece of potential evidence of any conceivable wrong could possibly be missed, Clara kept an accurate account of everything she saw. And from her front window overlooking Horsehead Point Road, Clara Zondich saw a great deal.

"What's this person's name, Mrs. Zondich?" the deputy asked politely.

"Just a moment," she scolded him, "I am not done. In addition, this is the same juvenile person I reported on two previous occasions."

"Who we talkin' about here, Mrs. Zondich?" he said.

Such impatience. "The person is Bucky Foster."

"Bucky Foster, huh?"

"Yes," she told him icily. "It appears your discussions with his parents were not taken seriously. I must now insist you talk to them again."

She could hear his sigh of resignation on the line all the way from the county seat in Port Gloster. "Well, I'll be damned," he said. "Okay, Mrs. Zondich, I'll try to get out first thing in the morning. Thanks very much for letting us know."

In the morning? A quiver of fear gripped her. That wasn't good enough. Anything could happen by then. She was an old woman, a widow, without protection. "But I want you to come today. I—I insist." Her voice trembled.

Last Halloween she let an innocent-looking child in a clown costume come inside. He handed her a sack full of steaming excrement and ran. That would not happen again; the two new chain locks would insure that everybody stayed on the front porch where they belonged.

"I'm sorry, Mrs. Zondich, but it's Halloween and we're stretched pretty thin. I just can't make it this afternoon."

"But I've lived here for twenty-two years," she whined. "I am a property owner and a taxpayer. I am entitled to protection. *I am.*" There was nobody at home during the day to control the children, nobody. Even the mothers all worked.

"You certainly are, Mrs. Zondich, and I promise you I'll get right on it first thing in the morning. In the meantime, if you have any other problems, give us a call."

He wasn't going to help her! What would she do? Clara gripped the receiver so hard her hand shook. The parents seldom even apologized when she called. Most just listened and mumbled. A few became sullen and angry. They hated her because her house was paid for and she had money in the bank, and because she was old.

"But he may come back. He looked at me this afternoon when he got off the school bus. I don't like him." She babbled desperately, trying to keep the deputy talking.

"Who looked at you, Mrs. Zondich?"

"The Foster boy."

"Well, if he comes back, give us a call and I'll come right out. Okay?"

"Yes," she replied with resignation. She felt faint. She felt hot.

A hawk-faced woman was talking earnestly to the handsome doctor on television. The chicken-embryo treatment had not only increased her energy level but also trimmed three inches from her hips and thighs.

"Oh, Deputy, you won't tell them who complained, will you?" Clara asked.

"No, ma'am, we never tell them who complained," he assured her. "Goodby, Mrs. Zondich."

Clara hung up. Halloween was one of the few times she missed her late husband Walter. At least he could answer the door and distribute candy.

She sighed and hobbled back to the living room. And this year was even worse. The Millers, of all people, had sent her an invitation to a Halloween party.

Clara sat down heavily in her faded blue overstuffed chair. Milly hung close, trembling and shaking. Of course, it was a mistake. She hardly knew the Millers. My goodness, they'd just moved in. They were young and loud and had a dog.

Yet there it was on the end table, a pumpkin-shaped piece of orange construction paper. "You're invited to the first annual Horsehead Point Gala Halloween Party," it said in big green block letters printed in a childish hand.

Clara gave her dog a reassuring pat. The TV doctor had been interrupted by the local weatherman with a special bulletin. The high-pressure system protecting the Washington coast, he said, was now deteriorating rapidly.

Clara slumped in the chair and stared gloomily at the confusing weathermap with its mysterious whorls and arrows. A major disturbance was sweeping down out of the Gulf of Alaska, bringing high winds and heavy rains, the weatherman said, smiling confidently. Horsehead Point, jutting out into Puget Sound, was directly in its path.

"Big, big, storm, Milly, wind and rain," Clara explained, translating for the old dog. But Milly ignored her mistress. She was looking for fleas.

"Oh dear," Clara worried out loud to the empty

23

room. It was all too much for her. She fingered the orange invitation. There was no mistake. It was clearly addressed to "Mrs. Clara Zondich." Surely they didn't expect her to actually come. It was just not possible. Children would be there—horrible children like Bucky Foster and his friends.

Clara Zondich reread the amazing invitation. "P.S.," it noted on the bottom, "Costumes are optional for adults."

CHAPTER 4

Jeff Myers adjusted his skeleton costume in the mirror. It was the same one he had worn last year. The arms were too short and so were the legs.

"You're not supposed to leave me alone," his sister Belinda lectured him.

He tried to ignore her. It just wasn't much. The black suit was faded gray; the white bones were cracked and peeling. It would never stand up against Bucky Foster's mystery costume.

"Come on, Belinda, be nice," Jeff pleaded, putting on his red, white and blue star-burst crash helmet. It didn't help. It made the costume seem even smaller. He looked like a little boy dressed up for Halloween, which was not the effect Jeff Myers wanted at all.

"I am being nice. You're the one who's being nasty, stupid," Belinda sassed, little hands firmly on little hips.

It wasn't fair. He never told on her when she watched cartoons in the afternoon. "I won't be gone very long. I'll be right back. Don't be such a jerk."

"I'm not a jerk, but you're a big, big drip," she countered gaily, whirling around the polished hardwood floor of the Myers' living room, her Princess Leia costume flowing behind.

It was really a nothing costume, but it would have to do. "Don't tell Mom and Dad, Belinda," he ordered her, "or you'll get in a lot of trouble." He had to go. Bucky didn't like it when he was late.

"You're the one who's going to get in trouble," she replied. Her tinny voice grated on his ears like fingernails on a blackboard. ·

"Come on, Belinda," he protested, pleading with her, "please, just this once. I'll take you for a ride on the driveway when I get back."

She looked dubious; it wasn't much of a bargain. "Take me with you now," she suggested brightly.

"No," he said, "you can't come." She didn't understand what seventh graders did on Halloween. And he could never let her see what they had in the cave.

"Why not?"

"Because."

"I want to come," the little girl insisted stubbornly, blocking his way into the hall.

"No."

Tonight the whole family had to go to the Millers' dumb Halloween party. His dad would be home. He'd never get another chance to paint the bridge. "I'll be right back. Stay in the house, understand?"

26

He didn't want to make her cry. Heck, he really liked Belinda. Once it was even fun to play with her. They had their own secret camp up in the woods and ate lunch there in the summer. Belinda was smart. She made a good pioneer woman.

But things had changed. He was in the middle school now. And although still fond of his sister, he just couldn't play cowboys with her anymore. Bucky would think he was queer or something.

He was going whether she liked it or not. "Maybe some other time," he said, pushing her aside.

"Jeffrey," she called after him in a teary voice, "you're being a bad boy again."

Jeffrey didn't care. He slammed the front door behind him and got on his red minibike. He felt guilty about leaving her, but Belinda probably wouldn't tell. And even if she did, facing his father was a lot easier than being ridiculed by Bucky Foster.

CHAPTER 5

Bucky Foster swung off Horsehead Point Road with a noisy downshifting of gears and stormed out the narrow causeway leading to the beach. His black Captain Terror suit glistened in the fog as the gold scrambler snorted and lurched down the narrow road. Tall cattails rose out of the salt marsh on either side, standing like soldiers in the mist.

He rode in a semicrouch, absorbing each slamming impact, eyes on the far reach of the pale headlight, body tingling with the thrill of high speed. At the shoreline, the bike was going over seventy miles an hour as it launched itself, front wheel airborne, out onto the beach. Bucky flew with it clear to the water, downshifting and standing on the brakes before he could reign in and turn north toward the secret cave.

Racing along the wide swath of gray sand exposed by low tide, throttle wide open, the deafening roar of the chrome engine bounced off the clay bank that ran along the beach and echoed out onto the fog-covered bay.

Bucky sat back and let the wind try to rip him out of the saddle, his mind flashing ahead. First they would paint the bridge, that would be easy. Then on to more exciting things.

Jeff and Harry would be utterly astounded when he casually jumped Hilda Bryant's pasture fence. The blood drained from his face in anticipation. He was going to do it. Today was the day.

First one, then hundreds, of ducks feeding along the beach turned in alarm as the speeding gold motorcycle bore down on them. En masse they scattered, wings whirring, yellow legs pumping furiously through the shallows as they headed for the safety of deeper water.

Bucky Foster saw them through the blur of fog and dropped down flat on the seat. Digital readouts unreeled in his brain as he closed—500—400—300—

The ducks were flying now, just barely. The red-lined engine howled. A few tantalizing strays wobbled just over his head, fighting for altitude as the ragged line of ducks wheeled out to sea.

"Kill! Kill! Kill!" Bucky Foster screamed after them as he flashed by.

The shattering blast of the motorcycle going by on the beach rattled the windows in the Elias house. Fred closed the fireplace doors with a snap. "It's that Foster kid again," he called to his wife.

He couldn't see him in the fog but he knew the

sound only too well. And if there was one thing that irritated seventy-two-year-old Fred Elias, it was children riding motorcycles, particularly when they were on his beach in front of his house.

Still carrying the heavy metal poker he'd been using to stoke the alder fire, Fred rushed into the spacious kitchen of their rambling waterfront home. "He's not old enough to ride that machine," he told her. "He doesn't have a license."

His wife Sonia was baking bread. She kept her hands busy kneading the rich brown whole wheat dough and her eyes on the portable TV in front of her.

"Calm down, Fred. He's just a young boy having fun," she told him, watching *The World Turning.*

"That's not the point," he grumped. "Ed Foster doesn't give a hoot what kind of cain that boy raises just as long as it's on someone else's property."

She turned away from the set and smiled, a mirror of Fred in a woman's body, but without the heavy lines etched in her husband's face from thirty-two years on the railroad. In spite of her age, Sonia had clear, almost transluscent skin that glowed with health. They had aged well together.

"That's true," she agreed amiably, "but it's not worth getting excited about, honey. You remember how you and your brother Stan used to race that old Model T up and down the back roads in Montana? I recall you didn't have a license either."

Fred watched her work the dough, his clear blue eyes not blinking. "That was different; nobody had a license then."

"Well, maybe not so much different," she replied,

turning back to her soap opera. Sonia had a faint lisp that accentuated her soft modulation.

She was right, of course, as usual. It certainly wasn't worth having another heart attack over, that was for darn sure. One of those was about all Fred Elias figured he could stand.

"I think I'll talk to Jan about Bucky," he said, staring out the window into the dense fog.

"That's an excellent idea," Sonia agreed.

Their daughter Jan taught art at Three Corners Middle School and lived on the south end of Horsehead Point. She'd be at the Millers' Halloween party tonight. He'd bring it up then.

"Save me a piece of that bread when it's done," he told her, and padded back into the living room, where he had a broken cuckoo clock disassembled on the table.

The logs burned evenly in the wide granite fireplace, warming the entire room. There was nothing quite as cheerful as a fire on a cold, foggy autumn day. Fred Elias picked up his pipe and lit a kitchen match one-handed with his thumbnail. Applying flame to the blackened bowl, he sat down and examined the clockworks, looking for the broken piece.

He was rather proud of himself. He was learning to handle stress in nonstressful ways, just as the doctor had ordered. The heart attack had finally convinced him he couldn't remake the world to fit his own specifications.

Fred Elias drew slowly on the pipe, savoring the strong bite of the tobacco. It was his only remaining vice. He took his pills; he took his walk twice a day all the way around the Point. And he took his religion seriously; he always had.

That was the best he could do. The rest was up to the good Lord. He puffed and looked out the front window. The fog seemed to be getting thicker, but that might change. The barometer had been dropping steadily all afternoon, and Fred suspected there was a humdinger of a storm brewing out there he couldn't see just yet.

He stretched his lithe, angular frame, ran a hand through his thinning snow-white hair and went back to the clock. Something was wrong with it. All he had to do was find out what. There it was—big as a crow in a snow-covered cornfield. The clock had a broken triphammer. Fred Elias grinned with satisfaction.

He felt a lot better about everything now. A little noise shouldn't bother him that much. Let his daughter handle Bucky; she saw him at school every day. And she was young, with young ideas. That's what you needed to have to deal with kids like Bucky Foster.

CHAPTER 6

Harry George sat crosslegged in the entrance to the secret cave, looking at Dandy Candy, the Chick of the Month. Candy looked back between her long legs and obligingly spread the cheeks of her bare white ass.

The Indian boy burped loudly and took another swig from the quart beer bottle. His black leather jacket hung open; his eyes drooped. Actually Candy didn't do all that much for him.

Of course, he thought lazily, she was a big improvement over those silly girls on the school bus. At least she was a real woman. He dropped Candy and selected another *Cheap Thrills* magazine. The pages were damp and smelled of mildew from being stored in the cave.

He found a blonde in a hard hat, tool belt and nothing else. She didn't do it either. When Harry put beer on top of Valium, he just couldn't get it up, even though he had the biggest dick in Three Corners School.

"What the hell," he announced to a seagull gliding silently by in the fog, and let the magazine drop. Harry George Junior slumped forward, his raven hair falling over his face like a tent. He felt great. He liked it here. This was, after all, his beach.

For generations the Klehonia Indians had wandered this shore gathering clams, spearing salmon, building sweat lodges and generally going as they pleased. And as the last fullblooded Klehonias in the world, the Georges were carrying on as best they could.

Harry dozed and listened to the gentle wind stirring in the gnarled firs clinging precariously to the crest of Horsehead Point, two hundred feet above him. He heard the steady drip drip drip of water running down the almost vertical clay bank above the cave, a tiny slash at the base of this monumental prow of land pushing out into Puget Sound.

Somewhere in the fog, one seagull called to another with a piercing cry. Motorcycles were coming, somewhere down the beach. The loud one, Harry knew, belonged to Bucky Foster. The little one that sounded like a sewing machine was Jeff Myers'.

Harry George didn't move as they pulled up the beach and stopped in the tangle of driftwood below the cave. Now they saw his silver dirt bike.

"Harry's already here." Bucky sounded disappointed.

The Indian smiled to himself. He liked to beat

Bucky Foster every once in awhile just to remind himself that he was older and smarter.

"Wow. Hey. That's really a prime costume, Buck," Jeff Myers said enthusiastically.

Harry made a special point of not even opening his eyes. He didn't have a costume and wouldn't wear one if he had. Halloween was for kids.

They were climbing over the logs now, coming toward the cave entrance. "Man, that looks just like Captain Terror's uniform," Jeff said in amazement.

"That's because it *is* Captain Terror's uniform," Bucky Foster informed him smugly.

"It's really super, Buck."

Harry George snorted when he heard that. To him Captain Terror was nothing but an imaginary character who talked in silly balloons over his head with words Harry couldn't always read very well. He didn't like comic books, anyway. He liked real pictures, preferably of naked girls.

They were climbing up the rock seawall. "Did you see those goddamn ducks?" Bucky asked Jeff.

"No."

"Listen, I almost speared one going a hundred miles an hour. No shit, it was this close."

They spotted Harry sitting crosslegged in the cave entrance. He cracked one eyelid so he could see their feet.

"Hey, Harry, wake up, man. We're ready to go." Bucky yelled at him as if he were deaf.

Harry George Junior arranged his poker Indian face and slowly raised his head, feeling the long hair fall away. He opened his eyes. "Speak, white devil," he intoned.

Jeff Myers laughed nervously, glancing at the half bottle of beer. "Come on, Harry, we're gonna paint the Birch Slough Bridge."

"With this," Bucky Foster cut in, brandishing a can of Everlast Red Spray Enamel, "Captain Terror's Red Death."

"Yeah, we got to hurry. I gotta be home before my folks get there," Jeff added quickly.

"And after the bridge, we hit some moving targets," Bucky informed them both, pacing up and down, his hands behind his back. "Big, fat, slow white targets—namely Rich Bitch Bryant's sheep."

"What do you mean?" Jeff asked, alarmed.

"We'll brand them with Red Death," Bucky replied gleefully, still pacing. "Round 'em up like cowboys." He stopped and swung an invisible lariat over his head.

This conversation was moving too fast for Harry George. He didn't want to go anywhere. He didn't want to paint anything. Harry wanted to sit in front of the cave and get stoned and listen to the boat whistles. "You guys want a drink?" He extended the amber bottle.

"Ah, no thanks," Jeff stammered.

Harry George shrugged. "Okay, short horns," he said, "suit yourself." He watched Jeff blush. He was such a pussy sometimes. Once Jeff Myers had cried just because Harry was smashing little crabs with a rock. That only made him mad, so he smashed another hundred before he quit. By that time Jeff was ready to throw up.

Harry swung the bottle over to Bucky Foster, but Bucky ignored the offer and went right on talking as if he were giving everybody orders. "Tonight we all go the Millers' party. Wait till old lady Miller sees me in this outfit—she'll just shit, literally shit."

Harry George Junior hadn't even been invited to the Millers' fancy party, and he knew why. He lived on the wrong side of the Birch Slough Bridge.

"On the way we'll trick or treat Clara the Cow. Old Zondich needs a good scare. Then we're gonna..."

"Hey, Buck." Harry George interrupted him loudly in midsentence. "How'd ya like to get into that?" He extended the centerfold showing Dandy Candy.

Bucky Foster glared at him and grabbed the magazine angrily. "That's no big deal," he said, pulling his upper lip into a sneer. "I've seen a lot better stuff than that."

"Oh yeah?" Harry challenged him. "Where?"

"Stuff from the war, stuff you've never seen, man," Bucky snapped at him, turning his back and gazing out into the fog.

"But I'm talking about cunt," Harry insisted, confused by the strange answer.

"Come on, you guys," Jeff insisted, his voice breaking into a whine, "let's go." He looked at his wrist watch. "It's after four o'clock already."

Harry George Junior shrugged his big shoulders and turned his attention to Jeff Myers. He knew just how to cool Jeff off. He rolled over and propped himself up on one elbow, a sly smile on his face. "Hey, Jeff, I got a good idea so you won't be late. We could all go over to your house right now and see if your sister wants to fuck around with my

39

heavy-duty cock."

Jeff went pale under his freckles. "That's not funny," he gasped, screwing up his face.

Harry George sighed heavily. "Oh, for Christ's sake," he said, staggering to his feet, "I was only kidding. Can't you guys take a joke?"

He surveyed the sorry mess he'd created. Bucky Foster was still pissed off about something, and Jeff was starting to whimper. Harry fished around for another Valium from the handful he'd stolen off his mother's nightstand after school.

"Okay, okay," he appealed to them. "You guys want to paint something? Let's go paint something. What da ya say, Buck?" Harry chased down another pill with a mouthful of beer. He didn't care what they did. He felt fine. He wanted everybody else to feel fine too.

Bucky Foster did a stiff, military about-face. Suddenly he looked very, very happy. "All right, all right!" he said enthusiastically, slapping an open hand on his neoprene suit with a loud pop. "That's more like it. I say we can sit around reading fuck books anytime. Halloween only comes once a year."

Even Jeff Myers perked up. Harry was ready to go along with anything that made his friends happy. They were both good guys. "Whatever," Harry George told them with a vague wave of the hand. "Let's get on it!"

CHAPTER 7

Bucky Foster led them onto the narrow bridge where the fog, heated by the exposed mud of Birch Slough below, thickened to the consistency of light misting rain. He crept commando style, hunched over, head down, and Jeff followed, doing his best to mimic his blond friend. Harry George Junior brought up the rear, standing upright, lumbering along, swinging his shoulders.

"We have exactly five minutes to do this job," Bucky whispered. "Not a second more."

Jeff nodded eagerly. Harry guffawed. He was too old for kid stuff. He was just along for the ride; he didn't have to play Army.

Bucky Foster handed out the paint tubes from his secret Captain Terror pockets and they began spraying. The hissing lacquer tickled Harry's nose. He sneezed.

41

"Quiet!" Bucky ordered.

Harry laughed. "Up yours, white man." He had intended to paint "Fuck You" across the planking, but with only the "F" and the "U" complete he'd run out of room.

He stood up and watched Jeff finish a lopsided red happy face. Bucky was flourishing his can of red lacquer with professional skill. "What the hell is it?" Harry asked him.

"It's your big dick," Bucky said with a knowing smile. "It's the Harry George Memorial Hot Dick, see?"

Harry saw now. He grinned stupidly. He was famous. "Now I'm gonna put your name on it," Bucky Foster told his Indian pal.

"Hey," Jeff Myers shouted, stopping in the middle of his second smiling face, "somebody's coming."

It was the unmistakable sound of a car engine coming from the mainland, and it was close. Harry George dropped his paint can. A faint cone of headlights popped out of the fog, reducing the mist to a curtain of watery slivers dancing in space.

"Run, run!" Jeff Myers shouted as he sprinted for their motorcycles, parked on the Horsehead Point end of the bridge. Harry stumbled after him. Bucky Foster didn't go anywhere. He painted on, ignoring the onrushing lights, attaching the first of two huge round red balls to the monument-sized penis.

Harry turned and saw the blue pickup coming up the bridge approach. It belonged to Ivan Olsen, a commercial fisherman who lived on the Point. Ivan was a rough old bastard.

42

Olsen saw the bridge and the boys at the same time and stomped on the brakes. The pint of rye on the seat beside him pitched onto the floor.

Olsen swore in Norwegian, fumbling for the bottle. Kids dressed like crazy people. Two of them were running, the other was still painting something. Ivan Olsen was in a bad mood. He'd driven clear to Port Gloster to get parts for the generator on his halibut schooner and when he got there, no damn parts.

He lurched down out of the cab, a big, red-faced, stooped man with bushy white eyebrows that swept upward in flared wings. The collar on his bulky pea jacket was pulled high under his chin, the black watch cap low over his ears.

"Hey, you boy, vat you doin'?" he challenged Bucky Foster, the crude Scandinavian accent blunting each word.

"I'm painting the bridge," Bucky told him, continuing to spray. "You know, it's Halloween, Mr. Olsen," he added respectfully.

Halloween? He didn't care if it was Christmas! Just another working day. Miller the banker had invited him to some party. New people. City big shots. Leeches. He had no use for them. He had thrown the invitation away.

This boy was in some kind of funny monkeyman suit. Ivan recognized him but couldn't put a name to the face. He didn't care for children anyway. Women produced them; women should take care of them.

"Git uff," he ordered him abruptly.

"Just as soon as I'm finished," Bucky replied, politeness hardening into what sounded to Olsen like defiance.

The old man glanced at the art for the first time and saw it was an enormous, stiff, red penis. Sex was something you did to women behind closed doors. This hippy queer was putting it on a public bridge.

"Go home, dirty boy!" he shouted.

Bucky looked up from his work, surprised. "But, Mr. Olsen," he objected, "I'm not quite done."

Olsen didn't argue, not with anybody. He told people what to do. "Gimme dat!"

In a rage, the old fisherman tore the paint tube out of Bucky's hand and threw it over the rail into the Birch Slough mud. "Dare, you wise-guy boy, now git home!"

Bucky hesitated, rubbing his hand where he'd been holding the can. Olsen advanced a step. "Go, shithead, or I kick you in dah ass," he threatened. The boy took a pace backward. Good; now he knew who was boss. Olsen laughed a series of huffing guttural barks.

The boy watched him with narrowing eyes. "See you later tonight, Mr. Olsen," he said evenly. "Make sure you have plenty of candy." Then he turned and began walking off the bridge.

The old fisherman's face went crimson with fury. The boy strutted like a girl in front of a band, wiggling his ass. Olsen spit a great glob of phlegm at his back. "I see yuh in hell, yuh asshole yuh," he called after him.

Olsen knew who it was now: the Foster kid, son of that fat asshole real estate man who was always sniffing around trying to buy his property. But

Olsen wasn't selling. He knew how much his big house on Horsehead Point was worth.

Mr. Fancy Real Estate Man with a big-wheel car. A goddamn college football player. Olsen snorted with contempt and lurched back into the truck cab.

Football players did not impress him; neither did college boys. At their age he was already making a good living all alone in the Bering Sea. Season after season, he was the top boat. The other fishermen tried to follow him when he left port to find out his secret, but they never got close. He rammed the truck in gear and roared across the bridge, sending the planks clattering.

All three boys were rushing to get their motorcycles out of the way. Olsen stepped on the gas. He knew that black hair—one of those worthless, thieving George kids, salmon stealers, welfare Indians. He leaned on the horn. "Go to hell, you boys," he bellowed through the open window as he went by.

"Jesus," Jeff gasped, "who was that?"

"Ivan Olsen," Harry said, his glazed eyes open wide.

Bucky Foster glared down the road after the truck, breathing heavily.

"What did he do, Buck?" Jeff asked him, pulling at his arm.

Bucky threw him off and spun around. "That fucker doesn't scare me," he told them. "He doesn't scare me at all."

Harry laughed a slow laugh. "Uh, uh, uh," he chuckled in slow motion.

"He doesn't," Bucky Foster insisted. He put on

45

his gold helmet and cinched the chin strap hard.

"Sure, you just left cause you ran out of paint."
Harry giggled, his words slurring over each other.

Bucky started his bike and revved the engine. "I
told him I'd see him later," he shouted over the
roar. "You guys can come with me trick or treating
over there tonight. Then we'll see who's a chicken."
He slammed down his silver-coated face shield.

"That's a fuckin' deal!" Harry shouted back.

"You gonna come too, Jeff?" Bucky yelled. The
reply was lost in the smoky bellowing engines.

Bucky Foster raised his arm. "Let's go brand
some sheep, guys!"

He took off in a spray of gravel, his gold scrambler fishtailing wildly across the road, and then
slowed to let Harry and Jeff catch up. Three
abreast, they jockeyed down Horsehead Point
Road in the heavy fog.

Bucky stayed on the inside lane, sitting straight
in the saddle, relaxed, just like Captain Terror did
it. He saw the fence line in his head, visualized the
exact point of takeoff, felt himself rising through
the air like a great bird. An avenging golden eagle,
he would swoop down out of the sky on the helpless
white sheep. Would they ever be surprised!

When he got to the turn by the bus stop, and the
mighty roar of his engine blanked out all other
sound, Bucky Foster was going to make his big
move.

CHAPTER 8

"Trick or treat," Jan Elias called, throwing the door open so hard it banged against the wall.

"I'm in here," he replied.

She propped the school art portfolio against the wall and unzipped her high sheepskin-lined boots. Anybody who knew Fred and Sonia Elias instantly recognized Jan as their daughter.

She pulled off the boots, first balancing on one foot and then on the other. Jan combined Fred's clear blue eyes and lithe physique with her mother's radiant skin and serenity. At twenty-eight, she was one of the most beautiful and vivacious women ever to teach at Three Corners Middle School.

Jan let her heavy green wool car coat fall on the floor and rushed into the living room where Jim Wentworth, her lover, fiance and remodeler, was sitting on the couch in his stocking feet. His curly brown beard was full of wood shavings and the house smelled of freshly cut pine. There was a smoldering fire in the Ben Franklin stove.

"I'm sorry, lady, we're all out of candy," he said.

She felt her face flush with excitement. "Darn," Jan said, leaning over to kiss him, "and I came straight home from school too. What else you got for the teacher?" she asked, pressing her lips to his neck, tasting the salty sweat and gritty sawdust.

"Oh, I guess we could cook something up."

She sat back. "First show me what you've been up to." The Elias-Wentworth house on Horsehead Point had been in a constant state of remodeling, inside and out, ever since the young couple had taken up residence three years ago.

"Exhibit one," he told her, motioning toward the kitchen cupboards.

She jumped up and went over to inspect them. They looked beautiful. Jim Wentworth was a craftsman. He did quality work, and he never hurried, which meant that he seldom finished anything on time.

He was also the sexiest man she had ever met. She opened a door, feeling the smooth texture of the bare wood. "Where's exhibit two? Where's my sink?" she called to him, still opening and closing cupboard doors.

"In the garage still in the crate."

"What have you been doing all day?"

"A volunteer fireman's work is never done. There was a cave-in down at Three Corners this morning, a sewer job. Nobody got hurt; we dug them out."

She pulled her sweater over her head. Jan Elias

48

had not rushed home from her classroom to inspect kitchen cupboards. It was just a little game they played.

He watched her come back across the room, ample breasts bouncing under the peach-colored bra. She sat down beside him on the couch. Like everything else in their lives, it was slightly dilapidated and only half recovered.

The plasterboard in the dining room was half done. Their old Cape Cod house, sitting back from the beach on a sandy treeless lot next to Birch Slough, was half shingled. Half the hardwood floor was down.

She didn't care. She could live with things half finished as long as Jim Wentworth did the half finishing. He reached back and undid her bra.

It had been a very basic decision in her life. Would she give up her independence and marry a nice dull boy who would take care of her, or go with her feelings, opt for independence, and take a man who not only loved her mind but her body as well? The decision was surprisingly easy, even though it went against everything she had been taught.

She pulled away, stood up and stepped out of the skirt, while he got out of his dusty jeans and peeled off his filthy T-shirt. Both naked, they settled back on the couch and began to stroke each other gently. Outside, the fog rolled up against the window, hiding them from the outside world.

Her father didn't know it yet, but there was a good possibility she would never marry Jim Wentworth. She kissed his hard nipple and ran her tongue over the dark hair on his chest.

It might always be this way. She had no definite

plans one way or the other. When he finally entered her, she was lost in a velvety heat that blanketed her body. Cupping her hands under his balls, she joined in his rolling thrusts that slowly brought her back, again and again, to the tingling pangs she wanted.

Jan listened to the foghorns on the bay. She tried to imagine what kind of whistles went with which kind of boat, and where they were, blindly feeling their way toward each other in the mist.

They seldom talked while they made love; they didn't need to. "That was marvelous," she murmured.

"Happy Halloween," he said.

According to her strict upbringing Jan was living in sin, and, of course, her father disapproved. She smiled. If Fred only knew Jim also occasionally smoked pot, that would be the end.

"What's so funny?" he asked her.

"Oh nothing. I was just thinking that while this activity is traditionally done at night, it's really much nicer in the afternoon."

"That's because only lazy, wicked people do it in the afternoon, while all the pilgrims are working their asses off."

"So that's your secret." Jan shivered.

"Cold?"

"A little."

As he rolled off she felt a trickle of cold semen run down the inside of her leg. He stretched, went to the closet and returned with two down jackets.

Without dressing, they slipped into the jackets and sat back on the couch. She was hungry. She hugged him, feeling the heat of the down against her bare skin.

"What's for dinner?" she asked. Jim Wentworth was not only a considerate lover, he was also a fair cook.

"Pizza at Three Corners. We've got to be at the Millers' Halloween party at 7:30."

"Oh damn, I forgot about the Millers."

"Well, the Millers haven't forgotten about us. Everybody's going to be there." He glanced at his watch. "If we want to eat, we'd better get going."

The Millers were new on the Point, and everybody had been surprised when the invitations showed up. Jan Elias thought it was a great idea. New people usually just moved in and waved as they went by to work. That was the beginning and end of most socializing.

Jim stood up; his limp penis peeked out from under his jacket. "I think I'll put on some pants, just for fun," he told her.

"Good idea."

He pulled on the jeans, not bothering with his underwear. "Shirt," he announced, and sprinted across the room and up the stairs, taking them two at a time.

She watched him go. He was a handsome man. Maybe she should just marry him and be done with it. Jan slipped into her panties.

"Incidentally," she called to him, "when you come down I want to show you something. I need your advice."

"Okay."

She went to the kitchen to get her art portfolio. When she got back he was sitting on the couch sporting a blue-and-gold cowboy shirt with red roses stitched over the pockets. She unzipped the leather folder and pulled out a pencil drawing.

"Here," she said. "Tell me what you think of this."

He examined the picture, holding it out in front of him as if he were a serious collector.

"The subject matter's a little weird," he said, suppressing a laugh, "but, on the other hand, it's a pretty good drawing. Very realistic."

It showed a huge, obscenely fat, naked woman, weighed down with chains and manacles, being strangled by a pair of oversize hands. The terror in the old woman's eyes was quite graphic.

"I don't think it's funny at all," she said quietly.

"Who's the artist?"

"Bernard Foster."

"Big Ed Foster's kid Bucky?"

She nodded and took the picture back. "Yes. Bernard has real talent. You know, for a long time he wouldn't draw anything. He'd just sit. So finally I said, 'Bernard, there must be something you want to draw.' "

"Oh yeah," Jim said, pulling on his boots, "I remember. He came up with a big hand giving everybody the finger." He laughed again.

"Jim, it's not funny," she repeated, beginning to get angry. How could a man be so sensitive one minute and so callous the next? She replaced the drawing and zipped the folio shut with a jerk.

"Honey, I'm sorry, but that kid reminds me of Mick Jagger with a hangover. I always thought what he needed was a swift kick in the ass."

Oh God, Jim could be infuriating. "Bernard is a sensitive boy. I just wish I knew how to steer him away from this ugliness, this obscene ugliness that comes out in what he draws."

"Come on," he suggested, "let's forget Bucky Foster. I'm hungry. You encouraged him to draw so he's drawing. Now you either have to tell him to knock it off, or he'll end up drawing porn and making a million dollars."

She pulled her boots on, feeling the smooth warmth of the sheepskin against her legs. How could she marry him? She couldn't even talk to him.

Outside, the fog was wet and cold on her face. In the distance she heard the annoying rattle of loud engines on the road. "What's that?" she asked, while he searched for the keys to his Bronco.

"Kids on motorcycles," he replied, finding the keys and unlocking the door on her side. "They came by about an hour ago. I imagine your little pornographer is one of them."

She hated the noise; it was so male, all smoke and flame and speed. The clatter became a throbbing roar. A cloud of crows burst out of the mist, came wheeling overhead and scattered, uttering their guttural cries as they went.

She climbed into the Bronco. "Damn it. I wish they'd slow down," she said. Jim put his arm around her. She could still smell the sticky aroma of sex clinging to his soft beard.

"Some of your kind, sensitive children having a little fun," he told her, kissing her gently. "Don't worry, they're just little boys getting warmed up for Halloween."

53

CHAPTER 9

With the ease of a great gold bird, Bucky Foster rose on the motorcycle, standing in the stirrups, leaning slightly forward, and soared across the pasture fence to a perfect touchdown in the tall wet grass. It was a feat worthy of Captain Terror, a stunt that couldn't fail to impress Jeff and Harry, and the start of a successful search-and-destroy mission.

Everything was in place for a perfect hammer-and-anvil sweep. His friends held the blocking anvil position at the end of the pasture. Bucky kicked the bike in a wide, searching arc through the grass. I am the hammer!

There they were. His headlight swept across the wooly, helpless little creatures all huddled together down by the trees. The search was over.

Trying to hide in the fog? Nobody could hide

from Captain Terror. Bad! Bad! Now to destroy! He revved the engine and headed straight for them. "Come here, little sheepy," Bucky crooned to himself. "Come to Daddy."

They waited, dumb and placid, chewing their cuds in the mist, ignoring him. Not for long. Now they were running, bolting in all directions, bounding desperately away. He spun around and overtook them from the side, herding them toward the corner. The stampeding animals streaked through the high grass, dodging and turning, but to no avail. He was everywhere.

When they finally decided to bunch up and run for it, he got behind them and closed the gap. "I'm coming right up your ass!" he screamed.

Jeff and Harry waited, spray cans poised. "Open up! Open up! Smash 'em!" Bucky whooped.

The sheep charged into the corner, stumbling over each other into a red cloud of hissing, blinding lacquer. Unable to stop, they piled into the triangle of fence, bleating and crying.

Some lowered their heads and tried to back out, but Bucky, shouting and racing back and forth in the fog, kept them hemmed in, butting the nervier ones with the front tire of his bike. Finally one broke and, in a frenzy, dashed by him, heading for open pasture.

"Let him go," Jeff shouted, but Bucky was already after the escapee. Nobody could cut and run on Bucky Foster.

With the Japanese scrambler in hot pursuit, the bleating animal charged blindly down the field, short legs pumping furiously, and slammed into the wire mesh fence at the opposite end. Bucky Foster hit the brakes too late.

The huge animal rebounded back into the skidding motorcycle, knocking Bucky off and sending the bike careening to one side, where it fell sputtering into the grass. The blow stunned him only momentarily. He was up in a supersonic flash, Captain Terror, ready to right wrongs. The goddamn stupid shitty beast had tried to kill him! It had ruined his beautiful bike!

He rushed to the fallen animal, driven by a towering rage. It was on its side, wheezing, eyes rolling, trying to get up.

No such luck, asshole. Bucky reared back and drove the point of his boot into the soft belly. Crying and raging, again and again he kicked into the quivering gut. It would not give.

The stupid animal was still alive, bleating faintly. He redoubled his effort, using the last of his superhuman strength. He would not be denied. Take that, you bitch, take that! He could feel the power rising in him, the body twitching and submissive.

Oh yes, it was coming. A numbing thrill raced through him, renewing his strength. But now somebody was trying to pull him back. He fought against them. He threw them off. "I'll teach you," he screamed.

"Come on, Buck, let's get out of here."

"No," he protested, crying now, "I'm gonna kill the fucker."

"You already did," Harry told him, grabbing him from behind.

Harry was too strong. Bucky went limp in his arms. "What's wrong with him?" he heard Jeff ask Harry Geroge.

Bucky panted for breath. "Nothing. Nothing. I'm all right."

The cool breeze caressed his face. He smiled easily at them. "It's going to be all right, really." Harry released his hold.

Jeff had pulled the scrambler upright. There were pieces of grass and mud plastered all over one side.

"Come on, man," Harry George urged him.

Bucky walked stiff legged over to the bike and mounted it, looked down at the fallen sheep and smiled a friendly smile. "See you in my dreams," he told the bleeding mound of stomped flesh.

Clara Zondich pressed the cold telephone receiver to her ear. She could hardly breathe. Beads of sweat glistened in the fine mustache on her upper lip. She couldn't see them, but she knew good and well who it was, although the motorcycle engines had stopped now.

"Hello," Hilda Bryant answered. She sounded angry, and harsh static clicked and screeched on the line.

"Oh, hello?" Clara, momentarily taken aback by the unfriendliness of the answer, pulled herself together. "Mrs. Bryant? This is Mrs. Clara Zondich." She put special emphasis on the "Mrs."

"Who?" the rich widow Bryant asked.

"Mrs. Zondich, right across the road? I just thought you'd like to know that Bucky Foster and some of his friends are riding motorcycles in your lower sheep pasture."

"I see."

"I've—I've had trouble with those boys before," Clara stammered, trying to find some common ground to prolong the conversation.

"Thank you for calling," her aloof neighbor interrupted. "The girl should be down there soon. She can chase them out."

Clara was considering asking Hilda Bryant if she had received an invitation to the Millers' Halloween party too. Was she as surprised as Clara had been? Why were the Millers doing this?

Clara Zondich was arranging these questions in the proper order when Hilda Bryant abruptly hung up.

CHAPTER 10

By 5:15 that afternoon, the Millers were ready for the First Annual Horsehead Point Gala Halloween Party. The lower level of their new cedar-and-brick home, just across the green belt from Hilda Bryant's sheep pasture, had been transformed into a fully equipped haunted house.

There were paper skeletons dangling from the rafters, rubber cobwebs in the doorways, electric pumpkins on the window sills, a big plastic bowl of pure apple juice, several pyramids of homemade oatmeal cookies containing no sugar or preservatives, and a small dance floor with a few modest strobe lights so the older children could boogie to *Saturday Night Fever.*

Dave and Kathy Miller were anxious to have their first social function on Horsehead Point go off smoothly. Dave, the youngest senior vice president in Seattle City Bank history, left work early to personally supervise installation of the "witches' kitchen," a large box with holes in the top just big enough to admit a child's hand and arm.

In order to gain admittance to the party, youngsters would have to reach into "the kitchen" and feel the contents—which, Dave had to admit, were pretty darn realistic. The peeled grapes felt just like eyeballs, and the cold clammy spaghetti was a dead ringer for sheep guts.

Dave Miller surveyed the setup one last time. Everything was in place. He emptied one bag of shiny red Washington Delicious apples into a tub of water, stashed another bag behind the door, and headed upstairs.

In the sunken living room that looked north up Puget Sound, everything was dusted and polished. Kathy Miller was one of the few nonworking wives on the Point, and certainly the most organized.

This was simply another day for her. Already she was second vice president of the Three Corners PTO and assistant chairman of the Sealth County United Way Drive. And only four months ago the Millers had been living in Pacific Palisades, where Dave had been with the Bank of California. He was definitely a young jet on a fast track, and Kathy was right behind him.

There were piles of coasters on the bar, cocktail napkins at strategic places, polished silver ashtrays, and a catered layout, covering three tables, of hors d'oeuvres from the Port Gloster Golf and Tennis Club.

"It looks just great," Dave told his wife.

"Thank you, sir."

The kids were getting washed up. A nice quick spaghetti dinner simmered on the stove. Dave Miller felt even younger than his thirty years.

"And you look pretty great, too," he said enthusiastically. Short and bouncy and full of fun, Kathy Miller was as old as Dave but looked fourteen. They had actually laughed at her when she went in to get her Washington State driver's license.

"You're not old enough to drive here, young lady," the grizzled old patrolman had said.

"Oh yes I am," Kathy had insisted goodnaturedly, and proceeded to show the astounded officer pictures of her three children—Rocky, eleven, Carrie, ten, and Cathy, eight.

It was a great story, only one of many the Millers liked to tell their California friends about their new home in Washington State. And the weather had been wonderful until a few days ago, when the fog closed in, but they didn't mind. They liked having big fires in one of their three fireplaces, and the friendly unaffected people of Horsehead Point more than made up for the bad climate. Once again they had found paradise on earth.

"My gosh," Dave said as they shared a small glass of wine before the children presented themselves. "The fog was so thick out there tonight the ferry had to darn near stop a couple of times."

Kathy was surprised. The boats that crossed Puget Sound twenty times a day, taking commuters like Dave back and forth, were very big and well equipped.

"Don't they have radar?" she inquired.

He assured her they did.

"Oh," she said, "I hate to bring this up, but there

63

seems to be a small leak in Carrie's room. It's in the ceiling; the plasterboard is getting all soggy."

"I'll take a look at it." Dave Miller wasn't worried. He'd get Ed Foster to take care of it. Ed had given them a mighty good deal on the house. It was almost a steal, in fact, at $93,000, and Dave expected to make out like a bandit.

A leak was nothing to worry about. Ed would fix it for them. Of course, Ed Foster wasn't just being nice. Nobody knew that better than Dave Miller.

"Speaking of Carrie," he went on, "is that cute little friend of hers coming tonight—what's her name?"

"Belinda Myers?"

"Yeah, that's her. She's such a spunky little gal, ready for anything. I like that in a kid."

"Oh yes, she'll be here, and about thirty other people." Kathy smiled at her husband.

The smile told him everything was under control. Not only was the party all arranged, but Kathy would have a firm grip on the names of all the guests as well. He knew very few of his neighbors because he was seldom home. When Dave wasn't working late he was traveling.

"Any trick or treaters?" he asked. It was the one area he hadn't covered, and Dave Miller was a guy who covered all the bases.

"Not a one, at least not yet. We'll probably get some later."

"Boy, what a great place," he told her earnestly. "You remember in California how all those people brought kids in cars from clear across town?"

"Oh yes, the charity patrol."

He laughed. "I don't think we'll have that

problem here."

In fact, a visiting reporter from *The New York Times* had called Sealth County in general, and Horsehead Point in particular, "probably the most liveable suburb on the West Coast, and perhaps in the United States. The crime rate is so low and the trees so high," the article concluded, "it's a wonder half the country doesn't move out to this ideal little corner of the world."

Dave had his secretary send that clipping to an old Harvard classmate of his at the Chemical Bank in New York. "Next time you get tired of garbage and mindless violence," he wrote, "come and see me about a good job out here."

CHAPTER 11

At exactly 5:30, Mary Soames went to the lower
pasture to get Hilda Bryant's sheep. A fresh breeze
was thinning the fog, and it swept toward her in
long ripples across the tall grass. Up ahead she
heard her little dog, Charlie, barking furiously at
something in the dusky twilight.

Mary laughed into the wind. It was good. It filled
her mouth and made her feel like a balloon.
"Whee!" she shouted.

At the far end of the pasture bordering Horsehead Point Road an occasional car was hurrying by.
Whoosh, whoosh, they went. The early commuters
were coming home.

Mary Soames walked on her toes, leaning forward, slightly hunched. To others it was an odd
stance, appearing to be off balance, but it didn't
seem strange to Mary. She'd been walking that way

for twenty-six years.

She had on her Canadian Indian wool hat, her father's black-and-red-checked-wool cruiser jacket, and a light cotton dress over her blue jeans.

"Charlie," she called. "Oh, Charlie."

The dog kept barking, but she couldn't see him. Suddenly the moon broke through the mist and made Hilda Bryant's pasture glow with a white fire. Then it was gone and back to dark, undulating velvet.

"Pretty," Mary said out loud. "Pretty."

Charlie was down at the corner of the pasture. He wasn't supposed to be there; he was supposed to be driving the sheep back up to the loafing shed where they slept at night.

Every afternoon Mary Soames came and cleaned Hilda Bryant's house for her, although it was just a little log cabin and really didn't need it that often. In the summer she helped her in the garden, in the fall with canning, and in the winter Mary washed, waxed and polished the silver Rolls Royce until she could see her face in the door.

Hilda's late husband, a mining engineer, had taken the car all over the world with them. In Africa a houseboy polished it, in Mexico the chauffeur, and now Hilda had halfwit Mary.

The girl turned on her flashlight and played it down in the pasture corner where Charlie was barking. "Charlie, you bad doggy," Mary called out. Her voice was clear and forceful in the wind. She sang solos in the Three Corners Community Church choir, and everybody said if Mary hadn't been mentally retarded, the product of an inbred family, she'd be with the Metropolitan.

The Soameses were among the first home-
steaders in Sealth County, and most of them, including Mary, still lived in the original ramshackle
shingle house beside Birch Slough.

Over the years additions had been tacked on at
odd angles, and woodsmoke was always puffing
from one of the multitude of chimneys, for the
Soameses had no central heating. The yard was a
historical museum of old cars, wooden boats and
farm machinery, interspersed with sleeping dogs.
Each Soames was entitled to a dog.

While the Indians drifted to Seattle slums, the
Japanese berry farmers sold to land developers,
and the loggers retired, the Soames family remained and proliferated.

Even though they were all at least mildly
retarded—grandfather Soames had married his sister, and Mary's father had wed his first cousin—
they were hard workers. The Soameses were good
with animals and willing to labor for less than a
minimum wage, a combination enabling them to
make an adequate living without welfare.

"Charlie, Charlie," Mary singsonged, striding toward him. Her heavy insulated rubber boots
swished in the tall wet grass. As she approached,
Mary could see something lying on the ground. Her
little border collie was standing over it. It was one
of widow Bryant's prize-winning sheep, and it was
dead.

"Oh, oh, oh," Mary moaned in agony, dropping to
her knees. The sheep was covered with something
red that smelled like paint. Even its eyes had been
painted shut. There was paint, mixed with blood,
running out of its open mouth. A hind leg

was badly broken.

Mary sat back on her haunches and cried. One of her friends had died, a wonderful creature of God. She rocked back and forth. "Oh, Charlie," she cried. The dog moved close, his heavy coat matted with dirt and twigs from driving the rest of the flock out from under the trees.

He licked her face gently with his rough hot tongue. It tickled, and she giggled. Charlie smelled good.

Mary stood up. "Oh, Charlie," she said, "a bad person hurt the sheep. Mrs. Bryant is really going to be mad."

While Mary Soames rushed to tell Hilda Bryant what she'd found, and the Millers enjoyed their pre-Halloween wine, Big Ed Foster was watching his young wife get dressed. It was only 5:45, and already Bucky's stepfather was on his third martini.

Damn, he thought, draping himself across the Ames chair in Linda's sitting room, she had one hell of a body for a woman who was almost thirty— hard and young-looking—especially young-looking. Small cupcake tits. She looked like a little girl with mascara. He drained the glass.

The all-white Foster house stood out like a beacon among the dark greens and grays on the north side of Horsehead Point. Built in the style and on the scale of a southern mansion, it was a dream come true for Linda Foster. To him it was just a good investment.

"I closed the deal on the Three Corners Mall," he said casually, belching slightly. "That'll net me a cool quarter million or my name isn't Big

Ed Foster."

He liked being called Big Ed. He'd cultivated the nickname since college, where, as a defensive end for the Washington State Cougars, he had cut down opponents like a John Deere combine.

Linda Foster looked at him in the mirror while she applied her makeup. The naturally blonde hair piled high on her head made her seem taller than she really was. Bucky had his mother's hair and the same milk-white skin.

"That's a lot of money." She showed no emotion.

"Damn right," Ed snorted, pouring himself another drink from the glass pitcher at chairside. The pitcher was beaded with water on the outside; it felt cold and good to the touch. He could lap up martinis faster than a Saint Bernard. "You want one?"

"No thanks," she said, fitting a false eyelash. "I have to drive."

"Oh, yeah," he grunted, and took a cigar out of his shirt pocket.

Being careful not to blink while the lash set, she reminded him she didn't like cigar smoke in her bedroom.

"Right," he said, stuffing the cigar into the corner of his meaty mouth but not lighting it. Just having it there to chew and taste made him feel better. It reminded him he could afford to buy and sell damn near everybody in Sealth County.

He worked the stogie around and eyed his wife. Foster was a big fish in a little pond, and he liked it that way. He also liked to smoke cigars as big as his cock. He sucked down half the martini. They didn't call him Big Ed for nothing.

"You look good enough to fuck," he said, staring

71

at her back. He felt hot and powerful. It was the highest compliment Big Ed could give.

She started on the eyebrows. "Thanks," she said, with total concentration on the arching pencil. "But I'm due back at the club in half an hour."

He finished the martini and smacked his lips. Yes, sir, he could still get it up on command. "So drive fast," he said.

He could hear Bucky's TV blaring away upstairs. When he put his car away, Ed had noticed that the boy's motorcycle was hot as a pistol and covered with mud. The kid would probably stay glued to the TV set for another hour. Plenty of time to give Mommy a quick tumble.

"You're expected at the Millers' tonight," she said.

"Don't change the subject."

"The subject was where you're going. Bucky's invited too."

Ed Foster slumped back. All he wanted was a fast one. "He'll probably go out trick or treating, won't he?"

"I suppose," Linda said. She hadn't seen Bucky since she got home from the Port Gloster Golf and Tennis Club, where she was the manager.

She'd worked most of the day, and tonight was the annual Harvest Moon Ball. Ed didn't like dances; they interfered with talking business.

"I'll drop by the Millers'. I guess Bucky can make it on his own."

"You should drop by," she said, sitting back to admire her makeup. "You sold them that house, and Dave is in a position to help you."

"Listen to the businesswoman," he said, with

more than a trace of admiration in his voice. "He can help us. You're damn right he can. It's the rest of the guests I'm not so keen on."

Linda surprised him. She'd surprised a lot of people. Ed had married her because she looked just like a twelve-year-old whore he'd pounced in San Antonio. But more important, she had solved his big problem. As he cruised city streets in his long Lincoln Continental with the "SOLD" license plates, he knew that sooner or later he was going to get caught. Then the world would know that Big Ed Foster, former all-American honorable mention, now successful real estate developer, molested little girls.

They had to be young, so Linda was perfect. That she was also a very smart girl with a keen business sense was a bonus he had never expected. She not only ran the country club with a firm hand; with her hard elegance she lured schools of valuable clients into his net.

Linda Foster gave her hair a final pat and stood up. She slipped into a plain black sheath, adjusted it and stepped into her high heels. Dressed, she was the picture of a highly successful real estate developer's wife. But Big Ed didn't give a shit what she looked like dressed. It was the little girl underneath that he loved.

He lumbered to his feet. His shoulders were still wide, and he could break bones with his huge paws, but the rest of him had gone to fat. The tailored clothes couldn't hide the huge gut, and the flab on his breasts showed through the white-on-white monogramed shirt he was wearing.

"How 'bout a quick one?" he asked her, unzipping his pants. "I won't even mess up your lipstick; I promise."

"Jesus, Ed. What do you want me to do, set the goddamn timer on the oven?" She wasn't unduly upset; in fact she wasn't upset at all.

Ed Foster was a pig, but he had some redeeming qualities, like money. And basically he wasn't a violent man. Also he didn't ask a lot of questions.

"Really, Ed, I'm late."

She kissed him on the cheek and gave him a squeeze in the balls just for good measure. "Hang in there, baby," she said, and walked out.

"Shit," Ed Foster swore, standing in the middle of her room and defiantly lighting his cigar.

CHAPTER 12

By 6:30 traffic was heavy on the Three Corners highway, and a steady stream of cars turned off at Horsehead Point and rattled across the Birch Slough Bridge. A few of the tired commuters noticed the fresh red paint but didn't slow down to see what was written on the rough planking.

The fog was almost gone and a gusting wind bumped against the cars as they snaked down the narrow, curving road. Brakelights began to flash as the residents of Horsehead Point turned off to their homes.

Wet hungry dogs, barking and wagging their tails, rushed to meet them. Lights came on in the darkened houses; fires cut the damp chill and filled the air with woodsmoke. Whiskey gurgled into glasses. Plastic sacks of Halloween candy were hurriedly torn open and emptied onto trays; porch lights came on. Grinning pumpkins appeared on doorsteps, their yellow candle glow flickering wildly as the wind rose.

Harold and Su Myers faced each other across the spacious kitchen of their custom-designed home. "I said, if we want to get to the Millers' Halloween party on time, you've got to take Belinda and Jeff out trick or treating while I throw something together," Su insisted.

"For God's sake, I walk in the door and you try to push me right back out," he complained. "Why can't they go alone?"

Harold Myers was a big, slightly overweight man, and his sagging thirty-seven-year-old face was pale with fatigue. He was still in his gas company vice president uniform, conservative gray suit and wingtip shoes.

"Because I don't want them out alone on a night like this. The wind's blowing right now. It's supposed to get worse," she said, slamming the refrigerator door shut.

Su Myers was in her uniform too—conservative gray suit and black pumps. Today she was a teller at the Three Corners Savings and Loan. Mondays and Fridays she was a reporter for the *South Sound Weekly.*

Harold ripped open his wilted white collar and sat down at the bar. He was exhausted. His company was going to ask the state for a massive rate increase in the morning, and it was Harold's responsibility to get it. He already knew the request would not be well received.

"When are we going to have something besides last night's leftovers?" he groused.

And why couldn't his own children at least come to say hello when he got home? Was it asking too much? Especially Jeffrey. He was turning into a sullen teenager sitting up in his room all the time. He must have told him ten times not to leave his damn motorcycle out overnight, and there it was, as big as life, right in the middle of the driveway.

Su Myers slammed down a stainless steel bowl with a crash and stomped around the kitchen, opening and closing doors in a fury. "Why am I always supposed to do it all?" she shouted at him.

"Jesus Christ, Su, I'm sorry, but ever since you started on that paper we never get to sit down for a meal."

Su Myers leaned back against the counter. She had been a high-school cheerleader and a Phi Beta Kappa, and she was not getting any younger. She still held her trim figure at 122 pounds, but dark circles were beginning to take up permanent residence under her tired eyes.

"Now wait a minute, just a damn minute. Why is it always my job? What about your job? When was the last time you made dinner?"

"Su, that's not the point." Harold rubbed his balding head in frustration. He was so tired he could die.

"Oh, yes it is." Her voice was getting shrill. "First," she said, stepping over to the bar where Harold sat slumped, "I went to work because we couldn't make it on your salary, right? We had this house and then the cars, the kids, and the sailboat you had to have. You remember that?"

She was so angry she lost her train of thought. "Second, second," she repeated.

"Mommy, where's dinner? Are we going out? You said Daddy would take us trick or treating." Their eight-year-old daughter Belinda was pulling on her skirt.

"Just a minute, dear." She took the little girl's hand away, but it came right back.

"You promised," she cried.

"Not right now, Belinda. In a minute. Go play with Jeff."

"He doesn't want to play. He locked his door."

"Go play anyway," Su said kindly, trying to ignore her.

"Do as your mother says, and do it now!" Harold shouted. "How many goddamn times do we have to say things around here?"

Belinda, wide eyed at her father's outburst but not cowed, stayed put.

"Do as your father says," Su told the little girl, her voice shaking with fury.

"Oh, okay, but Jeff won't play and we won't get to go out," Belinda said, retreating reluctantly.

"Well, I'm going to have a drink first," Harold said, moving around the bar to the liquor cabinet. He was being unreasonable. He knew how much the newspaper meant to Su; he shouldn't get on her about it. He was just tense; he was under a lot of pressure. She didn't understand that.

The Myerses kitchen was the kitchen Su had always wanted. It was huge, with wide butcher block counters, built-in appliances at waist level or above so you didn't have to bend over, and an array of electric gadgets that did everything from make ice cubes to broil steaks in thirty seconds.

Harold pulled out a bottle of Scotch and poured

himself a generous portion. "You want one?" he asked. He intended the question as a tentative peace offering. There was no reply. Su was removing something from one of the cabinets.

Harold hesitated. He was being awful. "We could just have a drink before I take the kids out."

"Do whatever you want," she said coldly, without looking up.

"Well, aren't we going to the Millers' Halloween party? What time is it, anyway?"

"You accepted the invitation," she said, opening a can of creamed corn.

"Honey, please. . . ." Harold took a long drink of Scotch; it burned all the way down. She'd be sorry if he just dropped dead someday.

"What do you want from me?" She slammed a tray of frozen pork chops into the microwave oven. "You don't want leftovers; we'll have pork chops."

"That's not what I meant."

"You can't even be nice to your own kids. I don't care about myself, but to poor little Belinda trick or treating is a big thing, Harold. Just as big as anything at your damn office."

So that was it. "I know that. I know that. I'll take them."

"It's not just a matter of taking them."

What the hell did that mean? He took another drink and lit a cigarette.

"I thought you were going to quit," she said, gathering up silverware noisily.

"The hell with it."

"Oh, Harold, please don't be that way. The doctor told you that you had to quit."

He took a long drag. "I'm sorry," he said quietly.

She stopped by his stool, silverware in hand. "I'm sorry too."

She was crying. He put his arm around her and kissed her on the cheek. Her skin was cold. "I'll go up and get Jeff and Belinda and hit the road. We'll eat at the party. We'll meet you over there."

"Okay," she said. "Harold, forget I said those things."

"Sure."

He walked slowly up the stairs. His legs were tired. His head ached. The drink had not relaxed him—in fact, exactly the opposite; he felt more on edge.

"Hey, guys," he called to his children without enthusiasm, "let's go out and do some trick or treating."

Belinda appeared in her Princess Leia costume. She looked magical. She was a beautiful little girl, as pretty as her mother. Harold tried to remember how Su had looked that first time he'd seen her standing in front of the Kappa Gamma sorority, but the memory was gone. He was getting old.

Where the hell was Jeffrey? Damn! The boy was always late. Why wasn't he out here, with Belinda, ready to go?

CHAPTER 13

Big Ed Foster filled Linda's sitting room with a satisfactory layer of strong cigar smoke, still marveling at how adeptly his young wife had slipped out of having a little quickie. He smiled. She hated the smoke. It was the only comeback he had.

Ed was turning to leave when the telephone rang. "Hell," he cursed, scooping up the pink bedside telephone. "Foster."

"This is Mrs. Bryant, Mr. Foster," she said sharply. "I want to talk to you about your son Bucky."

"Yes?" the big man said, sitting down heavily on his wife's bed. It smelled of powder and perfume.

"He just killed one of my sheep—mutilated, I think, is a better word—he and some of his friends, apparently."

Ed puffed slowly. Mutilated? It was obvious

Hilda Bryant was both furious and drunk. If it weren't for the fact that he had a continuing interest in the old gal's property, he would have told her to kiss his ass.

"My stepson," he told her very precisely, examining his cigar as he talked, "is upstairs watching television; he has been for quite awhile now."

"Well, according to a reliable witness, he was out in my pasture this afternoon on a motorcycle, harassing my sheep," she snapped.

Ed burped a deep, rumbling, satisfying belch that brought a renewed martini taste into his mouth over the essence of cigar. As well off as she was, he knew that Hilda was land poor. Daren Bryant might have been one of the world's most renowned mining engineers, but he had been a lousy investor, and he was long dead. Inflation must be eating her alive.

"Did you hear me, Mr. Foster?" she demanded.

Yes, Hilda, I heard you. Someday he'd bring her down a couple of pegs. But not quite yet. "Yes, I heard you." It wasn't very smart. Linda's kid had to understand he just couldn't keep bailing him out of jams. He'd already greased the skids for Bucky on a complaint from that old bitch Zondich. Not that he minded—a bunch of kids raising a little hell was nothing to worry about.

"Well?" she demanded imperiously.

The queen of Spain. He balanced a piece of tobacco on the end of his tongue and spit it across the room. It stuck on the opposite wall. "Who's this witness, Mrs. Bryant?" he asked her, his voice hard and even.

There was a pause. "That's not the point."

Probably that fat Zondich broad again, goddamn busybody. That was irrelevant, however. The thing to keep in mind was that she hadn't called the sheriff, not yet anyway. "What do you want me to do, Hilda?" he asked her calmly.

"Those are prize-winning Yorkshire sheep, breeding stock. And in addition to that he tore up my pasture. Clearly, I'd be perfectly justified in calling the authorities."

He puffed again. No cause for alarm. He rubbed his groin. That goddamn Linda had pulled a fast one, slipping out on him with his pants unzipped. Smart; he liked that in a woman. Hilda Byrant was intelligent enough, but she was just about a hundred years behind the times, and she understood nothing about men like Ed Foster.

"I'm sure you would be, Hilda, but I don't think that'll be necessary."

"Really?" she demanded, her voice rising. "And why not?"

Her imperial drunken majesty. Booze was her great weakness. He could hardly wait for the day when she had to pawn that goddamn pretentious Rolls Royce to pay her taxes; he'd give her a financial screwing she'd never forget.

"How much would you say the animal's worth? And the damage to the pasture, of course—just a ballpark figure?" he asked her.

"The rest of the sheep, at least most of them, were painted red," she quickly added.

Clearly this was the bargaining session the cheap bitch had had in mind when she called. "Red?" Ed Foster made an effort to mask his bellylaugh. He ground out his cigar in Linda's soap dish.

"Yes, and I fail to see the humor in it. We're talking about an economic asset of some consequence here, Mr. Foster."

He let her ramble. She was full of poison and wanted to spit it out. That was fine with him as long as she kept everything on a monetary level. Bucky and his friends had obviously been having a little Halloween fun—pranks, nothing more. He couldn't be bothered. He wouldn't be bothered.

"This is criminal behavior your son has engaged in, Mr. Foster—criminal."

This "your son" shit was beginning to irritate him. Everybody knew Bucky wasn't his son. Bucky came with Linda. He wasn't a bad kid; he always said thank you for the things Ed gave him, and he stayed out of the way. So he wasn't an angel. So what? Big Ed Foster was no angel either.

"Listen, Hilda. Number one, I don't think calling the police is the thing to do here," he told her with authority.

"And why not?"

"Because there's no need for it," he said. "That'd just create a lot of unnecessary animosity. Hell, I painted a lot of things red in my day."

"Damage has been done. An animal has been killed, Mr. Foster. This is not a boyish prank."

He had to take a piss in the worst way. The conversation could go on all night. This old broad was trying to push him around. "Listen, Hilda, let's get one thing straight. You call the law, I don't give a damn who your witness is, I'll sue the hell out of you. Is that clear?" He couldn't hold it much longer. The five martinis were going to burst his bladder. He could hear the old bitch huffing and puffing on the other end of the line.

"I don't have to tolerate this kind of behavior," she finally replied, but her voice had grown subdued.

Finally she was beginning to realize he wasn't some shoe salesman. "I agree," he replied abruptly. "How much?"

"I beg your pardon?"

'How much to cover the damage?" Come on, Hilda.

"The sheep is worth four hundred fifty dollars."

"Four hundred fifty dollars for a goddamn sheep?"

"That, of course, includes shipping and so forth," she told him primly.

Yes ma'am, and ten percent for you, he thought. "Okay, and let's add a hundred for the rest of the damage—$550. I'll send you a certified check in the morning."

"I see," she replied coolly.

He had to go like a racehorse. That's the deal, baby. Take it or leave it. Silence from Hilda Bryant. Her imperial majesty liked to deal from her throne. No common businessmen for her. "What do you say, Hilda?"

"All right, Mr. Foster."

Atta girl. "First thing in the morning. And, Hilda, you forget this ever happened. That's the deal. Agreed?"

"All right."

"Good. Good night."

He slammed down the phone. Dumb broad. He rolled over to Linda's bathroom, unzipping his pants as he walked. He'd have to talk to Bucky.

That wasn't smart, leaving tracks all over the place. He pissed and pissed, yellow urine splattering on the virgin white fluffy carpet around the toilet. Jesus, sweet relief.

"Hey, Bucky," he shouted, his deep bass voice booming through the house.

He listened. The TV was still going. Ed Foster clumped up the stairs. Painting sheep—not bad, not bad at all. At least it was original.

The boy's bedroom door was open. "Hey, Buck," he called, walking in. The point Ed Foster wanted to make was that a smart operator, whether he was pulling off a prank or a shady million-dollar real estate deal, never got caught.

The walls were covered with Captain Terror posters. The bed was unmade. The room smelled like a stable. Christ, Ed thought, the kid must be pissing in his bed. Bucky wasn't there. The wind whistled faintly in the eves. A rerun of *Clint McDonald, Private Eye,* was flickering on the color set. Clint's girlfriend was about to be raped by a drug-dealing motorcycle gang. Ed watched as the camera panned around the circle of greasy riders staring down at the helpless girl.

"Oh please, no!" she screamed as they descended. And the scene quickly shifted to where Clint McDonald was roughing up the front man for the gang, the owner of a funeral home where the drugs were stored in coffins.

"You hurt her and I'll kill you," the detective snarled at the poor terrorized schmuck.

Big Ed Foster snapped off the TV. What the hell, he'd catch up with his stepson later at the Millers' Halloween party. The call from Hilda Bryant had started him calculating again. That place would make a much better subdivision than sheep farm, and the Foster Land and Development Company was just the outfit to do the dividing.

CHAPTER 14

Now that Harold Myers had decided to take his children trick or treating just to please his wife, he was impatient. "Where's Jeff?" he demanded, pacing the upstairs hall.

"In his room like I told you, Daddy," Belinda said. "Let's go." She ran down the stairs, her white Princess Leia costume billowing behind her.

"Just a minute, sweetheart, just a minute." Harold knocked on Jeff's door. There was no reply.

"Let's go," Belinda shouted impatiently again from the bottom of the stairs.

Harold turned the knob. The door was locked. "Open the door," he ordered abruptly. Silence. "Jeffrey, I'll give you till the count of three to open this door," he told his son. He was furious but trying hard not to let it show. Calm down, he kept telling himself. "One, two. . . . " he began. The door opened. His son stood there, head down to one side. How he hated that hangdog look!

"I don't want to go with you, Dad. I want to go with some of the guys," he said in a muffled, mumbling voice.

"Speak up," Harold ordered him.

"I want to go with some of the guys," Jeff replied, louder.

"Who?" Harold demanded.

"Bucky Foster and some other guys," Jeff replied vaguely.

The blood rushed to Harold's face. The evasive little bastard! He did the same damn thing with track. Harold knew his son could be a champion but, for some reason he would never understand, Jeff wasn't interested. The boy had a great deal of ability. If I had his natural coordination, thought Harold, my whole life would have been different.

"Daaaa—dddeeeee!" Belinda screamed shrilly.

"Come on," Harold urged his son with the last reserves of goodwill he could muster, "come on with Belinda and me. We'll make it a family night."

After working hard all day, he was offering to take his children with him out of the goodness of his own heart. They didn't realize what a sacrifice that was, how tired he was, how worried he was. His son couldn't reject him.

"I got to go with Bucky Foster."

"Goddamn it," Harold shouted at him, grabbing his arm, "you're coming with us." His son was a coward, unable to stand on his own two feet, face life like a man and have a little consideration for others.

Jeff resisted, pulling back. Harold tightened his

grip and yanked him violently into the hall. The resistance infuriated him. The boy was just like him.

"Stop it!" Su shouted, rushing up the stairs.

He turned Jeff loose. "What I'm doing is informing your son that he's coming trick or treating with us and not with his friends," Harold explained.

She was the one who had urged him to take the children in the first place. Now, to his astonishment, she sided with the boy. Jeff looked like a beaten dog.

"Did it ever occur to you he might have made other arrangements?" she scolded him, her voice cracking with emotion.

Harold wanted to hit her. He clenched his fists. He wanted to throw them all out the window. He locked his jaw muscles until his teeth hurt. He wanted to scream for everybody and God to hear. How much is a man supposed to take? he wondered. But he didn't hit or scream. They would all hate him no matter what he did. They would turn on him and he would be alone.

Jeff kept his eyes on the rug, trembling. He really didn't want to go with Bucky Foster. Every time he closed his eyes the image of the dying sheep came to him—the fear in the rolling red eyes, the horrible sound of the boot slamming into the soft stomach. Did sheep hurt like people? He was sure they did. He knew just how the animal felt—the nausea, the helplessness.

"I think Jeffrey ought to make up his own mind," his mother was telling his father.

Jeff didn't want to do that. He couldn't look at either of them. Why did they fight over him all the time? Why didn't they just tell him what to do? If he didn't show up at Bucky's, they'd call him a chicken. Everybody at school would know that he had to go with his father and little sister. But if he went, he might get in even worse trouble. He was sure the telephone or the doorbell would ring at any moment, and there would be Mrs. Bryant with her dead sheep.

"Jeffrey?" his mother was saying. "You decide, Jeff."

"Come with us, please," Belinda asked him kindly.

Daddy liked her. She never got punished for anything. Tears filled his eyes. He wanted to go with Belinda and be safe. He didn't want to get in any more trouble.

"Jeff, I think you ought to go with your friends," his mother suggested, forcefully squeezing his shoulder. "You go have a good time, and we can all meet over at the Millers' Halloween party about eight."

"Well, goddamnit to hell!" his father shouted at him. "Just forget it then!" Harold picked up Belinda. "Come on, honey, we'll go have a good time all by ourselves," he said, and started down the stairs.

"Harold!" Su called after him in alarm.

But he slammed the front door violently on her, and stomped off into the night.

CHAPTER 15

In the brown log cabin sitting on the edge of the
bluff at the tip of Horsehead Point, halfwit Mary
Soames cried softly while Hilda Bryant marched
up and down the tiny living room, scolding the
hired girl in a shrill voice.

"How many times must I tell you to get those
sheep in before dark? I've said it and said it. Now
look what you've done."

The conversation with Ed Foster had infuriated
her, and now the gin she'd been drinking since view-
ing the mutilated animal in her lower pasture was
eating away her thin veneer of self-control.

"I tried," Mary whimpered, standing before the
angry woman like a dumb animal herself, tears
coursing down her comely face.

Hilda carried a riding crop in her right hand, and
as she paced she popped it in her left palm. She had

a head that belonged on a Roman coin, and a plastic surgeon in charge of preserving it until she died.

Her blonde, streaked hair was the responsibility of Maxim of Maxine's, and the body, still hard, tan and shapely at sixty-nine, was serviced once a week by the exclusive Vashon Fitness Salon in the city.

"You stupid, stupid girl. You cost me my finest ewe. Irreplaceable, one of a kind. Damn you to hell!"

She turned and shook the riding crop at her. Mary stepped back in fear.

"Please don't hit me."

If only I could, Hilda thought, if only I could. God, it was impossible to hire anything but idiots and morons in this country. They should sterilize people like the Soameses and be done with it.

"I'm sorry. I'm sorry," Mary kept repeating earnestly as she backed toward the door.

Hilda Bryant's mouth and jaws worked at a furious pace as she overrode the girl's feeble explanations. She had seen crawling beggars in India and starving children in Africa, but she had never seen anything that disturbed her as much as her precious animal slaughtered by that vicious, albino-looking child Bucky Foster.

"If you ever fail to do your job properly again, if you ever fail to do exactly as you're told, I *will* hit you. I have every right, and I will."

Even in her drunken fury she knew that wasn't true. God, if only her late husband Daren were here to deal with Ed Foster, he would make short work of that disgusting fat man. But Daren was gone, and Hilda's three children were scattered all over the world. They sent her Christmas cards and called her on her birthday. They were waiting for her to die so they could split the money. They would have a long wait.

The gall of that nouveau riche Foster, that Iowa corn farmer turned real estate magnate. She resumed her angry pacing. She had a witness to the crime, Clara Zondich. Thank God the pitiful woman at least had had the intestinal fortitude to call her.

How dare that Foster boy do something like this to her? It was like slapping her in the face. Money! What did she care about money? Ed Foster had offered her money. "That's the deal, Hilda."

Well, maybe Foster thought that was the end of it, but it wasn't. She had expected a more conciliatory attitude; she had expected an abject apology. Well, she still could call the sheriff. But she'd made an agreement. Why had she done that? Fear? She would not be coerced. The horrible boy would be punished.

"Can I go?" Mary asked timidly in a quiet little voice.

How Hilda longed to lay her whip into that pretty face and beat her into submission. She wanted to strike out at something, anything, but Mary was such a pitiful target.

"Yes, you may," she replied, her unnaturally smooth face tight with anger, "but you make damn sure you lock the gate, girl, damn sure. You understand?"

"Yes, Mrs. Bryant."

"Check twice so you're sure. Look twice, you understand? I don't want anybody else coming up here. I'm not giving anything away tonight." She let her hard green eyes settle on Mary.

"Yes, Mrs. Bryant."

That boy who called himself a bank officer, David Miller, actually had the gall to invite her to a Halloween party. He probably thought that gave him license to send up his costumed brats to beg for food. Well, he had another think coming. It was a long, dark driveway, and a locked gate on the road should discourage them.

Hilda felt powerless in the modern world, and it made her furious. Here she was, a woman of substance and means, forced to live in a neighborhood taken over by money lenders and tradesmen, reduced to depending on a halfwit peasant girl.

"Good night," she told Mary abruptly, and went into the kitchen.

"Good night, Mrs. Bryant," Mary called after her with childish sincerity.

Hilda poured a water glass of gin. It didn't warm her anymore. Nothing did. She was going to freeze to death in this ghastly climate. She went back into the living room and turned up the oil heater. It glowed in the dimly lighted room.

He could be out creeping around in the fog right now, up to no good. Hilda Bryant liked boys well enough—brown-skinned obedient ones, or solicitous, flattering, ignorant ones.

"Manuel, come here."

"Ah, señorita, you have such a beautiful body."

The gin made the whole room turn gently. She sat down heavily in her rocking chair. She would go to Acapulco this Christmas. She closed her eyes and listened to the wind bumping against the sides of the little cabin.

She imagined herself sinking into the warm, sugar-white sand, where the wind was a warm, gentle caress. She could smell the suntan lotion, feel it being massaged into her back by those strong brown hands. "Ah, señorita, such a beautiful body."

The wind pushed against Mary Soames, then pulled her along, as it whirled over Horsehead Point. It brought her the smell of the mud flats, and made scraping, crunchy noises in the darkness on either side of the road. She walked fast, with Charlie ranging on ahead. Her daddy's warm cruiser jacket felt good, collar pulled high around her cheeks.

When she got to the road she closed the wrought-iron gate on Hilda Bryant's driveway, wrapped the heavy case-hardened chain around the post and the gate, then pushed the heavy hasp lock together. She doublechecked, just as Mrs. Bryant had said, to make sure it was shut tight, and then set off for home.

Mary walked down the south side of the Point, the wind blowing her this way and that. The tide was high now and she could hear the driftwood booming as it slammed into the bulkheads along the beach.

Charlie occasionally barked at a flying leaf, but soon settled down to a steady walk beside her. That was nice. She loved Charlie. He made her feel safe. Charlie was never mean to her. The fog was almost gone. She could see the friendly lights of the houses blinking at her. "Hello, Mary," they called out as she passed.

There was food cooking—the wonderful smell of fresh coffee, somebody frying onions. It made her tummy growl. She wanted to be home with Grandfather in front of a hot fire, where she wouldn't feel bad and stupid. When she saw the spotlights on Ivan Olsen's house reaching out for her, she crossed to the other side of the road and trotted along in the waving shadows.

"Shhh," she warned Charlie.

The old fisherman had been mean to her too. Once, a long time ago, when Mrs. Olsen was shopping, he'd made her take all her clothes off just because she had knocked a little vase off a table while she was dusting it.

He tried to make her drink whiskey, and when she wouldn't, he tried to push his thing into her, but it was too soft. It reminded Mary of a big white slug, and she giggled, and he hit her and made her cry. She told her brother about it and then Mr. Olsen was never mean to her again.

She loved brother Henry. He was smart. He'd gone to the sixth grade and had a good job at the Three Corners Seed and Hardware. He could lift a hundred-pound sack of feed with one hand.

She still cleaned at Mr. Olsen's every Friday morning, but Mrs. Olsen was gone now, and Mr. Olsen didn't even talk to her anymore. He left piles of long underwear in the bathroom and never washed the dishes.

She hurried on toward the bridge, forgetting Ivan Olsen and Hilda Bryant, feeling better surrounded by the moaning, sighing darkness. The wind was trying tp push her over; she pushed back.

To Mary it was a friendly contest, and she gaily

called out to her adversary, "You can't push me, Mr. Wind." Charlie barked his encouragement. She saw two huge pumpkins on a fence, their candles blown out by the wind. They had wide, smiling faces, but to Mary they looked sad and lonely, like two old orange clowns.

Here and there she passed groups of children all dressed up in their costumes, swinging flashlights, calling to each other as they went from house to house.

"Hello, have a nice time," Mary greeted them shyly.

A few answered back. Most didn't. They were a little afraid of Crazy Mary, who lived by the swamp.

The water under the Birch Slough Bridge hissed and roared at her as she crossed. It was angry and foaming. Mary Soames bolted into a longlegged run and kept running until she saw the happy lights of home and heard the chorus of Soameses' dogs calling to her.

They came out of the darkness, racing the wind, to surround her—all sizes, all shapes, barking and jumping and playing with Charlie. "Hello doggies, hello doggies," Mary cried, patting and hugging them.

CHAPTER 16

All her friends were running by in the dark, having a good time, but Belinda Myers had to walk by the side of the road holding her father's hand. It would have been a lot more fun to go trick or treating with big brother Jeff. It would have been a lot more fun if her father had stayed home. He was so slow!

"Come on, Daddy," Belinda urged, tugging at Harold's gloved hand.

He wouldn't even talk to her since he'd shouted at Mommy and they left the house. She knew why, it was the whiskey. Her teacher, Mrs. McCrakken, said whiskey destroyed your brain cells.

When she told her father, Harold said, "Ask Mrs. McCrakken if she ever had a drink."

"Hi, Belinda," somebody in a Dracula cape yelled at her. "You want to trade a caramel apple for something good?"

It looked like Rocky Miller. "Sure." But her father kept walking, towing her along. "Daddy," she protested, trying to pull away.

That just made him squeeze her hand tighter. "You shouldn't take things that aren't wrapped," he told her.

It was no fun if you couldn't trade and talk to your friends. She walked beside him, head down, white Princess Leia costume trailing in the wind. "Why not?"

"Because they might be poisoned."

She snuffed. It was cold, and her nose hurt. "Are you cold, honey?"

"No." She was freezing, and all up and down Horsehead Point Road she could hear her friends' voices. They were having fun. She never got to do anything. Another group of children passed, but she decided not to speak to them.

"You sure you're not cold?" He sounded worried, and stopped walking.

But she was looking at the green light in Clara the Cow's front window. That would be neat! And the rest of her friends were afraid to trick or treat Mrs. Zondich. She could tell everybody about that.

"Come on, Daddy," she said enthusiastically, "let's go up there."

With Daddy holding her hand, Mrs. Zondich would have to be nice. It made her shiver all over, but she hammered on the front door anyway.

"Take it easy." Harold cleared his throat.

Wait until Jeff heard about this! Even bigmouth Bucky Foster was afraid to get this close. There was a rattle behind the door. She grabbed her father's hand and held on tight. The door opened.

There were gold chains across the inside. Mrs. Zondich was back in the shadows, making a funny whistling noise. It looked like she didn't have any eyes. How really weird!

"Ah, hello, good evening," her father stumbled.

Clara the Cow didn't say anything. She just kept whistling like she couldn't breathe, and stuck a bowl through the crack in the door with only three pieces of candy in it. Her hands were all twisted and shaking and covered with brown spots. How yucky! How sick!

Jeff would never believe her if she didn't get some candy. Belinda snatched a piece and stepped back quickly. The bowl disappeared inside.

"Say thank you," her father ordered.

"Thank you." She had the candy. She had gone up to the front door and trick or treated Clara the Cow. What a scary, neat story to tell all her friends at the Millers' party.

"Let's go," her father said. He was mad. "I'm sorry she didn't give you more. The cheap old bitch."

"Oh, I've got lots of stuff, Daddy. I don't care," she told him. "Let's go across the street to the Eliases' house."

And then they could go to the Jacobis' and the Harringtons', and her bag would be full, and they could go to the Millers' Halloween party. Everybody in the neighborhood would be there. Her friend Carrie Miller said they could even dance if they wanted to. Carrie liked that stuff; Belinda wasn't so sure.

She'd rather play cowboys with Jeff, except he wouldn't play with her any more. It was hard to figure out why. Jeff was a super cowboy, and he used to be nice to her. Now he said she was too bossy, and he was always running around on his stupid motorcycle with his stupid friends, going down to their stupid secret cave.

It was all because of Bucky Foster. Ever since dumb Bucky had moved in, Jeff followed him around everywhere. Jeff thought Bucky was a big shot. She knew better. Bucky Foster was nothing but a bossy bully who liked to be mean to people.

Belinda knocked on the Eliases' front door. It was a pretty door with carvings on it in square blocks. There were goats with curved horns, a mountain lion sitting in a tree, and a big bear standing on its back legs, holding a fish. Mrs. Elias answered and, instead of just letting them stand on the porch, she invited them inside where it was warm.

She had Belinda sit over by the fire. "You must be a cold little princess," she said.

"I'm not cold. I'm having fun," Belinda told her cheerfully. But it was good to be out of the chilly wind.

Mr. Elias laughed. "That's because you're young."

He had a happy, rosy face, even if it was wrinkled and saggy. He told her father to take off his coat and stay awhile.

"Well, maybe just for a minute," Harold Myers said.

Mr. and Mrs. Elias were like her grandparents. Their house smelled like fresh, hot food, and when you came over, they always talked to you. Mrs. Elias brought out a tray of popcorn balls, cookies, sliced oranges and a cup of hot chocolate. It made Belinda's tummy hungry just to look at them. "Can I, Daddy?" she asked him.

"Sure, why not? Have at it, honey," her father said.

Now he was all kind and friendly. Maybe he was cold outside and that was what made him cranky. The chocolate chips in the cookies were still hot; she could mash them with her tongue and rub the sweet chocolate on the roof of her mouth.

Mrs. Elias sat down beside her and looked at her charm bracelet. "That's beautiful," she said, taking Belinda's hand. "I used to have one just like that when I was a little girl, but I gave it to my daughter Jan when she graduated from high school. She teaches at the junior high now, right next to your school at Three Corners. Did you know that?"

Her hand was warm and soft and smelled of cream that smelled like roses. "You mean the middle school where my brother Jeff goes?" she asked the old lady.

"Oh, I see," Mrs. Elias said. "Is that what you call it? They used to call it junior high."

"Now it's the middle school," Belinda corrected her. It wasn't a big mistake, just a little one.

"Well, that makes sense," Mrs. Elias replied. "It is a school for the middle years."

"Jeff thinks Miss Elias is the prettiest teacher in the school," Belinda confided. She took a big drink of hot chocolate milk. It was warm and sweet, and it made you feel like you had hot little trees in your chest.

"Does he now? Well, my daughter is awfully pretty."

"Maybe I'll give this bracelet to my pretty daughter." Belinda thought that might make Mrs. Elias happy, and it did.

She smiled at her. "That's a wonderful idea. Why don't you try one of these oranges, dear?"

Belinda took an orange wedge. The first taste was sour, but the second one was better. Mrs. Elias had a funny little hiss in her voice when she talked and Belinda liked to listen to her. Her father and Mr. Elias were talking about the weather. Belinda took a third orange slice. They were pretty good now.

"We've got a humdinger of a storm brewing up out there," Mr. Elias was saying.

"Really?" her daddy answered.

"It could be as bad as the blow we had in—was it '52 or '53, Mother?"

"It was 1952," Mrs. Elias told him.

"I remember that because we were on the ferry that night. Heck, they were just little puddle jumpers then, and the darn water came right over the car deck. Remember that, Mother?"

"I remember it very well," Mrs. Elias said. "But I imagine this little girl would rather be out trick or treating than listening to you tell us about the good old days, Fred."

That wasn't really true. She was beginning to enjoy the warm toasty fire. It made her sleepy. She took another cookie while nobody was looking.

"Sonia always reminds me these are the good old days," Mr. Elias told Harold.

At the door, Mr. Elias gave her a great big hug. "You sure are the prettiest little princess I ever saw," he said. "You remind me of my granddaughter in Florida. She's a beautiful little girl, and so are you." Her face got hot, and she smiled. Mr. Elias smiled back. He always smiled at everything.

"Thanks," her father muttered. "We think she's pretty special too."

It was a funny thing to say. He didn't think she was special enough to let her go trick or treating alone with Jeff.

"Where's your brother?" Mr. Elias asked her.

Before she could answer, her father interrupted. "Jeff?"

"Yes. Great little lad. Fine runner, as I recall."

Her father was buttoning up his coat. "Oh, he's out with some of his friends. Got to let kids have a little rope once in awhile, I guess." Now he was looking at the ground. She knew better than to interrupt back. That was something only Moms and Dads did.

"Well, come back and stay longer some time. You know where we are," Mr. Elias said to them, putting his arm around Mrs. Elias. "We sure enjoyed your visit, little princess."

"Goodby," she said, waving.

Her father walked faster now, and she felt happy and warm. "Let's go to the Jacobis' and the Harringtons'," she suggested. Two more houses and her trick or treat bag would be full to the top.

"Oh, honey, it's getting late." He stopped walking and looked at his wrist watch. "It's after 7:30. We're supposed to be at the Millers' party right now."

"Just two more, please, Daddy?"

"No," he said sharply. "It's too late."

It was not too late. He just didn't want to go. It

107

wasn't fair. She was going to cry. He had spoiled her Halloween. "You promised."

"I did not."

"Please, oh, please." He had promised to take her trick or treating, he had! A big cold drop of rain hit her in the face.

"It's raining," her father said quickly.

"Not very much." It was only one tiny drop. "We could run." If they ran, the rain wouldn't catch them.

"You can't stay out in the rain," he said, gripping her hand tightly again.

He was squeezing too hard. "Please!"

"No!" her father said, starting to drag her along the road. He was mad again. He was always mad about something.

She let her bag of candy drag. "I don't want to go to the Millers' party," she whined. "I want to go home." Her whole evening was ruined. She was going to sit down in the middle of the road and cry until her father was nice to her.

"Don't pull that crap on me, Belinda." Harold jerked her along roughly. "Putting up with Jeffrey is enough to contend with. I don't need any of that from you."

"Where is Jeffrey?" she cried. When she found out, she was going to run away and go to him. He'd be nice to her. They still could have fun together.

"God only knows," Harold Myers said, dragging his reluctant daughter toward the Millers'. "Wherever it is, I'll bet my ass he's up to no damn good."

CHAPTER 17

The rain squall swept the length of Horsehead
Point, a black fastmoving curtain overlaying the
darkness of night, bending the tall stands of fir as it
passed. It rattled in the thick underbrush and
muted bright porch lights to a fuzzy glow.

Clara Zondich leaned forward in her overstuffed
chair, holding the front window curtain back just
enough to give her a good view of the road. The
night air was filled with leaves; raindrops hammered on the roof. The ghosts and ghouls and bears
and frogs were getting soaking wet. Good! She
imagined their little hands becoming red with cold,
lips quivering as the wetness soaked through their
ridiculous costumes.

Yes, she could see them bunching up as they
trudged along the road in front of her house. They
were no longer so happy and gay, jumping at

shadows and giggling. They leaned silently into the wind. A paper sack of candy broke. The children went on their knees in the freezing mud to retrieve the prizes.

Clara's old face screwed up, the lines of perverse satisfaction fanning out from her tight mouth. Soon they would all be gone. A yellow pumpkin rolled down the road and a garbage can lid clattered somewhere in the night. The children moved off.

"Bad bad boys and girls go home, Milly," Clara baby talked the old poodle shivering by her side.

But no! Three more children stopped in front of her house. They were bigger. With a jolt that took her breath away, Clara recognized them—Bernard Foster in a black shiny suit, Jeff Myers, and that dirty Indian Harry George Junior. Clara shuddered. If they put one foot on her property she would call the sheriff again. But they were turning, walking away.

She swallowed nervously and watched. Thank heavens! It looked as if they were going toward Ivan Olsen's house. She clicked her tongue. Served the old lecher right. It was common knowledge he had seduced the halfwit Soames girl who did his cleaning. The boys were going up Ivan's front walk. She settled down for a long vigil, keeping the curtain back enough to see but not enough for her to be observed.

"What are dose baddy boys going to do, Milly?" she asked the poodle.

"I don't want to go up there," Jeff Myers insisted. "Olsen will kill us."

"No, he won't," Bucky assured him scornfully,

110

slipping his ultrathin Captain Terror flashlight into a secret pocket. "He owes me candy."

Harry George Junior was hanging back too, breath sour with beer, eyes blank with Valium. "Say hello for me, Buck," the Indian drawled slowly.

Bucky Foster swaggered around in the wind and rain, hands on hips. "You know what?" he told them. "You guys are chicken shit. You haven't got the guts to go up there."

Harry George laughed carelessly. Jeff Myers jammed his hands deeper into his pants pockets and looked down at Ivan Olsen's front walk.

"Okay, I'll show you how it's done," Bucky Foster said. He didn't need them. He could face Ivan Olsen alone. He was looking forward to it. He bounced up the four steps to the heavy oak door and mashed the bell with his thumb. A harsh electric buzzing sounded somewhere deep inside. Bucky waited. The plants in the yard stood out under the harsh glare of the spotlights mounted on each corner of the house. The artificial light made the rain look like blowing snow.

"Hello, Mr. Olsen," he would say politely. "I'll bet you didn't expect to see me again."

He gave the bell a second push, shivering in anticipation. He was ready. Maybe Olsen was deaf. Bucky Foster doubled his fist and banged on the door. Still no answer.

"Come on, Buck. Let's get out of here," Jeff urged in a whisper. He was shaking all over.

Maybe the old man was pretending not to be home. They did that sometimes. Bucky Foster left the door and came back down the steps. "I'm gonna look around," he announced aggressively.

Reluctantly Jeff Myers followed him around the side of the house, glancing behind to make sure Harry was coming too. The house sat on a small knoll overlooking the bay. The spotlights illuminated the wide sloping lawn leading to the water and the narrow pier where Olsen moored his halibut schooner.

Bucky surveyed the white, cedar-planked boat as it rolled in the long swells, tire fenders chafing and squeaking against the dock. A brilliant idea had come to him. Olsen wouldn't dare ignore him.

He turned to Jeff. "Let's play a little trick on Mr. Olsen," he suggested.

"I—I think we ought to get over to the Millers' party, you know?" Jeff stammered.

"Well, I don't," Bucky sneered. "Mr. Olsen didn't give us a treat, and now we're gonna play a trick on him. We're gonna paint a nice red stripe down the side of that fish boat." That would bring the old man running.

Harry George Junior giggled and swayed in the wind, his long, tangled black hair flying.

"Well," Bucky demanded impatiently, "who's coming with me?"

Sheets of rain fell on them. "I'm cold," Jeff whimpered.

"I'm cold," Bucky mimicked back loudly. He wasn't cold. Sealed in his black neoprene Captain Terror suit, he was burning. The old man would come. He wouldn't have any choice.

It was better to go without Jeff and Harry anyway. They didn't understand what to do. "All right," he told them, "you watch." Bucky drew two

112

paint cans from the secret pockets.

Jeff Myers uttered a single panicky cry and ran back toward the road. Harry George hesitated, confused, then stumbled after him. Bucky Foster didn't see them go. A fiery tingle crawled up his back; he was already striding down the lawn, out onto the dock.

Thor, the black letters on the bow read. He stared at them, watching them go up and down as the boat rolled. He was lightheaded and breathless, shaking with excitement. He'd start with the name. He would obliterate it forever with his mark. Hot burning worms crawled over him as he brought the spray cans into firing position. The erection was pounding against his leg inside his skintight suit. He couldn't hold it much longer.

And then it happened. The pilothouse door above him slammed open and a huge, shadowy figure lurched out. Bucky Foster let out a sigh of relief. Everything was going to work out. He relaxed, paint tubes in hand, breathing easily now, obediently waiting for whatever would happen next.

Ivan Olsen loomed over the rail, the same red-faced old man who had chased him off the Birch Slough Bridge. He was wearing the black pea jacket and yellow southwester hip boots turned down at the knees. "Vat ve gut har?" he thundered, glaring down at Bucky. "Ve gut sum vis guys," he answered his own question, bracing his feet apart on the rolling deck.

Bucky walked over, paint cans extended. "Hi, Mr. Olsen," he said calmly. "Remember me? I'll bet you didn't expect to see me again."

And before the astonished fisherman could answer, Bucky Foster sprayed red lacquer in his face. "Yaaa!" Olsen howled, stumbling sideways off balance, trying to wipe the paint out of his eyes.

"Trick or treat! Trick or treat!" Bucky laughed, dancing a little jig on the dock. "What will it be, Mr. Olsen?" He ached with pleasure. This was it!

Olsen hung on a stanchion by the pilothouse, blinking his eyes. "I giff you a damn treat, you boy," he said, swinging into the cabin and coming back with a fire ax. The maul and cutting edge were painted bright green. He held the ax in front of him like a rifle at port arms as he lurched back to the railing. "Git offa my dock, you asshole, you!"

Bucky didn't move. "Go fuck yourself!" he told the old man, crossing his arms and smiling like a choirboy. Now it was close. Come on, Mr. Olsen. Please!

Olsen shook the ax at him, confused by his calm. "I call dah police, you boy. They put you in jail," he threatened, puffing with rage.

"Go ahead," Bucky replied, still smiling up at him, "and I'll tell them you fuck your cleaning lady." Come on, Mr. Olsen, do something!

"By gar, I fix you," Olsen snarled, crashing across the gangway and onto the dock.

Bucky waited for him. "Yeah, though I walk through the valley of the shadow of death," he recited under his breath. "I will fear no evil, for I am the meanest son-of-a-bitch in the valley!"

"Off, off!" Olsen shouted, charging him.

Bucky Foster took one step back and one quick step to the left. Olsen staggered clumsily by, completely befuddled by his sudden move. But he turned in time to catch Bucky with his back to

Puget Sound. He had him trapped.

The fisherman advanced now, cocking the ax. Calmly Bucky retreated down the dock, jabbing and thrusting with the paint cans, a bullfighter teasing the bull. Hiss! Whoosh! Before Ivan knew what had happened, Bucky had darted in and squirted him straight in the eye with a stream of red lacquer.

"Ahhhhh!" Olsen snarled from deep in his guts. He raised the ax over his head, whirling it like a battle sword of his Norse ancestors. Again Bucky danced back just out of the big man's reach. There were only a few feet of dock left behind him. He could hear the waves gurgling under the boards. Olsen raised the ax high over his head.

Bucky kept his eyes on the face. The old man wasn't going to chop him up; he was only trying to scare him. He stood his ground. With an angry grunt, Olsen brought the ax down, burying it in the spongy planking only inches in front of Bucky's feet.

"You missed! You missed!" Bucky taunted him, waving the spray cans.

Olsen spread his arms wide. Finally he looked serious. Now there was no escape. The moment had arrived.

"Come here, yu asshole boy, yu," he snorted.

"Hurt him! Hurt him! Hurt him!" Bucky's head screamed at his body, and he charged, snarling and spitting, driving his head into the big man's breastbone, cursing him, tearing, punching, kicking.

Olsen stepped back in surprise, stumbled over the ax, but managed to grab Bucky in a bearhug before they both fell on the dock. He was on top of him. "Kill! Kill! Kill!" Bucky screamed, and clamped his hands around the old man's neck. He could feel the slow chug chug of the dark arterial blood coming to a strangling stop. Bucky Foster was poised on the tip of ecstasy.

The damn rubber suit was slippery. The boy's hands on Olsen's neck were surprisingly strong. This child was trying to choke him. Bewildered by the ferocity of the attack, Olsen first tried to pry the skinny wrists apart, but they were as solid as steel posts. The thumbs were crushing his windpipe.

He should never have tried to scare the boy with the ax. He would not make that mistake again. Grunting, he doubled his right hand into a fist and slammed it across the side of Bucky Foster's head.

The blow telegraphed straight to his shoulder, and the choking hands fell away from his throat. Olsen rolled over quickly and caught a wrist just as the boy was trying to pull away.

"Too bad, yu sonny boy," he grunted, wrestling the boy down and straddling him, a big knee driving down into his chest.

"Don't, oh don't!" Bucky cried in pain.

But Olsen bore down with all his weight, breathing like a switch engine, his breath hot and smelling of whiskey. "I make you cry," he told Bucky. "I make you sorry."

"Oh, Jesus, no!" Bucky screamed at him. "Don't, please!" Tears were running down his face.

Olsen got control of himself and looked down. This was, after all, only a small boy. He let up slightly on the knee pressure, but still Bucky couldn't catch his wind.

"Please, Mr. Olsen," he begged, "please don't hurt me."

Olsen could think of no reply. What was he to do with this boy, this child who had tried to kill him?

"Ohhh," Bucky moaned, writhing under him. "My ribs—they're broken."

"Huh?" Olsen released a little more pressure but kept Bucky's shoulders pinned to the dock.

The rain pelted down on them. Olsen's black pea jacket steamed from the sweat and heat generated in the struggle.

"I'm paralyzed! I'm paralyzed!" Bucky yelled, a sudden panic coming into his eyes. His face was chalk white.

Olsen sat back cautiously, letting go of one arm. Bucky's mouth twisted sideways in a spasm of pain, his fingers feebly twitched, and the arm lay helpless on the dock. Olsen let go of the other arm, still bracing his knee on the boy's chest. The arms were limp, lifeless. He had hurt the boy, hurt him bad. No matter, it was self-defense. The old fisherman took several deep breaths. It might be hard to explain. It *would* be hard to explain. He removed his knee cautiously. The boy squirmed feebly as if he were pinned to the dock with a spike.

"Got damn," Olsen cursed, climbing to his feet while Bucky Foster lay there, helpless. Olsen hurt all over. His eyes burned. He braced himself carefully with hands on knees and then stood slowly. Blood in his mouth. He spit. He grunted. He was used to pain.

Bucky Foster rolled his eyes. "Oh, God," he cried in a quavering voice. "For God's sake, help me, Mr. Olsen."

Help him! Funny boy. He had to get some help. The radio telephone on the *Thor* was the fastest way.

Olsen turned toward the boat. The wind was blowing harder. They would have to believe that the boy had tried to kill him. The old fisherman had taken only a few steps when he heard the ax being pulled out of the dock planking.

He made a half turn in surprise at the squeaking sound before the ax hit him flat sided in the back of the head. He staggered, a blinding light all around him, and plunged into the darkness, down into the cold, surging chop of Puget Sound.

This could not happen. It must not happen.

Bucky Foster strutted along the dock in his Captain Terror suit, the ax over his shoulder, logger style. What a stupid old geek! He watched as the purple-faced Olsen tried to stay afloat. He was still close to the dock, but already the current was sucking him away.

Half-conscious, Olsen struggled to swim in the rough dark water. In one last desperate effort to save himself, Olsen reached out for the receding dock, arms flailing in slow motion.

"Here," Bucky offered, smirking as he unlimbered the ax. "Grab onto this." He threw it to him. It fell short and sank.

Olsen's head went under and, as Bucky watched, the fastmoving waves pulled his half-submerged form toward the open bay, where he disappeared in the thrashing whitecaps.

Bucky Foster smiled. He felt just great.

"Goodby, Mr. Olsen," he called into the night. "Have a nice trip."

CHAPTER 18

While the Halloween party went on behind her, Su Myers stood in the window and watched the steep foaming waves smash up and over the Millers' bulkhead. Everybody else gathered in animated groups, talking loudly at each other, munching, drinking, waving arms and generally ignoring the storm raging just outside.

Su had never seen such big waves on the bay. The wind was blowing them into towering mountains of water that swept in toward the beach at frightening speed. She glanced at her watch and sipped her drink.

It was already eight o'clock. She had been a perfect bitch to Harold. Of course, he hadn't helped matters by stomping out of the house with Belinda like that. But what had seemed so important only an hour ago—her job with the weekly paper, her ambition to be a big-city newspaper woman, and her husband's callous, insensitive attitude about both—no longer mattered.

Harold and Belinda were out there somewhere in this horrible storm. So was Jeffrey. God, she wished she hadn't been so damn pushy about Jeff's going trick or treating with his friends. Maybe Harold was right. Maybe Jeff wasn't big enough to be out on his own.

She turned and watched the socializing groups behind her. She should really go over and join in; it was all good material for her column in the *South Sound Weekly.* Su Myers bit her lip and watched the raindrops running down the window in crazy, jerking patterns. Please God, she prayed silently, make them come now. Make them safe. Make everything all right.

The Millers had invited all sixty residents of Horsehead Point to the Halloween party, and already over thirty had showed up. Their white wall-to-wall carpet was stained with mud and pine needles around the door, and somebody had dropped pizza in front of the fireplace.

Kathy Miller expected this, and the rug cleaners were coming first thing in the morning. She seemed to be everywhere at once, greeting each new group of guests at the door as they came in dripping wet, taking their coats, remembering their names, getting everyone going in the right direction.

"Children down the stairs and to the right; there are plenty of cookies and ice cream and lots of great games to play." Off went the children.

Adults were given their choice of plain punch, party punch, hot wine or a drink of hard liquor from the bar. And once they had a glass in hand, they were guided to the tables of light snacks and hors d'oeuvres—cracked crab, stuffed mushrooms, crepes, pizza, smoked oysters, tacos, celery and cheese, deviled eggs and four salads, each made especially for the occasion by the head chef at the Port Gloster Golf and Tennis Club.

Once the food and drink were supplied, Kathy saw to it that the guests, now balancing plates and glasses, were sent into the mainstream of the party and introduced to the right people: people they might enjoy talking to, people they should talk to, or old friends they just might like to see again.

She did all this so smoothly there seemed to be a continuous flow from main door to sunken living room or to the children's party, as the case might be. Her cheeks glowed in the warm room where the air was heavy with the aroma of cigarette smoke and rich food.

She was a woman in her natural element, her husband Dave reflected as he loaded a silver tray with more cookies for the children. As for the young banker, the whole process made him a little dizzy. Dave Miller's job was to keep an eye on the children, relax and meet his neighbors, but it wasn't working out that way. The children confused him. He wasn't used to dealing with young people close to the riot stage.

Making his way carefully down the steps, he was assaulted by the driving primitive beat of disco music, and dizzied by the red and pink strobe lights sweeping the ceiling.

Before he could put the tray down, grubby little hands were tearing off cookies. None of them even said thank you.

"Having a good time, kids?" he timidly asked a boisterous group of younger children, all trying to play pin the tail on the skeleton at once.

"Yes!" they shouted, milling around. His own son Rocky was shouting the loudest as he tried to steal the mask from another smaller child.

"Here," Dave suggested. "Why don't you all get in line?"

"Cause we're having fun this way, Dad," Rocky replied.

Dave shrugged. He didn't know whether he should join in or fade out. Would his constant presence embarrass his children, or would his absence allow things to get out of control?

Out on the tiny sawdust floor, Carrie, his eight-year-old daughter, enthusiastically danced with a reluctant Billy Jacobi. Carrie had all the moves, Dave noted, including the come-hither glances. She threw her tiny hips around and snapped her fingers smoothly.

"Come on, silly," she called to her partner. Billy shuffled along, looking for a way out.

She was too young to act that way, wasn't she? Dave Miller didn't know; he'd have to ask Kathy. Where could Carrie have learned all that?

Fred and Sonia Elias always went their separate ways at parties. Sonia was shy and didn't enjoy small talk; she liked to be useful and busy. So at the Millers', after the formalities, she migrated to the kitchen to help behind the scenes.

Fred liked to circulate. He gave their hostess Kathy Miller a grandfatherly hug and told her she was looking younger every day. He also said the house looked beautiful, and then excused himself. He stoped briefly to kiss his daughter Jan and say hello to Jim Wentworth. But he could see it wasn't a good time to discuss Bucky Foster, so he moved on, making his way across the living room slowly, stopping to pat a shoulder here, shake a hand there.

Fred Elias was enjoying immensely his role as senior citizen in residence on Horsehead Point. By the fireplace, he latched onto the young telephone company couple, Donna and Bill Harrington. He praised Donna for her weekend landscaping around their new home and reminded Bill that he'd better get the New Jersey plates off his car soon or he might get a ticket.

Bill Harrington thanked him for the advice and told him he just hadn't found time. Donna took the opportunity to announce that she was going to have a baby. "Bill and I," she corrected herself, coloring slightly.

"Well, that's great news, just great." Fred gave her one of his patented grandfatherly squeezes. Donna had wide shoulders for such a short woman. "I'll bet it will be nice to stay home and not work for a change."

"Oh, well," she replied earnestly, "as soon as the baby's old enough I'll go back to work."

The Jacobis joined them. It was excellent timing as far as Fred was concerned. He really didn't approve of working mothers. "How's the boy?" Fred asked Wayne Jacobi. His son Hank was the starting fullback for the Captain Vancouver High School Panthers. But before Wayne could answer him, a blast of cold air swept through the front door, scattering napkins and halting conversation.

"Look who's here," Kathy Miller announced loudly.

Harold and Belinda Myers were soaking wet. They stood uncertainly in the doorway, blinking in the bright light. Belinda's white Princess Leia costume was splattered with mud.

"Come in," Dave Miller urged them. "Don't let all this hot air out. Gosh, we'd about given you up for dead."

"Not dead," Harold assured everybody, "just darn wet."

Su Myers rushed over to her husband and daughter, hugging them both. Her prayers had been answered. They were safe after all. "Where's Jeff?" she asked her husband.

He looked bewildered. "I don't know. Isn't he here?" With Dave Miller's help, he struggled out of his overcoat.

"No," Su Myers said quietly, "I haven't seen him all night." A deep irrational fear seized her. Something had happened to her son. Everybody in the room must help her look for him.

When the doorbell rang a second time, she instinctively rushed to answer it. This would be Jeff. But it was Ed Foster. He filled the doorway. His face was red, his camelhair overcoat flecked with dark raindrops.

"Hi, sweetheart," he boomed at Su, and pulled her into an embrace that flattened her breasts

126

against her ribcage.

She struggled angrily to get free. He ignored her. "I just love fighters," he breathed in her ear.

"Let me go," she hissed, conscious of everybody watching them.

He grunted and pushed her aside. "Where's the booze?" Ed Foster shouted to the assembled guests. "Let's get this party out of the huddle and onto the field."

Su Myers stood alone in the doorway looking out into the night. Wind-driven rain stung her face; anger and fear boiled and tangled inside her. God, how she hated pigs like Ed Foster. And where was her son? What in the world could have happened to him?

CHAPTER 19

Jeff Myers ran blindly down Horsehead Point Road, his pace slowed to a nightmarish crawl by the headwind. He sobbed with each tortured breath, a tiny struggling figure alone in the turbulent darkness. Footsteps paced him in the night, eyes watched from the black tossing woods, heavy breathing thundered in his ears. He had to get away.

By now Olsen had caught Bucky. He'd seen the old fisherman coming out of the cabin on the boat. He would grab Bucky by the neck and twist. Then Olsen would come after him. If he could just get to the Millers' it would be safe. Jeff didn't know how long he had been running. Minutes? Hours? His legs wobbled, his shoes slapped on the pavement.

Olsen might get in his truck and come looking for him. Jeff would be helpless, exhausted, caught in the middle of the road alone, with nobody to help him. There were lights ahead, twinkling lights in the trees. Adrenalin pouring into his system, Jeff Myers broke into his final sprint for safety. Behind him, blackness and fear pressed closer; the evil presence of Ivan Olsen pursued him.

He spotted the driveway by the faint glow of the white mailbox. He could clearly see the lights on at the Millers' house now. He surged ahead; only a few steps more. He slammed into a car parked in the darkness, his mouth striking a window. Stunned, he spun around, losing all sense of direction. Lights whirling, he fell face down in the driveway.

Harry George Junior waited quietly on Ivan Olsen's front steps. He saw nothing, heard nothing, felt nothing. His second Valium sucked fear, trouble, humiliation, cold and all other mental and physical discomforts into a wonderful pink-cotton whirlpool slowly revolving in his head.

There went his drunken daddy, his poor sick mom, his failing grades in school and other assorted humiliations of being a savage in a civilized world—right down the big pink drain. He was aware of his arms and legs and his location but indifferent to it all.

His long black hair hung in a wet, tangled mop. The wind shrieked around him. The rain blew into his face. Harry George hummed quietly, a little tune his father had taught him, *Wyamore's Blues.* "Got my name painted on my shirt, I ain't no ordinary dude, I don't have to work," Harry George Junior hummed.

He wasn't at all surprised to see Bucky Foster

130

come strutting across the lawn toward him. Harry was beyond surprise. He felt a lazy goodwill toward all. "Hello, stranger," he called. "And to all a good night." He chuckled quietly to himself, head falling forward, eyelids slowly opening and closing like giant manholes on his face. Bucky was going faster than a machine gun, arms waving, mouth flying, jumping up and down.

He looked funny, so Harry laughed. "Hey, Buck, what's happenin'?" he asked happily. There was another question he wanted to put to his good friend Bucky, something important. But it was gone, lost in the fluffy pink haze. Oh well, next year.

Bucky kept running, pointing. Mrs. Zondich. Goddamn it! Did he see Mrs. Zondich watching them? He knew her, Clara the fat old cow. They had to talk with her, Bucky said. Come with him. Come. Come. Harry sat. Bucky Foster pulled. Harry tried to stand. He *was* standing. Walk. Walk. Harry walked.

"The amazin' plastic man," he told Bucky Foster.

Clara Zondich, exhausted from her long vigil at the window, could not believe what she was seeing. Harry George and Bucky Foster were coming up her front walk. The Indian had been sitting on Olsen's front steps for some time. The Foster boy had suddenly reappeared from the other side of the house. He had been gone a long time to a place where she couldn't see him. "Oh, dear," Clara exclaimed to her best friend Milly. But the dog just twitched and moaned on the floor, lost in some old dog's dream.

She must call the sheriff again. This time he would have to send someone. She stood up as quickly as she could, groaning with the effort. Milly cocked one bloodshot eye. As Clara let the curtain fall, Bucky Foster broke into a run.

"Oh, dear," Clara bleated desperately. There was no time.

A fist crashed into the front door. Again and again it pounded, echoing through the empty house. "Trick or treat! Trick or treat!" Bucky called. The road was deserted.

"Just a minute," Clara Zondich croaked, her mouth so dry she could hardly speak. Most of the candy was gone; there were only a few pieces left. Clara picked up the bowl and hobbled to the door, checking the restraining chains as she approached. Laboriously she pulled back the locks, one at a time, and let the door open a crack.

"Trick or treat, Mrs. Zondich?" Bucky Foster said with exaggerated politeness, pushing his pimply face into the crack, forcing the door open until the chains snapped taut. Just over his head, the leering brown face of Harry George appeared. His eyes looked dead.

Clara Zondich locked her jaws in total disapproval. Without a word, she extended the bowl carefully toward Bucky. Thank God, this horrible young man would soon find himself face to face with a policeman. Bucky Foster snatched the bowl out of her hand.

"Stop that!" she protested, but her voice and body retreated. Her heart fluttered. The yellow death's head insignia on Bucky's Captain Terror suit glowed at her.

"Thank you, Mrs. Zondich," Bucky snickered from behind the door, his long thin hand pushing the bowl back through the crack. The candy was still there.

Gingerly she reached for it. He smiled at her encouragingly. Just as Clara felt the bowl touch her outstretched fingers, he dropped it. The cheap glass fractured on the flagstone entryway floor with a dull pop. Milly, startled by the noise, aroused herself and bravely rushed at the door, uttering hoarse desperate barks.

"Back, Fang." Harry George laughed his monster laugh.

"That's enough of that," Clara said angrily. "Quite enough."

"Oh, I'm so sorry," Bucky crooned. "Did I drop it?"

Clara was not fooled by this boy who could change voices like an actor. She was going to call the sheriff again. Stealthily she moved sideways in little crablike steps until she was directly behind the door.

"Oh, Mrs. Zondich," Bucky called sweetly, "have you been watching the trick we showed Mr. Olsen? Do you want to see the trick we have for you?"

She didn't answer. Carefully she placed both hands on the middle of the door and pushed, throwing her weight into it. It crashed shut with a satisfying double click of the spring locks. Quickly she slammed the deadbolt home and leaned against the door, her heart pounding with exertion.

They would go now, and she could call the police. Milly shuddered and whimpered and tried to climb up on her. "Just a minute, just a minute," Clara whispered to her. Then she became aware of another sound. It could not be! A hideous watery rattling, a steady squirting. It was! They were urinating on her door.

She stepped back in alarm, striking her head on the wall. Dazed, she braced herself and waited. Now she could smell it, the filthy disgusting stream of yellow urine on her door. She fled to the living room and to the telephone.

Slowly, hands trembling, she dialed 911. There were clicks and hisses. "Sealth Emergency," a coldly professional female voice answered.

"I need help," Clara whispered into the receiver. "I need help."

"I can't hear you," the voice stated in a flat lifeless tone. "Please speak up."

"This is Mrs. Zondich. I called this afternoon about a boy; he's here again."

"Yes, Mrs. Zondich."

"He's at the door." Her stomach turned over in protest at the thought.

"What's the boy doing?"

"He's—he's urinating."

"Urinating?"

"Yes."

"Stay inside, Mrs. Zondich, keep your door locked. We'll have an officer right out."

"Please tell him to hurry," Clara pleaded.

Sealth County Deputy Sheriff Bryan Emulooth heard the Zondich call, and there was no getting out of it, it was his beat. Emulooth swung his patrol car around and headed north down State Highway 410 toward Horsehead Point.

The driving rain came at him horizontally; the heavy-duty wipers were barely keeping up with it. Emulooth had driven more in the first three hours of his shift than he usually traveled in an entire evening. Already he'd quieted down three noisy Halloween parties, cleared up a minor traffic accident and filed reports on four broken windows.

He gripped the steering wheel tightly as he eased the cruiser out onto the Birch Slough Bridge, where the combination of high tide and wind set spray exploding over the railing. Horsehead Point was getting the full brunt of the storm. Fir boughs littered the road as he drove slowly down the south side of the Point.

Bryan Emulooth was young enough, at twenty-eight, still to have a philosophical attitude about Halloween and vandalism. They were as American as apple pie, he thought, and, all things considered, it hadn't been a bad night for him so far. The call was no big deal. The old lady was just crying wolf again. And Clara Zondich called wolf about once a week, on the average.

CHAPTER 20

The Millers' First Annual Horsehead Point Gala Halloween Party was in full swing. The steady monotonous beat of the disco music from the basement kept pace with the even drone of adult conversation upstairs. Excited children's voices mixed with the sedate clink of cocktail glasses. Everybody seemed to be having an awfully good time.

Harold Myers pulled out a cigarette and lit it. He had another bite of puréed shrimp on a cracker that tasted like wallpaper. He was stuffing himself. He took another swallow of his drink. It was bitter. He was drinking too much. He was damn worried about Jeffrey. He stood and listened absently while Dave Miller, Fred Elias and Ed Foster discussed development on the Point. He took a deep drag and glanced at his watch. It was nine o'clock, too late for Jeffrey to be out alone—much too late.

"There's no reason we can't fill up the slough," Ed Foster said. "It's a nuisance, it smells, and it could be turned into valuable, productive property. It's just a matter of financing."

Big Ed hitched up over his protruding stomach the $100 slacks with the expandable waistband. Bourbon-colored visions of ten or twelve flat bulldozed lots danced through his massive head.

"Seems to me that would change the whole character of the Point," Fred said mildly, puffing on his pipe while he seethed inside.

"Hell," boomed Foster, "change is what life is all about. That's why the goddamn Indians don't sit around here and bake clams anymore."

Dave Miller was a young but perceptive banker. He could feel the tension between the hulking, tipsy Foster and the older, slender, totally sober Fred Elias.

"Well, I'll tell you, Ed, I know what you mean, but there's a little more to it than just filling up the slough, as I'm sure you know. From the bank's point of view there's a rather high element of risk, I'm afraid."

"Oh yeah, the paperwork would stretch from here to Alaska," Ed agreed. "A lot of goddamn governmental crap to save some goddamn spiders."

That did it for Fred. Nobody was going to out-free enterprise him. Nobody had been a more passionate member of the Chamber of Commerce or the Kiwanis Club. "When you consider a development, don't you think you have a responsibility?" he asked Foster, his genial grin suddenly gone cold.

"Responsibility?" Ed Foster rolled the word

around on his thick tongue. "Responsibility? You bet, I have a responsibility to the guy looking for a house, to get him the best damn deal I can."

He downed the rest of the punch and looked around for somebody to pour him more. It was weak and tasted like Kool Aide. He didn't like guys like Fred Elias. They had gotten theirs and now they wanted to stop him from getting his.

"But what about the quality of life those people live?" Fred persisted.

"Oh sure," Dave Miller put in weakly, "that should be a consideration." He hoped that might deter Fred from getting in an argument.

Harold Myers shifted his feet nervously. He hated arguments of any kind. He liked everybody to get along, everything to be in its proper place. Jeffrey couldn't even keep his room picked up. If the boy didn't show up soon, Harold decided he'd have to go back outside in the storm and look for him.

"Do you know what a blue heron is?" Fred asked Ed Foster, staring straight into the big man's bloodshot eyes. He felt his heart banging on his ribs, but he couldn't just back down now. It was a matter of principle.

"Sure," Foster said, finally spotting Su Myers walking by with a tray of punch. "It's one of those birds with the big wings." He waved his empty cup at Su. "Hey, hon, I'll have another one of these."

Reluctantly she came over to the group. Fiesty broad, Ed Foster thought, remembering her struggle at the door when he came in. But he had about ten inches of good medicine for that. He liked what he had felt.

"When was the last time you saw more than one or two blue herons around here?" Fred Elias persisted.

"Hell, I don't know," Ed replied, taking a full glass and looking straight down Su Myers' open-necked dress. She had even bigger boobs than he had thought. He burped, and thanked her with a big wink.

She ignored him and went over to her husband. "Harold," she said, "I'm worried sick about Jeff. Where can he be? It's so late."

"I don't know," he told her, "but I can tell you one thing—he's never going out like this again. You just can't trust him."

It was the wrong thing to say. Harold could see the tears forming. "Su, honey," he started to say, but she brushed him off.

"My God, Harold, don't you care about anybody but your precious self and your precious goddamn feelings?" she asked loudly, and walked away.

Fred Elias didn't seem to notice. He kept after Ed Foster. "That's because when you filled in that lot down there where you built the Harrington house, you filled in their habitat." Fred shook his finger accusingly. "You chopped down all the old snags where the herons nest; you chased them out. The slough's the only place they have left."

Fred Elias was angry. He felt the tremors in his hands. He could imagine his arteries clogging. But he could not let people like Ed Foster run over everything decent just for a profit. Fred Elias didn't hate Ed Foster, but he sure didn't like anything about the man or the way he ran his business. He was, to Fred's way of thinking, totally irresponsible.

Ed Foster was about to tell Fred Elias that the fucking blue heron could go and live in a parking lot, and the old man could go with them, when he saw how uncomfortable the whole conversation was making banker Dave Miller. Ed didn't want to queer Dave at this stage of the game. His wife Linda was right: Dave could be a big help.

Harold Myers ground out his cigarette. He would find Su, apologize for whatever he was supposed to apologize for and then go look for Jeff.

"Fred, there you are," Sonia Elias called, coming over to take her husband's arm. "I've been looking all over for you. You're just the man we need to help with the kids' ice cream."

She didn't fool him. She'd been watching, and it was her way of getting him to calm down. "Excuse me," Fred told the men. "I believe I'm wanted."

Ed Foster grunted.

Then Harold Myers turned and saw Jeff running toward him from across the room. The boy's rusty hair was plastered to his head, his lip was badly cut and bleeding.

"Daddy," he cried, clinging to him fiercely.

"Jeff, goddamn it," Harold swore, but he couldn't sustain his anger. "What happened?"

"I fell," Jeff gasped, crying and panting. "I fell."

Harold looked around for Su, just as all the lights dimmed to a dull yellow. The children downstairs squealed and the adult conversation stopped. The disco music wound down. For a few seconds all the light bulbs in the Millers' house faded to tiny pinpricks; then they regained full power.

"What was that?" Dave Miller asked Fred. They

were standing in the kitchen.

"Probably a tree on the power line. Happens all the time," the old man told him. "Ten years ago we'd lose our power twice a day all winter long, didn't we, Sonia?"

She nodded, and presented the two men with aluminum ice cream scoops. "Dig in," she told them, "and don't stop till you hit bottom."

In the living room the conversation began to pick up again, but now several people went over to the front window and looked out.

"My God, look at those waves," Barbara Jacobi said.

Harold Myers still couldn't see Su anywhere. "Where have you been, Jeffrey?" he asked his son. "Your mom and I have been worried sick."

Jeff hung onto his father. He was safe. Olsen couldn't get him here. "I fell," he repeated, sobbing. "I fell in the dark."

The lights dimmed again and just as quickly came back up.

"Make up your mind," somebody joked. Then they went out completely, plunging Horsehead Point into total darkness.

CHAPTER 21

Clara Zondich sat in the dark, listening for the patrol car, watching for the welcome sweep of headlights coming down the road. The boys were gone. Milly whimpered at her feet. The wind hit the side of the house in deep, booming compressions. The darkness was complete. She couldn't see Ivan Olsen's house. She couldn't see the road or the shaking hand she tapped impatiently on the arm of the chair where she sat.

Milly had been afraid of the dark since she was a puppy; it was for that reason Clara kept the green Tiffany lamp burning day and night. Now she reached down to reassure the trembling dog. "No electricity," she explained, her own voice 'quavering. "No wites for poor Milly."

Clara had been sitting rigidly in the chair by the window since the lights went out. She heard the fir boughs scraping on the eaves in back of the house and the faint tick-tick of the baseboard heaters cooling. Where was that deputy?

As the room cooled in the darkness, she slowly became aware of another sensation—a river of frigid air running at floor level. At first it was a trickle around her feet; then it increased to a steady flow and began climbing up her legs.

All the doors were locked. All the windows were secure. Where could the draft be coming from? Her jaw trembled. She could not have left a window open; she was sure of it. She closed her eyes and mentally tried to picture herself making her once-daily check of security.

The icy invisible river rose higher. It was to her knees. She couldn't think clearly. It was impossible to concentrate. Oh dear, oh dear, why didn't the lights come on? When they first faded and then flashed back up, she had felt a burst of hope. But now that was gone too.

She had to find the open window, and to do that she had to have light. Slowly, carefully, Clara pulled herself upright in the chair and stood up. She was shaking all over; she must stop that. Milly let out a desperate howl, a low, hoarse rattle that rose to a piercing whine. "I'll be right back, darling," Clara called.

Slowly feeling her way along the plaster wall with her hands, she groped forward toward the kitchen. She must be very careful. If she fell and broke her hip she might be an invalid for life. Milly switched from wailing to barking. Clara could hear her scuttling around in the dark like a wounded beetle. For heaven's sake, what was it now? Sometimes that dog could be a trial.

She arrived at the kitchen counter and stopped to recover her breath. She felt faint and hot. A freezing layer of air whirled around her. A window was definitely open somewhere in the house.

"It's all right, Milly," she called to the old dog, fumbling in the counter drawer for candles and matches. Her hand shook so badly it took three matches before the wick on the half-burned candle finally caught and held, a tiny flame of hope in the darkness.

Her breath rasping, Clara set out down the hall, the candle flickering dangerously low, casting giant shadows along the walls. Everything depended on acting quickly. Obsessed with the vision of a window open at ground level where a man could easily climb in, she hobbled to her bedroom. All the windows were closed and locked.

The spare bedroom. Could it be in there? That window hadn't been opened since last summer. Somebody could already be in there waiting. She stopped, listening, the tiny candle flame quivering in her shaking hand. The rain was deafening on the roof. She opened the spare bedroom door; cold, stale air rushed out.

The bathroom; it could be the bathroom. Without closely checking the spare-room windows, she hobbled into the bathroom. The cold air grew stronger.

A freezing stream hit her at the waist and crawled up her body as she walked. It was in the bathroom! Holding her candle high, she saw that the small window over the tub was open. She couldn't reach it and hold the candle at the same time. She had opened it that morning to vent steam. How could she have been so stupid? Confused, she retreated, shutting the bathroom door behind her.

A man couldn't get through that window. But could a boy? She didn't know. Why didn't the lights come on? Panting, she headed back down the hall.

Clara Zondich, an old woman in ill health and badly frightened, couldn't go on much longer. She had to sit down. Milly was quieter now, but Clara could still hear the old dog crawling around looking for a safe corner.

As she entered the living room, a terrible thought occurred to her. Somebody was already in the house. The boys wouldn't do that. They were just trying to scare her, a helpless old lady. They wouldn't actually come into her house!

The candle shook violently in her hand. Oh please get here, she prayed silently for the deputy. Please come now. In answer to her fervent prayer, a bright light swept across the window. A firm knock sounded at the door. Thank God.

"I'm here," Clara called, rushing to the door.

"County Sheriff," the clear voice announced.

Thank God! Thank God! She fumbled one-handed with the locks. The first two came easily, the last deadbolt wouldn't budge.

"Take it easy, Mrs. Zondich."

Yes. Yes. The last bolt slid back. The door slammed open, almost knocking her over. The candle went out.

Something was coming for her. It was in the door. It was inside. Huge, bulking, gruffing and snorting

146

like an animal, it reached for her.

"Milly!" she shrieked, backing across the room, the cry choking off as her throat constricted, and her bowels gave way.

Clara's left foot caught on the corner of the fireplace and she fell heavily on the slate hearth, striking her head. It was there, a terrifying shapeless mass closing over her. "'No!" she shouted at it. "No!" trying to throw up her hands to protect herself.

The creature jumped astride, crushing the wind out of her body. Viselike hands closed on her skull and slammed it on the hearth. Clara Zondich screamed, but the suffocating, slippery thing forced the sound back inside her. Her eyes bulged, but they could no longer see the shape of the relentless black force that pushed her down into the cold, cold darkness.

Chapter 22

The hot cedar-scented blaze in the Millers' fireplace popped and snapped and sent dancing shadows streaking across the rough plaster ceiling. A row of flickering candles stood on the wide oak mantel. All the neighbors gathered around, warming themselves by the fire.

"We were out of power for a week in 1961," Sonia Elias was telling Barbara Jacobi.

"My goodness, what did you do?"

"We did our best," said Sonia matter-of-factly.

"My God, we'll lose all our frozen steaks," Su Myers moaned.

"Oh, they'll last a couple of days," Fred assured her. "If things get tough, I have a generator. You can bring them over to our house."

The wind whistled in the overhangs and shook the house. Without lights, the party became subdued. The neighbors drew closer together and spoke in lower voices. The children were quiet too as they sat behind the adults around the Millers' marble coffee table, having seconds on black-and-orange ice cream.

Even Ed Foster had mellowed in the darkness. "I wonder how hard it's blowing?" he asked Fred solicitously, knowing the old man would have an answer.

"Oh, I'd say we're getting gusts to fifty, maybe even sixty. I've seen it blow a lot harder though, believe me."

"Well, I hope they get us some power soon, or we'll have to let the kids eat all the ice cream," Dave Miller said. Some of the children cheered.

In spite of his little joke, however, the lack of electricity was making Dave distinctly uncomfortable. Nothing worked. Like Su Myers, he was worried about food in his freezer. Also the oil furnace wouldn't run because it required electricity for the burner fans, something he hadn't realized until Fred Elias explained it to him.

Soon, he saw, there would be no hot water. And there was no electricity to open his garage door, either. He'd tried to call the power company but he couldn't get through. That irritated him. It showed poor planning. He was going to give those people a piece of his mind in the morning.

What had been a great party, with everybody meeting everybody else, had turned into a very quiet gathering around the fireplace. And the discussion was dragging, as far as Dave was concerned.

The young teacher, Fred's daughter Jan Elias,

was saying she thought everybody should do without electricity once a month just to remind them what it was like. To Dave Miller that was just a stupid idea. Why turn back the clock?

"To experience what it's really like adds another dimension to our lives," she said earnestly. "Look at us: we're neighbors, but we're really strangers, and if the lights had stayed on that's all we'd ever be. But now, because we don't have our artificial light, we've been drawn closer together. We can relate better as people."

That sure was a lot of crap, but her bearded boyfriend, Jim Wentworth the volunteer fireman, just nodded as if he agreed with everything she said. He was a strange duck, didn't say much. Dave had heard he was a graduate of Stanford, but that was hard to believe.

David Miller certainly didn't feel closer to anybody because the lights were out. He felt uneasy. The kids were starting to get restless and run around the living room.

"Rocky, you come back and sit down," he ordered his son. He had no idea what they were doing, giggling and whispering back behind the couch. The kids were supposed to be downstairs, but with no electricity that wasn't a good idea either.

Dave sighed. Nobody was making a move to leave, and he couldn't think of any graceful way to break up the party yet. He'd just have to get some more wood for the fire and wait them out.

"Look what happened in New York City when they had a blackout," Jan was saying.

"Yeah, but look what happened in New York City the second time," Bill Harrington countered. (The

Harringtons, after all, were recently from New Jersey.) "The vandalism was terrible."

Good for you, thought Dave, wondering where he'd left the flashlight. Jan Elias certainly had a lot of radical opinions for a schoolteacher.

"That was just an illustration. We're an entirely different community than New York City. We don't have muggers and rapists on every street corner," Jan shot back defensively.

Well, the heck with it. He'd go without the flashlight. He made his way down the darkened hall, feeling for the door into the garage that he knew was directly in front of him.

Touché, score one for her. It was true. Compared to New York or L.A., Horsehead Point was heaven on earth. No smog, no traffic, no water problems, no sewage problems, no crime—nothing to worry about except a little growth and development. Why should anybody want to stop progress? It was the lifeblood of a growing economy.

Two kids ran by him, squealing in the darkness. "Hey," he called, but they were gone. He'd better speak to Kathy; that sort of thing had to stop. His wife would know what to do. Kids that age should not be running around in the dark unsupervised.

He twisted the knob on the garage door and pulled. It was stuck. He couldn't see his hand. He pulled again; the door wasn't stuck, somebody was holding it. It gave slightly and then pulled back.

An electrifying chill ran up his spine and he retracted his hand quickly. This couldn't be. He grasped the door handle again, turned and pulled. It gave a bit more this time and then was definitely snatched back.

152

"Hey," he called weakly, retreating in confusion. "Stop that." He heard the handle turning. What was going on here?

A tiny sliver of light appeared and then widened as the door swung slowly open. A shadowy figure, a grotesque, illuminated, chalk-white face, twisted and lopsided, appeared.

"Who is that?" Dave Miller shouted, panic just a few breaths away.

"Did I scare you?" Bucky Foster asked hopefully, a flashlight pointed upward into his face. He relaxed his features and lowered the light.

It was only the Foster kid. "What are you doing in the garage?" Dave Miller demanded, anger washing over retreating panic. The boy had a strange-looking rubber suit on. He looked like a scuba diver.

"Playing hide and seek with the rest of the kids," Bucky said, hurt in his voice.

"Oh," Dave replied, trying to get his bearings. He didn't remember Bucky Foster's coming in with his stepfather Ed.

"This is a great party, Mr. Miller. We're having lots of fun," Bucky went on in a juvenile bubble of enthusiasm. "Aren't we, Harry?"

Behind him, out of the shadows, came Harry George Junior, with his long black hair tangled in dripping wet ringlets. He looked like a damn zombie.

"Now see here," Dave snapped, angered to see George, "I don't want you guys playing around in my garage."

The Foster kid was all right, but who had invited Harry George Junior? The Georges didn't even live on the Point. He had nothing against them except that they were Indians, and Harry was too old to be creeping around in the dark with his kids.

"Go out in the living room," he ordered them abruptly.

"Sure, Mr. Miller. We were just playing with the kids," Bucky repeated innocently.

"Fine. Go and play in the living room."

The two boys brushed past. The truth was they'd scared the living hell right out of him. He felt his way to the woodpile, running his hand along the familiar fender of the Thunderbird. It was smooth and clean and parked right where'd he'd left it. That made him feel a little better. He loaded up his arms with wood. There was no way to deny it; the encounter had shaken him badly.

It was silly, but he'd always been a little afraid of the dark as a boy. He could remember lying in bed in Indianapolis, imagining Geronimo coming to get him in his sleep—the cruel eyes, the dusky darkness of the man, the poised tomahawk.

He kicked the door shut behind him and hurried down the hall toward the light. Maybe that was why he disliked Harry George. There's something behind me; I've got to hurry. It was a game he'd played as a child. No, it wasn't a game; it was a phobia, and he still felt there was something back there, and tonight it was very close.

Dave Miller was glad to get back to candles and people. The fire cast a welcome light out into the dark room. He dropped the wood and selected a few pieces.

"Thank God you're back. We were about to send out a search party," Barbara Jacobi joked.

Very funny lady. He put a good-sized piece of dry cedar on the fire. It caught with an explosion of sparks, sending those closest to the blaze jumping back.

"Hey, take it easy, David." Ed Foster joined in the joking. "You'll burn down the house."

What Dave Miller wanted was more fire and light. He had a sudden need for both. Here he was, thirty years old, a senior vice president at the biggest bank in Washington State, afraid of a movie-lot Geronimo. Maybe he needed to see a headshrinker. That was a silly idea. Now he thought about it, the movie Geronimo probably wasn't even a real Indian. There were so few of them who could do anything. Was Geronimo really Burt Lancaster? It might have been; it was so long ago that he had seen the frightening movie. Funny that the childhood fear was still with him.

Dave Miller rubbed his hands together briskly. He hated the dark. He hated uncertainty. If these outages were as frequent as Fred Elias indicated, perhaps he should look for a nice condo for them in Seattle where Kathy and the kids would be safe.

The candles on the mantel were burning low. What if Kathy didn't have any more—what then? Would the stores in Three Corners be open on Halloween?

"Kathy, we do have more candles, don't we?" he asked her, trying to keep the fear suppressed. For some reason he didn't fully understand, Dave Miller was terrified of being trapped in the dark surrounded by his good neighbors.

CHAPTER 23

It was strange not to see the lights along Horsehead Point Road. Even though the houses were widely separated on large lots, the residents favored lots of outdoor lighting on their porches, driveways and patios. Some even had spotlights on the trees to illuminate the clusters of mailboxes alongside the road. At night the boxes, under their miniature shake roofs, reminded Deputy Bryan Emulooth of deserted little country bus stations.

The sudden power outage had transformed the glowing all-electric suburb back into a primitive dark evergreen forest. The Point must have looked like this when the Klehonia Indians used it as a fish camp—except that even the Klehonia Indians were smart enough to withdraw to the shelter of the mainland at the approach of winter, Emulooth reflected.

He smoked as he drove and played the patrol-car spotlight along the overhead power lines. Broken tree limbs dangled and flapped in the wind like tattered laundry on the wires. The rain rushed at the windshield in tight little patterns.

Deputy Emulooth took a long drag on his cigarette. The glowing red tip and harsh taste reminded him of other, more lonely nights in Germany. Driving Horsehead Point on Halloween sure beat the hell out of patroling the Czech border in an unheated tank.

Just across from the Myers' house a huge tree had come down, completely blocking the narrow road. There was the source of the outage. It meant he would have to walk over to Clara Zondich's house, just beyond.

"Christ," he said to himself. If this was another of her hysterical calls because she was lonely and wanted some attention, he was going to be more than pissed. He had better things to do. He locked the spotlight on the tree and struggled into his knee-length rubberized raincoat. The downed tree was a fir. Its mushroom-shaped shallow roots stuck up as high as a house in front of the car.

Emulooth took the flashlight off the dash, put the portable walkie-talkie in his jacket pocket and got out. The force of the wind took him by surprise, catching the door as he opened it. It wrenched the handle out of his hand, snapping the hinges backward.

"Goddamn it," he swore, pulling back the door, wincing at the sound of screeching metal against metal. He slammed the door shut. The latch caught, but the door itself was definitely sprung.

Fighting the howling wind, he looked for a way across the downed fir.

The limbs sticking into the air formed a forest of their own, and in climbing through them he loosened showers of water down his neck. People like Clara Zondich gave him a pain in the ass. His slicker was wet on the inside; so was his wool jacket. In fact he was wet all over. What a way to make a living, he thought, as he walked down the deserted road.

There were no candles in Clara's window—no light whatsoever. That was odd, very odd. How long had it been since she called? Not over five minutes, maybe ten? Worried, he broke into a jog and headed up the front walk.

At the base of the stairs the light hit what looked like a bundle of white laundry. He looked closer. It was Milly, the old lady's poodle.

He reached down: she was still warm but dead. "Son-of-a-bitch," Emulooth muttered. He left the dog and took the steps two at a time. The front door was wide open and banging. He should have hurried. *There is no such thing as a routine call. Treat every call like an emergency.* He knew all that.

"Goddamn it." Emulooth swore out loud at himself as he rushed into the house, sweeping the room with his light. "Goddamn it all to hell."

He found Clara Zondich on the first pass, crumpled in front of the cold fireplace. Emulooth knelt beside her. He could smell shit. There was blood all over her face, a lot of it. It had pooled on the flagstone hearth.

"Mrs. Zondich?" He held himself steady and took her wrist. She groaned. There was still

159

a faint pulse.

Emulooth pulled the walkie-talkie out of his jacket. Step one: call the medics. Step two: stabilize the victim and treat for shock. And pray his own stupidity had not cost the old lady her life.

The harsh buzz of Jim Wentworth's pocket pager stopped the lagging conversation in front of the Millers' fireplace instantly.

"What in the world was that?" Kathy Miller asked.

Jim got up and showed her the gray cylinder he kept on his belt for fire calls. "Where's the phone?" he asked her.

She led him into the kitchen. "How can there be a fire when it's raining so hard?" somebody in the dark asked.

Fred Elias was going to answer, but he caught himself. He was getting tired and irritable. Sometimes his younger neighbors amazed him. They knew very little about the power of fire, wind and water. They all lived very warm, comfortable, orderly lives. Fred Elias wondered how long they could survive without their modern conveniences. He knew what a windswept fire could do, and it frightened him to think Jim might have to go out and fight one on a night like this.

"Got to go," Jim Wentworth announced, coming back. He already had his yellow parka on.

"What's up?" Fred asked him.

"Clara Zondich had an accident."

"Bad?"

"Bad enough to call the aide car. I've got to run." He gave Jan Elias a quick kiss.

160

"Jan can stay over at our place until you get back," Fred offered.

Jim waved his hand in agreement and was gone.

"That's terrible," Su Myers said, but she also realized it was something to put in her weekly Horsehead Point Ramblings column.

Jeff leaned against her. His lip was badly swollen, and he looked pale, but otherwise he seemed all right. He said he didn't feel like playing, and she didn't mind. Su enjoyed having her son next to her—it happened so seldom.

"That's the old lady at the corner?" Bill Harrington asked.

"Yes, she's the bitchy one that calls the police all the time about the kids at the bus stop," Barbara Jacobi added.

"Oh, that one," somebody else said.

"What happened to Mrs. Zondich?" Bucky Foster asked, from the marble table where he was playing a battery-operated computer game with Rocky Miller.

Harry George Junior was asleep against the back wall, his long hair across his face.

"She fell down or something," Ed Foster told his stepson. "Come on, it's time for us to go."

He wanted to advise the boy that Hilda Bryant had called him about his sheep-painting caper, and let the kid know he would be shelling out $550 in the morning so she wouldn't call the police about the one that had died.

"Gee, that's too bad," Bucky replied absently. "Just one more game, Ed. It will only take a minute."

"One more," Foster grumbled. "But step on it."

He wasn't going to chew Bucky out. He just wanted to let him know he'd better wise up or he was going to get his skinny little ass in a bad jam someday.

The tiny electronic blips flashed back and forth across the darkened board, buzzing as they moved. It was Rocky Miller's game, and he was maneuvering Bucky's blip into a corner for the kill.

"Whatever is that hideous costume supposed to represent?" Barbara Jacobi asked Jan Elias, referring to Bucky's shiny black suit.

"I think it's Captain Terror; that's a comic-book character," Jan replied.

"My God, it's ugly. It looks so sinister. Why can't they wear nice things and be cowboys and Indians anymore?"

Bucky's trapped blip came charging back, feinting, dodging, driving. It went straight for Rocky and hit him head on. The enemy blip exploded in a shower of electronic bits.

"I blasted you! I blasted the shit out of you!" Bucky Foster shouted, to the astonishment of the Millers' remaining guests.

CHAPTER 24

Jim Wentworth pushed the Bronco hard down the perimeter road, blue trouble lights flashing. The sealed-beam Cunningham spotlights mounted on the front bumper picked up limbs and branches in the road, but he went straight over them. They clanged and slapped at the underside of the high-sprung vehicle. It was too dangerous to swerve, and he didn't have time to find a path through the debris from the storm.

By the time he arrived at the Zondich house the county ambulance was already there. He parked in the street and ran up the front steps, noting the dead dog as he passed.

Inside, the volunteer firemen had already loaded Clara on a stretcher. Her face was badly bruised on the left side. "It's okay, lady, we got you," Pinky Hart assured her.

Emulooth carried the IV as they maneuvered her around the living room and headed for the door. Her eyes were open; her tongue made wet clicking sounds.

"What's the situation?" Jim asked Pinky.

"Fall. She's stabilized, looks like a bad concussion." Pinky Hart was short and square and could smile at anything. "Give us a hand, old buddy."

They eased her down the front steps, heads down, holding her steady in the gusting wind. Jim Wentworth looked at the old lady's eyes. The irises were brown and cloudy, the pupils dilated all out of proportion.

The wind tore at them while they loaded her into the back of the ambulance, their breath puffing out in little smoke signals that were snatched away into the night. The rain had finally stopped.

"Thanks, guys." Emulooth slapped Hart on the back.

"All part of the service," Hart said. "It's lucky we got here. Our man on the Point has a hard time getting out of bed." He leered at Jim Wentworth.

Jim grinned back. "That's your problem, you horny little bastard."

The firemen didn't waste time. Pinky slammed the back doors shut and the ambulance pulled out, siren wailing. They watched it until the flashing red lights were gone, and then Jim followed the deputy back up the walk toward the house.

Jim Wentworth and Bryan Emulooth were about the same age. They played for rival slow-pitch baseball teams and had covered a lot of emergencies together. Jim knew something was bothering the deputy.

164

"What's the trouble, Bryan?" he asked. Emulooth's uniform was soaked; he must be freezing.

"That, for one," the deputy said, pointing at the poodle's body.

Jim knelt down, putting his flashlight on the dog. The body seemed cold, but rigor mortis hadn't set in. He turned the dog over. "Old dog," he said.

"Yeah," the deputy agreed noncommittally, leading Jim into the house. His flashlight shone around the living room.

"Not much furniture," Jim said, seeing the candles piled on the kitchen table.

The deputy stood in the middle of the room.

"What's bothering you, Bryan?"

"Oh, I shoulda got out here faster. I coulda got out here a lot faster. I thought it was just the old gal raising hell again."

"You got a call earlier?"

"Yeah. We got a call this afternoon and then later this evening."

"What was the trouble?"

Emulooth put his long silver flashlight in the crook of his arm and tried to light a cigarette. It was bent and wet on one side. He snapped his lighter and held the flame until he finally got the cigarette going.

"Kids, motorcycles, the usual. Kid named Foster. Know him?"

"Yeah," Jim Wentworth replied, running his light around the room. "He was at the Halloween party where I was tonight, as a matter of fact."

Emulooth spit out a long stream of smoke. "The old lady's paranoid about kids, always has been. She's complained about Foster before." The cigarette smoke smelled strong in the cold house.

"What was the call tonight?" Jim asked. The place hardly looked lived in.

"Trick or treaters apparently. She didn't say who, just that somebody was pissing on her door. Scared her, I guess."

"Yeah, well, that doesn't have much to do with her falling down."

The deputy drew hard on his cigarette. "No, doesn't look like it. It's the dog that really bothers me."

"Well, like I said, it's an old dog," Jim offered. "Old dogs die."

"Yeah."

"Want to take a look around?" Jim suggested.

"Sure."

Emulooth led the way. The bareness of the front room was only a preview. The few pieces of furniture scattered around in the various rooms reminded Jim of props for a play that had never opened. The entire back half of the basement was piled with paper boxes filled with paper sacks.

"Looks like she saved every grocery sack she ever got," Jim remarked. His voice echoed in the concrete room.

"Yeah, looks like it."

Upstairs, they found the open bathroom window. Jim reached over the tub and shut it.

"Goddamn it to hell," Emulooth swore as they walked back to the front room.

"What's the matter?"

"I shoulda got here quicker." The deputy sounded depressed.

"Bullshit," Jim Wentworth replied. "It probably

wouldn't have made any difference at all."

Jim Wentworth did not have a vivid imagination. He didn't believe in fairies or ghosts, and every accident, every house fire he'd ever covered had a perfectly logical explanation. Sometimes it wasn't apparent, but it was always there. He worked with figures and angles. If something didn't fit, there was a reason, always.

"Maybe the dog just died. The old lady was already upset over the kids. It was stormy, the lights went out, she found the dog. She panicked, ran back inside and either collapsed or fell."

"Sounds reasonable to me," Emulooth said, still standing in the center of the room.

"Was the door open?"

"What?" the deputy said.

"Was the door open?"

"Yeah, the door was open."

"Well," Jim went on, feeling that everything fit, "she ran out, found the dog, panicked—I mean, here's this old gal, and the dog means everything to her, right?—she panics, runs back in and, like I said, collapses or falls in the dark."

"Sounds good," Emulooth said, looking for a place to put out his cigarette.

"Find a flashlight?"

"No, no flashlight, just those candles." Emulooth walked to the door, knocked off the burning cigarette tip and field stripped the butt, scattering the remaining tobacco in the wind.

"Doesn't look to me like anything's disturbed. I mean nothing is turned upside down or anything," Jim said.

"No, doesn't look like it," Emulooth replied,

swinging the light around the living room aimlessly.

"When was the last time you had an assault in connection with a house robbery in this county, Bryan?"

The deputy stopped moving the light. "I don't remember one."

"So why are we standing around here freezing our asses off?" Jim asked him. It was silly. Bryan Emulooth was making up stories in his head.

"I don't know."

"Good. Let's close this place up," Jim suggested, "and you can talk to the old gal in the morning. No more mystery."

"Sounds good to me." Emulooth shook himself, trying to get the stiffness out of his shoulders.

"What are we going to do with the dog?"

"Take her in, I guess. Maybe the pound can figure out what happened." Emulooth put on his raincoat and led the way out on the porch.

The wind was dying and the temperature was dropping. "Bryan, old buddy," Jim told him as they walked down the front steps, "I'll bet you a drink, I'll bet you two drinks, that's exactly the way it happened. The old lady will tell you herself."

"I sure hope so," Emulooth said, shaking Jim's hand. He knelt and picked up the dog, cradling it carefully in his arms.

"Damn it, Bryan, don't act so guilty," Jim told him, slapping his friend on the back. He'd never seen Emulooth so down.

"Yeah, well, I can't help it. I shoulda put my foot on the floor when I first got the call."

"Like hell. You came, man, that's what counts,"

Jim Wentworth told him, walking his friend down to the road. "Get off this thing, Bryan. Forget it; it's over."

Overhead, a sharp sliver of moon sliced through the clouds and then was gone.

"Yeah, I guess it is. I'll see you tomorrow."

CHAPTER 25

The kerosene lamps spread a soft, rich glow around the Eliases' living room, where Fred and Sonia sat with their daughter, waiting for Jim Wentworth. The power outage gave Sonia a perfect excuse for using the old-fashioned method of lighting, which she preferred anyway.

Sonia Elias had kept every lamp she and Fred had collected over the years, and they were all in perfect working order. The tall stately railroad models from Montana sat over the fireplace. The rose-tinted wall hangers with the delicate curved chimneys, from her mother's farm in Kansas, burned at each end of the spacious room. And the brass hurricane lamps they had bought their first year on Horsehead Point were permanently fixed in the entryway.

"The Millers seem like nice people," she said,

pouring Fred and Jan tiny glasses of homemade peach brandy from a gallon apple juice bottle. Sonia herself didn't drink. She never had and she never would.

"Yes," Jan agreed.

"I thought that remark about Clara that Barbara Jacobi made was really uncalled for," Fred said, putting more wood on the fire.

Jan smiled. "Well, Daddy, Clara Zondich does harass those kids all the time. Let's face it, she's not the most popular woman in the neighborhood."

He stood up, satisfied the fire was going. "Yes, but the kids also go out of their way to bother her. Don't forget that."

"But if she'd try being nice to them once in awhile, you know, they'd be nicer to her. I'm sorry, but if you go out of your way to be mean to children, they'll go out of their way to be mean to you."

"Clara's just old," Sonia remarked, capping the brandy.

Fred joined them on the wide, comfortable leather couch where they could look out the front window. The weather was definitely clearing. They could see the lights of Seattle across the bay, and the white crests on the waves sweeping around the end of the Point.

Fred sipped his brandy. It was a good batch, maybe the best he'd ever made. For just an instant he saw a piece of the moon slip between the clouds. He might be able to get some fishing in tomorrow after all.

"Getting old is no excuse," Jan told her mother. "That's just a copout people like Clara use."

Sonia started to interrupt, but Jan held up her

hands. "I know, I know. The poor lady just had an accident. I'm as sorry as you are, Mom, I really am. But I doubt that she's ever been very nice to children even when she was young."

"Well, I hope she's all right," Fred said, glancing at his barometer on the wall. It was still down, not a good sign, but maybe there would at least be a lull before the next weather front hit. It would be cold on the water. He'd have to get out his long johns. Fred could feel the cold wind on his face, the gentle motion of the boat; he could imagine the rod bending double. He'd have to put it to Sonia just right or she'd ground him.

"Honey," Sonia told her daughter kindly, taking her hand, "you have to remember that Clara has not had an easy life. You know she took care of poor old Walter for, what was it, Fred, almost four years?"

"Just about four," Fred agreed. He remembered Clara's leading her husband Walter out on his daily walks to the mailbox, nothing but skin and bone. A bad heart was better than cancer. Fred Elias thanked God for being kind to him.

"Walter was not an easy man to take care of when he was well, honey," Sonia explained, "and he just made life miserable for her when he was sick. Clara never complained, never. And we'd see her at church, sitting all alone, so pale and drawn. My heart just went out to her. It still does."

Jan sampled the brandy. She would never have the honest Christian charity of her mother, she thought. How could Sonia say that about a woman who had never spoken a kind word to her?

Jan knew that for a fact. The old lady had deliberately snubbed her mother. Half the time she wouldn't even return her "Good days," but Sonia kept right on offering them. "The only point I was trying to make is that Mrs. Zondich could be a little nicer to the kids. Kids don't go running across your lawn. Kids don't harass you. That's because both of you are nice to them. You like kids."

Fred smiled at his daughter. She was right. He loved children, always had. "And we're old and feeble, right?" he kidded her gently. "Just as old as Clara."

Jan had deliberately avoided saying that. "That's not what I meant." She had never thought of her parents as old until just recently.

"I wonder what's keeping Jim?" Sonia said.

"He'll get here when he gets here," Fred told her, looking back out the window.

He decided he'd take the positive approach, tell Sonia he was going fishing right after his walk in the morning. She knew how much fishing meant to him. There was nothing dangerous about sitting in a boat.

"Wasn't that just a horrible costume the Foster boy was wearing tonight?" Sonia asked her daughter.

"It was a little odd," Jan agreed.

"It looked like one of those frogmen suits or something. Goodness."

"He was supposed to be Captain Terror. He's a comic-book character, Mother." Bernard Foster's grotesque picture in her art portfolio flashed through her mind.

"Captain Terror?" Sonia asked. "What in the world does he do?"

174

"Terrorizes people, I guess. All for a worthy cause, I suppose," Jan told her absently. It was a powerful drawing. She could see the face of the old woman in the drawing quite clearly. It was not a pleasant thought.

"Well, I never," her mother said. "Whatever you call that ugly suit, it was certainly out of place with all those darling costumes everybody else was wearing. That little Belinda Myers in her princess outfit was as cute as a bug's ear."

"Speaking of Bucky Foster," Fred cut in, reminded of his vow that afternoon to mention the motorcycle incident to his daughter, "I want to talk to you about that boy."

"Bernard?" Jan sipped her brandy.

"Yes, Bernard—Bucky—and his loud motorcycle."

"Fred," Sonia warned him, taking his hand, "if you're going to discuss that, do it calmly."

"Calmly? Sure." He smiled grimly at Jan. "That boy rode his motorcycle by here today going a hundred miles an hour, or my name isn't Fred Elias. Made a terrible racket. I thought maybe you could talk to him, you know, in a nice sort of way."

"Sure I could. In fact, I heard them myself this afternoon." Right after making love on the couch, she thought, and a hot glow burned on each cheek.

Her father didn't seem to notice. "I don't want to call the sheriff, the boy's just having fun," he went on. "But I've talked to Ed, and believe me, that doesn't do any good."

Fred considered the scene that might have erupted at the Millers' Halloween party if he'd followed up his blue heron argument by berating Ed

Foster about his stepson. Sonia was right; he should let Jan handle it.

"I'll be glad to talk to him, Dad," Jan said, wondering if she were still blushing. Would her parents ever understand her passion for Jim Wentworth? Probably not. "In fact, I'll talk to him tomorrow. He's a very bright child but a classic underachiever. I need to spend some time with him anyway."

"I'd really appreciate it, honey, and so would your dear old mom," Fred said, patting his wife on the back. "She was afraid I'd run out there and stand in the middle of the road."

"Well, don't worry any more, Mom. Daughter dear will take care of it," Jan told her mother, giving her a warm hug. She loved Sonia very much. If her mother didn't understand the sexual revolution it was probably because she'd been too busy raising five kids.

Jan stood up and stretched. Speaking of sex, where was Jim? And what would her dad say about Bernard's picture of the helpless old woman, naked and chained? Would he call it filthy trash or see it as she did, the manifestation of deep problems that needed to be resolved?

Jan Elias didn't know. She was tired. The Big Ben chime clock over the fireplace began its midnight tolling. As it started into the twelfth cycle she heard the Bronco pulling into the driveway.

Jim Wentworth came through the door, puffing and stripping off his yellow parka. "Sorry to be so long," he apologized.

Sonia got up and poured him some brandy. Jim downed it in one gulp, licking his lips and shaking the water out of his dark brown beard.

"So what happened?" Jan asked him impatiently as he sat down on the leather couch beside her.

"Mrs. Zondich fell and hit her head pretty bad. She's on the way to the hospital."

Fred Elias sat up straight. "Fell? Is she all right?"

"Yeah, well, she's unconscious, but she had a bad fall. She was in shock."

"But why did she fall?" Fred insisted impatiently.

"Daddy, this isn't an inquisition, you know," Jan reminded him.

"I know that," Fred said, smiling at both of them. "I just want to know what happened—all of what happened."

"Because he's a nosy old man," Sonia added. "They talk about women gossiping; they've never heard Fred, by golly." She laughed.

"Now listen," Fred said, sipping his brandy, "I want the details, that's all,or—" he paused slyly— "the wedding's off."

"No more for this man, bartender," Jim said, laughing.

"Come on," Fred urged, "even Sonia wants to know."

"Do you, Sonia?" Jim asked her seriously.

"Yes," she said. They all laughed nervously.

And Jim Wentworth, normally a man of few words, told them everything—the open door, the dead dog and even his impression of Bryan Emulooth's uneasiness. "He gets so many calls from her he figured there was no hurry; besides, you know, the kids were long gone by the time she fell. Poor Bryan, it'll take him weeks to get over it."

177

"The poor lady," Sonia said.

Fred stared out the window, his eyes fixed on some distant point. "It's very odd," he said.

"What's odd?" Jim asked him.

"That Clara would leave her door open."

They sat in silence for a moment. It was an awkward pause. Finally Jim picked up the conversation, providing them with his theory which by now he considered to be absolute truth. "She went outside to find the dog, probably, and got excited. The dog was dead and she rushed back in. The lights were out by then; she fell and hit her head."

Fred continued to stare out the window. The lights of Seattle came and went with the passing of the low-hanging clouds.

"She couldn't tell you what happened?" he asked Jim.

"No, I told you, she was just out of it. Her eyes were open but she couldn't talk."

"What a horrible thing," Jan said. "She must have been terribly frightened."

"Listen, she hit her head really hard," Jim replied, without answering the question. He yawned. He had as much sympathy for Clara Zondich as the next person, but he made it a practice never to get personally involved with victims. Over the years he'd responded to dozens of calls where old people had attacks of one kind or another and fell in the process. It happened all the time.

Fred turned and looked directly at Jim. "Clara Zondich kept her doors and windows locked at all times." He knew the lady. He knew her habits.

"Not tonight," Jim replied nonchalantly. Fred was challenging him, but there was no reason to argue. There was no sense in mentioning the open bathroom window either, he reflected. That would only complicate things. Jim Wentworth wanted to get home and go to bed—with Fred's daughter. He put his hand around the curve of Jan's hip and squeezed. She pulled away.

"And she never let the dog out at night," Fred went on stubbornly.

"Now how do you know that?" Sonia said, her exasperation showing. Sometimes Fred Elias could be a know-it-all, but almost fifty years of marriage had confirmed that he was frequently wrong.

"Because I know Clara Zondich," Fred told them, his lined face reddening. "I've known the woman for twenty years, and I knew her late husband too."

"Fred." Sonia reached out to warn him.

He pushed her back gently and became insistent. "Now look, I may not know much about a lot of things, but I do know Clara Zondich would never go out at night, especially on Halloween. I also know she wouldn't let the dog out at night. The animal's older than she is, relatively speaking. Milly couldn't stand the cold or the excitement. It would kill her."

"Well, it did," Jim said harshly, "and that's exactly what happened."

Fred pointedly ignored him. "I walk around this Point twice a day. You get to know people, see things. You know when something's wrong."

Sonia twisted her hands uncomfortably. Men could get in the darndest arguments sometimes.

Jim Wentworth stood up impatiently. Jan could see he was angry. "Daddy," she said reasonably,

179

"something *is* wrong. Mrs. Zondich had a terrible accident, and you're upset by it. That's perfectly natural."

Fred stared out the window sullenly. That was very unlike him, and Jan had seen Fred under great stress before. When they got the news that Jerry, his middle son and Jan's favorite brother, had been killed in Viet Nam, Fred had grieved, but he never, never felt sorry for himself.

"He was a good boy, a wonderful son. We just didn't have him very long," he would explain to those who offered sympathy.

Jan stood up and took Jim Wentworth's arm. She gave him one of her "be nicer to my parents, please" looks.

Jim got the message and went over to Fred. "The weather's clearing," he said awkwardly. "Might be a good day to drop a hook. What do you say?"

He was genuinely fond of Fred Elias and he didn't want to hurt his feelings. It was also his habit to put fire calls out of his mind as quickly as possible. Dwelling on them was a good way not to sleep at night.

"Thanks, but I don't think I'm up to fishing tomorrow," Fred replied gloomily, staring straight ahead.

He resented not being taken seriously. It was the greatest humiliation of old age, worse than having to pop nitroglycerin pills just to keep your heart going.

"Daddy, are you okay?" Jan said, going over and giving him a firm kiss on the mouth.

She knew that beneath his polite deference to Jim he was still upset, and it frightened her. Although she'd been on her own for eight years, Jan still looked to Fred for strength when things got really bad.

He put his arm around her, but the arm wasn't as

firm and steady as she remembered it. For the first time since they'd moved to the Point, Jan wanted to stay with her parents rather than go home with Jim Wentworth. Unfortunately she couldn't do that gracefully.

Fred walked her to the door and patted Jim on the back. "You kids get on home now, and don't get lost in the dark."

He was putting her off. "Daddy," she insisted, "you're not answering my question."

"It's nothing, sweetheart, nothing for you to worry about. It will all look better in the morning."

CHAPTER 26

Dawn was a thin band of washed pink running across the horizon. Below it, a faint mist rose off the water. Overhead, dirty white clouds, pushed along by a brisk wind, drifted and separated into long strings trailing across the sky. Fred Elias walked quickly, watching as the pinkish band grew wider, the red intensified, and the shadowy Cascade Mountain range popped into focus across Puget Sound.

The Birch Slough mud flat, exposed by low tide, was littered with piles of driftwood and long streamers of cinnamon-colored kelp torn loose by the storm. He walked onto the bridge, paused to lean over the railing and examine the barnacle-encrusted pilings underneath. They were thirty years old but still looked sound.

Then Fred saw the red penis and smiling face. Instinctively, his chest tightened just for an instant before he controlled his anger. Kids would always draw filthy pictures, and somebody always painted the bridge on Halloween. It was a routine job for the highway department to clean up.

He took several deep breaths and checked his pulse, concentrating on the putrid smell of the mud and the raw salty breeze he liked to feel on his face. Normal as a twenty-year-old kid. Fred definitely had himself under control.

And he felt much better this morning. Some time after slipping on the soft white duofold long underwear, but before putting on his blue down parka and leaving the darkened house, Fred realized that old people sometimes did crazy things.

He'd thought about it very carefully while he dressed himself in layers. After the underwear came rough corduroy pants, a wool hunting shirt, two pairs of socks, and the silk scarf his father had given him.

Last summer he'd put his boat in the wrong slip at the Three Corners Marina. It looked like the regular docking spot, but it was the wrong pier, and there was no logical explanation but old age.

Fred had donned his red pile cap and kissed his sleeping Sonia, pausing to look carefully at the woman he had known and loved for fifty years, and tiptoed outside. Clara's accident had frightened him more than he was willing to admit. He and Sonia knew people their age who fell, broke bones, and never even emerged from the hospital. Jim's explanation of Clara's fall was probably exactly the way it happened, or at least pretty darn close.

For some reason she had let the dog out, or she

made a mistake and the dog got out on its own. Whatever happened, her lights had failed, as they had all over Horsehead Point. The dog got in trouble. Clara went out, or opened the door, and somewhere in all the confusion she took a nasty spill. And that was that.

It was a relief not to brood about it any more. Fred turned and headed back toward the Point, stepping out at a brisk pace. Call Jim and apologize; that was the thing to do. There was nothing worse than grouchy, morbid old people taking out their disappointments and fears on younger folks.

The bay was robin's egg blue on the horizon, changing to purple as it neared the Point. Only an occasional whitecap flashed out in the low rolling waves. If the weather held he would invite Jim Wentworth to go fishing.

As he passed the Elias-Wentworth mailbox he heard the whine of the power saw. Jim was up early and hard at it. The boy might take hold of himself after all. He had the stuff, if he'd just use it.

Across the water, the buildings in Seattle were beginning to get some backlighting. He tried to pick them out, but the skyline was changing too rapidly.

When he and Sonia had moved to Horsehead Point the Smith Tower was the tallest structure west of the Mississippi. Now it was just another building. Change came too fast; it came faster with old age. Everybody in Sealth County used to know everybody else. Now Fred Elias hardly knew some of his neighbors.

A black Porsche went by. That would be Linda Foster, a strange hard woman who was always coming or going somewhere. He hoped Jan remembered to talk to Bucky about his motorcycle.

Fred unzipped his down parka as he walked, letting the heat out and the refreshing cool air in. A half century of living in the Pacific Northwest had taught him that a morning like this could bring anything from snow to a false spring; you had to be prepared.

The huge tree that had gone down in front of the Myers' house had been reduced to a pyramid of log rounds by the side of the road. Some time during the early morning the power company had sawed up the tree and reconnected their overhead cable. Everything was back to normal. Everybody would have hot coffee and toast for breakfast.

The sun was rising, pushing through the overcast, forming a blazing white path of light across the water, turning the clouds a fiery red. It put a gold sheen on the dark brown tree trunks alongside the road and revealed a shimmering coat of fresh snow on the mountains behind the city. Winter was poised. He stopped to watch. The sunrise was always unique, and it never failed to bring him a sense of renewal and peace.

It would only last an instant and then it would be gone forever. As the intensity of the light began to fade he heard the sounds of children, tinkling chimes on the wind. Fred smiled and resumed his walk. That glorious burst of childhood and innocence was as spectacular as the sunrise and just as brief. They were all precious gifts of God to be treasured.

The schoolchildren huddled in the road at the foot of Clara Zondich's lawn, a mixture of yellow rain slickers and quilted jackets, bundled up against the cold breeze.

"Hi," he greeted little Carrie Miller as she ran up to him. "That sure was a nice party you had last night."

"I'm glad you liked it, Mr. Elias," she replied very formally. "See what I got?"

She showed him a big orange Halloween cookie. There was a gap in her front teeth. Jan had had teeth just like that once.

Fred was surprised to see Hank Jacobi waiting for the bus in his blue-and-gold letter jacket. The big fullback for the Vancouver High football team usually drove to school.

"Hi, Hank," he called.

"Hello, Mr. Elias."

"Car break down?"

"No, Mom wanted me to come up here with the little kids, what with Mrs. Zondich getting hurt and all. I don't know, I guess she thought it would scare 'em or something."

He shrugged elaborately. Tall, blue eyed, broad shouldered, he really didn't understand. Fred did. He looked over at the huge brick house. It was the first time he could remember not seeing Clara standing in the front window.

Bucky Foster was sitting on her front steps, wearing silver reflecting glasses. Hank Jacobi followed Fred's gaze. "Hey," the boy said, "I didn't see that creep up there. Want me to kick him off?"

Fred knew the boy was eager to do just that. The blue veins stood out in his massive neck; he curled a solid hand into a ham-sized fist.

"No," Fred said evenly. "Let me talk to him."

The old man went straight up the walk, never taking his eyes off Bucky as he closed the gap between them. The silver glasses stared back. "Young man," Fred said firmly but without anger, "just because Mrs. Zondich isn't here doesn't mean you're free to sit on her steps."

Bucky didn't say anything. He looked tired; his face was pasty white, the scattered pimples stood out like angry berries, and his hair was uncombed.

It was hard to tell what the boy's reaction was although he tilted the mirrors up at Fred.

"Why don't you go down and wait with the rest of the kids?" Fred suggested, keeping his tone neutral.

"Because I like it here," Bucky replied quietly.

Fred remained calm. "Wait in the street," he ordered him.

Bucky hesitated, then shrugged, lifting his shoulders nonchalantly. But Fred sensed his intense anger.

"Whatever you say, Mr. Elias." Bucky stood, stretched and ambled down the walk, his slightly bowed legs strutting lazily as he went. Fred watched him go, uneasy and disturbed.

He'd dealt with rebellious adolescents before. His own son Jerry, God rest his soul, had not been an easy child to raise. Fred would never forget the day when the boy, then a sophomore in high school, had casually offered him a cigarette.

But Bucky Foster was a real puzzle. Fred didn't know what to make of him. The boy seemed to create moods around himself. Those moods affected Fred, and he didn't like the feeling of being manipulated.

One minute he felt Bucky was a slightly unruly child; the next minute, a surly, unbalanced adult. He seemed harmless, then suddenly dangerous. He looked like an innocent victim of circumstances, giving a boyish shrug, then became a seasoned manipulator, hiding his motives behind silver glasses.

The yellow-and-black school bus was coming around the bend, its noisy diesel engine throbbing in the early morning stillness. Perhaps it was just the boy's age. Fred started slowly back down Clara's walk while the children lined up to get on board.

Maybe he resented youth, Fred thought, watching them pushing and crowding and shouting. Children never knew just how lucky they were. Was that another sign of advancing age? Fred Elias knew one thing for sure: he was darn glad he didn't have to raise five kids again. He enjoyed being a grandfather; when the kids got out of hand he could send them home.

Fred was at the end of Clara's walk, and all the children were on the bus, when he saw Jeff Myers running. Fred waved at the driver to wait.

"Well, hello there, Jeff. You're a little late this morning." Fred greeted him enthusiastically as he puffed up.

Jeff's normally ruddy face was pinched. His upper lip was purple and badly swollen where he'd collided with the car the night before. He glanced at Fred but showed no sign of recognition, and hurried by without saying anything.

Fred Elias was taken aback. He always made it a point to greet each child by name. Well, he thought, as the bus pulled out, spewing diesel fumes into the clear air, maybe Halloween was a little too much for Jeff Myers. The poor kid must be tired.

He jammed his hands in his jacket pockets, his mood strangely altered. Somewhere, between the time he'd first heard the children's voices and the odd rebuff by Jeff Myers, something had happened.

Fred kicked a rock and watched it bounce onto the road. He was used to the ups and downs of life, but he was optimistic by nature, and seldom if ever gave in to the bad moments. Now, however, he felt the light grip of that same mild but very definite despair that had hit him when Jim Wentworth broke the news about Clara Zondich.

Only a few moments ago he'd been sure that incident was completely behind him. Apparently not. As he stood in front of her house the doubts reentered his mind.

The vivid colors of dawn were muted now, the sky had paled. He knew the signs: the slight chill, the darkening clouds. There would be no salmon fishing today. Another storm was coming.

Doggone it, Fred lectured himself, raising his head and vowing to improve his outlook, let's look on the bright side of things.

CHAPTER 27

"We leave at 7:20, sonny, on the dot," the school bus driver sarcastically called after Jeff Myers as he went by. The little girls sitting in front giggled and pointed at his swollen lip.

"He looks just like a little piggy," Carrie Miller snickered to Jeff's sister Belinda.

Belinda didn't say anything. She felt sorry for Jeff. She knew his face hurt, but he seemed unhappy, too, and wouldn't talk to her at all, and she didn't know why.

Jeff went directly to the back of the bus, where Bucky Foster slouched in his silver reflecting glasses. "Where you been?" he asked Jeff sharply, not mentioning his friend's fat lip.

"I didn't feel good. I'm sick, but my mom wouldn't let me stay home," Jeff replied in a flat voice, throwing himself down in the seat opposite

Bucky and staring out the window as the bus pulled out. He put his hand over his lip to hide it.

"Did you get sick at Ivan Olsen's house too? Is that why you left so soon?" Bucky asked, leaning toward him.

"I—I was supposed to meet my dad; I had to leave. I told you I had to go to the Millers'," Jeff replied weakly.

"Sure, sure, I understand, Jeff-rey," Bucky sneered. "Well, it just so happens Harry and I had a great time."

"You did?" Jeff turned halfway toward his friend but stayed up against the window.

"Yeah. Mr. Olsen isn't such a bad old guy. He even apologized, and he gave me this candy bar. See?" Bucky held up a Big Rocky Hunk Bar.

Jeff permitted himself a quick darting glance. Bucky's silver mirrors reflected his own round frightened and bruised face.

"I know," Bucky went on in a hard, teasing voice, "you were having so much fun with Mommy and Daddy at the party you wouldn't even talk to Harry and me." He slapped himself on the forehead dramatically. "Now why didn't I see that? I've been thinking you were just being a little chicken shithead."

Jeff curled up in his seat, hiding his face completely.

"Hey, look," Bucky shouted, grabbing Jeff's shoulder and pulling him out of his protective cocoon. "Look at that. It's the rich bitch."

Hilda Bryant's magnificent silver Rolls Royce chugged quietly beside the road while she locked the iron gate in front of her driveway. Her blonde-streaked hair was pulled back in a bun. She wore tight-fitting designer blue jeans, high, polished calfskin boots, and a waist-length wolfskin coat.

The widow Bryant felt like hell. Her head ached, her mouth was full of sand, and the small jigger of Scotch she'd added to the coffee had only worsened her already foul mood. She wrapped the chain around the gate, wrenching it tight. Her fury over the vandalism to her sheep was only heightened by the humiliation of her agreement with Ed Foster. The absolute unmitigated gall, offering her money and speaking to her like that!

Hilda Bryant pulled on her soft pigskin driving gloves. She was going to the city to get her hair done and her body massaged and creamed, then have a fashionable lunch in an excellent restaurant. Afterward she might even call on her lawyer. She was having second thoughts about taking the money from Ed Foster. Revenge was on her mind.

The school bus approached just as she turned to get back into the Rolls, and it was then that she saw him. It was unmistakably Bucky Foster in the mirror glasses. As the bus pulled even with the car, he put his lips to the window, flattening them into a grotesque leer, and mouthed the words "Fuck you." To insure there was no misunderstanding, his middle fingers on each hand pumped up and down vigorously as the bus swept by, shifting gears and laboring.

"Did you see that?" Bucky Foster punched Jeff in the shoulder. "Did you see the rich bitch's face?"

Jeff Myers had seen. His stomach tightened, and he pulled himself down lower in the seat so Mrs. Bryant wouldn't see him.

"She called my stepfather last night about her dumb fucking sheep."

Jeff grabbed the armrest in alarm. "What did she say?"

Bucky Foster laughed. "Don't worry. He told her to screw off. She isn't gonna do shit."

The blood rushed to Hilda Bryant's head. That was the last straw, the final humiliation. She would not take the money. There would be no dealing with Ed Foster, not ever.

She got into her car. This contemptible boy wouldn't get away with it. She would cancel her hair appointment and forgo lunch. She would put a stop to this once and for all. She was going straight to the Sealth County sheriff.

When Hilda Bryant drove by in that monstrous foreign car without even bothering to acknowledge his cheerful wave, Fred Elias knew that a once promising day had definitely gone sour. He zipped his jacket back up so the goose-down filled collar was tight against his neck, and watched her speed away. Hilda Bryant was driving like she wanted to kill somebody—but then that was the way she always drove.

The bright band of dawn on the horizon was turning a muddy gray, and Fred's spirits sank with the fading light. He'd known Hilda a long time, but there was no friendship involved; there never had been. He was simply an acceptable member of the lower class, a nice fellow who was always willing to help his neighbor fix a leaking faucet. And he'd helped Hilda with quite a few.

Still, all things considered, she could at least have waved back, made some small sign. Fred

Elias shivered. Maybe he was sick. One of the symptoms of flu was a mild depression, wasn't it? He considered the possibility as he stared across the water. The bay, so brilliant blue and purple when he'd left the Birch Slough Bridge, had turned a light green, and the flash of whitecaps was more frequent. It was certainly going to be too rough for fishing.

He didn't feel sick. Ten minutes ago he had felt just fine. The flu was not likely. The snub by Hilda Bryant? He didn't resent Hilda; he pitied her.

Because Jeff Myers had walked by him without saying hello? That was ridiculous. Jeff was barely a teenager, and boys that age seldom realized how their actions affected other people. His brief encounter with Bucky Foster? Admittedly the boy made him uneasy, but he'd moved off the steps after a normally rebellious pause.

Clara Zondich? Jim Wentworth's ridiculous version of the accident? That was a lot closer. He should really go to see Clara in the hospital. Fred heard the faint cry of seagulls out on the bay.

Then again, maybe he should go back to the house and clean up his workshop. A little hard work was always good medicine when things weren't going quite right. There was nothing like an orderly workshop to lift a man's spirits.

Whatever he did, he couldn't stand around in front of Clara's house any longer like a bump on a log. Resolutely, Fred Elias stepped out for home, his boots squishing on the packed, rainsoaked leaves by the side of the road. Just moving made him feel a little better. He hadn't taken more than a dozen steps when he heard somebody calling his

195

name. He looked back and saw Mary Soames waving at him from Ivan Olsen's front steps across the road.

Well, that's the spirit, he told himself. You start to think positive and good things happen. Fred waved back. He frequently saw the retarded girl on Fridays. It was the day she cleaned for the old fisherman when he was in port.

But this time Mary came running after him, long brown hair flying in the wind, her little dog right behind her. "Mr. Elias, Mr. Elias," she called out to him as she came, excited about something, her cheeks red with cold.

"Mary, how are you?"

"Mr. Olsen's not here," she said, worry creasing her young face.

"He's probably gone to town," Fred replied. Poor Mary, things could get complicated for her so fast. Still, she was a very pretty girl with a wonderful disposition. Maybe not being smart enough to see all the ugliness in life was what made her that way.

"The doors are locked," she said, pointing with excitement.

"Maybe he forgot to leave one open, Mary."

"Mr. Elias, the door is always open for me."

"Well," he told the girl kindly, "Let's see what the problem is."

First they tried the front door of the low rambling house and, just as Mary had reported, it was locked and he got no answer. "Come on," he said briskly, leading her around the side. The house was an undistinguished structure reflecting the utilitarian squarenesss of the Fifties, when it was built. The cedar siding ran horizontally and was painted pale green, a color Fred associated with government buildings. A daylight basement ran along the front facing the water. The wind whirled around the house. There was a banging noise somewhere. Could it be a shutter? Fred looked up. There were no shutters to bang.

"Do you always come on Friday?" he asked her.

"Yes, Friday," she replied. Now that Fred was in charge, Mary looked relieved.

He'd accomplished one positive thing today, he thought grimly, trying the brass knob on the basement door: He'd put a little light into sweet Mary's face.

The door was locked. Where was that darn banging? "I don't know, Mary, I guess maybe he went away."

"Where would he go, Mr. Elias?"

"Good question."

The *Thor!* That was where the banging was. The wheelhouse door on the halibut schooner was open and slamming. "Wait here," he told the girl.

Fred Elias headed for the dock. The door banged back and forth. That wasn't like Ivan at all. The wooden schooner was his pride and joy. It had been in his family for generations. "Ivan," he called, as he strode down the dock. He fellt an extreme sense of urgency now and found it difficult not to run. "Ivan!" There was no answer.

The *Thor* rode even with the dock on the flood tide. He'd been aboard only once, for a rather gloomy cruise arranged by the ex-Mrs. Olsen. Fred went cautiously across the gangplank and stepped onto the gently rolling deck.

He was used to boats, but now he sensed danger

and stepped carefully. "Ivan," he called again, hearing a strange hopelessness in his own voice.

Fred Elias really didn't expect an answer. The uneasiness over Clara's accident, the depression on his walk, congealed into a cold heavy fear. Fred secured the banging door with a brass hasp and entered the wheelhouse. The windows were fogged and running with condensation on the inside. Something was terribly wrong. He felt his heart laboring in the dank salty air.

There was an empty bottle of whiskey on the chart table to the rear and a glass half filled. A large multiple-band radio had been left on. The hissing static murmured in the empty wheelhouse. He shut off the radio.

"Ivan," he called, stepping down the companionway leading to the narrow cabin. "Ivan?" The bunks were empty.

Olsen would never leave the boat open like this; Fred was sure of it. He went back to the pilothouse and cleared one of the windowpanes with his jacket sleeve. He could see Mary waiting up on the lawn with her dog. She looked eager, happy, convinced he would take care of everything and make it right. She was wearing those silly blue jeans under her dress, like a little girl.

Fred Elias felt the boat roll under him, heard the squeaking and moaning of the rigging, smelled the tar and teak oil in the air. He couldn't take care of this. He couldn't. A trembling swept through him. Something was squeezing him inside, making him weak.

It wasn't anything like the terrible sense of loss he'd felt when his son was killed. This was far worse. It was a nameless, formless dread that was threatening to paralyze him. Fred Elias forced himself out the wheelhouse door, across the gangplank and onto the narrow dock. He had to get help. He had to find somebody quickly. He would call Jim Wentworth; Jim would know what to do.

CHAPTER 28

Jim Wentworth zipped up his wetsuit and watched the milling throng of gray and white seagulls riding a raft on the dark green waves out beyond Ivan Olsen's dock. "Ready, partner?" he asked Pinky Hart. The little fireman nodded, and Jim helped him boost the silver scuba tanks onto his back.

"I hope this isn't what I think it is," Pinky told Jim, adjusting the tanks.

The gulls pecked and thrashed and screamed their high-pitched cries. More were coming; the word was out. They moved across the water on a high, effortless, searching glide, sleek scavengers riding the wind. On spotting the raft, they dropped down on the wavetops and hurtled along like jet fighters closing on a target.

"Let's take a shot under the dock and then go out along the kelp line." Jim shouted at his partner so he could be heard through the hood that left only Pinky's round face exposed.

On the bulkhead behind them, Fred Elias waited with Mary Soames and Sealth County Deputy Bryan Emulooth, who was in his street clothes. Mary's collie ran back and forth on the grass, barking at the two divers on the beach.

They backed slowly into the water, feeling the coldness of the sound pressing against their wetsuits. Jim checked his watch and underwater lantern. Pinky was already up to his armpits and breathing compressed air. Jim turned and eyed the raft full of birds with distaste. The new arrivals pushed their way in, screaming angrily, expelling other birds into the air, wings flapping.

He bit down on his mouthpiece, waved at Emulooth and Fred, and followed Pinky into the muddy green water. They stayed on the surface until they were clear of the breaking waves and then sank, leaving a thin trail of bubbles to mark their course under the dock.

Emulooth jammed his hands in his pockets and waited. He was damn glad he didn't have to go looking for Ivan Olsen. He was a poor swimmer, and just imagining himself in the cold water frightened him. Fred Elias stood with him, not saying anything, rubbing a hand over his leathery face. He'd removed his cap and his white hair stuck up in the wind.

Su Myers saw Fred standing on the bulkhead as she pulled out of her driveway onto the Horsehead Point Road. But she continued to drive with one hand as she hastily ate her burnt toast, until she noticed the fire department aide car parked in front of

Ivan Olsen's house. She was already pushing the deadline on her Clara Zondich story but, with the instinct of a good reporter, she pulled over immediately and set the parking brake, her heart pounding. The Zondich story could wait. This might be bigger. She didn't bother to lock the car. This could be it!

Dear God, thought the mother, housewife and bank teller as she hurried down the wet lawn, not another accident. Please God, prayed the novice reporter, if it's an accident, make it a big one worthy of wire service coverage.

As she broke into a run, Su Myers mentally prepared herself. She would endure any hardship, bear any burden, face any cruel or unusual suffering, as long as there was a story with her byline on it. She desperately needed a triumph, any little success, some scrap of genuine recognition. She set her face into tight professional lines. She was becoming quite adept at not showing her emotions.

Su had even managed to maintain the reasonable semblance of a devoted smile all through breakfast, while Harold ate his scrambled eggs with his mouth open and fussed about his rate-increase presentation for the gas company. She held the smile firmly pasted to her face as she kissed him goodby, before he dashed to catch the 7:10 ferry without so much as a "Thanks for the breakfast."

But the façade collapsed once she heard his car start. She felt used. Once again he was leaving her with the problem of how to handle Jeffrey. He hadn't said one word to the boy after the Millers' Halloween party, and this morning he was so preoccupied with his damn business problems he hadn't even asked his son why he was so upset.

Jeffrey had been sullen and uncommunicative and had not eaten his breakfast. He claimed he was sick. Maybe he was, but it was probably just his swollen lip. That certainly didn't look serious to her. Besides she didn't have time to baby him. She had to write the Clara Zondich piece and get it to the paper by nine o'clock. For once she had decided to take care of herself first.

"Good morning," she greeted Deputy Emulooth. "What's going on?"

He was out of uniform, wearing boots, jeans and a windbreaker. He hadn't shaved and he looked exhausted. "Oh hello, Mrs. Myers. Ivan Olsen's missing, at least it looks that way. We're still investigating."

She pulled out her notebook. "You think he drowned?"

"It's a possibility," he told her, rubbing his eyes. Emulooth pulled a double shift on Halloween and had been within a mile of home, after finishing, when he got the call. In spite of his fatigue, he was not going to get caught short twice. Clara Zondich, collapsed and bleeding, was still on his mind. He had wheeled the car around in a U-turn and responded to the call himself.

Su greeted Fred Elias, who was standing with Mary Soames and her little collie.

"Hello, Su." The old man turned, gave her a weary grin and then looked back at the water where Jim and Pinky were searching. The gulls out beyond the dock continued to chatter and thrash.

"Are there divers out there now?" she asked Emulooth, seeing two more firemen standing on

204

the beach. He wasn't supplying much information, and that irritated her. She was not going to get the brushoff from a $17,000-a-year deputy sheriff, just because she was a woman.

"In the water, in the water," Mary told her eagerly, her radiant face glowing pink in the cold air.

"Yes," Emulooth replied abruptly. He was so tired that when people talked it sounded like screams inside his head. Too much coffee, too many cigarettes.

He lit another one, cupping his hands against the wind. There was something about the Soames girl and Ivan Olsen, but he couldn't remember what it was. A report had been filed.

"I see," Su Myers replied coolly, waiting for more, pencil poised.

He let a slow stream of smoke trickle out the corner of his mouth. The cigarette tasted like horse manure. "Jim Wentworth and Pinky—Richard—Hart are out there," he added in what he hoped was an apologetic tone.

He liked Mrs. Myers. She was trying hard to be a good reporter, and her column was just trivial social stuff anyway.

"Thank you," she replied, writing steadily. Her hands shook with anticipation. She had never actually seen a dead body.

"Mr. Olsen wasn't here," Mary said.

"I see," Su Myers answered politely. The Soames family was a mystery to her. How could people like that exist in this day and age? This sweet-looking girl was the product of incest, a subject Su couldn't even bring herself to think about, it was so disgusting.

"I certainly hope they don't find him out there," she remarked to Fred. But secretly she hoped they did; it would be a front-page story.

"I don't think he fell in," Fred said absently.

A uniform grayness had blotted out all the morning light except a small hole on the far horizon, and even that was becoming streaked with invading black clouds.

"Why not?" she asked, surprised.

"Because he made his living on boats. Before he fished halibut he was a salmon troller in Alaska. He went out alone; it's very dangerous work. How could a man like that fall overboard at his own dock?"

"Well, maybe he had a heart attack," she suggested.

"Maybe."

Fred had already given Emulooth his theory, and it irritated the deputy that the old man would offer this wild speculation to a reporter, even if she was only from the local paper.

"Look, Mrs. Myers," Emulooth interrupted, "Olsen's house is locked, the car's in the garage, the boat was wide open. A radio was still playing in the cabin. That all indicates he fell overboard."

"They think it was because he was drinking," Fred Elias shot back.

"Was he drinking?" Su Myers asked Emulooth, grateful to Fred for the lead.

Bryan Emulooth exhaled loudly, pushing a column of cigarette smoke into the wind. "Maybe," he replied angrily. "Could be."

"Olsen's been a drinker for years. It still doesn't make any sense," Fred insisted.

206

Su Myers stopped writing. Missing, presumed drowned, she thought. That was the story to this point. But maybe, just maybe, there was something more to it. She could only hope.

Emulooth fumbled in his jacket pocket for a piece of paper and scribbled down "Henry Soames." He remembered the report now. Mary's brother Henry, a big brute, had threatened Ivan Olsen over something. Nothing ever came of it.

Su decided to push him. This might just finally be her day. "What do you really think, Deputy?"

"I don't know," he replied sourly, looking out at the bay. "We'll soon find out."

But regardless of what Jim and Pinky found there, Emulooth intended to reread the Henry Soames record just as soon as he reported for his regular afternoon shift in Port Gloster. He was also going to call on Clara Zondich after he got this mess cleaned up. Things were not going to get away from him again. He didn't want any lingering doubts about either incident.

"How about you, Mr. Elias?" She turned to Fred. "I'm interested. If Ivan Olsen didn't fall overboard, what in the world could have happened to him?"

Fred was looking back up the lawn and across the road at the red composition shingle roof on Clara Zondich's house. He was going to check on Clara. He would drive over and visit her in the hospital. She might be able to tell him what really happened last night.

He turned back to Su Myers. "I don't know either," he said. Fred Elias looked directly at her, his clear blue eyes steady and unwavering. "But I'll tell you something, young lady. Something is very wrong on Horsehead Point—very, very wrong. I'm absolutely convinced of it."

CHAPTER 29

Jim Wentworth couldn't see a thing under the dock. A dark haze of mud stirred up, obscuring even the closest pilings, and the bottom was covered with a constantly shifting layer of dull green seaweed that stood as high as a man. Their searching lights flushed perch, and the fish darted off as the two men worked their way toward the schooner. It was slow going. They had to swim down through the seaweed, forcing it back with their arms until they felt the mud on the bottom.

Even though Pinky was right beside him, all Jim could see was his yellow weight belt. He checked his depth gauge: twenty-six feet. The light from above came down in pale shafts, fading badly toward the bottom. He signaled a slow turn and, as they passed under the schooner, looked up. The bottom was in good shape. Ivan must have had it on the ways recently; there was no marine life at all clinging to the rust-red paint.

Just beyond the dock, the seaweed ended and the bottom was sandy. They kicked slowly out toward the kelp line, staying close enough to see each other, scanning the bottom as they went. It was a chancy thing at best, and it depended on the wind and tide and prevailing currents. Sometimes they found a body right away; sometimes it took a week, or even months. The floaters who came up that way were not a job for the squeamish.

Pinky tugged at his arm, pointing at something, a long dark shape, protruding out of the sand. Jim felt the excitement pounding in his neck as they swam down into the twilight darkness. He'd done this before, but it was a nasty job, and he didn't look forward to finding anything. Sometimes he still dreamed about the streaming chutes of the two Navy pilots strapped in their trainer in forty feet of water off Skiff Point.

Jim Wentworth forced himself to go closer. It was just an old piling, a water-soaked deadhead, finally so heavy it had sunk to the bottom. They turned away, relieved, and continued the search.

Moving toward the kelp bed that marked the edge of the shelf running around Horsehead Point, Jim kept looking up, trying to spot the seagulls. The water was clear now and the long slanting shafts of light probed to the bottom. Finally Jim saw a ruffling above them, and signaled Pinky. They rose slowly, searching for whatever the gulls were feeding on. Unaware of the approaching divers, the birds continued thrashing and pecking at a bulky dark form floating on the surface. It was as big as a man. Pinky came in from the other side, his light waving back and forth.

Jim reached out; the birds exploded out of the water, whipping the surface into a white froth. The object was soft and spongy to the touch and turned as he nudged it. The dead harbor seal, bloated and floating high, slowly rolled over until Jim Wentworth was looking it in the face. The eyes were gone; empty sockets looked back. The long whiskers seemed erect and alive, but the flippers hung down motionless in the water.

He tried to grin at Pinky. Pinky tried to grin back, but it was a pale grimace behind his face mask. Jim was tense and breathing too fast. They had twelve minutes of air left before they had to head back in.

The sandy shelf where the two men were swimming ran a quarter mile out and then abruptly dropped off to depths of over three hundred feet. At the lip of this underwater cliff a thick forest of bulb kelp grew, its thin stems reaching heights of over sixty feet.

The brown bulbs floated on the surface, trailing long streamers that followed the deep currents moving along the edge of the dropoff. When the tide was running a rip developed just beyond the kelp, creating slow-moving whirlpools. Pinky and Jim felt the pull of this deep current and relaxed in its grip, letting it tow them along. Coming back they'd have to swim hard against it.

The light grew fainter as they neared the kelp bed, the pale rays of the sun taking on a deep brownish tinge. The tangled kelp stems loomed like a dark wall in front of them. They hung in the water, being sucked toward the dropoff, running their lights along the edge of the kelp forest. Small fish scattered into the gloom when the beam touched them.

And then Jim saw Olsen standing in front of the wall of kelp directly below them. His thinning white hair streamed out in the current, the winglike eyebrows were cocked in surprise, his black jacket was buttoned to the throat against the cold. Ivan Olsen looked up at them, mouth open. He swayed gently in the current, anchored firmly to the bottom by his bright yellow southwester boots.

The last person in the world Sealth County Sheriff Burt Rogers wanted to see that morning was Hilda Bryant. The entire county was in disarray from the Halloween storm, another was on the way, and he had a Kiwanis speech to give at noon.

"Send her in," he told his secretary, slumping back in his swivel chair. His office, on the third floor of the remodeled and expanded county courthouse, overlooked Port Gloster and the harbor beyond. Hilda Bryant swept in, wearing her blue jeans, high boots and fur coat. The sheriff was no judge of clothes, but he wondered why a woman of that age, in that income bracket, would wear Levis. She smelled of expensive perfume.

"Good morning, Mrs. Bryant," he greeted her with guarded enthusiasm, rising politely.

"Good morning, Sheriff." Hilda Bryant sat down opposite his desk without being asked. He knew the woman by reputation; she drove the only Rolls in Sealth County.

"What can I do for you, Mrs. Bryant?" He took

out a cigarette, considered asking her permission to smoke, then rejected the idea. It would give her the upper hand.

"I'll get right to the point, Sheriff." She sat straight in her chair, green eyes staring at him. "There is a young man in my neighborhood, a young man I've had problems with before—mostly about riding his motorcycle on my property and in my pasture. Last night, yesterday afternoon to be exact, he and possibly one or two of his friends—I'm fairly sure of their identity too—rode a motorcycle onto my property and proceeded to spray my sheep—Yorkshire breeding stock—with red paint."

She paused, but he could see she wasn't finished. He lit the cigarette very carefully with his 11th Cav Army lighter, a souvenir of the recent unpleasantness in southeast Asia.

"In the course of this mindless prank they killed a particularly expensive ewe. I want you to arrest this boy."

He leaned forward, letting the cigarette burn in his left hand. He was young, his face chubby and unlined. "Did you report this at the time?"

"No. I wasn't sure."

"You weren't sure of what?"

"I wasn't sure who did it, but a subsequent conversation with the boy's father confirmed my suspicions."

"How so?"

"The man offered to pay me for the damage."

"I see."

The sheriff sat back. "What's the boy's name?"

"Bucky Foster—Bernard, I believe."

"Ed Foster's son?" Now there was a name that

rang a big bell.

"Yes."

He could see she wanted to push him around, so he sat back, parked the cigarette in his Harrah's Club ashtray and steepled his hands. "Would you like a cup of coffee, Mrs. Bryant?"

"No." She was getting angry now. Tiny lines formed around her eyes and mouth, odd lines, stress cracks on her otherwise smooth skin.

"You don't mind if I have some, do you?"

He didn't wait for an answer but stood up and went to the door. He was tall, well over six feet, stoop shouldered and soft. His wash-and-wear nylon blue pants were baggy in the seat.

He asked his secretary to bring him a carafe of coffee and two cups. "Just in case you change your mind," he told her, smiling, as he returned to his desk.

He carefully put out his cigarette. The walk had given him time to think. This lady could make things very uncomfortable for him, but basically she wasn't a threat. People like her still ran the Gloster Golf and Tennis Club, built back in the days when lumber schooners tied up right down the street, but they no longer ran the city of Port Gloster or Sealth County.

"Mrs. Bryant, I'm going to need a statement from you. I'll need to know when this happened, if you saw them. . . ."

"There's no doubt who it was. His father as much as admitted it to me," she snapped, not bothering to hide her irritation.

"Yes, but were there witnesses?"

"Yes, one. Clara Zondich; she's a neighbor."

He remained reasonable. "We'll certainly have to get statements from any witnesses and then, of course, talk to Mr. and Mrs. Foster and naturally the boy."

She stood up, rage sending dark blood into her tanned face. "This boy, as you call him, has been driving a motorcycle around Horsehead Point for the past year with a little gang of helpers, terrorizing residents and destroying property."

"Well, we'll certainly look into all that, Mrs. Bryant."

"Look into it? Look into it?"

She put her hands on the front of his desk and leaned over at him. The hands were stringy and long, filled with crevasses and broken veins. They gave her age away. She had a ring on every finger of her right hand.

"That incompetent deputy Bryan Emulooth that you have assigned over there has been 'looking into it' for a year. He has done nothing. We're entitled to equal protection, and if you can't provide it we'll just find somebody who can."

"Now, Mrs. Bryant," he said, standing up.

"Don't you now me," she screamed at him, suddenly on the verge of losing control.

"Mrs. Bryant, please. You know we just can't get anywhere like this." He wasn't backing up from this bitch. It was unpleasant, but people like Hilda Bryant didn't elect him to office.

"I will repeat what I just said. I will repeat it just once," she said, facing him, breathing fiercely. "This boy has been terrorizing the neighborhood on that machine. I want it stopped."

"Terrorizing?" he asked, allowing a baffled look

to show on his plain face. "I'm not sure what you mean."

He was trying to come up with a way to get rid of her gracefully, but if not, he was prepared to get rid of her any way he could.

"This morning he threatened me. He made threatening gestures. I want him arrested. I want him stopped."

"What sort of gestures?"

"He made faces; he glared at me." She faltered and then plunged on. "He made obscene gestures, threatening obscene gestures."

For the first time the assertiveness weakened as a hint of fear crept in, and her hands trembled. She clasped them together in front of her.

"I see."

He turned and looked out the window at the harbor. Directly below him the old onion-tower turret of the original Grand Hotel stood out among the rest of the modern office buildings and retail stores. The lumber wharfs had been replaced by marinas. The lumber barons were replaced by real estate magnates like Ed Foster. He turned back.

"Mrs. Bryant, I'll be glad to investigate each and every allegation involving Bucky Foster, just as this department, I'm sure, has investigated previous allegations."

"Allegations?" Her face was pale. "These aren't allegations."

"They are allegations," he insisted. "And until such time as we investigate them, I'm afraid I can't, and I certainly won't, arrest anybody."

That took the wind out of her sails. She went pale. "This boy," she said very quietly, sitting down as if she'd never screamed at him or made a scene, "is after me."

His secretary came in with the coffee. Excellent timing, he thought, excellent timing. "Let me pour you some coffee, Mrs. Bryant."

"Thank you." Her hands, still clasped together, were shaking.

"Mrs. Bryant, believe me, I do want to help," he told her kindly.

But not to the extent it will upset Big Ed Foster, he reminded himself. The sheriff knew little about sophisticated law enforcement beyond his eight years' experience as a deputy sheriff, but politically he was a very astute young man. Mrs. Bryant couldn't elect a dog catcher in Sealth County; Ed Foster could make a congressman.

"And I understand your concern. I want you to know that, Mrs. Bryant."

"Well, there's something wrong with that boy. He does horrible things."

"You're referring to the sheep?"

"Yes, but also his attitude. I felt that in making the threatening gesture, he really was threatening me in a physical sense."

"Did he raise his hand to strike you? Anything overt?"

"No, but that's hardly the point," she replied sharply. The old gal was regaining her momentum.

It was the time to extract himself. "I'll personally talk to Deputy Emulooth, Mrs. Bryant. He's out there now, as a matter of fact. Just as soon as he wraps up his current business I'll have him look into this."

"How soon will that be?" The steel was coming

back into her voice.

"I don't know, Mrs. Bryant. He's working on a missing-person problem. I can't exactly say, but I assure you he will give full attention to your complaint just as soon as possible."

"Missing person?"

"Yes, a gentleman named Olsen. Know him?"

"Yes." She hesitated. The hesitation became a pause. She looked worried. "What happened?"

"We don't know yet," he said.

And you will never know, Hilda Bryant thought bitterly. His incompetence was very obvious. My God, Ivan Olsen was probably dead drunk in the basement with that halfwit whore Mary Soames. Why couldn't they see that her problem took priority? She felt angry and helpless. This boy, this child playing sheriff, had just about maneuvered her out the door with his smooth promises to investigate.

And naturally they would investigate. But Hilda knew Clara Zondich would be a poor witness. The woman was so flighty she could hardly carry on a coherent conversation. Hilda hadn't seen the crime in her pasture; that was the problem. There were tire tracks, of course, but they wouldn't prove anything. She squeezed her hands tightly together. The tremors persisted.

Why were they doing this to her? Hilda was afraid of the Fosters. They had absolutely no respect for her position or financial standing in the community. They only knew raw, crude power. Ed Foster would be furious when he found out she'd broken their agreement. And if the sheriff wouldn't help her, she was trapped.

She had tried to convey all this to the sheriff in her own way, but he was insensitive to everything. He was rough, common.

A drink. Absolutely. It was the only answer. To feel the burning warmth and confidence spreading through her body—so sensuous, so royally uplifting.

Hilda wanted to plead. She wanted to beg for help, but she could never bring herself that low. Never. What could she do? Threaten to go to the county attorney? Another polyester-suited peasant, another boy in a man's job. Impossible! She had to pull herself together, maintain her control and dignity and find the nearest bar quickly.

"I'll expect to see your deputy today, Sheriff," she told him.

He stood and held out his hand. "I certainly hope so, Mrs. Bryant. At any rate, as soon as possible."

She took the offered hand; it was soft and sweaty. He was welshing on her. She dearly wanted to leap on this fat lump and rip his eyes out. She could call her attorney in Seattle. Roger would listen. Roger was influential. He could do things for her. It was a good idea. She would have a drink and then call him.

She dropped the sheriff's limp hand. "I certainly hope you will investigate immediately and take some action. If not I shall have to take this matter to a higher authority," she told him.

Hilda Bryant turned and walked out. She did not say thank you. He had done absolutely nothing for her; he did not deserve the privilege of social amenities.

Sheriff Burt Rogers waited until she was gone. "Goddamn," he said aloud. Then he sat down at his desk and called Big Ed Foster.

CHAPTER 30

The third-period bell sent a sea of children pouring out of the classrooms into the halls, pushing, shoving, slamming lockers, calling to one another and comparing Halloween stories. Friday was always a particularly disruptive time at the Three Corners Middle School, but Jan Elias moved through this midmorning confusion with the sureness of an experienced navigator. The children parted in front of her. "Hello, Miss Elias," they greeted the art teacher cheerfully.

She knew most of them by name and took the time to answer each one. They were at a fascinating age, a time of fundamental change, all charged with tremendous but undirected energy.

One boy had the voice of an adult male, the next was still a child. A girl in the seventh grade, with the body of Farah Fawcett, waved; her shy friend would blossom much later. It was a time when guidance from adults could be of critical importance. Jan felt better already. She was on her way to do something she should have done a long time ago, review Bernard Foster's records.

She'd meant to do it last year when he arrived in midterm, some time around Thanksgiving, but for some reason she hadn't given it the priority she was now convinced it deserved. At any rate, her father's request last night to speak with the boy about his motorcycle had finally swung her into action. Jan had a free period—one hour to find some answers before she talked to Bernard this afternoon in his art class.

Why was the boy such a loner? Where had he gone to school before? Why did he persist in drawing horrible pictures, despite her best efforts to channel his obvious talent in a more productive direction? Where had Bernard acquired this fascination with violence? More important, what would the records contain to help her give this boy the new perspective he needed?

The bell rang again, a sharp piercing jolt that angered her. Surely there must be a better way to signal children for class. But then again, maybe not. Magically the halls emptied, and Jan was walking alone, her low heels clicking on the tile floor.

The worst part about obtaining any child's record was Henry Barret, the school counselor and custodian of the files. "Who's getting the ax today?" he asked her, feet on the desk. She noted that there was a large hole in his left shoe and a smaller one in the right.

"Nobody. I'd like to see Bernard Foster's

222

records, please.''

''Oh, Bucky Foster. Now there's a familiar name.''

''You've seen him?''

''Not once but several times, as they say.'' Henry Barret sat there, a lecherous grin on his crumpled, puffy face. It reminded Jan of raw cookie dough.

''May I see the records, please?''

Henry never complied with a straightforward request when a woman was involved. He fancied himself irresistible. ''What's in it for me?''

''Nothing, Henry.''

''Foster is a weird kid. I guess you already know that.''

''No, I don't.'' She was getting exasperated.

''You're beautiful when you're mad,'' he told her, letting his feet down with a crash, getting up and going over to the bank of file cabinets behind him. He was shaped exactly like a pyramid. While he rummaged through the F's, he kept talking. ''You've heard of a borderline schizophrenic? Well, baby, this kid is borderline weird.'' He handed her the file. ''Happy reading.''

''Henry,'' she said, not leaving, ''what are you talking about?''

''Aha, a spark of interest. Perhaps lunch in our magnificent cafeteria?''

''Some other time, Henry. What are you talking about?''

''I've seen this kid several times. He's hopeless.''

''There is no such thing as a hopeless child, Henry,'' she said, the anger rising in her voice.

''No such thing as a bad boy, eh? All God's little children? This punk might change your mind,

223

sweetheart," he said smugly.

"What is that supposed to mean?"

"It's supposed to mean that last year, his first year at our fair school, he was sent to me for constantly disrupting his math class. Not only disrupting but threatening his teacher with bodily harm. He made a face and told her he was going to cut her up and put her in a jar. That was Emily Caradeen, you know? It scared the hell out of her. I hauled Bucky in for a little heart to heart, and he was just wonderful."

"Wonderful?"

"Wonderful. Wonderful manners. Wonderful kid. So sorry that he had scared Emily; he couldn't have been nicer. Bright, too. Wanted to know if I was a psychiatrist, psychologist or paraprofessional counselor."

"What did you tell him?"

"Why, I told him I was a specialist in the female posterior, of course."

Jan Elias made it a point not to smile at his little joke, but she felt the hot flush on her face. That seemed to be enough for Henry, and he became quite chatty.

"I remember at the time, I wondered if your friend Master Foster wouldn't be a good candidate for a real psychiatrist instead of a humble school counselor like me."

"Why didn't you send him?" she asked sharply.

He spread his hands wide. Henry Barret had short stubby fingers like Mickey Mouse. "Risk my precious job because some kid made me feel uneasy? Parents don't like suggestions like that; neither do school principals!"

He leaned forward, a serious look on his lumpy face. "Between you and me—and I sure wish there were something between you and me—I probably shoulda done it anyway."

"Why? Did something else happen?" She deliberately sat down on the edge of his desk. It was a calculated sexual gesture; Jan wanted Henry Barret to keep talking.

"Yeah, well, yes," he admitted in surprise. "There was, ah, another incident." He seemed torn between looking up at her face and examining the panty line she knew was showing through her dress.

"What did it involve?"

"A little girl over at the grade school. She said Bernard—Bucky—was following her around on the playground and that he followed her into the girls' restroom."

"What?" This was more than she had bargained for.

He seemed pleased to have shocked her. He sat back and looked her up and down, apparently convinced he was finally getting someplace with the elusive Miss Elias.

"Into the restroom," he repeated.

"What happened?"

"Nothing. Seems he wanted to scare her, not look down her pants. At any rate, he made some sort of face. Did a Dracula act, from what I could understand, and left. I chewed him out, told him that the next time I was going to call his folks and maybe the police. I finished off with my standard sex-and-the-single-boy lecture about why the sexes don't mix." He snickered knowingly, smiling at Jan.

Henry Barret needed his teeth cleaned. They were an ugly green.

"What did *he* say?"

"Not much. It was odd—he seemed bored by the whole thing. He gave me some phony excuse about how she had dropped a pen and he was returning it. Didn't see the sign on the door. I told him that was a lot of bullshit, and you know what he did?"

"No."

"He smiled at me, told me the girl made the whole thing up, swore he was telling the truth. It was such a good act I almost believed him."

"Maybe he *was* telling the truth," Jan replied briskly. "I don't suppose that ever occurred to you." She removed her buttocks from his desk and walked out with Bernard Foster's file under her arm.

"You-all come back," he called after her.

Jan Elias was not beyond using sex to get what she wanted. After all, it got Jim Wentworth. But what she had gotten for her minor flirtation with Henry Barret disturbed her. She knew Bucky wasn't a model student, but the counselor's report was upsetting.

She turned into the empty cafeteria, waved at the head cook and poured herself a cup of coffee. Henry's flip attitude made her very angry. She was serious about her work, serious about providing children the opportunity to express themselves through the arts. Henry Barret was supposed to be helping kids, not making fun of them. Maybe he was the one who ought to be seeing the real psychiatrist.

She sat down at one of the rear tables and opened

the folder. The kitchen steamed and rattled. The food defied identification by smell—some sort of overcooked vegetable and bland institutional meat.

Bernard David Foster, age 13, born September 19, 1967, Louisville, Kentucky. Mother, Linda Foster, born October 21, 1952. Father, Staff Sergeant E-6 Bernardo DeFalion, deceased. Entered Three Corners Middle School, October 1978.

Jan sipped her coffee; it burned her tongue. She blew across the cup and did a little quick math based on Linda Foster's birthdate. She was only fifteen when Bernard was born.

His IQ was listed as 136. That surprised her; he appeared to be a borderline genius. Yet his grades, with a few exceptions, were uniformly bad. It was a thick file. She turned over the summary sheet and ran down the "Schools Attended" column. There were lots of them. She tried the coffee again cautiously and found it had stopped boiling.

Bernard started school in Louisville, Kentucky. From there he moved continually: Atlanta, Georgia; Tacoma, Washington; back east to Louisville; on to Lawrence, Kansas; Bozeman, Montana; Wallace, Idaho; Sandpoint, Idaho; and finally Spokane, Washington.

That was a lot of moving. She pulled out the sheaf of academic and counseling reports. The name listed on the cover of the older report was Bernard DeFalion.

Jan spread out the reports in order on the polished tabletop. No wonder the boy was a little unstable, all that changing and adapting during eight years of schooling. Consistency, a feeling of belonging, a chance to relate to a constant environment were all missing. She got up and walked slowly back to the coffeepot on the serving line. Today's special was meat loaf. She could see it, meat loaf and limp cooked carrots. Jan refilled her cup and, balancing it carefully, went back to the table and Bernard Foster's reports.

Bernard DeFalion entered the Hughes Elementary School in Louisville at age five, according to a yellowing sheet from that institution. He had received unsatisfactory marks in all subjects except reading. His behavior had been disruptive, and he was subsequently placed in a special class for children with learning disabilities. Jan knew that could refer to anything from a dumping ground for little troublemakers to small group classes for specialized problems.

At any rate, there was no indication what the outcome was, because the next report was from Lincoln Elementary School in Tacoma, Washington, where Bernard DeFalion was enrolled in November 1973. Here a lengthy report was attached from a school counselor who saw Bernard 12-9-73 regarding threatening and abusive language used in the classroom. "Bernard seemed cooperative and contrite but absolutely refused to admit that any of the alleged behavior ever occurred," the report noted.

"In view of the complete divergence of the facts in this matter, it was concluded that a general session on classroom behavior would be most productive, and subject was returned to class for such counseling by his teacher." That meant nothing was done, Jan concluded. There followed, however, a second report from the same counselor. The subject was: "Teacher complaint: Rock throwing."

Mrs. Elvira Costello, his fifty-year-old third-grade teacher, had filed a report with the Lincoln School principal alleging that on the afternoon of 12-14, two days before Christmas vacation, Bernard DeFalion, in the company of another small unidentified boy of approximately the same age, had dropped a huge rock "the size of a volley ball" off an elevated roadway, narrowly missing her.

Bernard's mother, who resided at Fort Lewis, Washington, was notified, and she came to school the following day. During the conference "Bernard DeFalion was extremely polite, but absolutely denied that any such incident took place," the counselor noted.

Mrs. Costello, however, was adamant that such an incident had occurred, and stated that if the school did not take action she was going to the police.

On 12-16, the counselor noted, Mrs. Costello called him at home, advising him she was now receiving abusive telephone calls and was of the opinion that Bernard was the caller. The counselor had attempted to contact Mrs. Linda DeFalion, but there was no answer, and he assumed that she had taken the boy on a vacation.

At this point the counselor's notes indicated he had made a recommendation that Bernard DeFalion be seen by the school district's counseling service. However, that was the end of the report. An orange rubber stamp at the bottom of the page noted: Transferred 1-1-74.

In September 1977, Bucky was in the fifth grade in Wallace, Idaho. Here his grades improved, although, once again, a report was appended, this time from the school principal.

On September 19th, Bernard had been sent to the office by the district's physical education specialist, Mr. Ted Pike. Mr. Pike complained that Bernard DeFalion called him an obscene name and refused to apologize. "In the company of the proper witnesses," the school principal noted, "I gave Bernard DeFalion five strokes with a wooden paddle in my office."

On September 21st, however, the next scheduled physical education session for fifth graders, the same Mr. Pike reported he was struck in the back of the head with a baseball thrown by Bernard DeFalion. Angry, he had shouted at Bernard, "What do you think you're doing?" or words to that effect.

According to Pike, Bernard had replied, "Stand still and I'll do it again, asshole," and he had, according to Pike, picked up a baseball bat and menaced him.

This time the school principal had called in Mrs. DeFalion for consultation, and "in her presence Bernard absolutely and positively denied such incidents ever took place."

"He was," the principal noted, "or seemed to be, perfectly sincere, and it was difficult to imagine this student could have done such a thing."

Mr. Pike thought differently. On September 22nd he advised the principal he would not teach if Bernard were present. Apparently the boy was removed, although the report didn't indicate one way or another.

On October 5th the same Mr. Pike reported to the Wallace, Idaho, school principal that all four tires on his pickup truck had been slashed in the school parking lot, and he suspected Bernard. A police report, Mr. Pike claimed, would also be filed.

Jan finished her second cup of coffee. These reports were confusing. Much of what was written was heresay. Actually, she reflected, the reports shouldn't be attached at all. What emerged was the picture of a boy moved from place to place, a string of unproven accusations following him wherever he went. Not once had any of the people involved taken the time to look for a cause, to sit down with the boy and find out if he was a victim of circumstances or a genuine troublemaker.

And what was worse, the pattern had continued here at the Three Corners Middle School. People like Henry Barret had passed the buck again. Somebody had to take responsibility. Here was a bright boy, Jan thought, perhaps even brilliant. He was only thirteen years old, and the school system in a half-dozen states had completely failed him.

And what about his parents? Father deceased, but when? There was no mention of Bernardo DeFalion in any of the reports. But it was obvious that, at least up to Bucky's fifth grade year, Linda DeFalion had been living on an Army post. And what had she been doing all this time?

Jan knew what talent Bernard had. The technical skill could be seen in every drawing, regardless of the offensive subject matter. But what did the drawings mean? She was convinced they might be the key to dealing with Bucky's problem—if he had one. But analyzing those problems, she knew, could be extremely complex. It was way beyond her expertise.

If Henry Barret wouldn't do anything, she would. She would call Dr. Hertog at the University of Washington, for starters. She had discussed her master's project with him; he'd have some good suggestions on where to begin.

She turned back to the Wallace, Idaho, papers, distinguished by their pale green heading on every page. On November 1, 1977, the principal was contacted by the Wallace, Idaho, police regarding an automobile accident in which the same Mr. Ted Pike had been seriously injured. Mr. Pike stated that somebody in a ghost costume had darted in front of his pickup truck near his home the previous evening, causing him to swerve off the road and over a steep embankment.

Mr. Pike sustained a broken neck. He told police he had reason to believe that Bernard DeFalion "might be responsible." The reasons given were numerous threatening phone calls Mr. Pike had received off and on since the first incident involving Bernard.

The principal's notes indicated he talked with the boy's mother again, but this time she advised him they were harrassing her child and that, if they persisted, she would file suit. The principal told the police that as far as he was concerned the matter was closed. There were no further notations. That June Bernard DeFalion left Wallace for Sandpoint; he stayed only three months before moving to Spokane.

Jan Elias sat back in the steel folding chair and glanced at her watch. There wasn't time to read

Henry Barret's report. Her next class started in five minutes. Besides, she had more than enough to think about.

She collected the papers, refiled them neatly in the folder and got up, smoothing her dress. She thanked the cook for the coffee and walked quickly down the hall.

A ghost costume. That was interesting. But what did it mean? She'd like to meet Mr. Pike. Jan Elias had a very low opinion of most gym teachers.

In front of the office, the school secretary flagged her down. "Miss Elias, you have an emergency call from Jim Wentworth." That was highly unusual; Jim would never call her at school unless it were important. Jan hurried to the telephone.

"Hello, honey," she answered apprehensively.

"Hi. Say listen, I just wanted to let you know Ivan Olsen fell off his dock this morning and drowned."

"That's awful."

"Your dad called me just after you left. The Soames girl—what's her name, Mary?—came out while he was on his walk and said the old guy was missing."

"Poor Daddy."

"Yeah, he was pretty shook up," Jim told her, concern in his voice. "I'm worried about him."

"Worried?"

"Well, he's argumentative as hell. You remember the stuff about Clara last night? Now he's taking the same attitude about this."

"I don't understand," Jan said, bewildered.

"He told me there was no way Ivan could fall off his own boat. When we pulled the body out, he just

233

walked away. Said he was going to see Clara Zondich. I didn't have time to ask him why."

CHAPTER 31

Fred Elias followed the nurse, antiseptic hospital smells forcing him to recall his own recent trip down these same corridors flat on his back, rubber tires squeaking on the linoleum. The nurse smiled reassuringly and ushered him into the room. She was young, maybe younger than his daughter Jan. Her look told him that she probably had him pegged for a sweet old man who could hardly take care of himself. Fred Elias didn't like that look. He'd only been in a hospital twice in his life—the heart attack and a hernia operation when he was thirty-nine. He planned to die at home in bed.

It was a semiprivate room, and Clara's roommate was an old woman who looked dead already. Her body was arched back, propped up by pillows, eyes closed. She breathed in long gasps.

"One foot in the grave, the other on a banana

peel," Fred's grandmother used to say with a toothless smile as she surveyed the younger residents of her nursing home in Nebraska. Fred was determined to be cheerful no matter how bad Clara Zondich looked.

He arranged a suitably confident smile on his face in spite of the unnerving recollection of Olsen's body still on his mind. But Fred was through brooding; he was done worrying. He had undertaken the forty-five minute drive to the Port Gloster Memorial Hospital to get some answers. And he wasn't going to leave without them!

Clara was on the other side of the screen. "Now just a few moments, Mr. Elias," the nurse said, her birdy blue eyes batting.

"Thank you, nurse," Elias replied, humbly grateful. There was no reason to spoil her illusions about life. She'd soon learn. That bouncy little body would get tired of bouncing, and then she wouldn't be so condescending to old men who moved slow.

"Mrs. Zondich, oh, Mrs. Zondich." The nurse shook her gently. "Somebody's here to see you."

One side of her face was encased in bandages. They ran over her head, covering it like a helmet. Only a few gray hairs stuck out.

"Hello, Clara, it's me, Fred Elias," he said, feeling slightly foolish, and glad to see that the nurse was about to go.

Clara Zondich opened her eyes slowly and kept opening them until they were wide and staring. Fred squirmed and had to look away. "Ghhhh," she said, a guttural sound coming from inside her.

"Only a few minutes, Mr. Elias." The nurse patted his hand as she left in a swish of white nylon.

"Sonia sends her love," Fred said, rather stiffly. "We'll look after the place for you until you get better."

'Ghhhhh," she said, saliva dripping down the side of her mouth. Her upper lip was covered with fine white hair. Fred had never noticed that before. He forced himself to look at her. Horror looked back; there was no other word for it. It was frozen permanently in the failing brown eyes.

The old lady tried to lift her hands in a pleading motion, IV tubes trailing. "Here, don't do that," Fred said, pushing her back gently. "It's all right. It's all right," he reassured her. But nothing was right. He'd just seen his worst fears looking back at him.

"Clara," he said urgently, bending close, "I want you to answer a question for me by shaking your head yes or no."

Fred Elias had to know what it was that frightened him so, what was wrong on Horsehead Point. And here in this quiet hospital room he was close to finding out. Clara Zondich could tell him.

"Clara," he said, keeping his voice low so her roommate, struggling for breath on the other side of the curtain, wouldn't overhear. "I came to see you because I have a feeling, and nobody will believe me because it's just a feeling, that what happened last night was not an accident."

The brown marble eyes never wavered, never blinked.

"Jim Wentworth thinks you went outside to get the dog, and that when you found her—ah—hurt—that you panicked and fell in the dark."

"Ahhhhggggh," she moaned, a rising wail.

Fred pushed on. "That's not what happened, is it?"

A loudspeaker echoed in the corridor. "Calling Dr. Mason. Dr. Mason to OR, please."

Clara's whole body stiffened and she flung both hands back violently, the wail building to a shrieking crescendo. "Ahhhhggghh."

For an instant, Fred Elias felt what Clara Zondich felt, knew what she knew. It was the same lurking cold evil that had touched him on the deck of Ivan Olsen's schooner that morning.

His pulse raced. "Nurse," he yelled, jumping forward to restrain the old woman. "Nurse!"

He found the dangling call button and punched it. She would not lie back. She was reaching for him, trying to pull him close, clawing, grasping at him. The low desperate cry of a mortally stricken animal rose in her throat.

"Let me," the nurse ordered briskly, pushing him away. He obeyed, shocked at the old lady's response.

Fred stood back while the nurse unraveled the tubes and forced Clara Zondich down. "There, you must lie still. You must lie down, Mrs. Zondich."

The young nurse knew nothing about horror, especially horror for the old, and she easily overcame the old woman's protests with her crisp professional orders. Clara collapsed on the pillows, defeated.

"Please wait outside," the nurse told Fred.

He met the doctor at the door. They passed without a word, and Fred waited in the corridor. An old man in an oversize hospital robe was making his way painfully along, using an aluminum walker.

"Great day for a stroll; just listen to them birds," he told Fred, grinning wolfishly.

"Yes, sir," Fred replied. All he could hear was the faint Musak. They were playing the organ version of *Bridge on the River Kwai.*

It never hurt to have illusions. Everybody needed some, he thought. Fred sighed and began pacing the corridor. The nurse needed hers; so did the old man with the walker. And if he'd told Clara her dog was dead and her neighbor Ivan Olsen had just drowned under suspicious circumstances, he might have killed her.

But Fred needed some answers, and he needed them quickly. The illusion that Ivan and Clara had suffered unfortunate but unrelated accidents wasn't something he could accept any longer. He had to come to grips with this dreadful feeling he could not shake. He had to find the danger, identify it, and put a stop to it.

He made a turn at the water fountain and started back toward Clara's room. He had to do something, but what? Fred Elias usually got all the guidance he needed from the family Bible. In this case, however, he might have to appeal directly to higher authority. He put his head down and stopped. Fred would never ask God for help on his own behalf, but there were others involved here, others in terrible and immediate danger.

The man with the walker drew abreast. "You do hear them birds, don't you?" the old boy asked.

"Sure," Fred told him. "Sure I do." But he didn't. He didn't have any answers, either.

The doctor came out of Clara's room. "We've got her stabilized," he said, taking Fred's elbow and steering him over to the wall. "What happened in there, anyway?"

"I don't know," Fred lied. The doctor looked young too. Everybody looked young here but the patients.

"Well," the doctor told him, "Mrs. Zondich is a very upset woman."

"What's really wrong with her, Doctor?" Fred asked as innocently as he could. It was so easy to fool people when you were old. That was one advantage to not being taken seriously.

"You mean beyond the concussion and obvious shock?"

"Yes, beyond that."

"She seems to have suffered a severe trauma—precipitated by something other than the injuries themselves, that is. Combined with hysteria, that would seem to account for most of her condition."

"But what happened to her, Doctor? What's your best guess?" Fred coaxed.

"Come on, I'll get you pointed in the right direction," the doctor said, firmly guiding Fred toward the elevator with a hand locked on his elbow.

They liked to steer you around, these young bright medical people. They were so self-assured, there didn't seem to be anything they couldn't handle. But this young man hadn't answered his question. Was it possible he didn't know either?

"Don't you guys ever guess?" Fred asked mildly, as they both watched the green numbers march down the display board above the elevator.

"We don't like to guess, Mr. Elias," the doctor said, looking straight ahead. "But if I had to in this case, I'd say something or somebody is scaring

Mrs. Zondich to death."

CHAPTER 32

Linda Foster sat alone in the Port Gloster Golf and
Tennis Club bar, slowly stirring her first Bloody
Mary of the day. The lunch crowd was gone and, as
club manager, this was the only real break she took
all day.

In spite of the solid oak furnishings and black
leather booths, the room looked a little shabby in
the natural light. Some wilted orange crepe paper
still hung over the dancefloor, remnants of the Halloween dance. She made a mental note to get that
taken down.

The club sat on a round, almost symmetrical, hill
overlooking the harbor. The bar where she sat, and
the main dining room adjoining it, were all part of
the original house built by Clarence Mullens, who
founded the Port Gloster Mill Company in 1869. In
fact all the club property was still owned by the mill

which, now the timber was gone, had converted it-self into a real estate holding firm.

Linda Foster shivered and lit a cigarette. It was cold in the big empty room, but she liked to sit at the end of the bar, look out through the French doors and watch the fall leaves eddy across the ninth green.

Ed saw the club simply as a good place to make business contacts, but to Linda the Port Gloster Golf and Tennis Club was something very special. For her it was a complete world in itself, a place with its own rules and customs, a place where she was accepted and liked to be.

"Hi, beautiful," the club tennis pro said, sitting down next to her without an invitation. "Can I help?"

"Do I look as if I need help?" she said in her neutral voice, sipping the Bloody Mary.

"Yes."

"And you're just the boy to do it, right?"

"Right." He put a hand on her shoulder.

She let it stay there. He was not a very good tennis player, but the women seemed to like his style. She had no idea how good he was at anything else, and had no intention of finding out. "It's my neck. What do you have for a stiff neck?"

"Oh, I've got all kinds of good stuff. We could start with this." He stood up, came around behind her and began massaging her spine from just below the shoulders to the base of her skull.

'Umm," she said lazily. Maybe she'd hire him as a masseur and get a new pro. A good masseur was hard to find.

"How's that?"

"Good."

She let her cigarette burn in the ashtray. She'd been at the club until after midnight on Halloween, not arriving home until two in the morning. Fortunately Ed had been snoring like a chainsaw. Then up at eight and out the door. She was always busy and that was the way she wanted it. She had life under control.

"You ought to let me really give you a rubdown sometime," he suggested, the eager tremor in his voice giving him away.

"Forget it," she said, picking up her cigarette. The hands stopped.

His serve smoked when he coiled those Charles Atlas arms, but his footwork was none too good. She wondered what Ed would do if she actually did decide to screw the pro. She took a long drag. Sex didn't interest her except as a means of keeping what she had, and Ed Foster was her only true love.

"Don't you think you better go hit a couple of balls or something, Elliot?" she asked, spitting out a stream of smoke.

"Sure," he replied sullenly.

He was such a child. She downed her drink. Behind the bar the mustached faces of Port Gloster's founding fathers stared back at her: Lt. Commander William Stevenson, who came with Captain Vancouver; Clarence Mullens, timber baron and mill owner. They looked so noble. Men didn't look like that anymore.

"Telephone," the bartender called from his post at the far end.

"Okay." She put out the cigarette and walked down the thick maroon carpet. The weekend would find Sealth County's finest, richest and oldest filling the place shoulder to shoulder.

It was Ed, and he sounded mad. "That Bryant broad went to the goddamn police," he fumed.

"Police?" she asked sharply. The blue jugular vein in her neck jumped to life.

"Yeah, County Sheriff Burt Rogers. She went to see him personally this morning."

"You didn't tell me anything about the police."

Her hands tightened on the receiver until the knuckles were white. She kept her voice low, her face expressionless. The bartender was busy rinsing glasses, out of earshot.

"That's 'cause you weren't around to tell. To make a long story short, your son and some of his friends played a little Halloweeen prank on Hilda Bryant. She didn't appreciate it. She called me and raised hell."

"What did they do?" Linda motioned the bartender to bring her the pack of cigarettes she'd left on the bar. She needed a smoke.

"Painted some of the old bat's sheep; one of them died."

"Painted?"

"With a spray can," he said.

Linda Foster ground her teeth. She knew the bartender noticed the muscles working in her jaw as he handed her the cigarettes in the gold-trimmed leather pouch, but he paid no attention. It was his business to pay no attention. He liked his job.

"Jesus," Linda breathed, lighting up and inhaling deeply.

"Yeah, well, I had it all fixed. I offered to pay her for the loss and she agreed. But apparently the kid

246

did something this morning on the way to school, gave her the finger from what I can understand, and she ran right down to the county sheriff."

Linda Foster nervously twisted the telephone cord around her finger. It could not happen again. For over a year she had been safe. It had to be stopped. "What's the sheriff going to do?" Think. Figure all the angles. She couldn't run this time. There was too much to lose.

"Burt's got to go through the motions. He wouldn't really do anything 'cause he knows what I'd do. But he's got to send somebody over here to talk to us, talk to Bucky."

She had to play this just right. The motorcycle complaint had been innocent enough. The boy was simply making noise; that was nothing to worry about. But this was serious, very serious.

"Maybe you ought to talk to him?" she suggested tentatively. Ed seemed to be able to handle the boy; at least Bucky had never disobeyed him. Whether it was out of fear, or a sure knowledge that his stepfather held some very large pursestrings that could provide motorcycles and speedboats, she didn't know. Nor did she care, as long as Bucky realized this was the best they could ever expect. She'd told him that right after she met Big Ed, and she warned him not to queer this deal.

"I *have* talked to the boy," Ed told her. He wasn't angry, but she could tell by the way he chopped off his words that he was going to issue a pronouncement and there would be no argument. "I talked to him last night. I told him I bought the old lady off and it was goddamn stupid of him to get caught. Jesus Christ, if I were that careless I'd

247

be in jail. It's time for you to talk to him. I'm not going to go around fixing things twice."

She ran the tip of her tongue lightly across the glossy frosted lipstick on her lower lip and focused her eyes on the half-empty glass she had left on the bar. Somewhere a door slammed.

"All right," she replied shortly. "I will."

Linda Foster examined the cigarette between her fingers. Her hand was steady; not a quiver showed. Talk to the boy, she thought. Run, run, the voice of survival whispered. Run like hell before it's too late. Linda Foster's hard shapely body leaned on the bar, her face a mask of indifference. She carefully put out the cigarette.

"And maybe if you're home tonight," Ed said, his tone faintly sarcastic, "you could do a couple of things for me too."

A thin cosmetic smile appeared on her alabaster face. She ran a long perfectly manicured hand down to her cheek where a six-inch scar had once cut an ugly furrow. "Sure," she told him, her voice purring with just the right sexual resonance. "I can hardly wait."

She hung up and walked the length of the bar. There was no trace of the scar now; that was what money could buy. "Billy," Linda told the bartender as she finished the drink, "fix me another one of these, will you, lover?"

CHAPTER 33

The three boys came forward in what Jan Elias called the seventh-grade-what-did-I-do-now shuffle. They drew up in front of her desk in a ragged line. Jeff Myers looked at the floor, trying to hide the purple swollen lip that distorted his whole face. Harry George Junior stared past her, apparently toward something more interesting on the blackboard, which was totally blank.

Jan couldn't tell where Bernard Foster was looking because he was wearing silver mirror sunglasses. She didn't trust people who habitually wore dark glasses. Jan liked to see who she was talking to, and it was irritating to have a thirteen-year-old boy keep the glasses on in her art class.

There wasn't time, however, to get into all that now. She had a serious matter to discuss with these three boys from Horsehead Point. The rest of the class worked diligently on their assignment, glancing up every time the clock jumped another minute with a noisy electric click toward the magic hour of 2:10 P.M. It was the last period of the day, the last day of the week. That, combined with the excitement of Halloween's having been on Thursday, meant there was more foot shuffling being done than work.

She turned to the boys. "I called you up here to give you some bad news, I'm afraid," she told them, leaning over the desk. "I wanted to let you know exactly what happened so you won't hear rumors on the way home."

She paused. Jeff Myers looked up. His normally ruddy face was pale and twisted into a grotesque mask by the swollen lip. Bernard Foster contributed a rather phony solicitous smile, Jan thought, but she pushed on anyway.

"You all know Mr. Olsen, our neighbor? Harry," she asked the Indian boy, "are you with us?"

Harry George looked at the wall over her head. "Yeah," he replied without blinking.

"Mr. Olsen fell off his dock and drowned. The fire department found him this morning. I know you're all just as sorry as I am. The sudden accidental death of one of our friends is just one of those things we're never quite prepared for." It was a bit flowery, she thought, listening to herself, but it seemed to go pretty well.

Jeff Myers recoiled as if she had struck him. Harry George continued to commune with unseen things.

"That's just terrible," Bernard offered, sounding like a polite adult. "We're all very sorry to hear

250

that. Aren't we, guys?"

"Yeah," Harry George agreed, eyes blank. "Can I sit down now?"

She wanted to reach out and grab them both—to shake them, to tear them out of their sullen adolescent boyish indifference, to tell them it was all right to show emotions, to cry, to react.

Jeff Myers was the only one who seemed to be affected, and he was slowly curling up, still standing but with his head lowered almost between his knees. She quickly waved the two other boys to their seats. The whole class was now giving Jeff Myers their undivided attention.

"Jeffrey, are you all right?" Jan asked, coming around her desk.

"No," he answered in a muffled voice.

She put her arm around him. He was trembling. "What's wrong, dear?"

"I don't feel good," he snuffed.

"Do you want to see the nurse?"

"Yes," he responded, groaning.

"I'll be glad to take him," Bernard volunteered enthusiastically, suddenly at her elbow.

Jan stared at herself in his mirror glasses. She hadn't quite decided how to handle her talk with him yet, and his polite, cool reaction to her announcement of the drowning confused her.

"No," she replied firmly, "thank you very much."

"Okay," he responded cheerfully.

What had Henry Barret said? Bernard absolutely denied everything, with a smile on his face? "Bernard," she called after him, "I do, however, want to see you right after class."

"Yes, ma'am," he answered with a military snap.

"Whatever you say, ma'am." He returned to his seat with his peculiar grasshopper stride, blond hair bouncing with each step. It was a wiseass gesture designed to draw attention, and it did. A faint titter ran through the class.

Jan ignored that. "Come on, Jeffrey," she told him, putting her arm around his shoulder, encouraging him to uncoil from his hunched position.

He came in halting steps. Once in the hall, she stopped and lifted up his face with a hand under his chin. "Jeffrey," she asked kindly, "are you sure there isn't something else wrong? Something you want to tell me?"

Even as she asked it, she realized it was a peculiar question. What could possibly be wrong with Jeff Myers other than the shock of hearing about the sudden death of a neighbor? He'd always been a sensitive boy, but even so he was acting strange. His eyelids fluttered and he leaned against her, barely able to stand. Sometimes it was hard being a teacher.

"Come on, honey," she said, thinking of how much she sounded like her mother. "Nothing can be that bad. We'll get you a quiet place to lay down for awhile and you'll be as good as new." If you can't do anything else, Sonia Elias had always told her daughter, remember to be kind.

CHAPTER 34

By the middle of the afternoon Hilda Bryant had managed to forget all about her poor mutilated sheep, her fear of Bucky Foster, Ivan Olsen's drowning, and her anger at Sealth County Sheriff Burt Rogers. "I like you, I really do. You're my kind of man," she told the bartender at the Viking House on Port Gloster's waterfront.

Wolfy the bartender had a relief-map face and almost no hair. What was left was on the sides, dyed black and slicked against his bullet-shaped head. "I'm all yours, Mrs. Bryant, believe me," Wolfy said, his voice gravelly and hoarse.

From the nice spot he had saved for her at the bar, Hilda could look out at the sailboats in the marina, and to the harbor beyond. The forest of aluminum masts rocked in the heavy chop, and the wire rigging kept up a loud musical pinging and clanging in the wind. Gray waves of rain came across the bay, one miniature weather front after another, sweeping down on Port Gloster.

Normally Hilda would not frequent a place like the Viking House, but Wolfy was such a dear. He got her drinks; he talked with her. He was a man of small kindnesses. "Sit over here, Mrs. Bryant, the view's much better. I've been saving this place just for you."

It was really a tasteless dive, she thought. The flowers were plastic and dusty, some of the Naugahyde stools showed traces of white stuffing. The art was abysmal: crudely done sailing ships, the oil fairly dripping down the frame; and, of course, the usual barebreasted seagirls painted on black velvet. Mermaids, she corrected herself. She must be careful to stop at her normal limit of drinks. She had to drive.

And she knew that Wolfy—whatever his real name was—might be an old lecher, a man with a sordid past and no prospects for the future, but he listened to her and mixed a good solid gin fizz. Also the Viking House was close to the courthouse, and she had needed a quick port in the storm today where somebody would listen to her. The only other choice was the country club, but with Linda Foster as the manager that was out of the question.

Besides, the club was such a stuffy place. People knew you. They would gossip to other people, and she would be talked about by all those ancient fuddyduddies who sat around clipping their coupons.

None of that for her. At first she always sat in back at the Viking House where she wouldn't be noticed, but after a couple of drinks she came up front with Wolfy. After a couple of drinks the Viking House became her kind of place.

"This is my kind of place," she told Wolfy dreamily. Hilda crossed her legs, making sure Wolfy saw they were still shapely in their stylish designer jeans.

"It's a lot better for having you here, Mrs. Bryant," he told her, lighting a cigarette.

He didn't tell her it was his normal practice to put gin in only her first two drinks; from then on they were pure fizz. It didn't seem to make any difference, she got drunk just the same.

"Let me have one of those, will you, Wolfy?"

"I didn't know you smoked."

"I don't, dear boy, I just thought I'd have one with you."

"It's your funeral, Mrs. Bryant." Wolfy smiled and shook out a cigarette.

"Like most things that are enjoyable, they're also bad for you," she told him confidentially. "You know what I mean?"

She carefully adjusted her coat so he was able to see her breasts. Not bad for a sixty-nine-year-old lady, Wolfy, not bad at all.

He inspected them while he lit her cigarette. "Oh, I know, Mrs. Bryant, I know. You bet," he agreed, his voice gurgling in his throat.

She blew a cloud of smoke at the ceiling with a theatrical gesture. The Viking House was like a second home; in fact it was the only place where she felt safe, away from the prying eyes of her contemporaries, those boring rich people. She loved the common man.

"Be a darling and fix me another one of these,"

she ordered him.

"Coming right up, Mrs. Bryant."

The slights of Sheriff Rogers were forgotten for the moment. Her plans to call her lawyer in Seattle could be postponed. The fear of Ed Foster and his ridiculous son had vanished in a river of gin and good friends. Well, one good friend, anyway.

"Wolfy, you're just a darling," she told him.

"I'm all yours," he repeated mechanically. He knew she wouldn't remember he'd used that remark only moments before. He mixed the drink without gin, stirred it and made a lot of unnecessary motions around the sink.

"If you only knew how very much that meant to me," she told him, tears welling in her eyes. Real tears. Wolfy brought out the best in her. His dark bar was protection, a fortress, hiding her from people who said Hilda Bryant was nothing but a rich drunk.

"You know," she told him, graciously accepting his proffered drink with a Marlene Dietrichlike wave of the hand, cigarette smoke trailing romantically through the air, "this reminds me of a little place on the Costa Del Sol."

"Yeah," he replied noncommittally, putting his hands in his pockets and looking out into the uniform gray drabness of the Port Gloster harbor.

"Oh, Wolfy, if we'd only known each other then, things might have been different."

"Never too late, Mrs. Bryant, never too late."

But she wasn't listening. She rambled on. Neither was he, he'd heard it all before. The only tropical beaches Wolfy had ever been on were alive with Japs. He didn't mind. She was a nice old broad, not bad looking for her age, and that silver chariot out front was good for business.

"Did I ever tell you about Puerto Vallarta, Wolfy, before it was discovered by the tourists?"

"No, Mrs. Bryant, you never did."

"My God, you have no idea of the breathtaking expanse, the richness in the air." She did not add the cooperative brown boys. She wasn't that drunk.

He had no idea, but he'd listen again. Everybody in the county knew that when Hilda Bryant wanted to tie one on in public she went to the Viking House, and that didn't hurt business either. It gave the place a touch of class.

"It fills you with a love of life," she announced, sweeping her ringed hands before her. *Sí, señorita, you like it like this?*

She was a real showpiece. Wolfy smiled. He got a percentage of the take at the bar.

Hilda Bryant smiled back, her lipstick only slightly lopsided. "Be a darling and freshen this up just a tad," she begged him coyly, extending the glass. "Then I simply must be on my merry way."

CHAPTER 35

"Miss Elias, you wanted to see me?" He was formally polite.

"Yes, Bernard, I did."

"Please call me Bucky; everybody else does," he said with beguiling charm.

Jan was determined to like him. She could honestly say she liked every child who had ever come into her classroom.

He could be a handsome boy, she thought, surveying his face. His pale skin, where it wasn't marred by red pimples, was smooth, almost delicate. And yet there was also a certain solid vitality in the features she hadn't noticed before. He was still wearing the mirror glasses.

"All right. Bucky it is," Jan agreed. There seemed to be a restless energy, that wasn't obvious at first, in the rather thin, perpetually stooped body. The slouch, she realized in surprise, was a coil of strength rather than a slump of weakness.

"I—I wanted a chance to have this talk with you, Bernard—Bucky—about several things. Things that have probably been bothering both of us."

He waited in childlike anticipation to find out what those things might be, feet shuffling nervously, a deferential smile on his face. The long blond hair was in such close color coordination with his skin, they seemed to melt together under the fluorescent lights that hummed noisily overhead in the empty classroom.

She felt herself fumbling. Jan Elias was nervous, and that was unusual. Suddenly she wasn't quite sure what she was dealing with. "I believe that when something is bothering people, it's best to get it out in the open where they—we—can discuss it. Don't you?"

"Do you want to see my sketch?" he asked suddenly, as if he hadn't heard her question at all. "It's very good."

"Bucky. . . ."

"It will just take a minute." He stood up, insistent.

"All right." She was impatient, but perhaps this was a good way to get into the art end of things quickly.

He ran to the back of the room, returned with the paper and spread it out on her desk. She bent over to examine it. It was even more horrible than the drawing she'd shown Jim. A burning nausea stirred in her stomach and climbed toward her throat; she forced it back. Bucky Foster's drawing paper was covered with graphic pen-and-ink medi-

260

eval horrors, executed in his usual thoroughly professional style.

He smiled at her, the blind silver eyes bobbing up and down with excitement, the eager child waiting for praise. There were bodies hanging from trees, eyes bulging, tongues distended, excrement dripping down, a naked woman being torn apart by two huge draft horses; a man impaled on a stake, entrails bursting out; another nailed to the ground, a post through his ear. Dog-sized rats ran everywhere in a blood frenzy, tearing off chunks of their fat, old, helpless victims.

In the middle of all this, playing ringmaster for this macabre circus of agony, was Captain Terror, his costume authentic down to the death's head over the right breast. There was a knowing smile on his face. He looked very much like Bucky Foster without the pimples.

If there was one thing Jan could not tolerate, one thing that enraged her, one thing that made her weak with pity and horror, it was one human being hurting another. In fact, Jan Elias couldn't stand to see any living thing harmed or abused—and that included fish. Jim used to kid her about it until he realized it was not a laughing matter. After that he no longer took her salmon fishing.

Logical arguments based on the fact that she ate both meat and fish failed to take. "I wouldn't eat them if I had to kill them," she said, and talked, from time to time, about becoming a vegetarian.

She was determined to maintain her control in front of Bucky Foster, however. "The technique is very good, Bucky. In fact, it's excellent, the best I've ever seen in a seventh-grade class."

He basked in the glory.

"But you will recall that the assignment was to do something original, something abstract based on the way you, and only you, see things in your head."

The boyish grin faded and was replaced by a mouth tight with alarm. "But this is what I see," he argued, a high shrillness creeping into his voice.

Jan swallowed hard. Now was the time to come to grips with this. "Aren't these representations almost direct copies of things you've seen or read about somewhere else?"

"Yes," he answered eagerly, the smile making a faint comeback.

Perhaps he didn't understand. She leaned toward him, putting as much warmth into her voice as she could muster. She did not look at the picture. She didn't know if she could. "Maybe you didn't understand what I was trying to say. Let me put it another way. It's something you feel, a very personal statement. And as you may recall, I said it should be something that makes you feel *good.*"

She went on eagerly, trying to read his reaction. "It could be a shape. A graceful curve could make you feel good. The Indians, for example, liked the security and completeness of circles. It could be a color and a shape." Bucky seemed to be taking it all in. With an IQ of 136, he should be. She was reaching him; she was breaking through.

"What you've done here is, as I said, very good as far as the drawing goes—excellent, in fact. But you've taken somebody else's idea of . . . uh . . . something . . . ." She stopped. What *had* he done? She wasn't sure. The subject matter reminded her of the fourteenth century, but he'd put himself, looking thoroughly modern, right in the center. The whole scene revolved around him.

Finding no answer, she pulled herself together and tried another approach, still watching Bucky and avoiding the horrible drawing. "And it, uh, certainly doesn't make me feel good. I'm sure it upsets you as well."

"I like it," he replied stubbornly.

"Bucky, I'm not criticizing your talent or ability. It's the ideas. . . ."

"I like the ideas too."

"You like the ideas?" A cold chill settled on her shoulders, as if a door had opened somewhere in the empty school. The electric clock lurched forward with a hollow click.

"Yes, and they aren't copies." His voice grew in strength as he talked. The high boyish timbre dropped lower.

"I don't understand," Jan said. She reached for the sweater normally hanging on her chair. It wasn't there.

"Well, like the rats—I didn't copy those from anywhere. I made them up. They're sort of like the rats in *Super Rodent* but they're not the same. Or this, it's like Captain Terror, but he never did anything that neat."

She forced herself to look. His slender finger was tracing the outlines of the decapitated nude woman. Jan's insides tightened. "What's *Super Rodent?*" she asked him, looking away. She had to keep him talking.

"It's a movie," he said eagerly. "I saw it five times. It was really cool. This big pack of rats in

New York City attacked these old bums and dumb guys in the slums, you know, and ate them."

"I think that's horrible, just horrible," she said honestly.

"I think it's cool," he retorted, a mannish arrogance invading his childish voice.

Jan Elias made herself sound interested. "And Captain Terror, I don't know much about him."

"He's my favorite." The voice went back to a thirteen-year-old level, high and eager. "He's cool. I've got a hundred of his comics. I've even got a suit, you know, the one I wore to the Millers' party."

He sounded very innocent. In spite of Sonia's reaction to the costume, Jan actually thought the boy looked rather good in it.

"What does your friend Captain Terror do for a living?" she asked him. Now they were getting somewhere. Counseling might be her field after all. It was fun once she settled down and was calm enough to observe how he was reacting to her statements.

Jan's dream was to be able to return to school: to study with Dr. Hertog at the U of W; to get her master's, perhaps even her PhD in psychology; and to specialize in treating disturbed children by using the creative arts. As soon as Jim Wentworth got his development business going, she was determined to leave teaching and become a pioneer in this exciting new field.

"He rights wrongs on a universal scale. He stands for truth and justice," Bucky Foster recited.

"But you said some of his ideas—" she held up

264

her hand, seeing he was about to object—"at least some of the inspiration for this picture—" she pretended to look at the drawing but actually concentrated on the table—"came from Captain Terror. These," she said, spreading her hand over the drawn figures but again really not looking directly at them, "don't seem to involve people righting wrongs."

Bucky Foster suddenly stood up. Alone in the empty classroom, he seemed bigger. He stared down at her with blank silver eyes. "He lives by the intergalactic golden rule. He calls it the Times Two Rule."

He began to pace back and forth. It made her nervous. She was also tired of talking to a silvery blank. "Please, Bernard, Bucky, take off those glasses and sit down. I like to see who I'm talking to."

He stopped pacing and faced her. Slowly he peeled off the glasses. He narrowed his eyes to slits in the bright light, giving her an appraising look. Then he defiantly resumed pacing.

"The Times Two Intergalactic Golden Rule is this," he continued in a monotone. "Do unto others as they would do unto you—only do it twice." He whirled around, startling her. "If they beat you with a stick, hit them with a hammer. If they hit you with a hammer, use a club."

He spread his lips into a superior smile, sensing her discomfort. "If zeh take ze money, take ze life." He stopped to see if she was appreciating his imitation Gestapo accent. "If zeh call you stupid, drink zer brains for breakfast."

He broke into a Dracula laugh. "If they cut you,

slice them in two and drain their blood. Times two, times two." He stopped to survey the scene, his stage, back arched, hands on hips.

Jan was surprised to find she was shaking. "Sit down," she said, as firmly as she could.

He watched her carefully, his eyes roving over her body. It was not a sexual look. Then his triumphant visage collapsed as suddenly as it had appeared. "Sure," he said meekly, and he sat.

"We can continue this discussion of your picture on Monday," she told him briskly in her best efficient-teacher voice, her confidence coming back. "I don't want you to miss your bus."

He started to get up. She stopped him. "But before you go, there is something else I want to talk to you about." He looked at her, a wary, sullen look coming over him, shoulders slumping. "I fully understand your attraction to that beautiful motorcycle you have." She didn't, but that was beside the point. "And I'm sure it's lots of fun to ride."

She paused and pinned him with her blue eyes. Her Elias dander was up and she was no longer shaking inside. "But I'd like you to consider that it makes a great deal of noise, and that some of your neighbors might be annoyed because you're riding back and forth all the time. Have you ever thought of it that way?"

"No," he said, voice muffled, looking at the floor. He seemed to be on the verge of tears.

She softened her voice. "Well, you should. I'm sure these same people, adults, do things that annoy you, and they should consider your feelings as well. It should work both ways."

He made no reply. He probably didn't under-

266

stand what she was trying to say. The best approach, as her father constantly reminded her, was the direct approach.

"It's been brought to my attention that you've been riding that motorcycle after school, that you've been riding it too fast, disturbing people. You're not even supposed to be on a public highway without a license. Are you aware of that?" It was too preachy. Perhaps she shouldn't be a counselor after all. She was falling over her own words, making a mess of it.

He slowly looked up at her, his face blotchy with anger. The stooped shoulders pulled up and back. "Who squealed?" he demanded roughly.

The anger flared before she could stop it. "Bernard, I've had just about enough of your lip. Nobody squealed. My father asked me very nicely to remind you there were others to consider. He could have called the sheriff, you know."

"He'll be sorry." Bucky crouched in his chair.

Jan Elias stood up, furious now. How dare he threaten her father? "Young man, I want you to go home and think over what we've talked about here this afternoon. This picture, well, I don't like it. You can do better, on better themes, instead of depicting people hurting other people. As for the motorcycle, I'm going to speak to your mother about that, and I'm going to do it today. I've had it with your belligerence."

Her anger deflated him. He slumped forward; his pale body seemed to shrink. "I was just trying to do what you said," he whined softly.

He was crying. The tears came as easily as water out of a faucet. That was a woman's trick, Jan thought. Don't pull that stuff on me, buster. But then, he was barely an adolescent, and she was a grown woman. She had turned on him rather abruptly; perhaps that wasn't fair.

"Bucky, Bucky," she said kindly, reaching out to touch him, "I'm really sorry we let this discussion get away from us. It's my fault as much as yours. Your best will always be good enough for me." She touched his arm. It was cold and covered with goose bumps.

But his face lit up. "You won't talk to my mother?"

"You'd better run for your bus." She would have to consider that. The electric clock jumped to 2:25.

"Say you won't talk to my mother," he demanded, pulling his arm away.

The conversation was exhausting her. One minute she felt threatened, almost in physical danger, then she felt sorry for the boy. She was being manipulated by a clever child. Jan Elias would not allow that. "Bucky," she said, "I'm still going to talk to your mother, but that doesn't mean. . . ."

He rose out of the chair, nostrils distending in anger, and pushed his face close to hers. "You do," he snarled, "and I'll kill you."

CHAPTER 36

He took the call because it sounded as if somebody wanted to congratulate him on the "Law Enforcement in the 1980s" speech he'd given that noon at the Port Gloster Kiwanis. Sheriff Burt Rogers was always interested in praise, or even constructive criticism, of his public speaking because his real ambition in the Eighties wasn't law enforcement at all. It was the Democratic congressional nomination—which, in Sealth County, was tantamount to election.

"This is Fred Elias," the caller informed him. "I live down on Horsehead Point. We met last year at the Three Corners combined Rotary-Kiwanis."

"Oh yes, Fred." He remembered the meeting; he didn't remember the man. "What can I do for you?"

The reply was overcome by background traffic

noise and either terrible static, a howling wind or both. "I'm sorry, Fred, I didn't catch that," he said loudly, putting his feet up on the desk and lighting a cigarette with his battered 11th Cav lighter. The weather was kicking up something awful out in the harbor.

"I'm sorry, I'm in a phone booth. Can you hear me now?"

"Yes, that's much better." As he recalled, the speech he gave at Three Corners was also "Law Enforcement in the 1980s." That was all right. It was a damn good speech.

"There was a drowning this morning on the Point. At least that's what it appeared to be. Are you familiar with it? The name was Olsen."

Faint alarm bells went off in the sheriff's head. Appeared-to-be drowning? "Yes, I am." Now he had him pegged. Elias lived over on the north side of Horsehead Point. Nice old guy, active in service clubs and church, probably a Republican like almost everybody else over there.

"Are you going to do an autopsy on Ivan, that is, Mr. Olsen?"

"I'm sorry, I didn't quite catch that. Could you speak up a little, Mr. Elias?" Burt Rogers had heard the question very well, but he carefully watched the end of his burning cigarette while he waited for it again. What was this all about? What had gone wrong? Could the department be blamed for something?

"Are you going to do, or have you done, an autopsy on Ivan Olsen?" Fred shouted into the receiver. His voice sounded hoarse and tired.

"I'm sure we are," Rogers replied carefully,

270

bringing his feet down off the desk and giving the conversation his full attention. "It's standard procedure."

"Has it been done yet?"

"I have no idea, Mr. Elias. Why do you ask?" Best to cut this short. Rogers wouldn't win any elections on Horsehead Point. As far as he knew, Ed Foster was the only Democrat of any influence over there. Besides, he had an important county budget committee meeting in just a few minutes, and the Sonics were playing at 6:30. Sheriff Burt Rogers never missed a good basketball game.

"Because I don't think he drowned." Fred Elias was shouting to be heard. "I told your deputy that this morning. It just doesn't make sense to me at all."

Jesus H. Christ on a crutch, the sheriff thought, leaning forward in his chair to stub out the smoke in the overflowing Harrah's ashtray. First that dingy Hilda Bryant broad bitching about her damn sheep, and now some senile old coot who reads too much Perry Mason. He had to get these calls screened better and passed on to somebody else. "The coroner's report will tell us exactly what happened, Mr. Elias. In the meantime, we'll just have to be satisfied with the preliminary finding of drowning which was made by trained observers on the scene."

There was a long pause on the other end of the line. The sheriff could hear the traffic roaring by in the background. Old Fred Elias must be right out in the middle of Interstate 410 making the call.

"When will the autopsy be done, Sheriff?" the old man asked rather formally.

Rogers stiffened in his chair. "Soon, Mr. Elias, as soon as possible. I'm sure you're aware that Dr. Mathew is not a full-time coroner. Let me assure you, however, that an autopsy will be done, and I'm sure it will dispel any doubt."

Hell, there wasn't any doubt now. Rogers twisted in the chair and looked at his wrist watch. He had ten minutes until his 3:30 meeting with the county budget committee. He also wanted to talk to Emulooth personally about the Foster situation. The investigation into the sheep killing had to be handled just right. And while he was talking to Deputy Emulooth, he might just tell him to keep these damn Horsehead Point people off his back. Twice in one day was two times too many.

"Last night, Sheriff, right across the street from Ivan Olsen's house, an older lady by the name of Clara Zondich apparently fell and hurt herself very bad. She's in the hospital now, still suffering from severe shock." Fred Elias's voice was straining. To Burt Rogers he sounded like one of those street-corner evangelists, desperately trying to get his point across while you walked away.

"I'm sorry to hear that, Mr. Elias," he said sympathetically. The old boy must have a screw loose. What did Zondich have to do with Olsen? Zondich? The sheriff had a very good memory, and he had never heard of the lady or the accident. Probably another Republican.

"I know this is going to sound a little crazy, Sheriff, but please listen. It's very important."

"Go ahead," Rogers replied, rubbing his eyes. The worst thing about being a public servant, the young sheriff thought, is dealing with the damn public. In congress he'd have a staff to handle this sort of garbage.

"The circumstances were very odd," Fred went on quickly. "When they found her the door was open, and I know for a fact that she always kept the doors locked and never went out at night."

"Did we investigate? Did we have a man there?" Rogers asked, picking up the budget folio. He needed to look at the figures one more time.

"Yes, your deputy Emulooth was there. I wasn't on the scene personally, but, ah, a good friend, a fireman, described the situation to me."

The trouble was these old guys needed a hobby. They worked all their lives, and then they retired and didn't have anything better to do than mess around with his business. Sheriff Burt Rogers did not intend to retire. He intended to be a U.S. congressman and keep working forever.

Opening the budget folder, he decided to bring this conversation to an end. "I'm sure we looked at all the circumstances, Mr. Elias. You say she fell, well, that's a fairly common occurrence."

"But I was just down to see her," the old man interrupted him. "That's why I didn't wait till I got home to call you. This is too important. I know this woman. She's a member of our church, you see, and I want to tell you she's a very frightened lady, extremely frightened. She can't talk, she can't talk at all. But she didn't just fall, doggone it. If you'd go down there and look in her eyes you'd see what I'm saying."

Yes, Mr. Elias, yes, yes, yes. My God, these old coots would talk your ear off if you let them. The look in her eyes. Jesus! The sheriff made sure he

273

had enough copies of the study indicating that the average county in the United States had four more deputies per thousand people than Sealth County did. The accompanying Chamber of Commerce study showed that Sealth County was the fastest growing county in the state of Washington.

"For an older person, like your friend," the sheriff explained patiently, "a serious fall is a frightening experience, Mr. Elias. I'm sure that's what's bothering her." That Chamber study would really knock their socks off. And then he'd remind them that the growing population was the new electorate. And they wanted—demanded—efficient law enforcement.

"It's more than that, Sheriff, much more," Fred shouted over the wind and static. "Your deputy is ignoring, and now you are ignoring, the very real possibility that neither of these things were accidents at all."

Sheriff Burt Rogers was absolutely confident his department was ignoring no such thing. He was also confident that if he kept his record clean and handled Ed Foster and his son just right, he had more than an even shot at getting the congressional nomination.

The daily report sheet told him Ivan Olsen was a probable drowning—which, in 9,999 cases out of ten thousand, meant that the old fisherman had gone down for the deep six. He didn't even know Clara Zondich.

"We're not ignoring anything, Mr. Elias," he told the old man in a polite, official voice that masked his inattention. The Sonics were regaining their form. He wanted to be in front of his TV when they blew Milwaukee off the court. "Let me assure you, we will make a full investigation of each case on its

274

merits, and we appreciate your input."

"I'm not giving you input," Fred Elias insisted angrily. "I'm telling you that neither of these people was accident prone. I'm warning you, Sheriff, there's something terrible going on at Horsehead Point."

Let him talk, the sheriff thought, holding the receiver out from his ear, allowing a private sardonic grin on his round, unlined face. Let the old man get it out and then he would get rid of him.

"I'm darn worried," Fred Elias went on, talking faster. "Listen, I'm not a young man, and I wouldn't be out here in this weather, freezing in this phone booth, if I didn't think it was important."

The sheriff of Sealth County examined his nails and cuticles. A man's hands were as important as his face when you met people for the first time.

"I'm worried about the safety of my wife and daughter. There's something terrible going on; something's going to happen. I can't tell you what . . ." His voice trailed off, overwhelmed by the howling wind.

That did it. The sheriff stood up. Halloween pranks, painting sheep for Christ's sake, and now a raving, certified loony. "Don't worry, Mr. Elias, nothing's going to happen on Horsehead Point, nothing at all. Take my word for it."

There was no reply. Finally maybe the old character would listen and calm down. Sheriff Rogers cleared his throat. "Mr. Elias," he said very firmly, as if he were addressing a child, "I want you to put it out of your mind, completely out of your mind. Let us take care of things out there. Okay?" Christ, he was going to be late for his budget meeting.

"I can't do that, Sheriff." The voice was weak and fading.

He's finally shot his wad, the sheriff thought with satisfaction, and he began gathering together his budget exhibits while he delivered what he hoped was his parting lecture to a disturbed senior citizen. "Well, you must try, Mr. Elias. Really it's a statistical fact that every day in this county people die. Some die in bed. Some die in hospitals. And some die in accidents. Unfortunately, Mr. Elias, a lot of these people are older folk," he went on smoothly, trying to inject a little kindness into his voice. "And as much as you and I don't want to admit it, every once in awhile these people are going to be our neighbors and friends."

There was no reply from Fred Elias. The traffic rushed by like a mechanical heartbeat over the phone line. Sheriff Rogers pressed the receiver closer to his ear. "Mr. Elias, are you there?"

"Yes." The voice was faint, old and defeated.

"I'm afraid," the sheriff concluded somewhat clumsily, his mind already concentrating on the county budget, "that old people drop dead in this county every day."

"Yes, I'm aware of that," Fred Elias said. And he hung up.

"I'll be damned," the sheriff announced out loud. He shrugged and put down the receiver. Well, the hell with it, he thought. It was odd, though, two old folks almost on the same day in the same neighborhood.

But on to more important things. Sheriff Burt Rogers stood up and snapped shut the county budget portfolio. Deputies per thousand—that was the key statistic.

CHAPTER 37

"He's dead, he's dead," Jeff Myers mumbeld, hunching over as tight as he could against the window while the school bus made its way toward Horsehead Point. Jeff wanted to hide, to get under the covers and sleep. When he woke up the nightmare would be over and Ivan Olsen would be alive again.

"Yeah, it's really weird," Bucky said in a confidential tone, leaning across the aisle so the rest of the kids wouldn't overhear. "He was so nice last night, give me a candy bar and everything, and this morning he falls in the water."

The three boys were sitting in the back of the bus. Harry George nodded and snored beside Bucky. He was down to his last Valium but still up in the air, bumping around in the pleasant pink clouds, while outside the wind shook the bus and a light rain fogged the windows.

277

Olsen couldn't really be dead, Jeff thought. It was not possible. He'd been alive on the bridge yesterday. He'd been alive last night. Jeff had seen him, standing on the deck of the *Thor,* yelling at Bucky Foster. Then he gave Bucky a Big Rocky Hunk Bar.

The bus stopped frequently along the highway, and each time the doors hissed open Jeff Myers felt the cold rush of the wind forcing its way in. Jeff had seen the candy bar, Bucky showed it to him this morning. At least he was almost sure he'd seen it.

"What kind of a candy bar was it?" he asked Bucky timidly, turning away from the window but keeping a hand over his swollen lip. It was pounding and throbbing worse than ever.

"A cheap fuckin' candy bar, I'll tell ya," Bucky replied lightly, rummaging around in his jacket pocket and pulling out the Big Rocky Hunk Bar. It was bent, squashed and melted. "Jezz, that coulda ruined my jacket," he said, holding it out in front of him. "Hey, Harry, you want my present from Mr. Olsen?"

Harry grunted and took the mangled bar in his powerful brown right hand and squeezed until the white cream stuffing oozed between his fingers. "Me like candy bar," he growled slowly in his monster voice.

"Man, I wonder what he looked like? I wonder if he was all stiff, or blown up like a big fuckin' balloon?" Bucky asked them both.

Jeff didn't want to think about it. He didn't want to know. Bucky just sat there in his shiny glasses and talked about death as if it weren't important, as

278

if it were the movies. But to Jeff Myers it was utterly terrifying. It was the end. But what happened after that?

"If he was a balloon he'd float away," Harry George offered slowly and seriously.

"You don't blow up like a balloon right away. Don't you know anything?" Bucky said.

Jeff put his hands over his ears and curled up in his corner. He didn't want to hear; bad thoughts were pressing in on him. All morning he'd been frightened that Mrs. Bryant would call his father about the sheep. Now Ivan Olsen was dead. Drowned, Miss Elias had said. Did you pass out, Jeff wondered, or did you hold your breath until you couldn't hold any more? Did the water rush in while you choked and gagged?

Jeff gasped for breath, feeling it happen to him. The whine of the dual tires screamed in his ears. When he woke up from bad dreams his mother was always there. She pulled back the curtains and let the sunshine in. There would be hot chocolate. She would sit beside him on the bed.

"It's all right, darling. It's just a bad dream. Bad dreams aren't real."

Jeff Myers pressed his sore lip against the cold metal window frame. That was real. He could feel it. Bucky Foster was real. He was sitting right next to him. Jeff sat up with a start. Just a minute ago Bucky had been across the aisle.

"Dead people," Bucky was telling Harry George, "don't blow up like balloons until a coupla days later."

Harry George chuckled. "If I get me some of those Mr. Cool biker shades," he asked Bucky, "will that make me smart like you?" He drew the words out slowly, and in his tranquil mind's eye they formed comic-book-style little circles over his head.

"They aren't biker glasses," Bucky corrected him sharply. "They're chopper glasses."

Harry snorted. "Oh—yeah?" he challenged him in slow motion, the words not sticking together properly.

"Door gunners use 'em, man, so they can see into the sun. So they can waste gooks."

"Door—gunners?" Harry asked.

Death, to Jeff Myers, was a huge ball filling the sky—the dark suffocating blob that had pursued him relentlessly through his dreams ever since he could remember. He ran but he was never fast enough. He would fall, down and down, in a bottomless sickening tumble, until finally, after an eternity, he woke suddenly, alive and sweating and tangled in the bedsheets. If you died, Jeff imagined, you would never stop falling. He couldn't stand that.

No matter how hard he tried to pretend, he couldn't wake up now. He was already awake; he was sure of it. He was on the way home. They would pass Mrs. Bryant's pasture soon. Would the dead sheep still be lying there? Would it be blown up like a balloon? And then Ivan Olsen. He had seen him last night, stepping out toward Bucky in the dark.

The school bus slowed for the Horsehead Point turnoff and shifted gears as it jolted over the Birch Slough Bridge. The tide was low and the wind whipped up over the mud flat, rocking the heavy bus as it crossed.

"Chopper, helicopter door gunners," Bucky told Harry George in a loud voice. "Don't you know anything?"

Harry smiled. His face was pleasantly numb. He had already forgotten the question.

Jeff Myers didn't know what they were talking about. He was thinking about Ivan Olsen. He groaned out loud.

"What's the matter with you?" Bucky asked him.

Jeff Myers twisted in the seat. "What if somebody saw us last night?" he blurted.

"Saw us where?" Bucky's mouth pulled tight.

"At Mr. Olsen's."

"What's that got to do with anything?" Bucky asked, suddenly tensing. He'd just realized what Jeff was thinking.

"I—I don't know. I—I wasn't there anyway," Jeff stammered, trying to pull himself farther into the corner. He was at the Millers' party. If anybody asked he could tell them he was with his father.

The thoughts were pouring into Jeff Myers' head: Dead bloated sheep; floating people with eyes open, staring at him, pointing fingers; the sickening fall into nowhere. He tried to concentrate all his attention on a battered sign just below the window. He didn't want to talk to Bucky Foster anymore. The sign read, "In Case of Emergency, Twist Handle." Jeff could see nothing to twist.

"Hey, wait a minute," Bucky said, putting a hand on Jeff's shoulder and starting to crowd against him. "We were all there at Mr. Olsen's. Right?"

"I wasn't there. I was at the Millers' party with

281

my dad," Jeff mumbled, trying to pull away. But the hand clamped harder. Bucky was hurting him. "We all went to Mr. Olsen's and then we all went to the party. Right, Harry?" Bucky Foster demanded.

"Ri-ght," Harry agreed cheerfully. And why not? He remembered very little. He remembered sitting on Olsen's front steps in the rain, and knocking on Clara the Cow's front door. It was warm at the Millers' party. Groovy party. He went to school. Far out, far away.

"You, me and Harry, we were all there." Bucky pulled Jeff out of his huddling crouch across the seat toward him.

"Yes, yes," Jeff agreed feebly, trying to get Bucky's hand loose. "But I wasn't at Mr. Olsen's," he added in a protesting whine.

"Yes you were, you little chicken shit. I saw you," Bucky snarled, his voice hard and tough. He pushed his silver glasses close to Jeff's face.

"No fighting, no fighting on the bus!" the driver yelled, eyeing the boys in his rear-view mirror. "I'll give you another warning ticket, Foster, and your mommy will have to drive you to school."

The entire busload of children turned uneasily in their seats. Bucky Foster still held Jeff Myers by a hunk of twisted jacket. There was a nervous undercurrent of concerned whispers.

Bucky pushed Jeff back and let go. He stood up, braced his feet on either side of the aisle and turned the blind silvery glasses on the driver. The driver glanced back and his confident look faded.

The children grew silent. The bus driver warily eased off the gas. "Foster, sit down or you're going to walk," he warned.

Bucky smiled. The sting was going out of the driver's voice. He was beginning to get the picture.

"Lay chilly, mutha fuck. You ready to buy the farm?" he murmured under his breath.

"Sit down," the driver repeated, his voice cracking. He carefully applied the brakes.

"Me?" Bucky asked loudly and innocently.

"Yes, you," the driver called back. He seemed relieved. The children were all very quiet.

"Okay," Bucky agreed cheerfully, and sat down next to Jeff again. "Someday I'm gonna rearrange that fucker's face for him," he said loudly.

Harry George Junior yucked his slow yuk.

"Listen, guys," Bucky told them with childish enthusiasm, "let's not worry about Mr. Olsen. We have more important things to do."

Jeff Myers was lost. What could be more important than a dead man?

"We got to figure out what to do about Mrs. Bryant. The thing is, she knows who painted her sheep."

"She does?" Jeff asked fearfully.

"It's like I told you, she called my dad last night. And, Jeff, she mentioned your name."

"You didn't say that!" Jeff cried.

"Oh yes I did. You just weren't listening," Bucky corrected him, smiling. "Too bad, we're all in trouble. But we'll figure something out."

Jeff needed time to think. What if Mrs. Bryant had already called his father at work? What if his father came home early? He needed to tell somebody what happened, but his father would never listen now. He'd have to hide someplace, but where?

The bus stopped with a whoosh of airbrakes in front of Clara Zondich's house. Jeff could see Mrs. Miller waiting, hands deep in her green raincoat pockets.

A surge of hope swept through him. He could ask Mrs. Miller for help. She could tell him what to do. But the hope died as he watched her hugging Rocky and Carrie. He hardly knew her. She might not even remember him. She might not understand what he was trying to say.

"Hey, you missed your stop, Harry," Bucky smirked.

Jeff slumped in the seat. He was going to cry, he couldn't help it. Bucky sounded happy. How could he be happy when everything was going wrong?

"No—shit," Harry said, staggering to his feet, looking around.

Jeff got slowly up and stood in the aisle. He felt sick to his stomach.

"Let's all meet at the cave and make a plan," Bucky suggested as they waited to get off.

"I can't," Jeff replied in a whisper.

"Oh yeah, why not?" Bucky demanded loudly, turning on him. "The rich bitch is gonna call your father, don't forget that. We better get a good story together or your ass is grass."

"What kind of a story?"

"A good lie, stupid." Bucky slapped him on the back.

They filed past the bus driver: Harry hanging onto the chrome seatbacks with both hands to steady himself; Bucky strutting; Jeff bringing up the rear in a slump. A fine cold wind-driven rain hit them with a hail of pinpricks as they stepped off.

"Hello, Bernard," Mrs. Miller called, gathering her children around her. "How are you?"

"Super, Mrs. Miller. Just super. Wonderful party," Bucky called back, steering Jeff with a vice grip on the shoulder over to the side of the road. Harry shuffled along after them.

Bucky sounded to Jeff just like his dad did when he was being polite to somebody he didn't like. Jeff could never talk to adults like that. He didn't know how.

It was a subdued group of Horsehead Point children that fanned out from the bus stop and started to trudge home in the rain. By now they'd all heard about Clara's fall, and, even though her window was empty, the green tiffany light still burned and nobody walked on her grass.

"Why can't you come down to the cave?" Bucky demanded.

"Because—because—my father said I'm not supposed to play with you anymore. He said he'd kick my ass if he ever caught me near you again." Jeff Myers blurted out the lie full force. It was what his father should have said, instead of ignoring him.

Jeff swallowed hard. He could feel Bucky looking at him behind the intimidating silver glasses, searching for the lie in his face, probing with his clever mind. Jeff tried to pull away, but the bigger boy held him.

"I'm not afraid of your old man, Jeff," Bucky told him matter-of-factly.

"Well, I am," Jeff said.

285

"Daddy never told you to stay away from Bucky," his sister Belinda interrupted, her blue eyes wide with coyness. She had on a yellow Donald Duck raincoat.

"He didn't?" Bucky asked her quickly.

"He never did," Belinda sang gaily. "He never did, never did."

"He did too, Belinda," Jeff cried desperately. "You just didn't hear him." Jeff felt the dark anger in Bucky Foster building, an anger that could hurt him. He cringed.

"What's the matter, little chicken, don't you like me anymore?" Bucky asked him sarcastically.

"Sure I do, it's just that. . . ."

"Piss on your old man. Come on down to the cave."

"I'm coming too," Belinda happily interjected, finally seeing the opening she needed to get close to Jeff again.

"No," Jeff shouted at his little sister angrily. "No!" He twisted out of Bucky's grip.

"Why not, Jeff?" Bucky said, grinning. "What do you think, Harry? Shall we let Belinda come?"

Harry didn't answer.

"I can do anything I want," Belinda announced to all of them, setting her jaw defiantly.

"No you can't," Jeff shouted, his voice hoarse.

"Oh come on, Jeff. Why not?" Bucky challenged him. "Because your dad says you can't play with me anymore? What a bunch of shit. He never said that; Belinda just told us."

Jeff grabbed Belinda's hand. "Come on," he ordered her.

"No." She tried to pull away.

286

"You have to," he cried, tugging at her.

"See you two at the cave," Bucky chortled. "Come on, Harry, you can ride with me."

"We're not coming," Jeff yelled, still tussling with his sister. She was a strong little girl.

Bucky turned. "Oh yes you are, Jeff-rey, or Harry and I will come down to play at your house. Won't we, Harry? See how your daddy likes that!"

Harry George nodded, standing in the rain, his mouth open. He finally knew where he was. "See you soon, little girl," he said with a stupid grin.

"Oh, neato, I get to go to the cave." Belinda got away from Jeff and clapped her hands in excitement.

"We're gonna have lots of fun," Bucky promised her. His silver glasses were splattered with raindrops.

"Come on, come on, let's hurry," Belinda urged Jeff. "I get to ride on your motorcycle. I'll hang on real tight, I promise, and I won't tell. You don't have to worry, Jeff."

Jeff Myers didn't answer. He stood head down on the deserted road. The green light from Clara's window cast an eerie trail down the lawn; the wind moaned in the treetops.

There was a smashed pumpkin in the ditch directly in front of him, one side of its grinning orange face completely crushed. "Jeff," she called enthusiastically, running back to him.

Jeff Myers took her hand and slowly started walking home. He was defeated. He had nowhere to go. If he hid in the house they'd find him. Mrs. Miller might have helped, but it was too late, she was gone. He'd have to go to the cave with Belinda.

"Silly, what's the matter with you?" she chirped, squeezing his hand.

"Nothing." There wasn't another person in the whole world who knew how afraid he was at that moment. There was nobody to save him.

The rain fell in long, slanting curtains across Horsehead Point, turning the afternoon into dusky twilight.

CHAPTER 38

Jan Elias drove slowly up the long curving entranceway of the Port Gloster Golf and Tennis Club. The green golf course, on either side of the road, was dotted with white seagulls standing motionless in the downpour. She was calmer now; her confrontation with Bucky had put itself into perspective during the drive from school. She had allowed the conversation to get out of control. She had overreacted to his drawing.

That was her problem. Plenty of perfectly normal kids were attracted to what she considered horrible, ghoulish things, and God knew there were enough of them around. She no longer read popular paperback novels, and carefully checked movie reviews before she'd spend her good money.

She wasn't squeamish; she just didn't like ugliness, especially in the guise of entertainment. And although she was sure most children who saw violent TV shows wouldn't commit violent acts, it seemed reasonable to assume that the sum of all the entertainment to which a child was exposed must have some effect. The thing she could do, as a teacher, was counteract that negative destructive influence with an alternate perspective, one that stressed kindness and beauty, and that enabled children to create a more positive set of surroundings in their daily lives.

The indoor tennis courts looked like a landed spaceship, bright shafts of light glowing through the skylights into the late afternoon murk.

The single wiper was half dead, barely making it back and forth across the windshield, and water dripped through the top around the plastic side curtains. Her old Triumph was great in the summer, but it was a leaky rustbucket the rest of the year. Still, she loved the car, and nobody would ever get her to sell it.

Jan slowed and turned in the entrance to the main clubhouse, hidden behind a row of giant rhododendrons. She was actually looking forward to meeting Mrs. Foster.

The woman had sounded distant and hard on the telephone, but she hadn't refused the interview. And Jan did have some good news to mix with the bad. Bucky was one of the best art students she'd ever had the privilege of teaching.

The front of the Port Gloster clubhouse was imposing, with a silver awning and matching carpet running to the curb. She stopped and got out, careful to keep her legs together so the onrushing lot boy wouldn't be shocked.

"Yes, ma'am," he puffed, "I'll take care of your car."

Jan thanked him and hurried inside. If he expected a tip, it would be a small one.

The thick carpet deadened her footsteps. It was a stately old mansion and she felt uncomfortable. It wasn't her kind of place. Lots of old-money people, and a few young ones, held the club together, a monument to things past in Sealth County. Jan had played in several high school tennis tournaments here and had once dated the son of a member, little Denny Weeks. Actually he wasn't so little, she remembered.

"I'm looking for Mrs. Foster," she told the woman in the cloakroom. She was directed up the curving staircase to a balcony overlooking the lobby. The stairs swept past a massive chandelier that overhung the room, dripping crystal.

Denny Weeks had provided her with water skiing, rides on the family motor sailer, a guest's swimming pass at the club's Olympic-size pool, and a dozen dinner dances under the stars, the summer before she went to college. It was great fun, and she allowed him to place one hand at a time on one breast, until the night he lunged across the seat of his Cadillac convertible and jammed a groping hand between her legs.

Jan walked slowly around the balcony, thinking of poor Denny. "What do you take me for?" she had yelled at him angrily, taking his arm and twisting it back. He was properly apologetic, but it had done him absolutely no good. She had humiliated him.

Jan found the mahogany door with the brass plate marked "Manager," considered knocking but then decided to walk right in. It was a plain room compared to the rest of the club, with a desk in the center. Behind it a tense-looking Linda Foster rose to greet her. She was, Jan thought, a very pretty woman.

"Let me take your coat," Linda offered formally. "Sit down, please," she added politely, giving the chair a nudge toward her guest. "Would you like some coffee?"

Jan gratefully accepted. "It smells wonderful, just what the doctor ordered," she replied, but Linda Foster didn't blink.

The manager of the Port Gloster Golf and Tennis Club returned to her desk and chair, sat down and lit a cigarette. Surveying Jan, she inhaled deeply and asked as the smoke dribbled out, "You wanted to talk about Bernard?"

"Yes," Jan said, trying to put some warmth into the conversation, "I do."

"Well," Linda Foster replied, delaying just a touch, "I guess it's your move, Miss Elias."

"Please, call me Jan."

Linda tried another smile but fell short, a long way, Jan noted. The teacher sipped her coffee in the thin china cup. It was strong. She liked it that way. "This is excellent coffee," she said.

"I'm glad you like it." Linda Foster's composed face betrayed no emotions. "Miss Elias, Jan, just what is it you want?"

Linda had a body off a calendar, perfectly contoured, proportioned and brushed. But Jan noted the carefully controlled hand movements, the faint smudges of fatigue under her eyes.

Jan decided to plunge in. "I'm very worried

about your son, Mrs. Foster. Quite frankly, I think it's important enough for us to discuss right now, if you have the time."

Linda inhaled savagely. "I told you I did. I'm here," she said shortly, looking at the opposite wall.

Jan leaned forward. Now she was on the other side of the desk, and it felt awkward. "Bernard, Bucky, as I'm sure you're aware, is a very brilliant boy, and I'm not just talking about his achievements on aptitude tests. As an artist he already had technical skills some people never acquire in a lifetime, and I mean talented people, Mrs. Foster."

Linda provided a wintry smile and squashed out her cigarette in a plain gold ashtray, scraping it around until the paper squeaked against the metal.

"But I had occasion to talk with him this afternoon about several things, and it wasn't so much the things themselves that brought me over here as it was the tone of the conversation. Bernard and I did not have a pleasant talk, Mrs. Foster, and that was, as I told him, as much my fault as his. I'm afraid that I wasn't able to maintain the teacher-pupil relationship as well as I should have. Quite frankly, sometimes, in talking with Bernard, I feel as if I'm talking with an adult, and a rather rebellious one at that."

Linda Foster flicked her eyes. She picked up her coffee cup and sipped without making a sound. She sat perfectly straight. Jan was trying to think of a way to engage the woman in a give-and-take dialogue, but this obviously was not going to be that kind of conversation. In fact, this was not her day for conversations at all. Perky Jan felt herself slowly falling on her face. Still, she kept going.

"Anyway, I was somewhat appalled by a picture—pictures—he has turned in."

Linda's lips moved, flattening and narrowing. Her dark eyes fixed on Jan.

"Actually I was not somewhat appalled. I was thoroughly appalled, Mrs. Foster, and I told him so. It's not pornography or anything like that. It's, well, worse." Jan rushed on. "Now maybe I'm being unfair, but the pictures involve scenes of torture and all kinds of bizarre cruelty, terrible things being done to people." The memory made it hard to get the words out. "And it—the assignment—was supposed to be something that made him happy, or at least something that made him feel good. Maybe he didn't understand the assignment, but when I asked him, when I made it clear that it was supposed to be something joyful, or good, he said it was, he enjoyed that sort of thing. It upset me. I'll admit it. It made me feel awful. Most of all, I felt bad about Bernard. You see, I like him, I really do. He's a very gifted child."

Jan paused to check the words that were tumbling out. She had forgotten her planned approach. "Perhaps he didn't realize the effect it would have, but if he did, and it was meant as a joke, it certainly was a cruel one for such a young boy."

Jan was on the verge of tears. She had not meant to be so accusatory. Here she was supposed to be objectively discussing the woman's son, and instead she was close to hysteria. "Anyway," she concluded awkwardly, holding the tears back, "I thought we ought to talk about it. I'm sorry, it's been a long day." She smiled to show the other woman she regretted the emotional display.

Linda Foster watched impassively. "Is that all?" she said.

"No," Jan replied, gathering herself together. "I then proceeded to bring up another matter, not school related, regarding his use of a motorcycle in front of my parents' home at all hours."

She talked briskly. If this woman wanted to sit there like a statue, that was her business. Jan Elias's business was teaching children about beauty and truth in the world, and if Linda Foster didn't understand, that was too damn bad.

Linda put her right hand to her mouth and allowed her index finger and thumb to search for a piece of something that might be sticking to her golden frost lipstick. Finding nothing, the hand selected another cigarette out of the padded leather pouch and brought it to her lips. All this was accomplished without moving her head or removing her unblinking dark eyes from Jan.

To Jan Elias, the eyes looked black and were in startling contrast to the woman's milk-white skin. "I don't want to dwell on the details," Jan continued, "but the same sort of conversation ensued, and again I'm not putting the blame entirely on Bernard. I was right there getting upset again too. "Why did I get so uptight?" Jan said. "Why?" she repeated. "Because one minute I felt I was talking to a sulking boy, the next to an angry adult, then to a deeply disturbed, overly shy child, then, well, then, I just don't know how to describe it."

She paused. Linda lit the cigarette she had been holding poised between her fingers. Jan watched the heavy silver lighter go up and down. The windowless room smelled of leather and stale smoke.

"I'm sure I don't either," Linda replied in a flat tone, blowing smoke out her nostrils, "I wasn't there."

If it was a calculated attempt to dismiss her, Linda Foster had another think coming. "Well, I find that disturbing, Mrs. Foster, because I would be surprised if he didn't act the same way at home. I just thought we might get into that." Perhaps a mild frontal attack would shake his mother loose.

"Miss Elias," Linda said very formally, putting the cigarette down and folding her hands on the desk in an attempt to terminate the interview. "I appreciate your taking the time to come over here today and discuss Bernard's behavior with me. I'm also very sorry if he upset you. Bernard can do that, and I will speak to him about this incident."

It was perfect. Actually Jan had been prepared to meet a hard, brassy, arrogant woman. First married at fifteen, then married to Ed Foster, she could only be a nasty little bitch. Jan had been wrong. Now she understood how Linda had become the manager of the Gloster Club, how she fit into the quiet, sedate, withdrawn atmosphere that pervaded every corner of the old mansion.

Linda had what Jim called "class," much as Jan disliked the term. And this was nothing but a classy brushoff. Jan would not allow that, not yet. She knew she was doing the right thing; and, as her father told her over and over again, when you think you're right, stick to it. Jan Elias was absolutely convinced there was something very wrong about Bucky Foster.

She stood up quickly and braced her hands on the desk. "Mrs. Foster, when I told your son I was com-

ing over here to see you, he moved this close to me."
To demonstrate, she moved her face up against
Linda's until she could smell the vanilla-flavored
lipstick and see the faint spiderweb of lines around
her mouth and eyes, invisible a few feet away. "And
he said, 'You do that—' " she paused, still pressing,
leaning over the desk, "and he said it like he meant
it, 'you do that and I'll kill you.' "

Jan Elias stepped back. "And he walked out,"
she finished quietly. "At the door he turned around
and smiled and waved, just like a normal, happy
thirteen-year old boy. I think your son needs some
professional counseling, Mrs. Foster, and I think he
needs it now."

The room was so quiet Jan could hear the old
building creaking in the wind. Linda Foster sat perfectly still, her face an impassive mask.

Well, she had done it, and now she had to do the
rest. All the lady could do was tell her to mind her
own business. Jan went back to her chair and sat
down. "Mrs. Foster?" she asked tentatively.
"Linda?"

The tears ran silently down her porcelain cheeks,
leaving tiny rivulets in her heavy makeup. "Oh
God," Linda Foster said, her voice thickening, "it's
going to happen again."

297

CHAPTER 39

While the rain beaded perfectly in thousands of tiny, sparkling, quivering pearls on the waxed silver hood of her magnificent Rolls Royce, Hilda Bryant cruised toward home and considered various ways to rid Sealth County of Sheriff Burt Rogers once and for all.

She was willing to pay any price to run him out of office, but her cash flow was temporarily slowed to a trickle. It was a conspiracy against the upper classes mounted by the current Democratic, socialistic, communistic administration.

Her late husband Daren was right; it had all started with that fiend Franklin Roosevelt. She felt that her eyes were clear, her hands steady on the wheel. Still, the annoying sound of gravel pinging on the undercarriage had constantly interrupted her thoughts all the way from Port Gloster and the

Viking House bar. She turned the wheel ever so gently, made a slight adjustment, and the big car lurched off the shoulder where it had wandered and back onto the roadway where it belonged.

She was not drunk. On the contrary, Hilda Bryant knew she was driving beautifully. The Rolls gave her a great sense of power and continuity. When everything seemed to be falling apart, an afternoon with Wolfy at the Viking House and a drive in this wonderfully expensive, extravagant machine served to remind her that there was indeed a much better world.

The car still smelled new. The rich sensuous chocolate-colored leather seats showed no sign whatsoever of wear. Money, she reflected, could buy everything worth having. It most certainly had given her a new face, a longlasting body and the ability to stay well above the common rabble.

As she swept across the Birch Slough Bridge, tires humming in the rain, an utterly brilliant thought came to her. She'd sue the sheriff for failure to do his duty. That would cost far less than a fullblown public campaign to rid the county of an incompetent law officer.

Sheriff Rogers was a lout. And no wonder; consider the residents who had elected him. Consider her neighbors: Ed Foster, with his ham-handed threats; that milquetoast Fred Elias, walking around as if he were somethig more than a retired railroad clerk; and that boy Miller from the bank. Naturally her stocks were doing poorly.

Although it wasn't dark yet, it was stormy, and she flicked on the powerful headlights as she motored down Horsehead Point Road. Some urchin

300

was liable to dart out from the bushes and run under her tires. The Georges were capable of that, poor ignorant savages. She had seen the people of color throughout the world, at work and play, and nothing could ever convince her that the meek would inherit the earth.

Her late husband Daren had known how to handle them. You could buy their souls for a gold wrist watch, he had said, and on every mining job where he was superintendent he had ordered Timex watches by the carton.

Hilda didn't hear the motorcycle until it was right beside her. She looked to her left and saw a face shield looking back. She would know that gold motorcycle anywhere, and its black-costumed rider. It was Bucky Foster! She gripped the wheel and stepped on the gas. Bucky moved closer, staying with her. He had a passenger, Harry George Junior, his black hair streaming in the wind.

This was going too far. This was too much. This was the obviously malicious incident she needed to stop them once and for all. She glared at Bucky Foster, concentrating so hard she didn't see the second motorcycle driving slowly in front of the car. Hilda looked up and jammed her foot down hard on the brake; a little girl passenger on the second motorcycle turned around in alarm. The Rolls, its four superbly tuned disc brakes operating perfectly, slid to a graceful stop on the rain-slick road, wavering neither left nor right.

The cycle with the girl passenger drove on. Bucky Foster stopped in front of her left fender, blocking her escape. Hilda locked all the doors with the flick of a walnut button. It provided a reassuring sound of heavy greased metal sliding closed with a solid click. That gave her the confidence to put the car in reverse. The dual Fentress Foggers were working perfectly, but still it was difficult to see through the rear window. She backed anyway, and when there was sufficient distance to swing onto the road, she stopped and started to go around them.

These boys would not intimidate her! Show no fear. That was another lesson she had learned from her husband about dealing with the lesser peoples of the world. That attitude had allowed Cortez to conquer the Incas, and it had enabled her husband to face down two thousand angry, drunken laborers in Malaysia.

Hilda Bryant drove forward. Bucky cut directly in front of her. She mashed the brake pedal again. The big car lurched to a stop. Bucky Foster pulled up his face shield and laughed at her fury. Hilda Bryant ran down the electric window just enough to communicate. She had her hand on the button and her foot poised above the gas pedal. One move and she was prepared to run down both boys.

"I have just returned," she shrieked into the crack, "from talking to Sheriff Rogers about you, young man. I have reported to him that you killed my sheep and made certain threatening gestures this morning. I will now report that you attempted to force me off the road."

A surge of powerful 110-proof joy coursed through her as she saw the smile fade from Bucky Foster's face, the blood drain, the eyes narrow. "I'm going to see," she continued, emboldened by the impact of her opening remarks, "that you are sent where you belong, which is locked up away from civilized people."

She closed the window. Bucky Foster got off his bike. Hilda threw the shift level into reverse, but he was already at the window, pressing his face against the glass, creating a hideous distortion that spread wider and wider.

Panicked, she sent the car leaping forward and Bucky sprawling to the ground. As the Rolls Royce sped by, the front fender nicked the gold scrambler and the bike fell over on the asphalt with a dull crunch.

"Hey," Harry George called after her. All sudden movement irritated him. The Valium was wearing thin. Things were speeding up and jerking around. Somebody was talking to them, and then the person was gone. He was getting cold.

"That stupid bitch wrecked my bike," Bucky shouted at him. "Did you see that?"

Harry wasn't sure what he had seen. Was that Ivan Olsen who just drove off? No, it was Hilda Bryant. Ivan Olsen was dead. Dead. He had to get his head straight. His nose felt as if it were stuffed with iodine-flavored cotton.

"Where's Jeff and his sister?" Bucky demanded impatiently.

Harry George squinted at him. "I dunno." Why was Bucky Foster shouting? He could do without that.

"Come on, help me with this thing," Bucky ordered him, trying to pick up the bike from its side. Harry pushed, and together they righted the fallen machine. The handlebars were badly bent and the front light was broken.

"Come on, stupid, help me get it started," Bucky screamed at the confused Indian.

The pink clouds were gone. Harry George Junior was standing in the middle of Horsehead Point Road. It was raining hard and Bucky Foster was calling him stupid. "Don't call me stupid. I don't like that," he said slowly, not moving.

Bucky Foster looked at Harry closely. "Harry," he said reasonably, "come on, man, help me get this thing going. The old bat is gonnna call the police. We gotta stop her."

Harry smiled at his skinny friend. He rolled his shoulders, feeling the pectoral muscles lifting, the triceps flexing, taking his time. He was beginning to feel mean.

"Just don't call me stupid no more, Buck."

"It was old lady Bryant said you were stupid, Harry. The rich bitch in the big car."

"She did?" Harry put his foot on the kick starter while Bucky, sitting astride the battered scrambler, twisted the throttle.

"Stomp on it."

Harry stomped. The bike fired, sending a cloud of blue smoke boiling out the dual exhausts. Bucky revved it up, the engine rattling and banging.

As near as Harry George Junior could recall, the old broad hadn't said that. Was Bucky trying to blame something on him? For the first time Harry began to wonder what had really happened on Halloween night. What was all that crap Bucky was saying on the bus about Ivan Olsen?

"Jump on. Come on! We've got to catch Jeff and Belinda before that little chicken shit gets cold feet," Bucky shouted, slamming down his face shield.

Harry took his time. He was thinking, trying to remember going up to Clara's door. The Georges always took their time; it was their backward way. It gave you a chance, his old man said, to figure out what the white man was really driving at. Harry swung a leg over and sat. He'd already decided one thing—whatever Bucky had in mind with Mrs. Bryant, he wanted no part of it. He wasn't fuckin' stupid.

Bucky Foster jammed the bike in gear and took off so fast Harry almost went over backward. Shit, Harry George Junior thought, as they hurtled down the road. What the hell's going on here anyway?

CHAPTER 40

Now Fred Elias knew how the old Indians had felt when they could no longer keep up; when one of the respected elders was finally left in the snow to die and the tribe pushed on. He pulled the red-and-black Hudson Bay blanket tightly around himself and stared blankly into the alder fire across the living room.

At least that had some dignity, he thought, leaning back on the wide leather couch. It sure beat the heck out of being dismissed as an old fool. Fred had never hung up on anybody in his life, but he was glad he'd hung up on Sheriff Burt Rogers.

He slumped lower and looked out the rain-streaked front window. The bay was a mass of whitecaps and, from the south, low clouds, almost black in the fading afternoon light, swept toward Horsehead Point.

Sonia was humming in the kitchen as she fixed their traditional Friday-night dinner, with Jim Wentworth and Jan as guests. Sonia always hummed the same tune, "Surrey with the Fringe on Top." And she always fixed the same dinner: roast beef, country gravy, mashed potatoes and spring peas. It was Fred's favorite.

But he wasn't hungry. His body ached and his mind was wandering. He'd never felt so tired and discouraged. The truth was, Sheriff Rogers was only a little less polite and a little more abrupt than Jim and Bryan Emulooth. They were all of the same opinion: Clara and Ivan had had unfortunate accidents; Fred Elias's premonitions were the ramblings of an overwrought, slightly senile old man.

Maybe he was imagining it all. His body was old. There was a time when he could lift bale after bale of hay on a hot summer afternoon; he hadn't thought about that in a long time. He could see his father working ahead of him, his brown back heavy with muscle, sweat glistening in the Kansas sun. Now his father was long dead, and Fred couldn't even pull the outboard motor off his own boat without help. The wool blanket felt warm and secure, like his grandmother's comforter.

Maybe his mind was weakening right along with his body. Still, Fred Elias didn't feel senile. He sat a little straighter and watched Sonia moving easily around her kitchen.

At seventy she was still a beautiful woman, straight and graceful as she worked—more beautiful, Fred thought, than when I first saw her over fifty years ago. When they left him in the snow, Sonia would stay with him whether he was crazy or not. He was a very lucky man.

When he heard the doorbell Fred started to get up but Sonia waved him off. "You stay right where you are," she ordered. His wife had not been happy when he came back from Port Gloster looking, as she put it, "like a ghost at dawn."

Fred sank back, grateful he didn't have to move. Olsen's body, Clara's wordless agony, Sheriff Rogers's rude dismissal and the constant pervading sense of danger had pushed him to his limits. He hadn't told Sonia but, coming back from the hospital, he'd stopped the car twice just to rest and catch his breath.

He could hear Jim Wentworth at the door. Fred let his head fall on his chest. If this was old age, he wanted no part of it.

"What did you do, Fred, put in a hard day at the office?" Jim Wentworth joked as he took off his jacket. Nothing seemed to bother him, not even finding dead bodies in the surf.

"I'm just a little worn out," Fred said noncommittally. "Put another log on the fire, will you?"

Jim looked at him sharply. Fred knew why; he'd never before asked Jim to do anything for him— play a big fish, chop his wood or stoke the fire.

"He's been busy being his neighbor's keeper, instead of taking care of himself," Sonia told Jim tartly as she took his coat and went to the hall closet. "This man, who's already had one heart attack, drove all the way to Port Gloster in this storm to see Clara Zondich."

Jim put a round of alder on the fire.

"Now he has to rest, so don't you get him all worked up about anything," Sonia told Jim, before retreating to her kitchen.

Jim Wentworth came over and sat down at the foot of the couch. "Sonia seems pretty upset, Fred."

"Well, she's right. It was a stupid thing to do," Fred replied gloomily.

"How *is* Clara, anyway?"

"Not good," he said bitterly. "She still can't talk, and she'd been darn near scared to death by something."

"Scared to death?" Jim asked, incredulous.

"Now, Fred," Sonia interrupted over the kitchen counter from her work with the mashed potatoes and roast beef, "you'd better tell him the whole story."

"That's what the doctor said," Fred grumped.

"Yes, but he also said he didn't like to guess, and it was a guess," Sonia reminded him gently.

"He said that too," Fred admitted reluctantly.

Jim ran his hands through his beard and looked at the floor. "Well," he said uncomfortably, "whatever happened, however it happened, it's over, and thank God for that."

"Now that's something we can all agree on," Sonia called from her post in the kitchen.

But that only set Fred's adrenalin pumping again. There was life in his old body yet. "I don't think it's over, not by a long shot," he said combatively, letting the blanket fall from his shoulders. "That's why I called Sheriff Rogers this afternoon about doing an autopsy on Ivan." His energy was coming back. His mind seemed pretty sharp, too. Somebody had to come to grips with this thing.

"You did?" Jim asked him.

It was a condescending question, Fred couldn't help but notice. "Yes, I did, and he gave me nothing but a runaround, completely avoided the issue, told me a bunch of baloney about old people dying all the time."

"Fred, he probably didn't even have the autopsy report on his desk yet," Jim said, obviously exasperated.

"That's what he said," Fred snapped back. "Your friend the sheriff wasn't interested in my suggestion that he look into the Clara Zondich case, either," he added.

"Case? What case? And look, Fred, Sheriff Rogers isn't my friend," Jim said, angry. "I was just trying to say that he probably didn't have a report. Hell, the coroner might not even be in town."

"Okay, okay," Fred said testily. "You've made your point." Jim Wentworth simply would not believe there was anything he could not cut, measure and construct to fit his own narrow, unimaginative view of the world.

Jim put a hand awkwardly on his leg. "Come on, Fred, let's not argue. I'm sorry, I really am." He glanced uncomfortably at Sonia, who was looking steadily at her husband.

"I'm sorry, too," Fred said sincerely, trying to relax and let his anger go, "but this thing's really got me upset." There was a pause. Fred Elias could think of nothing to say that wouldn't start the battle again.

Jim finally broke the silence. "I wonder where Jan is?" He made a show of looking at his wrist watch.

"What time is it?" Fred asked politely.

311

"Quarter to five; she's late. I tried to get her to take my car today. I don't like her driving around in that old ragtop in weather like this."

"She'll be okay," Fred assured him. "The girl just has a mind of her own."

"Yes—it runs in the family," Sonia interrupted, serving them both a glass of freshly squeezed orange juice. "Now lie down, Fred, please."

Fred let her push him back. It would make her feel better. Sonia would always look out for him as best she could. He didn't mind being taken care of, that was something that was supposed to happen eventually when you got older. At some point the younger folks stepped up and just naturally took charge.

Fred closed his eyes and listened to the rain falling on the roof. His father had managed it rather gracefully, finally allowing him to carve the turkey one Christmas. Fred was forty years old, but it was a symbolic act. From that day on his father always consulted him about important decisions.

Now Fred was seventy-two, but there was nobody to take the responsibility from him. Jerry was dead; the rest of the family was scattered across the country.

"I wish she'd call when she's late," Jim complained.

"I worry about her too," Sonia told him. "But she's a big girl, Jim, she can take care of herself."

She certainly could, Fred thought. Maybe he'd have to teach Jan how to carve a turkey. She was quite a girl. He could still see her face the day he got her the Triumph. It was a Sunday in April, her senior year in high school. The car was used, of course, but that didn't make any difference to Jan. She was fiercely loyal to it, beyond all reason. Yet Jim had called it a ragtop.

Fred twisted uncomfortably on the couch. That was over ten years ago. A sudden sharp stab of fear caught him in the chest and he sat up.

"What's the matter?" Sonia asked, alarmed by his sudden movement.

"It's nothing," he assured her. "I was just thinking." Something ghastly was wrong, and somehow Jan was very close to it.

"You haven't stopped taking your nitro pills, have you?" Jim asked, eyeing him closely, sizing him up to apply first aid.

"No," Fred replied sharply. The boy was always asking the wrong question at the wrong time. He forced himself to sit up. "Well," he lied, "I feel better. What's for dinner?"

He was old, and maybe his mind did slip a cog now and then. But there were people in danger on Horsehead Point. And his daughter Jan was one of them.

CHAPTER 41

Linda Foster's tears stopped as suddenly as they had begun. "I'm sorry,"she told Jan, her voice strained with suppressed emotion.

"That's all right. It's a woman's prerogative," Jan assured her.

Bucky Foster's mother was fast recovering her glacial façade, but for a moment Jan Elias had glimpsed the frightened woman underneath.

"Perhaps we should try some more coffee," Jan offered helpfully. She had to know what had upset Linda so badly.

"Why not?" Linda Foster said, resuming a formal stance behind her desk. Music was playing downstairs in the bar, but only the throbbing beat of the bass was distinguishable through the thick paneled walls of the Port Gloster Golf and Tennis Club.

Jan poured the coffee. It steamed and the rich smell filled the bare room, mixing with the cigarette smoke. "May I ask what you meant by 'again,' Mrs. Foster? You said it was going to happen *again.*"

Linda Foster sipped her coffee and considered this schoolteacher over the razor-thin cup rim. Jan Elias was just a girl really, well meaning but terribly naive. That could be dangerous. On the other hand, she seemed sincere; that was a plus. The question was, should she trust her?

She sipped again. The girl looked back. Linda Foster made it a practice never to confide in anybody. However, unless she took Bucky and ran again, there was no choice.

"I've just discovered my son has gotten himself in a little trouble," Linda replied, choosing her words carefully. "It appears that he and some of his friends were involved in a Halloween prank that got out of hand."

"I see," Jan replied politely, waiting for the rest.

It wouldn't hurt to discuss the incident. The teacher would soon find out anyway. "They spray painted some sheep out on the Point—Mrs. Bryant's," Linda said. "Do you know her?"

"Oh, yes." The beat of the music throbbed in the floor. Jan could hear the faint tinkle of glasses.

"She was not amused. Apparently one of the animals died. She called the police."

Jan's stomach turned over. What a ghastly thing to do. She visualized the sheep staggering, blinded with paint. But that wouldn't kill them, would it? "Died? From being painted, I mean?"

"Apparently," Linda told her, busying herself

with yet another cigarette. The smoke was already drifting in layers. Linda Foster flipped open the lighter angrily, applied the flame and clicked it shut with a hard snap. "You're shocked, " she said to Jan in a hard voice. "Aren't you?"

"Yes," Jan admitted, "I am. I don't like ugliness. I tried to explain that to Bernard this afternoon. It was one of the things we talked about."

"What did Bernard say?"

"Well, we didn't agree on that point." Jan paused and thought back. That was putting it mildly. It was about time she got this conversation off dead center. "When he indicated to me he liked that sort of thing, the ugliness, the cruelty depicted in his drawings, I told him I couldn't believe that. I wouldn't accept it."

Linda Foster smoked silently and steadily. She had been right, Jan Elias was naive. She might have to deal with this herself, just as she'd always done. "Well, I'm sure Mrs. Bryant can be pacified," Linda remarked with seeming disinterest. "Boys will be boys," she added, biting off the words.

Jan could feel the blood rising, the redness crawling up her neck. If Linda Foster wanted to play the tough-cookie role, that was up to her. The fact was they were discussing the welfare of a very disturbed child, and here they were fencing like a couple of teenagers.

"This isn't the first time Bucky has been in trouble, is it, Mrs. Foster? You should know that I've reviewed his records so I'm aware of some of the problems. Instead of just kissing off this incident with the sheep and the threat to kill me, why don't we get down to cases?" Jan paused for breath.

317

There was no turning back now. She was off the diving board. A tiny muscle jumped in Linda Foster's jaw.

Jan was shaking with anger. "I'm here because I care about Bucky. I think he's a talented boy with great potential. But I'm also convinced he's got some serious, some very serious, psychiatric problems. Why don't we quite screwing around and see how we can help him?"

Linda Foster glared at her across the desk, her burning cigarette forgotten between two long shapely fingers. The jaw muscle quivered spasmodically.

The harsh jangle of the telephone made them both start. Linda jerked it to her ear and listened without taking her eyes off Jan. "No," she said emphatically. "I'll talk to you later. Goodby," she added, hanging up the phone. It sounded like an oath. The ciagrette butt had gone dead in her hand. "You're a real bitch, you know that?" Linda Foster told Jan quietly, breaking off each word with a snap.

So that was the way she wanted it. Very well, if it was to be a test of wills, Jan Elias would not be found wanting. "I'll be whatever I have to be to get to the bottom of this. I intend to see that Bucky gets the help he needs, with or without your cooperation, Mrs. Foster."

The teacher knew too much already. Linda no longer had any choice; it was cut and run, or spill her guts to Jan Elias. Now was the time. Linda Foster came to a decision. "All right, Miss Elias, Jan. Let's start at the beginning."

"Good," Jan replied cautiously.

"There's always been something wrong with Bucky, something very wrong. If you've reviewed his school records you probably have an idea what I'm talking about."

"He certainly seems to have an adjustment problem," Jan put in eagerly, glad to finally be getting somewhere. "That may have been caused by the frequent moves."

Linda Foster smiled wanly. She shook out another cigarette and laid it on the desk, and another, and another, until she had a half dozen. She carefully lined them up like soldiers while she talked, not looking up.

"Some of the moves were caused by his adjustment problem, Miss Elias, not the other way around."

"I don't follow you."

Linda looked up at her. "You need a goddamn map?" she said bitterly. "Bucky got in trouble, bad trouble. He threatened people, just like he threatened you. He couldn't get along; I—we—had to move. I kept thinking the next place would be better, the next place he'd straighten out, but he never did. It just got worse."

"I see," Jan replied, trying to put all her sincere concern into the words.

Linda Foster abruptly picked up one of the cigarettes and lit it. "I'm sorry, I'm a poor excuse for a mother, I always have been. I can't talk to the boy; he's absolutely beyond me."

"That's why I mentioned counseling, Mrs. Foster. Neither of us can do anything about the past, but let's look to the future. There are counseling services where the whole family could participate."

Jan felt the missionary zeal taking hold of her. There was always hope. Sometimes people were too close to situations to evaluate them properly.

"That wouldn't work," Linda said flatly, exhaling a cloud of smoke.

"Why not?"

"Ed doesn't know anything about this."

"He doesn't?"

"No." She permitted herself a short, staccato laugh. "He wouldn't go for counseling, anyway."

"Well, why don't you ask him?" Jan suggested.

Why indeed, Miss Elias, Linda thought, drawing a lungful of smoke down deep and holding it. Was it possible the girl really didn't understand why not?

She looked at the well-scrubbed, radiant-cheeked teacher. Clear blue eyes looked back. It *was* possible. Linda felt old in front of this pretty, innocent girl. She was probably an excellent teacher, but sugarplums danced in her head.

"Your husand has to take some responsibility here," Jan went on, oblivious to Linda's look. "If he's not aware of Bucky's past he has to be told."

"No," Linda repeated with finality. She stood up at her desk.

Linda looked down at Jan Elias and then resumed her seat. She loved this club, it was safe, respectable and secure. In her past there had been too many bars smelling of vomit, where your job depended on sex. She looked at her hand holding the burning cigarette. It was steady. She had done what was necessary and she had finally climbed all the way out of the shit. Or had she?

"Miss Elias, Ed married me, but Bucky is my responsibility, not his."

Jan started to protest. How could they be married and have so little communication?

But Linda went on. "Let me tell you something about my first husband, Bucky's father, because sometimes my son reminds me so much of Bernie that I hate the kid."

She pushed the cigarette butt into the overflowing ashtray and ground it out, the muscles bunching and contracting in her graceful hand. "That's an awful thing to say about your own child, but it's true. When I see Bucky it's just as if Bernie is right in the room with me. When he does these senseless, cruel things, I sometimes think the bastard's come back to haunt me."

"Your first husband was DeFalion?"

"You *have* been looking at the records, haven't you?" Linda folded her hands in a praying position. "Bernardo DeFalion," she mused. "My first true love. He raped me when I was fourteen; that was the golden moment when Bucky was conceived." The words conveyed sarcasm, but the tone was unemotional. "Nowadays it might be called rape. Back than it was just 'giving a girl what she wanted.' It doesn't matter. I liked the bastard. I must have, I stayed with him so long."

She dropped her hands and began rearranging the cigarettes in a triangle, wondering if she should go on or not. Linda had never shared these thoughts with anybody, and it was difficult. Why not? The dam was broken. All the water was going to run out anyway. And it felt good.

"He was a handsome man. He looked kinda like Sal Mineo with muscles, you know? All the girls thought I was one lucky kid. Bernie was witty, he

321

was charming, and he was a hell of a dancer." Linda paused. "He was also a lousy lover, and the meanest son-of-a-bitch I ever met."

She selected one of the cigarettes and examined it carefully, rolling it between her thumb and forefinger. The voices in the bar were getting louder. Jan shifted uncomfortably in the chair.

"It was like he had two personalities, know what I mean? And the good one, the one that complimented you on how nice you looked and brought you flowers, made you forget all about the bad side. It's amazing, Miss Elias, Jan," she told her, trying to force a warm smile and almost succeeding, "now that I look back, I don't know why I stuck it out with him. The bottom line on Bernie was that he liked to hurt people. That was the way he got his kicks."

"Did he—did he abuse you?" Jan was not sure if it was the right word or question, and she didn't know where all this was going. What about Bucky?

"You mean beat me, physically abuse me?"

"Yes."

"Yeah, he beat me. At least he didn't kill me."

She paused and ran her hand down her face. She could still feel the scar when she pressed her finger across the cheekbone. A tiny invisible spine of hard tissue would always be there.

"He did other things too, like offering me to his friends when he was in a generous mood. It was kinda like they paid him. You know? Hell, I was just a kid, a child. They took him up, you bet they did. All the time. Once a whole gang of them took him up."

Jan reddened. Linda casually lit the cigarette

she'd been holding. Tough luck, schoolteacher, she thought; that's the way it was. "If you didn't want to go along, well, Bernie had ways to make you." The delicate hand went back and forth across her cheek nervously. "I'm sorry, Miss Elias, this isn't a very nice story."

"That's all right, go on. It's important." Jan would let Linda get to Bucky in her own way.

"You could never figure out what Bernie would do next. You know? He carried grudges around like luggage; he kept a list in his head. If you got on the wrong side of him you were in trouble. He was unpredictable and mean as hell."

Linda Foster started to go on but stopped abruptly, exhaling a long stream of smoke and once again considering Jan Elias. What did the teacher think of her now? Had she made a mistake? If so, she had to live with it.

"He beat a man to death one night in a little roadhouse near Fort Knox; he was in the Army then." Linda pressed her fingers to her forehead; the cigarette burned furiously in the ashtray. "He just hit him and hit him."

Linda remembered how he had strutted into the courtroom: clean shaven and handsome, a faint smile on his lips, jump boots shining, combat ribbons all in a row, hawk eyes steady and probing.

"Bernardo DeFalion, how do you plead?"

"Not guilty, your honor."

She was the lovely wife in the front row. "This is a combat veteran, ladies and gentlemen," the defense lawyer told the jury. The victim was an alcoholic, third-rate piano player, Stormin' Norman O'Peale.

"He tried to mess around with my wife. He attempted to fondle her. I warned him, but he wouldn't stop, so I was like forced to physically restrain him," Bernie had lied confidently.

The truth: she had requested "Moon River," and poor Norman's hands shook so terribly he botched it. That was an insult! Bernardo DeFalion, already credited with nineteen kills from his Army service, decided to give Norman a piano lesson he would never forget.

"What happened?" Jan asked her.

"Oh," Linda replied, pulling herself back to reality, "he got off, claimed self-defense. Bernie actually cried on the stand. He was sorry, but the guy had tried to kill him." She looked at Jan, her dark eyes unreadable. "The tears were real. Like I said, Bernie was a real snake charmer."

Linda had to finish this now; she had to get it out. "Anyway, Bernie and the Army were a perfect match. They wanted him to kill people, and that's what he liked to do." Be a good girl and I'll send you my next string of ears. Ears? Just like scalps, babe.

"He did two tours in Viet Nam. He loved it. They got him on the third tour, just before the war ended. He was a door gunner. It was a helicopter crash. They listed him as missing in action until 1974. Finally somebody found what was left of his dog tags. He just burned up. There was nothing left to send home."

Jan bit her lip. Her brother Jerry had died in Viet Nam.

"I threw myself a party," Linda told her matter-of-factly. "I was free. Some little guy in black pajamas had done what I was afraid to do, what I should have done myself, which was to kill the bastard."

She pulled hard on the smoldering cigarette butt. Linda felt better. Finally, somebody else knew.

Jan struggled with her emotions. They had buried her brother in the rain in Portland, Oregon, and given Sonia the flag. Jan cleared her throat. Somehow she had become a spectator in this conversation. Jerry was not the topic. Jan was here to talk about Bucky Foster.

"How old was Bucky when your husband died?" she asked, firmly injecting the question.

"Oh, the last time he saw him Bucky was only four or five years old. Hell, he thought Bernie was a hero. He was, too. They gave him—me—the air medal, a silver star and a whole bunch of other crap. I threw it away. I put it in the trash can."

"Bucky was fond of his father? They had a good relationship?" Jan persisted.

"Nobody ever had a good relationship with Bernie except Bernie," Linda said bitterly. "Bucky was too young to know what his father really was. He listened to all the crap Bernie used to tell him about the war and how nobody ever crossed him. Bucky followed him around like he was God or something. It made me sick."

"Does Bucky know how you feel—felt—about your husband, your ex-husband, I mean?"

"I don't know. I suppose so. We don't talk about it; I won't have it. I never want to hear that name again." Linda paused, breathing hard, color in her pale cheeks. The blue vein pulsed steadily in her neck.

Jan sensed that the terrible anguish which had been hidden so deep for so long in Linda Foster was finally near the surface.

"Ah, hell," Linda said in a husky voice, "the think is, Bucky and I just don't talk at all." Her face twitched once, a wrenching, spasmodic tick, and then hardened. "I couldn't tell the kid his father didn't even like him. He said Bucky was too blond to be his. Bernie said all blond boys grew up to be faggots."

The room had gone cold. The barroom talk and music below them was reaching a gentle crescendo. Linda Foster went back to her cigarette triangle. She was done. "I don't know where that leaves me," she said very quietly, rearranging the sides and no longer looking at Jan Elias.

"Mrs. Foster, Linda," Jan said kindly, putting all her sympathy into every word, "it leaves you in a position where you have to take a stand. Where you have to turn and face the fact that your son, for whatever reason, has some very serious psychological problems.

"There are a lot of very good people who are willing to help, Linda. Believe me, all you have to do is ask. But first you have to go home, right now, and talk to your husband. Tell him the truth. Tell him that you must get some help for Bucky—quickly. I'll be glad to help you with that. I know some people."

Linda Foster folded her hands together, palm to palm, and examined them. Maybe Jan Elias was right, except for one thing. "Do you believe in bad blood?" she suddenly asked, looking up.

Startled, the teacher blurted, "No, not really. I

326

guess not. I never thought about it."

"You don't, or you just don't know?"

"You mean somebody could just be bad for no reason, because of faulty genes or something, passed on from a mother or a father?"

"Yes. That's exactly what I mean. That you inherit it, and there's just nothing anybody can do about it."

"No, I don't believe that, not at all."

"Well, Jan," Linda announced, standing up, "I'm going to take your advice. It's all I can do, and I appreciate your coming over here. But I've got to tell you something. Bucky is Bernie's son. Except for the blond hair, they even look exactly alike. And sometimes Bucky scares the hell out of me, just as Bernie did."

CHAPTER 42

Hilda Bryant drove the careening Rolls Royce up the driveway to the high bluff where her brown log cabin squatted under the onslaught of the storm battering the crest of Horsehead Point. Her head seethed with a toxic mixture of gin and fury.

Bucky Foster had actually tried to force her off the road. He had threatened her and mutilated her sheep; and now this naked, crude act of attempted intimidation. Hilda Bryant was going to retaliate with everything she had. First she would call the sheriff and demand immediate arrest and protection of herself and property; then lawsuits would be filed against everybody involved; and finally, if necessary, she was not adverse to using physical force, by God. She would put Bucky Foster under the wheel of the car and think nothing of it. Nothing!

Hilda whipped the Rolls across the meadow,

where the grass lay flat under the howling wind, and drove straight into the coach-house garage. But she applied the brakes too late; the big car skidded and hit the far wall with a splintering crash, sending a cloud of dust billowing out of the dry wood. She ignored the inconvenience and got out.

On top of everything else, that damn halfwit Mary Soames had left the gate on the road wide open to any itinerant peddler or tramp who felt like trespassing. She had given clear, explicit and final instructions about that. Hadn't she? She had.

Hilda stumbled and caught herself on the car door. That sly devil Wolfy, at the Viking House, mixed a volatile potion. She steadied herself on the door, breathing rapidly, trying to get her bearings, while the cooling engine tick-tick-ticked, and the wind outside rushed by like a continually passing subway train.

The annoying scratching was louder than the wind, however. Uneasily Hilda searched for the source. It was just outside the door leading to the breezeway. She froze against the car.

He wouldn't dare come up here. A hot sweat broke out on her tanned face. He wouldn't pursue her into the house, would he? The door opened slowly, squeaking as it swung.

Mary Soames's foolish dog wagged his tail eagerly. Mary followed. "Hello, Mrs. Bryant," she said shyly.

Relieved beyond belief, Hilda lashed out with the day's worth of pent up frustration. "Do you remember what I said I'd do the next time you left the gate open, you moron?"

Mary bowed her head in humiliation. "Yes, Mrs.

Bryant. I was just goin' to get the gate on my way home."

"Going? Going?" the old lady shouted at her.

"Yes, it's just time. See?" Mary proudly held out her wrist watch, a child's timepiece with yellow daffodils painted behind the numbers. It was exactly five in the afternoon, Mary's usual time to round up the sheep, shut the gate and go home.

But Hilda couldn't acknowledge her own mistakes. She had to turn on someone. "Don't give me that 'Yes, Mrs. Bryant.' Yes, like hell! I swear to God, if there were any justice I'd cane you."

Visions of humble brown servants feeling the lash filled her head. But, even drunk, she knew care must be exercised in the United States of America, with its sniveling gutless liberals who wanted inferior men to have superior rights.

"Get into the house," she ordered, pushing the girl in front of her out the door and through the breezeway. The wind caught Mary's long woolen scarf and both women had to lean sideways into the blast.

But as Hilda struggled between the coachhouse and the log cabin, she realized she was absolutely alone on her ten acres. Having somebody stay with her until the police arrived, even Mary Soames, was better than nothing. The dog could stand guard—outside.

"Sit down," she ordered Mary as they entered, "and get that filthy dog out of here. He's dirtying my carpets."

Mary mumbled apologies and showed Charlie the door. "I'll be right out, doggy. Don't worry," she reassured the eager little collie.

"You stay right there," Hilda said, as she marched to the telephone. She would not be pushed aside so easily this time. She dialed hurriedly, her hands clumsy and shaking. The sheriff was not in his office. She demanded to speak to the undersheriff. He was gone too.

"What was the nature of the complaint?" the young lady who answered inquired politely.

"Threats, threats against my person."

"What was the name?"

"Foster, Bernard Foster."

"No, ma'am, I meant your name."

"Bryant," Hilda told her coldly.

"An officer has been dispatched on your other complaint already."

"But I just encountered the boy again; he attempted to force me from the road not ten minutes ago."

"An officer has been dispatched, Mrs. Bryant. He can take care of it for you."

"But something has to be done now! This boy threatened me. Don't you understand?"

"Where are you now, ma'am?"

"I'm at home, you incompetent," Hilda snarled at her.

"Is the boy there now?"

"No, but ten minutes ago he was on Horsehead Point Road on his motorcycle," she said slowly.

"I'll contact the officer immediately, Mrs. Bryant. He'll be right there."

"What does that mean—some time tonight?" Hilda demanded angrily. The rage boiling inside made her voice quiver.

"As soon as possible, Mrs. Bryant."

"This is an emergency. The sheriff's going to hear about this, and he's going to hear about your attitude too."

"The officer will respond, Mrs. Bryant," the voice repeated calmly.

"Oh for Christ's sake," Hilda Bryant shouted, completely out of control. "All right, all right! Tell him to hurry, goddamnit!"

Hilda Bryant rang off. Her old crevassed hands were shaking with rage. Those people were no longer public servants, they were in charge in this upside-down world. She marched back into the living room.

The filthy dog had left two muddy pawprints on her rug. "Clean up that mess," she curtly ordered Mary, who had not even taken off her red-and-black cruiser jacket.

"I got to go, Mrs. Bryant," Mary said, crossing her hands nervously in front of her.

"You clean up the filthy mess that your filthy dog left on my carpet," Hilda ordered.

"Yes, ma'am," Mary said, shuffling to the kitchen to get a rag.

Hilda sat down heavily in the Spanish-leather chair. She had to think. She had to consider what should be done if the officer failed to appear. That was entirely possible, in any department run by that baggy-suited bureaucrat Burt Rogers.

She could call Fred Elias! Of course. He'd come; he always did. At least he was reliable. But Fred was such a grinning monkey of a man, so pious in his middle-class good-neighbor Christianity. The thought of pleading with him to protect her made Hilda Bryant want to throw up.

That left Mary Soames and her dog. It was settled; they would stay until the police arrived. What did she pay her for, anyway? To serve Hilda Bryant, of course!

She watched from the chair with hate-filled green eyes as the girl scrubbed. She was doing a terrible job, smearing the mud around instead of lifting it off. That was beside the point, however.

"That's fine, Mary," Hilda said, not unpleasantly, a contrived smile of approval stretched across her surgically smoothed face.

Mary rose to her knees. "Can I go now, Mrs. Bryant?" she asked eagerly.

The wind whined around the front windows that faced the steep bluff. Daylight was fading fast. Tiny beads of rain ran down the inside of the leaded windows. She must have that fixed. They'd intended to build a much larger house, naturally, but her late husband Daren hadn't been able to adjust to retirement. It had killed him.

Hilda sat up with a start. She must keep her mind on the present. "What did you say, dear?" she slurred, catching herself, frightened for a moment that she couldn't remember.

"Can I go?" the girl repeated.

"No," Hilda said pleasantly, with a wave of the hand. "I'd like you to stay for awhile." Hilda Bryant would play the beneficent employer. She might even prepare soup for herself and allow Mary to sit at the table with her.

Hilda was starting to feel much better. There was nothing to worry about. First she would have a light gin. "Take off your coat," she said kindly.

Mary stared at her and began edging toward the

334

door. "I got to go," she insisted.

"No, you're going to stay," Hilda countered firmly. The poor stupid child did not understand. Hilda Bryant was alone in this world. The girl simply could not leave her.

"I'm afraid," Mary whined. "I'm scared, Mrs. Bryant. I want to get home before it gets all dark."

"Afraid? Afraid of what?" Hilda demanded angrily.

"Bad things," Mary told her, brown eyes wide. "Bad things in the dark."

"What bad things in the dark?" Hilda Bryant said, her wrinkle-free face breaking into a net of fine lines.

Mary backed toward the door. "I saw Mr. Olsen today. He was dead."

So that was it—her little Norwegian playmate. "It serves him right," she said viciously. "He was nothing but a drunken old bastard."

"Mrs. Zondich is gone too," the girl continued, oblivious to her remark.

"Clara Zondich?" Hilda came out of the chair at the name.

"Yes." Mary's hand was on the doorknob. "The spooks got her on Halloween."

"Spooks? What are you talking about?"

"They hurt her. She's in the hospital." Mary opened the door; the dog jumped on her, barking happily.

"Wait a minute," Hilda said, rushing toward her. "Who told you that?" Clara was her only witness against Bucky Foster. Her only witness!

"My brother Henry. He said to be home by dark." She was outside now; the wind and rain

335

whirled into the cabin.

Hilda went out onto the porch after the girl. "Henry? What does he know? You come back here, young lady."

The sturdy little dog turned on her, growling, the friendly face transformed by exposed fangs and blank, killer eyes. "No, Charlie. Come," Mary called him, her clear high voice carrying on the wind.

"You can't go, you can't!" Hilda Bryant was pleading, and she cringed at the sound in her own voice.

The dog backed up, still watching her suspiciously. "Henry says I have to go," the girl called over her shoulder, already striding into the gathering darkness. "Goodby, Mrs. Bryant."

"Go ahead, you little bitch," Hilda shouted after her, "and don't ever come back, never! You understand?" The words were blown back down her throat; her perfectly coiffured hair sagged to one side. She slammed the door and leaned against it, hot blood pounding in her brain.

Clara Zondich in the hospital? Spooks? Why was all this happening? And then Hilda Bryant knew. Of course—why hadn't she thought of it before? It was a conspiracy, a conspiracy against her.

Suddenly it came clear; she saw the patterns, and the reasons arranged themselves. She was at the center of a plot! Ed Foster wanted her property. She owned the largest piece of undeveloped land on the Point, prime view property, ripe for subdivision. It was worth millions!

Hilda pressed her mouth against the rough wooden door and closed her eyes. But this was serious, much more serious than she had imagined. What would Ed Foster do to get her property?

Anything! Bucky Foster was only the instrument of his will, sent to intimidate her, frighten her into selling. The sheriff was somehow in league with them, and they had already removed Clara as a witness.

Was it possible? It was! Hilda embraced the door with her body, breathing hard. She was well acquainted with conspiracies against her. Her own husband had contrived to mask the scent of the native woman's sex, but Hilda could smell it still.

He had been very nonchalant, but the experience hardened her, and she had turned the tables on him. There would be no divorce; in fact, he would see that she was provided with limitless trips to Acapulco and Javea, where she could do anything she wanted. The alternative was a messy divorce and a fight for every penny. And her own children talked about love but plotted ways to lay their hands on her money too. Drunken tears of self-pity ran down her beautifully preserved face. Nobody had ever truly loved her, or understood her, or cared for her. It was a great pity; she had so much to give.

Hilda pushed herself back from the door and stood up, swaying slightly and blinking. The hell with them all. No love, no money! She didn't need anybody. She would not die. She would not be intimidated! All her life Hilda Bryant had bent people to her will, one way or another.

Her tears dried as she walked to the kitchen. She took down a bottle of gin and poured herself a generous water glass full. Conspiracies had maneuvered the country into two wars; indeed, the country was run by Jewish bankers and the Rocke-fellers.

She took a long satisfying drink and another before carrying the glass into the living room. She understood the plot now, and after two swallows she knew what had to be done. To preserve what was right and true and hers, she had to stand against them. And she would!

Hilda left the gin and went into the bedroom, a narrow cold room, smelling of humid salty air trapped between the pine walls. She knelt and opened the teak trunk from India. In it was folded layer upon layer of expensive, very old Chinese silk. And under the bottom layer was Hilda Bryant's ultimate weapon.

Daren had given her the pearl-handled .45-caliber automatic pistol in Honduras, so she could protect herself against roving bandidos while he was away, he said. The first time Hilda fired it, in the company of Renaldo, the houseboy, she suspected her husband was only trying to build false confidence. The bark of the weapon was frightening, deafening, and it numbed her arm to the shoulder. Renaldo broke into a contemptuous grin. However, the bandidos did not get Hilda Bryant.

She learned to master the gun. She had practiced until she could hold it steady and level and hit anything at ten yards with deadly accuracy. Renaldo stopped grinning. Hilda felt around in the corners, found the full clip and slid it into the gun. Carrying the pistol, muzzle down, she walked purposefully back into the living room.

She seated herself in the leather chair, pulled the slide back and let it go forward, feeding a stubby brass-jacketed round into the chamber. She released the safety and laid the heavy weapon on the table beside her.

She was quite calm, remarkably calm, she mused, raising the glass to her lips. Hilda metered the gin slowly into her mouth, swished it around and swallowed. She repeated the process and waited. Within a few seconds her lips went numb and a warm steady glow filled her head. She felt young, alert and confident.

Ed Foster had made a serious mistake. He had chosen the wrong woman to intimidate. The first spook through her front door would get a hole the size of a Susan B. Anthony dollar blown in his belly button!

CHAPTER 43

Big Ed Foster's Lincoln Continental with its
"SOLD" license plates was still dripping wet when
Linda pulled her Porsche into the triple-car garage
and the automatic door rolled down behind her. She
had driven fast, leaving the club right after her discussion with Jan Elias. Her gloved hand on the
gearshift of the $30,000 car was an illusion; the
nightmare was real. She thought of moving, moving, taking Bucky in the middle of the night on
buses across the country. She had to move again.

Behind them they left sharp-eyed principals in
gold-rimmed glasses. "Mrs. DeFalion, I'd like to
talk with you about your son, Bernard."

Busybody juvenile officers. "Mrs. DeFalion,
we're calling about your son."

"My son?"

"Yes, your son Bernard."

341

"Bucky, I want you to be home when I get here. Do you understand? You must be home."

"But you never come home. Why should I?"

"Because it's important."

"Where do you go?"

Out, Bernard. Out to where I work—the Moonlight Inn, the Flitter Inn, high-class bars. Men. Somewhere she had lost count and sex had become mechanical, unfeeling. "Hey, you gotta nice ass there, sweetheart."

If she drove fast enough, it would all be over on the looping curve just before the turnoff to Horsehead Point. If she pushed the tachometer higher above the red line, made the centrifugal force pull the little black car out toward the guard rail, she then could forget it all.

Forget Bernie DeFalion's dark probing eyes. "You don't like the way I treat you?" An open hardedged hand knocking her to the floor. The taste of blood, the familiar taste of blood.

"The child, Bernie, for God's sake."

"The child? Hey, kid, come here. I'm gonna beat the shit outta Mommy. See that? That's cause she don't do what I say. She don't bring home the bacon. The hell with the child, you whore." Whack. A piece of tooth. A combat boot to the head. "Nobody fucks with Daddy."

The car was designed for speed, tested for stability, intricately balanced. The all-weather radials would grip on the fastest track. The rail would not come any closer. Push it harder, Linda. Break loose, you worthless goddamn car. The Porsche howled around the corner, squat and low in the rain. She had failed to will it over the edge, to drive it end over end into the blue-green sea.

"Mrs. Linda Foster was reported missing last night when she failed to return home from the Port Gloster Golf and Tennis Club where she was employed as manager. Her husband, prominent real-estate developer Ed Foster. . . . "

It was no good. Linda Foster would hang on to the bitter end; she was no suicide. She allowed the speed to drop, let the car guide itself across the bridge, down the curving lane, driving lights blazing a trail through the wind and rain.

Jan Elias was right about one thing: For the first time in her life, she could afford to turn and fight. For the first time in her life she could be more than a survivor. She was Linda Foster, wife of prominent real-estate developer Ed Foster. That was the problem. What was Ed Foster? What would Ed do when she told him about Bucky?

The car gleamed under the garage lights, the water glistening on the coal-black surface. Linda went into the house, walking resolutely, and threw her coat on a chair in the hall. She could hear Ed mixing a drink. It was a reassuring, familiar sound.

"What's a nice girl doing in a place like this?" he had leered that first night, hand on her leg.

"Looking for a good fuck, fat man."

It was love at first sight. It had been better than love. It was safety, security.

"Hi," she said without enthusiasm, coming up behind him.

"So what's the matter?" He swung around. "You havin' your period or something?"

"No," Linda told him, giving him a kiss on the cheek, "I'm not."

343

"Well, good, cause you promised me a little nooky, honey."

"First I need a drink, Ed, and then we've got to talk."

He hadn't noticed she was pale and upset. She looked fine to him, she always did. "Hey," he said. "Talk?"

She poured herself a martini from the glass pitcher on the bar. Some of it spilled over the glass onto the oak floor. She let the puddle spread. They were in what Ed liked to call his lounge. He had built it, he told her, because it reminded him of where they met in Spokane. It was Ed's idea of a joke. Actually it was much prettier than the hotel bar, although the motif was familiar. The room was divided roughly in half, one portion carpeted in deep white shag. The balance of the floor was polished oak.

Ed Foster watched his wife fumbling with the drink. He'd screwed the daylights out of her more than once on that shag rug and was thinking about doing it again. It was his size of bed. She came back and sat down in a round, high-backed pale brown leather chair. The surface was tucked and pleated and the leather shone under the recessed lights.

"Ed, you never asked me any questions. I mean, we've been married almost two years now, and you never asked me where I was from or what I did." Her voice was unsteady.

He leaned forward. Then he saw the strain in her face. "No, and I don't want any answers, either," he said sharply.

"Why is that, Ed?"

He finished his martini. "I'm dry," he told her.

She flashed him a poor excuse for a sexy smile and went to refill his glass from the bar.

Big Ed Foster had once been on the cover of *The Seattle Times Sunday Pictorial.* He was an imposing figure in his football uniform, charging the camera, huge arms spread across the page, a ferocious smile baring the yawning gap between his eyeteeth. "Washington State's Monster Man Mows Them Down," read the yellow banner stretched across the right-hand side of the page.

He watched Linda at the bar. She was so trim and young, so much like the little girls he could not resist. She even shaved her pubic hair. It drove him wild. She never asked him why, she did it because it pleased him. No questions now, Linda, he thought, please. Questions were dangerous.

True, no charges had ever been filed, but there had been some close calls. He was too big, too recognizable. A little girl at a motel in Boise had almost tripped him up. Ed had just closed a deal with three cowboys from Sun Valley, and he was celebrating. They were in the pool. He hadn't really done anything. They were playing; she enticed him into putting just a hand under the loose-fitting suit.

There was the enraged father: "Now just a minute, fella! What the hell do you think you're doing?"

"Ed," Linda prompted him, holding out the glass.

"Thanks."

It had been close. The father was a joke. Ed told him to fuck off, but he was a noisy little guy. The girl started screaming. He'd just walked out, went to his room, packed, and drove and drove, expecting to see a patrol car in the rear-view mirror. It never came.

"Ed, we've got to talk. I had a very disturbing discussion with Bucky's teacher today."

So that was it. Well, no dice. He'd done his best for Bucky. That was her lookout now. She could talk to the Bryant dame. She could talk to the police, too.

"He in trouble?" he asked. It looked like the good stuff would have to wait. He'd give her five minutes, then he was going to give her a fucking she'd never forget.

"It's more than that. Please, Ed, listen to me."

She was acting goddamn serious. Jesus, he'd take care of Hilda Bryant, if that was bothering her. He'd take that old lady and ram her complaint right down her throat. "I'll talk to Bucky," he offered. "I'll talk to him again about the sheep. I'll square it with the cops. I'll fix it. Don't worry."

"Thanks, Ed." She gave him a little pat on the knee and a depressed smile.

What the hell was going on here?

"Ed, this is serious. I've got to tell you some things, things that happened before I met you. It's important."

Christ, there was always something to complicate a good lay. At least she had forgotten her question about why he preferred to avoid the past. Ed could never tell her about the fear, the shame, the humiliation, the relief of finding her, a grown woman of legal age who looked just like a child. Linda had saved him.

"So tell me," he said, sipping his drink. If he

346

didn't love her, he was damn fond of her, and he didn't like to see her upset.

"Ed, I—I—" She paused and then set herself to go on. "I moved around a lot before I met you. You know, I was married before, and he died."

"He died?"

"In the war, in Viet Nam."

In the war; that was something. He hadn't imagined that. In fact, he was never sure Linda had been married. Well, if that was the way she wanted it. "You don't have to tell me any of this," he said, reaching for her hand. It was an awkward gesture. Big Ed Foster was used to grabbing things, and to merely reach unbalanced him. Nevertheless, he saw she was distressed, so he restrained his grip and held her hand as gently as he could.

"I have to, Ed."

He nodded.

"I moved a lot. I had some pretty low-life jobs, cocktail waitress, bartender, oh, stuff like that. Hell, Ed, I was a hooker."

"Honey, that's no news to me," he told her.

She was not getting to the point. "But I didn't move because of that. Well, I did and I didn't."

He finished the drink. "I don't get it. I don't know what you're getting at. We could just forget the whole thing." He sensed she was going to tell him something he didn't want to hear.

"I moved because of Bucky. He got in trouble, Ed. No matter how hard I tried, he got in trouble everywhere we went."

Ed Foster sat up a little straighter. "Trouble? What kind of trouble?" He withdrew his hand from hers and rested his big paw on the cool leather

347

chair arm.

"He'd say things to teachers or other kids. Half the time he didn't mean anything by it. It was hard on him, Ed."

He watched her struggling. It hurt him to see her like this. What was wrong with his little sexpot Linda?

"I couldn't do anything about it, you know. I didn't have a hell of a lot of credibility in my line of work then. Bucky got in arguments at school, he talked back to teachers, he threatened them. A couple of those people had bad accidents."

"Accidents?"

"Yeah, and they blamed Bucky."

"What do you mean? Were they lying?" he asked, leaning forward in his chair.

"Well, who are you supposed to believe if you can't believe your own kid? He said he didn't do anything, but I wondered. I wondered because Bucky reminds me so much of my first husband Bernie." Linda Foster always approached the truth with extreme caution, circling it first to see what it would buy. Instinctively, she clung to that habit now.

"What was Bernie's problem?" Ed closed a massive fist and rubbed it across the stubble on his square chin. He didn't like the sound of this.

Linda cleared her throat and looked at her long, graceful hands, so perfectly manicured. "Nobody ever crossed Bernie. He was a maniac. He was a killer. I'm glad he's dead."

Ed didn't reply. He continued rubbing his fist across his chin, making a scraping sound.

"I just don't know," she repeated, still not committing herself directly. "Sometimes I think Bucky got it from him, the meanness, like he inherited it. You know? They're like two cats. Did you ever have cats, and one would die, and another one would come along, and sometimes you forgot there were two separate cats, they just seemed like the same cat?"

"No," he replied. "I never owned a cat."

"Anyway, I just couldn't believe Bucky would do those things, but sometimes I was convinced he did." She edged closer, watching him now, ready to jump back.

"Look, honey, what the hell do you mean—that the boy got pissed at people and arranged accidents?" He had to get a clear picture. It was important in covering tracks. Big Ed Foster knew a great deal about the techniques. There were no footprints behind him at all.

"Well, he always denied it, and it was never anything they could prove. But they didn't know what happened in those other places. I did. I knew. I knew it couldn't all be coincidence."

Linda looked closely at her husband. She had not imagined he would be the least bit sympathetic, but something was there—pity, understanding, sympathy, concern—she couldn't tell.

Whatever it was, it was enough for Linda to spill it all. "I'm just all screwed up over Bucky, Ed, and that's the truth. I know he hurt people, I know it, but I felt that I had to protect him. I didn't want them to put him away somewhere. I couldn't stand that. I love him—and I hate him. He's my son, for Christ's sake!" She wanted to reach out and hold onto Big Ed Foster. Linda felt the tears, but she couldn't do that. He'd turn on her. Ed Foster was a nice guy, but to him, Linda knew, she was nothing more than a warm piece of tail.

Ed Foster remained calm. He was going over the call from Sheriff Rogers in his mind. He could see Linda was at the point of shattering. He wasn't going to let that happen. Just for the hell of it, he was going to fix this thing for her. Nobody ever moved Big Ed Foster off the line once he decided to dig in. But he had to keep thinking; there was no time for any of this hearts-and-flowers shit.

"Exactly what happened at school today?" he asked her.

"He threatened to kill Jan Elias, his art teacher. You know, the lady who lives down by the bridge."

Oh, yes, he knew Jan Elias. Miss Goody-Two-Shoes, know-it-all bitch and her hippy boyfriend Jim Wentworth, the quality developer. The quality bankrupt developer, the kid who wouldn't know the right side of a dollar if it hit him square in the face. But Jan Elias was a bad woman to threaten. She had a big mouth.

"What did he do that for?"

"I don't know." Linda was through. It was an effort to raise her voice. "Jan came to see me," she added.

"Yeah, what's her angle?"

He was all business now. He could still fix the sheep thing with Bryant, and if Jan Elias hadn't shot her mouth off yet, he'd figure out a way to quiet her down too. What had happened in the past was done, nobody could touch the kid for that. But things could get out of control here if he didn't move quickly.

"Miss Elias, Jan, said we should get counseling for Bucky. She was really very nice about it. I mean, she drove all the way over to the club."

"Did she call the sheriff about the threat he made?"

"No, not then at least."

"Good." He had the picture. The Hilda Bryant thing alone was not serious, and Linda could handle Jan Elias. There was nothing else to implicate the boy.

The thing to do was to get the kid to a good head-shrinker. That would cover everybody's ass. The boy would be in treatment, so they couldn't touch him. End of problem. "I'll take care of it, don't worry," he told her. "Let's get Bucky down here and have a little talk with him."

So Bucky had been in trouble. Ed had been in a little trouble himself before he met Linda, but he had managed to straighten out. Bucky could do the same thing. Everybody had his little quirks.

"Ed," she asked him quietly, "do you think he's really crazy?"

He snorted. "You tell me. Hell, everybody's a little crazy. Don't sweat it, I know exactly what to do." He stood up and listened. There was no television set playing overhead. "Hey, Bucky," he shouted. Big Ed Foster's voice echoed through the empty house.

"I dont' think his motorcycle was in the garage," she told him.

Ed hadn't paid any attention. Together they went into the garage and looked. The wind rattled the wide door. There were puddles of rain water around the two cars. The motorcycle wasn't there.

Ed Foster wasn't worried. There was nothing that couldn't be fixed if you had the right tools. He already owned damn near half of Sealth County, and if Burt Rogers got the Democratic nomination he'd soon have a congressman to go with it.

He put his arm around Linda and led her back into the house. She was shivering. "Don't worry," he said reassuringly, giving her a Big Ed Foster-sized squeeze. "He'll be back. Who knows, maybe he finally got interested in girls or something."

CHAPTER 44

"Hey, this is neato," Belinda squealed, running into the secret cave. This was better than Disneyland; it was real.

"Don't go in there," Jeff warned her.

"Why not?" she asked gaily, ignoring her brother's warning. Belinda was thrilled by the motorcycle ride down the beach, and being included in the big boys' games. Besides, it was cold and wet outside; the cave was nice and toasty. It smelled funny inside though, and Harry was way in the back where she couldn't see him very well.

"What are you doing?" she asked, looking around in the dim light.

"Trying to find a good one," he muttered, fumbling through a year's worth of damp *Cheap Thrills* magazines. As the Valium faded, so did Harry George Junior. He was feeling way, way down. He needed the driving lift of a good crotch shot.

"One what?" she said.

"Belinda," Jeff pleaded. He had to stop her before she saw one of those pictures.

Bucky jumped in front of him. "What's the matter, Jeffrey?" he asked him gleefully. "Afraid your little sister will get some hot ideas?"

Bucky wouldn't let him by. "No," Jeff insisted, trying to see what Belinda was doing. He had to get her away. "Belinda, let's go."

"Not until we make our plans, Jeff." Bucky blocked the cave entrance, feet apart, hands on hips.

The incoming tide ripped through the kelp beds; steep waves thundered on the beach below them. Jeff looked up the cliff to the crest of Horsehead Point. The steepness made him feel weak, and Bucky Foster looked very big and strong in his Captain Terror uniform.

"The rich bitch squealed on us. She smashed my bike and she almost hit you. She must pay!" Bucky Foster said dramatically.

"Who has to pay?" Belinda asked him.

"Mrs. Bryant," Bucky told her, smiling. "And you get to help, Belinda. Hey, Harry, get out here, man. Have I got a totally cool idea!"

Harry George came out, blinking and carrying a magazine turned open to a naked woman straddling a donkey. Bucky Foster was getting on his raw nerves. He always wanted to do something; he could never just leave things alone.

Jeff tried to get between Belinda and Harry so she couldn't see. What if he just suddenly stood up, he thought, grabbed her and ran? They'd never make it; they weren't fast enough. Bucky would catch them for sure.

"Put that shitty fuck book down!" Bucky shouted at Harry.

The big Indian looked over the top of the magazine. By now Hilda Bryant had called the police and they were up to their asses in trouble, Harry George Junior thought. All because of Bucky Foster and his dumb ideas.

"We're all in this together," Bucky went on happily, starting to march back and forth like a mechanical toy soldier.

"In what?" Belinda asked innocently. To her, Bucky Foster looked just like the cover of a Captain Terror comic, except for those yucky pimples all over his face.

"Well," Bucky said, leaning close to her and lowering his voice to a confidential tone, "see, last night your brother and me and this Indian, we went trick or treating at Mr. Olsen's house. You know Mr. Olsen?"

"Yes," Belinda answered tentatively. He was the one who was dead. She had heard it on the school bus.

"He wouldn't give us any candy, Belinda. He was mean to us, so you know what we did?"

"No." She looked uneasily at her brother. Jeffrey seemed scared.

"Hey, Buck," Harry George interrupted, "Jeff and I weren't even there. Right, Jeff?"

"Right," Jeff agreed quickly. Maybe Harry George would help him.

Bucky Foster ignored them. He was speaking only to little Belinda Myers now, and she was fascinated. She was getting scared and he hadn't even done anything yet.

"So," he whispered loudly to her, "we pushed Mr. Olsen off his dock."

"No!" Jeff screamed, jumping to his feet. "No!" It couldn't be true. Bucky wouldn't do that. It was a bad, bad dream. It had to be.

Harry watched carefully, his dark eyes suddenly alert and wide open. What the hell was Bucky Foster talking about?

"We did," Bucky confided to Belinda, excited by her nervous little mouth that was quivering, "and Mrs. Zondich saw us, and your brother ran, but Chief and I fixed her fat ass. Didn't we, Chief?" He turned to Harry George and smiled proudly.

A resurgence of pleasure swept through him as he recalled his clever ruse with the flashlight, his deputy sheriff imitation, the scream of fear, his leaping onto her fat body. But it was all spoiled by the shit in her pants.

Harry George Junior got to his feet quickly, breathing hard. "How many times have I told you, goddamnit, don't call me Chief!" He glared at Bucky, clenching and unclenching his fists. He searched the dull corners of his mind for last night's memories.

Bucky Foster didn't answer him. Bucky didn't hear anything. The plan was unreeling swiftly in his mind. Now they were getting to the good part, Belinda's part and Mrs. Bryant's part. Just thinking about it made him hot with anticipation.

Mrs. Bryant's sentence would be an application of the Times Two Rule. She deserved it. Captain Terror would see that justice was done. The only question was, how? He could squeeze her neck. He knew the spot just under her hard face where the wrinkles showed. Or he could zap her from the air. He could swing the machine gun across its greased carriage until he saw her green eyes in the sights. The chopper would bank low over her house. By-by, gook.

And then there was Belinda. "We're gonna waste the rich bitch that lives at the top of this cliff," he confided to her, pointing up the clay bank, "and you get to help."

Jeff Myers trembled. Bucky Foster had killed Ivan Olsen. Now he was going to hurt Belinda.

"Hey, Buck," Harry George said angrily, "you hear me, man? I said don't call me Chief."

Belinda Myers backed toward the cave entrance. "I don't want to help you, Bucky," she said in a small voice.

"The tide's coming in; we've got to go." Jeff forced the words out of his mouth; they sounded weak and silly.

Bucky sneered at him. He didn't need anybody for his game but Belinda. They didn't understand why he had to hurt people; nobody did. He had to do it because people were bossy and pushed you around and made you eat their shit if you let them. Everybody was like that.

So you pushed back. It was fun to make them guess what you'd do, fun to surprise them. And then came the best part: to push down, feel them giving in, get the thrill of squeezing and shoving and jamming truth and justice down their throats.

Everybody had to die anyway; it was just a matter of who went first. Bucky Foster grabbed Be-

357

linda's wrist and squeezed—just as he'd squeezed the doggy's neck, not too hard, not too soft. Just right.

It was such a little wrist, his long pale fingers almost doubled around it. "Let's see now," he crooned, "how could you help us? How do we get Mrs. Bryant to come out and play?"

He squeezed harder. Belinda's pink flesh bunched up on either side of his tightening hand. "Stop," she whimpered. "You're hurting me."

"What kind of bullshit is this anyway?" Harry George demanded. He stood swaying in the wind, confused and angry. Did Bucky mean he had killed Ivan Olsen? Why was he pulling this little girl around?

"Hey, don't do that," Jeff pleaded. "Please don't." He broke into sobs.

"Oh, I know, I know. I've got it!" Bucky exclaimed. "We can use you for bait. It's a stormy night; she hears you crying. She comes out to look. Your clothes are all torn, you're bleeding, you need help. She comes closer. Wham! Justice is done!"

"Bucky," Jeff cried, barely able to get the words out, "please let go of my sister. Let us go home."

The water foamed up the beach toward the cave entrance. Another five minutes and they'd be trapped until the tide turned.

"No!" Bucky shouted, grabbing Belinda with both arms, pulling her to him. "Nobody leaves."

CHAPTER 45

"Sometimes I wonder if Bucky Foster shouldn't have been evaluated by a real psychiatrist a long time ago." All the way back from the Port Gloster Golf and Tennis Club, Jan Elias wondered why in God's name somebody hadn't done exactly that. His school records were a litany of failure, a laundry list of unsubstantiated and unresolved complaints. The blame clearly belonged to buck-passing school administrators and ineffective counselors like Henry Barret who would rather protect their jobs than help a child.

It had been a hellish drive, the old Triumph plowing through the heavy rain, swaying in the wind, while Jan mentally went over and over her conversation with Linda Foster. Her polo coat was soaked through on the left sleeve where the cracked plastic side curtain leaked. By the time she had pulled into her parents' driveway behind Jim's Bronco, she was exhausted.

While Jan was sympathetic to Linda Foster, the more she thought about it the more she saw extreme parental neglect as a major contributing cause to the child's instability. If Bucky's real father had been half as bad as Linda Foster indicated, Jan Elias could not understand why the woman didn't just walk out with the child. How was it possible to stay with someone who beat you?

She got out of the car and ran through the rain to the house. She went in without knocking, as was her habit, and hung her coat on the same hook she'd used since she was a little girl. The house smelled of roast beef and gravy. Jan Elias was glad to be home. After all these years, it still seemed like her home even though she hadn't actually lived there since college.

She rubbed her eyes and tried to twist the stiffness out of her neck. At any rate, Linda Foster had gone home convinced she had to come to grips with the problem and get Bucky some psychiatric help. That was a start. It was certainly the best Jan could do right now.

"You're just in time," Sonia greeted her from the kitchen. "We were about to eat without you."

"Except I wouldn't let them." Jim Wentworth crossed the room to meet her. He hugged her, pushing his pelvis against hers. It was just a suggestive little joke, but Jan was in no mood for it. With a perfunctory kiss she wiggled out of his embrace.

"How was your day?" she asked him without really caring. "I've had a hell of a day myself."

"Where have you been?" he asked her.

"With my lover," she said, as they walked into the living room.

"Honey, I wish you wouldn't say things like that."

Fred waved to her from the couch.

"Daddy, what's wrong?"

"Nothing. Nothing," he told her. "Your mother thought I looked tired, but it's just a case of old age." He sat up, threw off the blanket and gave her a kiss.

His lips felt hot as they brushed her cheek. "That's nothing to worry about," she said, trying to be casual.

"All right," Sonia called, "it's on the table."

The dining room was casually arranged, with family pictures lining the walls. Sonia's twin schefflera plants framed the floor-to-ceiling windows that looked out onto Puget Sound.

A tug and barge, its running lights fuzzy in the stormy twilight, stood just off the beach, struggling northward through heavy seas. Each time a comber hit the bow there was an explosion of white spray, and the little boat seemed to come to a dead stop, staggering under the impact before shaking off the white water in time to meet the next wave.

"I'll bet he wishes he'd stayed at home," Fred remarked, unfolding his linen napkin.

"Heading for Port Gloster," Jim said.

"He's going to be late for dinner." Sonia smiled at all of them. She was pleased to have her family together. "Fred, will you do the honors?"

They joined hands, and Fred Elias said grace as he did before every meal. "Dear Lord, we thank thee for this bountiful blessing we are about to

361

share, and for the love of a wonderful daughter, our Jan, and the privilege of sharing your blessing with our good friend, and your beloved servant, Jim. For this and more we thank thee. Amen."

"Please pass the meat," Jim said. It irritated the hell out of him when Fred threw in the beloved-servant stuff.

"First I have to cut it," Fred reminded him. "Mother, give that hungry man some potatoes."

"And now Jan's going to tell us where she's been all this time," Jim announced.

Sometimes Jan wondered if she could really stand living with Jim Wentworth the rest of her life. "Pass the peas, Dad." She ladled a few onto her plate.

"Jan?" Jim would not let it go.

"I went to see Bucky Foster's mother over at the Port Gloster Country Club. It was a long and involved conversation."

"They're not poison, honey," Sonia reminded her.

Jan Elias had never liked peas, even though her mother had insisted she have at least one spoonful with every meal when she was living at home. Jan obediently gulped them down with a glass of milk. They made her feel as if she were going to gag.

"Did you talk to the boy about riding that motorcycle?" Fred asked her, transferring razor-thin cuts of roast beef to a large serving plate.

"Yes, I did. He wasn't exactly receptive, and for that, as well as some other reasons, I went to see his mother."

"That kid give you some lip?" Jim asked aggressively, his plate heaped high with a mountain of white mashed potatoes.

"Wherever are you going to put the rest of your dinner?" Sonia asked him good-naturedly. Her rosy face glowed. She loved it when people liked her food. She was especially fond of men who ate large dinners.

Jim ladled rich dark gravy into a hole he'd excavated. "Jan, did the Foster kid get smart with you?" he repeated, annoyed at her failure to answer his questions.

Jan watched the tugboat. It shouldered its way through the storm, never giving in to the constant pressure of the wind and waves. She really didn't want to talk at the dinner table about the conversation with Linda. She wanted to discuss it alone with her father. It had been a confusing afternoon, and Jan needed advice and counsel. Fred Elias was still the best counselor she had.

"Jan," Jim Wentworth asked her again, "what did the kid say to you?"

She wanted to shout at him: Stop it! Leave me alone! But she couldn't do it, not in front of her parents.

"Bucky Foster threatened to kill me," Jan answered reluctantly. She jabbed a piece of meat from the serving plate and transferred it to her dinner plate. Two blood-red drops of juice fell on the white tablecloth.

"Sorry," she mumbled, and passed the plate to Jim, giving him a defiant look.

"He what?" Jim said sharply, gripping her arm.

She firmly removed his hand. "Bernard became slightly irrational. He threatened to kill me. I felt he was serious, absurd as that sounds, so I went to see his mother."

"Good for you," Sonia said firmly. "I certainly hope she's finally going to do something about that boy."

"What that boy needs is a good swift kick in the butt," Jim told them all, his neck reddening. "I'm going to tell that fat-assed Ed Foster the next god-damn time that punk raises his voice to you, I'm gonna personally beat his head in."

The Elias table fell silent. They all knew, Jim included, that Fred did not allow that sort of language in his house. He had explained that very carefully to Jim on several occasions.

They all turned to watch the tug as it moved northward in the darkness, its position marked only by the bobbing running lights on the mast.

"Sorry," Jim finally said. "I really am sorry. I know how you feel about profanity, but darn it all, that kid needs to be taken down a few pegs."

"He needs more than that," Jan replied quietly. "He needs psychiatric help, and that's exactly what I recommended to his mother."

"Why do you say that?" Fred asked her intently.

He hadn't touched his dinner. It waited for his fork, all neatly arranged and separated on his plate, meat, potatoes, a touch of gravy and a small mound of steaming peas.

"Because of his violent reaction to me, because of what I found in his school records, because of what his mother told me this afternoon about. . . ." She stopped.

"About what?" Jim asked.

"About her life with Bucky before she married Ed."

Jim sat back. "I'm sorry, hon, but I don't understand. Something you found in the school records? Something his mother said? What are you talking about?"

The Eliases Big Ben clock chimed a quarter of six. Fred started to intervene. He could sense that his daughter was about to turn on Jim. He could see the signs he'd learned to read: the tapping of the index finger, the tight look around her mouth. But he occupied himself by carefully sawing away on a piece of beef he had no intention of eating. He wanted to hear more about Bucky Foster.

"What I found was that Bernard, Bucky, has a near-genius IQ. I also found that he's been in trouble everywhere they moved, and they have moved often."

Jan put down her knife and fork. Nobody was eating. "He has a history of threatening people—teachers, others in authority. There's some indication he might have carried out some of these threats, that he actually hurt people. He was also in trouble on Halloween night here on the Point. He and some other boys killed one of Hilda Bryant's sheep."

Fred half rose out of his chair. "Killed one of Hilda's sheep?"

"Yes, they put spray paint on it."

Fred was standing now. "What kind of threats did he make to these other people? What happened?"

"One teacher, a woman, was almost hit by a large boulder after she had a run in with Bucky. Another, a gym teacher in Idaho, claimed Bucky—or somebody in a ghost costume—jumped in front of his truck and made him crash. He broke his neck."

365

"Jesus," Jim said loudly.

Sonia flinched and glanced at Fred, clearly worried about her husband. He was listening intently.

"Well," Jan went on, "the point is, the boy needs help and he's never received any. The system has been working against him. That's why I recommended to Linda Foster that she get psychiatric help for Bucky—immediately."

"Or maybe somebody should just lock the kid up and throw away the key," Jim said roughly.

"That never solves anything," Jan replied, the color rising in her face.

Fred Elias leaned over the table. "You know," he interrupted their argument, "in light of what you've just said, honey, maybe I'd better tell you what I've been doing today. As I already told your mom and Jim, I went to see Clara at the hospital."

Fred paused and eyed them all before he went on. "I'm convinced, absolutely convinced, Clara Zondich did not have an accident. I still think she was attacked by somebody or something."

"Hey, Fred," Jim cautioned him. "We've been over all that. . . ."

Fred Elias cut him off. "Now hold on just a minute here. The woman was terrorized. I saw her. She as much as told me so. Clara no more had an accident than Ivan Olsen did." The gnarled veins stood out in his tan, wrinkled neck.

"Fred, I don't want you to get excited all over again," Sonia told him, concern creasing her face. "You just can't allow yourself to do that."

"Mom's right, Dad," Jan added. She saw that her mother was frightened.

"I'm all right," Fred said firmly. "But I'll tell you

366

something, this feeling I have is not my imagination. There's something wrong in this neighborhood, and if you can't put two and two together, I can." Fred Elias looked directly at Jim.

Jan squirmed in her chair. "I just can't believe that Bucky could be involved somehow in what happened to Clara or Ivan. I just can't believe it."

"You don't want to believe it," Fred told her. "That's the problem. Neither do I."

Jim Wentworth was quiet now. He sat looking across the table at a picture of Fred's grandfather on the wall. The old gentleman looked back at him, with the fearless clear eyes of a God-fearing Christian, head held rigid by a high starched collar.

"What do you think, Jim?" Fred challenged him.

Jim kept his eyes on grandpa. Fred had that same look, he thought.

"Daddy," Jan cut in, "there just has to be another explanation. Bucky may be disturbed, but he can also be nice, and he's very talented."

Fred took his daughter's hand. "Honey, there are some things all the good intentions in the world can't cure. Some people, well, they're just not good people, I'm afraid."

"But he's only a boy, Daddy."

"That doesn't matter," Fred insisted. "It doesn't matter at all."

A real snake charmer—Linda's description of her late husband. Jan forced it back in her mind. Linda Foster's bad-blood argument was nothing more than mindless superstition.

"Fred, do you really believe the Foster boy did something to Clara and Ivan Olsen?" Sonia asked quietly, her faint lisp emphasizing "Foster."

"Yes."

"Now wait a minute, now wait just a minute," Jim said, leaning forward, elbows on the table. "I'm willing to buy the fact that Bucky Foster is a troubled kid, a bad kid. Jan's seen the evidence. It's in his school records."

He ticked off that point by holding out one finger on his left hand. "Apparently he's also in trouble over Hilda Bryant's sheep." Finger two came out. "And he threatened Jan this afternoon; we ought to go after him on that. I'm all for teaching the little punk a lesson he won't forget." Finger three. "But it's a long jump from there to saying he hurt Clara or killed Ivan. That's murder and attempted murder you're talking about."

He opened both hands, palms up. "You have no evidence, Fred, absolutely nothing. All you have is a bad feeling, a feeling that something isn't quite right. That doesn't count when you're talking about murder. To me it's absolutely inconceivable that a thirteen-year-old child, in a neighborhood like this, is a murderer. But that's exactly what you're saying." Jim looked around the table at them: Sonia full of motherly concern for everybody; Fred pale and drawn by his obsession; Jan flushed and very angry.

"And even if it's true, Fred," Jim went on, his brown beard showing streaks of red under the table light, "you make one hint of an accusation without something to back you up, just one hint, and Big Ed Foster will sue you for everything you've got. I know that man. He'll hit you with a lawsuit like you wouldn't believe."

"Spoken like a true bureaucrat," Jan snapped angrily. "You'd have to put your hands in the holes before you'd believe Christ was nailed to a cross."

"Jan!" her mother admonished, shocked by the sudden outburst of unChristian remarks.

It was, Jan thought, all very well for Sonia to defer to the man of the house. It just so happened her father had excellent judgment and a great deal of common sense, and Jan trusted his instincts implicitly. She could not say the same for Jim Wentworth.

"Mother," Jan said firmly, addressing her directly and ignoring Jim, "ever since Halloween night Daddy had been trying to tell all of us he felt something was wrong. Daddy's never been a person to brood over nothing or imagine he's sick or make things up. Wouldn't you agree?"

"Of course," Sonia told her promptly, recovering her equilibrium.

"Well, I think Daddy's right about this feeling of his."

"Christ on a crutch," Jim Wentworth swore under his breath, throwing his napkin down on the table and sullenly staring out the window.

"And if he's right, then we have to do something," Jan continued.

The tug was gone. Jim could hear the shriek of the wind outside, blowing the wave tops off.

Fred Elias sat down. "Jim has a point, you know," he said to his daughter thoughtfully. "We can't do anything without proof. The question is, where do we get it?"

"Maybe we could call the Fosters, or even go over there. I just don't know," she admitted.

Sonia Elias sighed heavily and picked up her

369

fork. "I really don't think that's a very good idea, dear."

Jim Wentworth turned back to his plate and shoveled a mound of mashed potatoes and gravy into his mouth. "You know, Fred, you were talking about autopsies," he said, swallowing the mixture in two gulps. "I wonder if Bryan Emulooth ever found out what killed Clara's dog? I know it sounds a little silly, but after what Jan said about the sheep I have to admit that part of it kinda bothers me."

Jan looked down at her plate. The gravy was congealed; the peas were wrinkled. She was not hungry. Now Jim was ignoring her. What an infuriating, typically male tactic, she thought bitterly. How big of him to finally admit, in the face of overwhelming evidence, that one minor little thing might just bother him, one piece of his precious puzzle didn't quite fit.

Jim Wentworth hadn't listened to one word she'd said all evening. And now he was admitting his doubts to her father, not to her. The hell with him, Jan thought, stirring the cold potatoes around. Whatever needed doing she'd have to do herself.

CHAPTER 46

The commuter traffic always peaked early on Friday, and Bryan Emulooth found himself in the thick of it all the way to Horsehead Point. It was exactly 6:30 P.M. when he turned his patrol car into the Fosters' driveway. The gusting southeast wind was stripping the remaining leaves off the alders along Horsehead Point Road, sending them hurtling across his windshield into the darkness.

It was, he thought, straightening his tie and adjusting his Smokey Bear hat, going to be another long, nasty night. Emulooth was not looking forward to talking with the Fosters about their son Bucky.

He knew exactly what Sheriff Rogers meant by "give Mr. Foster every consideration." It meant wear your dress hat and say "Yes sir" and "No sir." It meant give the boy every last benefit of the doubt. Unfortunately, Emulooth thought, checking his appearance in the rear-view mirror, I'm a country cop, not a politician.

And now on top of the original complaints from Hilda Bryant, he'd received another call en route. Mrs. Bryant claimed the boy had tried to run her off the road with his motorcycle that afternoon.

Emulooth stepped out of the car, not bothering with a raincoat. Considering the serious nature of this last allegation, he didn't know how he would handle the contact. Leaning into the wind and holding the flat hat on his head with both hands, he sprinted for the porch. All he could do was his best.

Deputy Sheriff Emulooth was in a foul mood, after only three hours' sleep. His throat was sore, and he hadn't been able to finish anything in the last twenty-four hours. He rang the doorbell and waited.

He had found the complaint filed by Ivan Olsen against Henry Soames. Henry claimed he had beaten up Olsen because Olsen had been molesting his sister Mary, a domestic, but the complaint had been dropped by mutual agreement. Emulooth wanted to talk with Mary but he didn't have time. He also wanted to talk with the vet who'd left a message for him about the white poodle he'd found last night at Clara Zondich's house, but the vet was out when he called back.

Emulooth was getting impatient. He rang again. It was a hell of a big house. Maybe, Emulooth thought bitterly, I'm in the wrong goddamn business. Finally Big Ed Foster himself answered the door. Emulooth had seen him around, but they'd never been introduced.

"Well, hello," the big man greeted him enthusiastically. "You must be Bryan Emulooth."

"Good evening," Emulooth said formally. "May I come in? I need to discuss a couple of matters involving your son Bucky."

"Stepson, actually." Big Ed clapped him on the back. "Hell of a night out there, isn't it, Bryan? Come on in."

Emulooth stepped inside, hat in hand. He didn't trust backslapping strangers who called you by your first name.

"Unfortunately," Foster said, relieving him of his hat, "Bucky's not here right now."

"Will he be back soon?"

"Sure." Foster ushered him down the hall and into the bar. "He's just out with his friends. You know how kids are; he'll be home for dinner."

"Yeah. I'd kinda like to talk to him too," Emulooth said uneasily, looking around the room. Everything was first class—a cut above what he was used to, that was for sure.

"Sit down, sit down and let me fix you something. How about a drink to take off the old chill? I think winter's here."

"I'm on duty," Emulooth replied dourly, still standing. The white carpet was three inches deep. He'd never been in a house where they actually kept booze in crystal decanters.

Foster turned and dropped the smile. He was a big, imposing man with a neck wider than his head. "Sure you are," he told him. "And believe me, son, I won't forget it."

Emulooth hitched up his pistol belt and met Big Ed Foster's look. The man was just a little too cute,

373

a little too sure of himself, like a lot of the new people on Horsehead Point. Emulooth couldn't figure out how they had made so much money honestly. But then he was only a simple patrolman, he thought.

"Might as well sit down, Deputy. The boy might be a little while."

"Might as well," Emulooth said. At least Foster had dropped the "Bryan" routine.

He sat, sinking into the soft leather chair. It dropped his ass lower than his knees, not a good position to be in if you had to get up fast. Emulooth decided to give it a few minutes. If Bucky didn't show up, he'd go up to see Hilda Bryant and her famous Rolls Royce. Another Horsehead Point heavyweight.

He had a clear set of instructions from Sealth County Sheriff Burt Rogers there too. "Whatever you do, keep that broad off my back."

CHAPTER 47

Su Myers had been running on adrenalin all day, chasing down leads on the Ivan Olsen story. It wasn't until after five o'clock that she managed to contact the coroner in Port Gloster, who confirmed in a bored voice that Ivan Olsen had, in fact, drowned.

"No wounds on the body?" Su inquired aggressively.

"Of course not," he said irritably. "Is that all?"

The doctor liked being a coroner because the patients never asked foolish questions. He didn't bother to tell her about the bruise on the skull or the red paint embedded in one eye; those weren't wounds. And neither had caused death.

"That's all for now," Su told him, determined not to be intimidated, "although we may want to talk with you again."

"Goodby," the coroner said, and hung up.

The day had gone by so fast she hadn't had time to eat, or even to think about dinner. The sight of Ivan's body, just that brief glimpse, was etched firmly on her mind—a dead man, green seaweed tangled in his clothes. It really was something. Then there were pictures, and lots of interviews.

"What did you see out there?" she had asked Jim Wentworth.

"Oh, the victim, you know. He was caught by the kelp."

The house was cold when she got home that evening; somebody had forgotten to turn on the heat. "Damn," she said, and cranked the thermostat to 75 degrees.

Su opened the refrigerator and found nothing—not a single TV dinner, no frozen chicken. She felt guilty, then reminded herself her career as a reporter was just as important as Harold's gas company job. He had to understand that.

"Kids?" she called, as she pulled down the pastry flour. They would have waffles; everybody loved waffles. There was no answer. Odd. "Hey, kids!" she shouted up the stairs.

Still no answer, but she could hear Harold's car pulling into the driveway. Thank God he was home. She had a thousand things to do. And Su could hardly wait to tell him about her story.

He came in looking pale and drawn. She kissed him enthusiastically and smelled the beer on his breath. "Been having a few on the ferry?" She meant it to be a joking accusation, not a serious one.

He hardly looked at her. "They ought to require

anybody on a state rate commission to pass an economics test," he said.

"Bad day?" Why didn't he ever ask her about her day, she wondered?

"Oh, this idiot interrupted my presentation, started arguing with me about the real price of Canadian gas. He's nothing but a cheap two-bit politician."

"That's too bad. Guess what?" she asked him eagerly. "Ivan Olsen drowned this morning. I'm going to get a front-page story, and the wire services picked it up too."

"That's great," he said wearily. "I mean it's too bad about Ivan. What happened? I'm going to have a drink. Want one?"

She remembered the children. "Did the kids call you at work?"

"No, why?"

"Because they're not here."

"Not here?" He looked at his watch. "It's almost seven. It's dark. My God, where are they?"

Why was it always her responsibility, she thought. She had a job too. I might very well ask you the same question. "I don't know," she answered.

"Jesus H. Christ! That goddamn Jeff is supposed to take care of his sister."

"Now don't get excited," she said, trying to stay calm herself.

But he *was* excited. He stormed to the garage door just off the kitchen and yanked it open. "Jeff's motorcycle's not here. That does it."

Harold Myers stormed right back. He'd come home to a cold house, no dinner and no sympathy.

377

He'd practically lost his job that afternoon—and now no kids. "Shit! It's dark. If he has Belinda out there riding around, I'll tan his ass so hard he'll never forget it."

"I'll call some of Belinda's friends," Su said, intimidated by his outburst.

He was like a madman. It wasn't her fault; they were all right together. It wasn't as if something had happened to them. Harold Myers, however, was easily frightened. He was afraid of his boss and he was afraid of his mother, but the thing that frightened him more than anything else was children. When their temperatures shot up erratically he thought they had spinal meningitis. When they failed to do exactly as they were told and were two or three minutes late, he imagined they'd been hit by a car or kidnaped by a sex pervert. When Jeff and Belinda were younger he'd checked on them two or three times a night, just to make sure they were still breathing.

Now he was panic-stricken. "Never mind," he shouted, throwing off his suit jacket with a dramatic gesture intended to demonstrate she had failed. "I'll go out and look for them myself."

His ranting upset her. Maybe she should have called home. But why couldn't Harold call once in a while? The one day, her day, when she immersed herself in her work with the concentration necessary to reach her goals, the kids took off. Harold always acted concerned, but he left the real worrying to her. As usual she'd have to take over.

"I'm going to call Fred Elias," she said.

"Fred? What for?" he yelled from the hall. "Where the hell is my slicker?"

"Because he walks around the Point every afternoon. Because he may have seen them."

"One goddamn slicker, and it's never where I hang it up," Harold raged. If something happened to his kids he would never forgive himself.

Su was already on the phone in the kitchen. He waited patiently while she called. Su always knew what to do; he had to admit that calling Fred was a good idea.

Harold reluctantly gave up the hunt for his slicker and put on a ski jacket. It was, he noted as he rushed toward the kitchen, still dirty from last season.

"Fred and Jim Wentworth are going to help us look. They're going out right now," she said, coming to meet him. "Fred is a great guy. He's always there when you need him."

"Yeah, Fred's okay," Harold Myers agreed grudgingly. It was easy to be helpful when you didn't work for a living and weren't dead tired every night.

She grabbed his arm. "Don't you have a hat?"

"No," Harold said. What did she think he was, a child? His own kids were out there somewhere. "I'll be back, you stay here," he ordered, and rushed out.

The freezing rain hit him full in the face. In a matter of minutes he would be soaked to the skin. It didn't matter; he was doing penance for not taking proper care of his children. Harold swore that if they were alive and well, he would spend more time with them playing games in front of the fire, reading books, things like that.

Why couldn't he be calm like Fred Elias? Because the old man saw everything from his narrow Christian outlook—God would take care of it. Harold had nothing against churches or God, except that in business you had to compromise.

Fred Elias did not compromise. He didn't have to. He'd saved his money; he hadn't spent it all, as Harold had, on boats, cars and houses. Fred Elias lived in another age. If Fred were out there today in the trenches where Harold was, he'd be seeing a headshrinker right now.

Harold Myers turned his back to the wind. He could feel things, sticks and leaves, flying by him in the darkness. The cold rain stung his face. He couldn't see anything. He needed a cigarette, but he'd never get it lit. Everything was going wrong. How was he going to find his children? It was useless. He didn't even know where he was. He felt like crying from sheer despair.

Harold Myers stood in the middle of Horsehead Point Road, slowly turning in a circle. "Jeff! Belinda! Where are you?" he shouted desperately.

CHAPTER 48

Bucky Foster held Belinda firmly from behind, arms wrapped tightly around her. "We're not going to hurt you," he said. "We'll just pretend."

Harry George Junior watched in astonishment as Bucky ripped open the little girl's dress, exposing her white chest.

"No!" Belinda screamed, but her tiny voice was lost in a blast of howling wind that sent a sheet of salt spray raining over them.

"Bucky, don't," Jeff Myers pleaded. He was paralyzed with fear.

"It's the only way," Bucky shouted. "She must be sacrificed." He held Belinda with one hand and tried to pull off her green tights with the other. She kicked and squirmed and then hit him with her tiny fist.

Jeff couldn't stand it any more. "Stop!" he cried,

rushing at them. Bucky caught him with a hard kick in the solar plexus, and Jeff went down in a heap.

"Hey," Harry George said, "what'd you do that for?"

Bucky Foster didn't hear him. Belinda's feeble blow only fueled his need, made his head sing with power. He wanted to squeeze the pretty little neck until her angel face turned purple. He wanted to hear her cry out in pain, again and again. He turned on the little girl and with a moan sank his teeth into her shoulder.

Belinda's piercing shriek brought Jeff to his feet. Frightened beyond reason, he rushed at them blindly, slamming his head into Bucky Foster's chin.

He folded with a groan, falling away from Belinda. Jeff felt his sister's body against him. They were free. This was their last chance. He grabbed Belinda's wrist and pulled her away.

Bucky Foster was up on one elbow in time to see them clambering over the seawall. He felt the raw wound where his teeth had torn into his lower lip.

Jeff knew the tide was too high. Whitecapped waves were breaking around the motorcycles and sucking the tangled drift of roots and logs out into the surf. In a few moments the beach would be gone.

"Come on, Belinda," he urged his sister, pulling her down the seawall.

She struggled against him, stiff with fear. "No! No!" she screamed.

Bucky got to his knees, rubbing his mouth in disbelief. Jeff Myers had hit him! "Grab her, grab her," he yelled at Harry George.

But Harry didn't move. He was finally figuring out what was happening, and he was getting a bad feeling—the kind of feeling he got when he was in serious trouble.

"Leave it alone," he said to Bucky, looking down at him.

Jeff pulled Belinda off the rock wall onto the beach. A freezing wave broke at her knees. Jeff held her up by the shoulders. "Run! Run! Run!" he shouted.

"I've got to hurt her," Bucky screamed, struggling to his feet. He was losing the delicious sensation of pins and needles in the groin. He had to get his hands on Belinda and make her so afraid she would die.

"You're fuckin' crazy," Harry said, watching him carefully.

Belinda struggled forward in the deep, slippery gravel. Another wave caught her at the waist and sent her tumbling back up the beach toward the cave.

Jeff staggered after his sister, fighting against the river of swiftly receding water cutting across his knees. He saw her coming toward him, a dark lump, face down in the foam, and he lunged, catching her by the hair.

Belinda came up, coughing and gasping. All the driftwood along the beach was shifting around them with an ominous hollow booming as heavy logs rolled into each other.

Jeff held her up until she could stand on her own. "Come on," he urged her, "we've got to get away quick." And they started off down the dark beach.

Bucky saw them running. "Get out of my way, you moron," he screamed at Harry George, trying to lunge past him.

Harry caught a fist full of the slippery Captain Terror suit in his right hand and sent a hard left bashing into Bucky's mouth. Bucky staggered back, hands over his face, blood leaking between his fingers.

"Don't call me no moron, you stupid fucker!" Harry warned him. He waited, ready to fight. "I didn't do nothing to any of those people; that was all you. You really are crazy, man, you know that?"

Bucky Foster started to whimper and sniffle, the blood streaming down his arms. "Please don't hurt me any more," he moaned.

Harry faced him. "Yeah, well, just don't fuck around with me." He couldn't think of anything else to say.

"Please help me," Bucky pleaded. "I'm bleeding to death."

The big Indian snorted. "All you have is a little nosebleed."

Bucky Foster could help himself, he decided. It was time for Harry George Junior to make himself very scarce. He left Bucky standing alone in front of the secret cave and stoically waded after Jeff and Belinda, who had already disappeared around the end of the Point.

They were staggering through freezing water that came to Jeff's armpits. He towed Belinda along by the collar of her torn dress, staying as close as possible to the band of driftwood girdling the steep cliff. Jeff could hear the driftwood shifting in the dark as the storm tide rose higher.

"Don't let go," Belinda cried weakly.

"Don't worry, I won't." His arms burned with the strain. He couldn't catch his breath in the cold water.

A wave washed over his shoulders, and Jeff felt his feet being swept off the gravel beach. Desperately he thrashed toward the bank, fighting the heavy undertow, barely able to keep a grip on Belinda.

They couldn't go any further. He led her through the churning driftwood until he felt the slime of the clay bank. The rushing water followed them in, rising to his knees before dropping again. They struggled along the base of the cliff until he found a narrow cut in the bank. The sand underfoot seemed firm. Jeff pulled Belinda into the cove and they both collapsed. He held her in his arms.

"We'll rest for a minute," he said, each word separated by several rasping breaths.

Belinda hugged him tightly, shivering. Jeff could hear the water only inches away, hissing as it crept back and forth in the sand, coming higher with each wave. They were close to safety. He could see the glow from Ivan Olsen's floodlights reaching out onto the bay. There were rafts of ducks floating just off his dock, riding out the storm.

If we were like them, Jeff thought wistfully, watching the ducks bob up and down like bathtub toys on the waves, we could fly home. But this wasn't a dream, this was real, and Jeff knew the truth now—all of it.

Bucky Foster was a murderer, and he was after them, somewhere back there in the dark. If they went on they would drown or be crushed by logs. If they stayed, the tide would cover the sand where they were sitting.

Jeff got to his feet. "Come on, Belinda," he said, pulling her up.

"Can't we stay here?" she asked weakly.

"Yes, but we've got to climb a little higher." Jeff felt along the slippery wall until his hand touched a protruding root. It curled above them, dangling from the overhanging bank, the last remnant of a tree that had fallen long ago.

Jeff pushed Belinda up and then climbed up after her. They clung to the coils of the root, heads hard against the dripping overhang, and waited as the black water rose toward them. It was as high as they could go. Jeff hoped it was high enough. He hoped somebody was out looking for them. He hoped somebody would find them before Bucky Foster did.

CHAPTER 49

Mary Soames pushed through the storm in her peculiar forward-leaning stride, knitted cap pulled low over her ears. She wasn't afraid of the wind and rain or the huge trees waving overhead in the darkness. Grandfather Soames had told her God would take care of her, and she believed him.

Mary was at peace with herself, having already forgotten the bad things that happened at Mrs. Bryant's house. Her dog Charlie trotted ahead, leading the way along the gravel shoulder of Horsehead Point Road. It felt good to walk fast, and before she realized it the floodlights of Ivan Olsen's house were splashing across the black asphalt road in front of her.

For a moment Mary thought Mr. Olsen had come back from the dead, and she stopped, unsure if it were safe to go on. Maple seeds, little wind-driven helicopters, filled the lights and whirled around her.

Instinctively she moved to the far side of the road. His ghost might be out there just beyond the floodlights, hiding in the tall grass or tangled blackberry vines. Charlie began to bark furiously at something. Then the little collie turned and started down Ivan Olsen's driveway.

"No," Mary called after him, frightened. "Charlie, no!" But the dog was gone. Timidly, she took one step across the road and then another.

"Charlie, come back," she called, turning her flashlight beam down the driveway. He was at the far end, down by the water, yipping and yapping at something.

"What are you doing down there, you bad doggy you?" she cried, going after him.

Fred Elias and Jim Wentworth just missed seeing Mary on Horsehead Point Road. They'd been out searching for over half an hour and Fred's legs were giving out on him.

"I'm getting darn worried about those kids," he shouted over the rush of the wind. Fred kept the beam of his electric lantern swinging back and forth across the asphalt road. The pelting rain ran off to either side in rivers.

Jim clapped the old man on the back and nodded as if to agree. But somewhere along the line Jim had lost his capacity for that kind of worry. He'd been on dozens of searches, and nine times out of ten the supposed victim—a child, a hunter or a fisherman—was eventually found safe and sound.

There was nothing to be gained by anticipating disaster, Jim Wentworth thought, stepping alongside Fred, deliberately slowing the pace.

"After we check this side, I think we ought to go back to the Myers'. The kids are probably there by now, drinking hot chocolate," he said, leaning close to Fred to be heard.

Fred nodded, keeping his head down. "Okay."

Jim eyed the old man carefully. He seemed to be walking slower and slower. The truth was, Jim was more concerned about Fred Elias than about the Myers kids. "Are you all right?" he asked. Up ahead he could see the firs lashing back and forth in the lights from Ivan Olsen's house.

"I'm fine, I'm fine," Fred insisted. "Let's worry about Jeff and Belinda. If they're still out in this, they're in a lot of trouble."

Jim couldn't argue with that. Fred could be a stubborn old bastard, he thought, but he had to admire his spirit. When it came to helping his fellow man, nothing could stop him except his own heart.

A hundred yards in front of them, Harold Myers was ready to give up and go home. First he'd gone north, then he'd turned back and headed south. Now he didn't know where to go. He'd never seen the wind blow this hard. At any moment, Harold was convinced, one of the giant fir trees in their yard would tear loose and drop on the house. Su was inside. He had to warn her.

He'd done everything that could reasonably be expected to find the children, hadn't he? Where could they be? Where would they go? Harold Myers had no idea whatsoever.

He started walking slowly. That's where the children must be, he thought: home. And the more

Harold thought about it, the more convinced he became that he was right. He walked faster and considered what his reaction should be when he got back and found them safe. He didn't want to fly off the handle, but if it turned out Jeffrey had been running around with Bucky Foster, he was going to lower the boom. Of all Jeffrey's friends, Harold liked Bucky Foster the least. He didn't know why; there was just something about the boy that vaguely disturbed him.

Bucky Foster stood alone in front of the secret cave, feet apart, chin thrust forward, hands on hips, shoulders arched back. The huge waves, their tops blowing off in the wind, slammed into the seawall with a shudder he could feel under his feet. Boom! Boom! Boom! The wind caressed him; he was oblivious of its chill. The rain came down; he was warm and secure inside the Captain Terror uniform.

The blood on his battered mouth had washed away, the tears were gone, he was no longer in pain. His friends—Jeff, Belinda and Harry—had deserted him, but he didn't need them. The foaming water surged around the motorcycles. Bucky didn't care. He was going up, straight up the cliff to Hilda Bryant's house to teach her the Times Two Rule and to show her the truth. But he had to hurry, while he was strong and hot. He had to do it now. Five, four. . . .

Bucky Foster turned his back to the wind and methodically ran down his checklist of weapons, lightly touching the bulge of Red Death in each secret pocket. Three, two. . . . He drew out the stiletto, holding the blade directly in front of his nose, testing it gently against his tongue. He felt the sharp bite; he tasted the warm blood. One. . . . it was carving sharp. He put it in the ankle scabbard. Zero!

Gliding noiselessly across the ledge in front of the cave, he approached the clay headwall, found a narrow path and sprang up it with catlike agility. The trail ended, but he felt a foothold just beyond and took it, stretching upward until his hand touched a slick madrona root. Long slender pale fingers curled around it and snapped tight. He pulled himself up.

Flattened against the towering wall, hanging over the rocks and breaking surf below, his searching fingers detected a niche, then another and another. On he went, higher and higher.

It was easy for Captain Terror. He was never afraid. He always won. He was always right, and he showed no mercy. None. Ever.

Bucky began rehearsing his opening lines.

"Hello, Hilda," he would say with easy familiarity. "I'll bet you never expected to see me again."

CHAPTER 50

"Charlie, you come back here," Mary Soames scolded her dog.

But the little border collie wouldn't mind. He just kept barking and running up and down Ivan Olsen's bulkhead. The waves exploded under the wooden cap, sending spray high into the air and leaving brackish pools of foam on the lawn. The ghostly white bulk of the *Thor* rose and fell, creaking and groaning against the dock.

"You be careful, doggy," she warned. But then she heard what Charlie had heard—a voice calling on the wind.

"Help, help," it called.

Mary ran her light down the bulkhead and over the water beyond. Something moved in the edge of the beam. There were two children clinging to the far bank, just above the black surging water.

"Help," they called weakly.

Mary Soames didn't hesitate. She took off her coat and jumped into the waist-deep water. The children needed her. She had to help them. Charlie swam after her, but he couldn't keep up in the rough water. "Go back, go back!" she told him.

The waves clashed in all directions, swooping and dipping in dizzying patterns, but Mary waded resolutely on, keeping her light on the children. "I'm coming," she called.

She was almost there, close enough to see their white faces, when a huge wave caught her from behind, lifting her feet off the bottom, throwing her forward. As the horrified children watched, the wave broke over her with a roar of white water and the flashlight went out. The children called to her, but Mary Soames had disappeared. Desperately, they tried to climb higher, but there was no place to go. The next wave slammed them roughly up against the overhang.

Jim Wentworth stopped on the road, listening. "You hear that dog?" he asked Fred.

Fred Elias had heard nothing but the relentless rush of the wind overhead. "No," he yelled back at the younger man.

Somewhere close behind them, a limb snapped with a pistol-shot crack. They both ducked, but nothing fell.

"I heard a dog on the beach," Jim insisted. "Come on." He started trotting down the driveway. Fred followed as fast as he could, but he was done in. His feet ached; he felt heavy and slow.

"Over here," Jim shouted. He was standing on

the bulkhead, swinging the light back and forth across the water. He'd found the dog, swimming near the bulkhead.

Fred caught up with him. "That's Mary Soames's dog. Come here, Charlie, come here, boy."

The little dog paddled toward them. Jim got down on his stomach and pulled the collie onto the bulkhead. "Hey, little fella, what are you doing here?"

The dog shook himself off, showering them with spray, and promptly jumped back in the water.

"Hey, Charlie," Jim shouted after him, "come back here." But the dog kept going, ears flat against his head, paddling over the huge waves toward the far bank.

Mary Soames was treading water in the darkness, wriggling out of her pants and shirt as she let the surge of the waves carry her toward the shore. Going under the breaking waves frightened her, but she felt better without the weight of her clothes, and she struck out toward the beach. She battled out of the troughs, swimming strongly, and felt herself speeding down the waves, being swept along faster than she could move her arms.

The closer she got to the beach, the choppier the water became; it splashed in her mouth, choking her. Mary pulled against the undertow with all her might until she saw the boy's white shirt just ahead.

It was like swimming up a river. The harder she tried, the slower she went. But Mary Soames was not a quitter; Grandpa had taught her that. She kicked and pulled and, with a final burst, got in close to the bank on a big wave.

As it rose toward the children, she reached out, grabbed the root and hung on tight. "Hello," she gasped. "Hello."

The children stared at her, uncomprehending. "Please help my sister," Jeff Myers croaked.

Mary tugged at the little girl with her free arm, but Belinda would not release her grip on Jeff. "Let go, let go," Mary pleaded.

"I won't," Belinda whined.

Jeff pried her hand off his arm. Belinda gave in, finger by finger, until she was clinging to Mary Soames.

"You come too, little boy," Mary told Jeff. "We'll go to the beach."

The children were heavy, but Mary felt strong, striding through the chest-high water. Charlie was barking somewhere ahead, helping her find the way. A light was searching up and down the bulkhead.

"We're over here, over here!" Mary called out to them.

The light swung back until it was shining in their faces. "Stay there, I'm coming," a man yelled. But Mary continued to wade, carrying Belinda. Jeff, staggering alongside her, kept slipping and falling.

Suddenly he fell up to his neck in the freezing water. "I can't feel my legs," he sputtered. Mary tried to pull him up, but he was too heavy.

Jim Wentworth jumped into the water and came out to meet them. He got Jeff on his feet and then swung him over his shoulders. "This is called the fireman's carry," he said cheerfully as he led them to the bulkhead. Jeff Myers hung limp, breathing hard.

Jim handed the children up to Fred and then helped Mary out of the water. "You did a real brave thing, young lady," he told the girl. "Your folks will be proud of you."

While the men wrapped their jackets around the children, Charlie raced around Mary, barking and wagging his tail.

"How do you feel?" Fred asked Belinda.

"Okay," Belinda chattered, huddling in his bulky down jacket. "I'm getting better!"

Jim Wentworth pulled Jeff tight against his body to warm the shivering boy. "Don't worry," he reassured him, "everything's going to be all right now."

Harold Myers stopped when he saw the lights on Olsen's waterfront. That could only mean one thing. The children weren't safe at home. They were dead! Slowly, reluctantly, he forced himself down the driveway, a suffocating fear pressing the breath out of him with each heavy step. He lowered his head and prayed as he walked.

"Please, please, please, please," he repeated over and over again.

"Daddy!" Belinda cried.

Startled, Harold looked up and saw her. "Belinda!" Jeff was there too. They were safe. They were alive. He ran to them. "Thank God, oh, thank God," he sobbed, hugging them both.

"Dad," Jeff said, his teeth chattering. "Bucky and Harry are still at the cave."

Harold pushed him back. "Cave, what cave?"

"The one on the Point. The one down below Mrs.

Bryant's house."

"Mrs. Bryant?"

"I know where it is," Jim Wentworth said. "Let's get everybody home. I'll call the fire department. We'll go get them."

The rain poured down, bouncing off the lawn like BBs. "Dad," Jeff persisted, "I've got to tell you about Bucky. It's important."

"Christ, not now," Harold said, hurriedly gathering up Belinda. "Everybody's freezing. Let Mr. Wentworth take care of Bucky Foster."

CHAPTER 51

Hilda Bryant was on her second glass of straight gin, and the more she drank the more incensed she became. She had been threatened—she was being threatened—and the authorities were deliberately ignoring her. This was unconscionable; this could not be tolerated. That woman in the Sealth County sheriff's department had assured her somebody was on the way. But here it was almost eight o'clock, and nobody had arrived.

The wind battered the little house on the bluff, blowing so hard Hilda could smell the smoke from the oil heater being forced back down the chimney into the room. She fingered her .45-caliber automatic on the table beside her. It was cold to the touch. She lifted it, staring at the oversized gun in her hands. A heavy weapon. Might makes right, she thought with dizzy cleverness, laying it gently back on the table. And she was right!

Hilda downed the rest of her gin and stood up. She was steady and calm, her body completely anesthetized. Moving like a queen, she went gliding across the living room, lightfooted and graceful. She would take control of this situation, once and for all, from the incompetents in Port Gloster.

Carefully she dialed the number of the sheriff's office. This time there would be no denying her. She had new information that would make everything clear even to Sheriff Rogers.

Ed Foster would do anything to get her property, including turning his psychopathic stepson loose to kill her animals and terrorize her. There was only one thing wrong with his crude strong-arm plan: it would not work.

The irritating ring continued. How many times had it rung? Total and complete incompetence. Finally a recording answered: "You have reached a business number of the Sealth County sheriff's office," a brittle female voice advised her. "If this is an emergency, please call 9-1-1. Thank you."

It sounded suspiciously like the woman she had talked to that afternoon. "Of course it's an emergency call, you whore," Hilda Bryant railed at her, slamming the instrument down.

At precisely that same instant there was a sharp thud against the door. She froze, momentarily confused, listening. The wind moaned in the eaves, the windows rattled. It was only her imagination; she was sure of it. How silly. She was allowing herself to become upset when in fact she felt quite serene and in control.

This would never do. You must never let others

dictate your mood, she thought. It was such a shame that people could never see her for what she really was: one of the nicest, most gracious women in the world.

"Ah, well," she said out loud, "so lonely at the pinnacle of power." And she dialed again, taking her time. 9-1-1.

"Sealth County Emergency Center." This time it was a man. Good. She always had great success at bullying men.

"This is Hilda Bryant. I would like to speak to Sheriff Rogers," she said with authority.

"I'm sorry, he's not available, ma'am. May I help you with something?"

"No, you may not," Hilda snapped. "This is an emergency."

There was a pause in the Sealth County Emergency Center. "What's the nature of the emergency, please?"

"Young man, I personally spoke with the sheriff this afternoon; I know very well that he is available tonight. He will be very displeased if you fail to put me in touch with him immediately. I have new and vital information for him."

It always worked. It was simply a matter of showing them you would not take no for an answer.

"Mrs. Bryant, may I have your number, please?"

"My number? What for?" she demanded.

"So that I can try to relay your message to the sheriff. If it's an emergency, however, you should tell me what the problem is so we can dispatch some help."

"My number," Hilda said grandly, "is 842-3356, and you may tell him that I have become aware of a conspiracy against me; that I know who the perpetrators are, and that I intend to amend my previous complaint to include this information."

"Mrs. Bryant, who was the complaint against?"

"Bernard Foster, and others. You may also advise the sheriff that his investigating officer has not arrived as promised, leaving me completely without protection this evening, a virtual prisoner in my own home. Tell him that if I don't hear back from him in five minutes, I shall call the governor of this state—a personal friend of my late husband, by the way. Do you understand?"

He paused, obviously impressed. "I'll do my best," the dispatcher said, resignation in his voice. "We do have an officer at the Fosters' right now, Mrs. Bryant," he added respectfully. "He should be arriving at your residence very shortly."

Hilda permitted herself a ladylike but horsey snort of disbelief. "Five minutes," she repeated imperiously. "Your job, quite simply, is to relay that message to Sheriff Rogers without delay. Is that clear?"

"Perfectly clear, yes, ma'am."

There. Very satisfactory. Hilda hung up.

This time it was unmistakable—a brisk rapping at her front door. Three crisp rhythmic thumps, dump-te-dump-te-dump.

Do my ears deceive me, thought Hilda, or has the errant deputy finally arrived? It was about goddamn time. "Who's there?" she asked sharply. She stood in the kitchen, waiting, but there was no answer, only the wind. Hilda narrowed her green eyes. "I said who's there?" she hurled the challenge at the silent door.

"Sealth County," a muffled voice called.

Hilda's nostrils flared. Really, what did they take her for, a weakminded fool? "Just a moment," she called back, reaching for the outside light switch.

She threw it and, with a hollow click, the entire front yard clear to the road lit up. She stepped quickly to the table and picked up the .45. The gin buzzed through her. Have a care, sir, this woman is armed.

Pistol held in the approved assault position, she cautiously approached the door, listening as her light steps set the warped floor to creaking. Nothing. Only the wind. Well, by God, she was tired of playing games. If that was a Sealth County deputy out there, he'd better identify himself properly or he was going to be a dead one. Hilda Bryant was so drunk she could hardly stand. She felt very courageous.

She was no more than three steps to the door when she noticed the blood. It wasn't just a drop or two, it was a sheet of flowing dark red arterial blood, flooding under the doorjamb, spreading out across the floor. She wrenched the door open and the sheep, which had been propped against it, fell partway in. It had been slit open from throat to anus.

CHAPTER 52

Sonia Elias only seemed like a passive woman because she graciously deferred to others. But Jan knew better. She knew that when the chips were down and Sonia finally took charge of something, there was no turning her.

The first thing her mother did was to get Fred wrapped in a blanket and drinking hot tea. Sonia said he looked gray, and she was right. Step two was getting Mary Soames dried off and into one of Fred's maroon-and-gold sweat suits. The dog, after a brisk toweling, went in the garage.

"Daddy," Jan insisted, "we have to talk to the Myers kids and find out what really went on at that cave. This is serious. It's just like the rest of the stuff Bucky's been involved in."

"Your dad is doing something," Sonia told her firmly. "He's getting thawed out."

"She's right, honey," Fred told his daughter quietly, huddling in his blanket. "Those poor kids are absolutely exhausted. They have to rest, and so do I." Fred was numb with fatigue and cold. His hands were so stiff he could barely open and close them.

"Stop talking and drink your tea," Sonia ordered. It was her special mint-lemon mixture with lots of clover honey stirred in. She turned to her daughter. "I know you're worried, honey, and so am I. But Jim's doing everything that can possibly be done. He'll find Bucky Foster, don't worry."

"Jim?" Jan Elias said the name with uncharacteristic contempt. "If Jim had listened to Daddy before, Clara Zondich might not be in the hospital and Ivan Olsen might be alive. Two lovely children were almost killed tonight." She was on the verge of tears.

"That's not fair, Jan," Sonia bristled. "That's not being fair to Jim at all. We don't know what happened tonight and we don't know for sure what happened on Halloween."

"He couldn't have known," Fred added quietly. "Your mom's got a point. He's doing his best."

"Jim Wentworth will do the right thing; I know he will. Until then, we need to carry on with what needs to be done right here," her mother said in a voice that would brook no argument. "Your father needs to rest. He's not young, but I expect him to bring home the salmon for a long time."

Sonia gave Fred the benefit of a loving smile. "And I'm going to call this young lady's family," she added briskly, patting Mary on the shoulder, "and tell them you're driving her home," she told Jan.

"Mother," she protested, "I want to stay here with you and Dad. My God, I just can't believe any of this is happening."

Sonia calmly brushed her objections aside. "Mary needs to go home, honey. And your father is in no shape to drive."

Reluctantly, Jan had to agree. There was nothing they could do until Jim found Bucky Foster. Kissing her father, she bundled Mary and the dog into Jim's Bronco and headed for the Birch Slough Bridge. As soon as she got down the driveway, Jan realized the storm was a great deal more violent than it had looked from her parents' living room.

She turned on the driving lights and peered through the streaked windshield. Huge fir boughs littered the road. The wind bumped and slammed against the jeep, causing the steering wheel to jump in her hands.

"Hang on, Mary," she said. "This could be a rough ride."

Sonia watched from the door until the red taillights disappeared. "My goodness," she remarked to Fred with determined cheerfulness as she shut the door, "what a storm."

"It's the worst one you and I are ever likely to see," he told her seriously.

"I know," she said, nervously picking up the empty teacup and napkin. "I hope Jim's all right."

"So do I."

They listened to the waves pounding in an irregular rhythm, the whistling wind, the clatter of sticks and leaves on the front window. They felt the steady shaking of the house, right down

407

to its foundations.

"Jan doesn't understand about evil in the world, Mother," Fred told Sonia, drawing her down on the couch beside him. He took her hand. It was wrinkled and nut brown but still strong. He squeezed it tightly.

"Neither did I, really, until all this happened," he went on. "We've been so happy and so lucky all our lives. I guess we never really had to face the dark side of things."

"Yes," she agreed, tucking the blanket around him, "we've had a good life, but we've also had our share of trying times, Fred Elias." Sonia was thinking about losing a son in a war everybody wanted to forget. Having five children in various small towns in Montana was no picnic either.

He knew by the set of her mouth that she was thinking about their son Jerry. "Oh, I know we've had some trials, but we always had each other, and our faith, to see us through," he told her seriously. "I was just thinking about Jan. She's so optimistic about people. She still thinks you can fix everything with good intentions and a university degree."

"She's young," Sonia reminded him. "She'll learn."

"Painfully." Fred was feeling much better. He wriggled an arm out of the blanket and put it around Sonia.

"Yes, I'm afraid so, but some of the best things in life involve pain. Children, for instance."

"Amen," Fred said.

The house shuddered in the grip of the gale winds. Sonia turned quickly at the sound of something tearing loose on the roof. An aluminum ventilator, most likely, Fred thought.

"Don't worry," he told his wife, pulling her close. "I've got this place anchored in bedrock."

"We should pray for Jim. It's no night to be out in a boat," Sonia told him, a worried concern darkening her normally rosy face.

"Yes," he agreed.

He didn't hear the phone at first, but gradually, by degrees, he distinguished the frantic ringing from the background noise of the storm. He jumped up. Nothing good could come from a ringing telephone on a night like this.

"Fred," Sonia called after him, but he was already in the kitchen.

"Fred, please come quick," a faint female voice rasped.

"Who is this?"

"Hilda Bryant. Oh God, Fred, it's awful."

"What? Where are you, Hilda?"

"Home. He killed another one of my sheep. There's blood everywhere. I can't stand it. Blood, blood, blood."

"Hang on," Fred snapped, "I'll be right there."

Sonia was beside him, holding him desperately. "You can't go."

"I have to go," Fred told her. "Call the sheriff. Tell them to get somebody up to Hilda's just as fast as they can."

CHAPTER 53

Su Myers was so glad to see Jeff and Belinda she couldn't stop talking. She pulled off their wet clothes, much to Jeff's embarrassment, and forced them both under some hot water—Belinda in the bathtub and Jeff in the upstairs shower.

"Thank God, thank God, thank God," she repeated over and over. "Oh, I love you so much; you'll never know how much."

Harold poured himself a drink and sat down in the living room. He wondered if he could ever forgive Jeff. And now that he thought about it, there had to be more to this whole incident. That was what really frightened him.

The whiskey sat in his stomach in a burning sour pool. He didn't want to find out the truth. He didn't want to know what else was involved. If it were something horrible to do with Belinda, something sexual, then he absolutely could not stand it.

He was very successful, yet there were many secret failures in his life. He heard Su moving around upstairs, chattering like a magpie. How could she ignore the ghastly possibilities, he wondered? And why wasn't she with him, helping him to cope? Harold closed his eyes in despair.

"Dad." Jeff addressed him loudly. He had a towel wrapped around his waist, his pink body was steaming, water was running all over the hardwood floor.

"For God's sake, Jeffrey," Harold shouted, startled at his son's sudden appearance. "Get dressed. You'll catch cold. How many times have I told you not to drip water on the damn floor? It warps it."

He could feel himself coming apart. It was finally happening. He hadn't intended to say any of those things, but he had. Jeff didn't seem to notice.

Jeff tried again, coming closer. "Dad, I've got to tell you something, not just about tonight, about other times, things that have happened."

Harold did not want to hear it. For Christ's sake, he thought, the boy hadn't even said he was sorry, he hadn't mentioned risking Belinda's life, he didn't care. That was damn clear, he didn't care.

"Young man," Harold told him, rising from the chair. "I hope you realize how fortunate you are that nothing happened to your sister."

"Dad," Jeff pleaded, "listen. Bucky Foster has done some bad things."

"I'm not interested in what Bucky Foster has done. He's not my son, you are, and I'm only interested in what you've done," Harold snarled. He wanted to punish Jeff for ruining his evening.

"Stop that," Su shouted at him. She was carrying Belinda, wrapped in a pink fuzzy blanket. "Stop jumping on the boy. Can't you see he can hardly stand up? Don't you understand what he's been through?"

"Christ," Harold shouted back at her, "why can't I ever say two words around here without somebody telling me I'm wrong? I'm wrong all day, goddamn it."

He got up and headed for the den with his drink, not sure what he was going to do once he got there.

"Dad," Jeff pleaded as Harold brushed past him, "you've got to listen!" But his father didn't even acknowledge him. Harold slammed the door.

"It's all right, Jeff," Su assured him, laying a motherly hand on his shoulder. "I want you to get right in bed. Your father's just tired. He was very worried about you."

"I know," Jeff insisted, "but I've got to tell him about Bucky."

"Mr. Wentworth is out looking for him right now, honey. Don't worry, you did just fine. It will all look better in the morning."

Jeff was crying. "Don't cry, Jeff," Belinda told him sleepily. "You saved me."

"That's right, honey," Su said, kissing her son lightly on the cheek, "and both your dad and I are real proud of you. You did the right thing."

Jeff had saved her. He knew he'd done his very best. But every time he closed his eyes he saw Bucky, his black Captain Terror suit glistening in the rain, grabbing Belinda and tearing her dress. Jeff clung to his mother's robe. He was

413

terrified of Bucky.

"I'll come in and sit down with you for awhile," she said kindly. "Just let me get Belinda tucked in first."

Jeff waited at the door to his room, shaking, watching the shadows of the tree limbs jump and twist on the walls in the howling wind that sent his curtains puffing out even though the windows were shut tight.

Where were Bucky and Harry George now? Would Bucky come looking for him later tonight, climbing up to his room when everyone was asleep? Jeff shuddered. He wished his mother would hurry.

CHAPTER 54

Hilda Bryant backed to the far corner of the room, as far as she could get from the advancing tide of sticky blood. The sheep carcass sprawled where it had fallen, entrails steaming, blocking the door open. The wind whirled around loose in the cabin, sending the curtains flapping.

She held the .45 with two shaking hands, keeping it pointed at the open doorway. She had badly underestimated the boy. She should have known better, after a lifetime of dealing with foreigners, many of whom looked and acted childlike while they were, in reality, murderous adults.

Hilda's designer blue jeans were dark with fresh blood, her white peasant blouse splattered with gore. The putrid slaughterhouse smell of death was everywhere. You must not weaken, she told herself, trying to steady the gun. Fred Elias is on the way.

At any moment this nightmare will be over. Fred was reliable; he always followed through.

"Come on, you son-of-a-bitch, hurry up," she muttered.

The pistol was getting heavy. It swung erratically; her hands quivered and twitched. She could not give in. She would not.

Hilda braced herself in the corner. How she hated them all: her dear late husband and his cheap little whores, her greedy children who despised her, and the dullwitted brown beach boys who would do anything for money. They always got what they richly deserved from her—complete and utter contempt. A lifetime of hating had sustained her through the worst of times and would give her the strength now to hold out against the Fosters and their multifarious evil designs.

Where was that idiot Fred Elias? The miserable little bastard was certainly taking his goddamn time. She listened, straining to catch the sound of his car. But there were too many distracting noises, things that clattered and banged and scraped in the night.

She needed another drink. She had to have one. Carefully, never taking her eyes off the open door, she moved along the wall toward the kitchen. She was getting tired, but a drink would fix all that. The gun sagged; she forced it back up. Slowly Hilda backed into the kitchen. There was the bottle with that wonderful miracle worker, waiting for her on the counter. She put down the pistol and picked up the gin bottle, lifted it to her lips and swallowed a deliciously long gulp. She inhaled the smell: another gulp.

The comforting warmth prickled through her. In just a moment she would be the old Hilda Bryant, the wonderfully imperious little rich girl sought after and loved by hundreds, literally hundreds, of young bachelors—her parents' most talented and gifted child.

The lights went out and she dropped the bottle in alarm. It hit the linoleum floor with a hollow thump. She could hear the gin running out—her lifeblood.

"No," she screamed, falling to the floor. Where was it? On her hands and knees, she searched desperately, bumping into a kitchen cupboard. She pawed the darkness, and then she heard the old floorboards creak. She paused, staring, seeing nothing, one hand in a puddle of gin.

She realized it was only Fred Elias. Of course. "Fred," she called him, staggering to her feet. "I'm in here."

It was so dark Hilda Bryant couldn't see her own hands as she groped along the counter. "I'm over here," she cried with relief, trying to put a little zing back in her voice. After all, she'd only called him to help remove the sheep carcass. If she had been somewhat excited at the time, that was understandable.

But now she had the situation well in hand as usual. "Turn on the flashlight," Hilda said irritably. My God, the stupidity of the man. She stopped. Somebody was breathing close by.

She was going to call out "Fred" again, just to confirm his presence, but the words would not come. She felt her mouth open and close but there was no sound.

417

"I'll bet you didn't expect to see me again, Hilda," a clear boyish voice said from a position directly behind her.

Hilda whirled. He was here in the room with her! Too late, she remembered the gun on the counter. There was no time. "Go away," she ordered him desperately. "Go away!"

"I just got here, Hilda, and I'm not finished yet," he crooned.

He was in front of her and getting closer. She turned and ran in the dark, slamming into the wall. Stunned, Hilda Bryant collapsed slowly on the floor.

He was over her, coming down. "I'm going to teach you something very important," he said. "It's called the Times Two Rule."

"Please," she whispered, "please don't."

CHAPTER 55

They found Harry George Junior just as he was rounding the Point, waist deep in the water, stolidly making his way through the debris and crud as though it were simply a distasteful job. Emulooth held the spotlight on him while Jim Wentworth maneuvered in close. The rubber boat pitched and yawed in the rough water.

"Hell, we ought to let him walk," Jim yelled over the noise of the outboard, giving the deputy sheriff a wide smile as they sideslipped down the side of a breaking wave.

"I don't think we'd better do that," Bryan Emulooth shouted back, not appreciating the attempt at humor.

He hung onto the lifeline with one hand and guided the light with the other. Emulooth was a poor swimmer, and the orange life jacket he was wearing did not reassure him. And he was confused. Where was Bucky Foster, and why had Jim told him the boy might be involved in more than sheep killing?

There hadn't been time for explanations then, and there certainly wasn't now. Jim Wentworth was easing the boat in toward the breakers while Harry George Junior waited in the waist-deep water, his dark eyes squinting into the bright light.

Harry wasn't pleased to see his rescuers. He had no illusions about who the law would blame for everything. Bucky Foster was white, lived in a house like George Washington's, and his father drove a big expensive car. Harry George Junior was an Indian, lived in a broken-down trailer, and his father was a chronic drunk.

Reluctantly, Harry waded deeper and stretched out his arm until Emulooth could reach him. He struggled to get in the boat, belly halfway over the side, while Emulooth pulled and Jim Wentworth backed the engine at full power.

They were on the crest of a wave that was carrying them straight toward a collision with the headwall. The outboard smoked and raced as it pulled them slowly off the wavetop and into the trough, where Jim could swing the boat around and head for open water. Harry jammed himself up against the middle seat and hung on to the lifelines so he wouldn't bounce out. This rescue was bad luck. Another fifteen minutes and he would have been long gone.

"Where's Bucky Foster?" Emulooth shouted at him through the spray.

Harry shrugged his big shoulders under the soaked leather jacket. "At the cave, I guess." Sure as hell I'm gonna get screwed, Harry thought.

"You guess?" the deputy sheriff shouted again.

"Was he with you or wasn't he?"

"He was there. I left." Harry's father always told him that when you got caught, the only way to avoid getting screwed was to squeal on somebody else quick. "That Bucky Foster's crazy as hell," Harry George Junior added helpfully.

It had stopped raining and a pale moon was trying to force its way through the high overcast. The boat wallowed in the long swells as the wind drove them south along the dark shoreline.

"I wasn't anywhere near old man Olsen. Ask Jeff Myers; we were clear up on the road. And I didn't touch Mrs. Zondich either."

"Olsen?" Jim moved the motor down to idle and turned into the wind. "What about Olsen?"

"He pushed him. I wasn't there, but he told me. He pushed him off the dock."

"Bucky Foster did that?" Emulooth asked, astonished. He wiped a cold hand across his face. His fingers smelled of gasoline.

"That's what I said," Harry replied.

"What about Mrs. Zondich?" Jim asked him.

"You know. Mrs. Zondich and. . . ."

"Hey, wait a minute," Emulooth interrupted him. "Let's find Bucky first. We're gonna get this all fucked up. I got to give this kid his rights. Come on, show us this cave," he told Harry.

The Indian gestured toward the beach. "It's over there."

Jim Wentworth gunned the motor and got the boat up on a plane. Slamming from wave to wave, they moved in close to the high bluff at the tip of Horsehead Point. The long finger of light from the hand-held spot revealed nothing except the two motorcycles still propped up on the beach, covered with seaweed.

"Where did he go?" Emulooth asked Harry.

Jim Wentworth fought to keep the little boat heading upwind; the waves hissed and broke over the side, drenching all of them.

"He was there," Harry insisted.

"Well, he's not there now," Emulooth retorted, "unless he's inside."

Jim got in as close as he dared. The current was running at full flood, and the wind-driven waves were battering the seawall right up to the cave entrance. The probing light went to the back of the cave. Bucky Foster was gone.

"Where the hell could he go?" Emulooth yelled to them both, cupping his hands to be heard.

Harry George Junior was pleased with the way things were going so far. The men were now concentrating all their attention on Bucky Foster. He decided it was time to be really helpful. "Buck was pissed at the Bryant dame. He said he was going to get her. He buzzed her on his bike this afternoon." Harry had almost slipped and said "We buzzed her."

"Hilda Bryant?" Jim asked him.

"Yeah, that's the one. He was pissed because she squealed on him for killing her sheep."

Without waiting for Emulooth to respond, Jim turned the boat back toward Ivan Olsen's dock and opened the throttle. He didn't know how he could have been so stupid. Old Fred Elias had known what he was talking about all along: something terrible was wrong. There was a murderous psychopath loose in the night somewhere on Horsehead Point, and his name was Bucky Foster.

CHAPTER 56

Now that Mary Soames was safely delivered, a new fear sent Jan Elias driving recklessly back down Horsehead Point Road. She never should have left Fred and Sonia alone in the house. Bucky Foster could be anywhere. He was capable of doing anything.

Every shadow was a potential hiding place. Jan hunched over the wheel and put the gas pedal on the floor. She knew exactly what had happened to Clara Zondich and Ivan Olsen. It was suddenly all very real to her, just as real as the overwhelming danger her father had sensed ever since Halloween night.

And he was faltering under the strain. Fred was no longer the changeless superfather she had imagined. One look at him, shivering in the blanket after bringing in the Myers kids, shattered the last of

Jan's girlish illusions. Fred's will might still be strong, but he was an old man and he needed her help to cope with this thing.

She could see the house lights and everything looked normal. Jan made a wide arc at high speed and pulled into the driveway, locking the brakes. She jumped out of the Bronco and dashed up the front walk. As she burst in the door, she was surprised to find Sonia standing alone in the entry hall looking distraught.

"Where's Daddy?" she asked her mother breathlessly.

"Gone to Hilda Bryant's. Somebody killed another one of her sheep."

"Just now?"

"Yes. She was hysterical. I begged him not to go," her mother said sadly, raising her hands in a helpless gesture.

"Call the sheriff, Mother, call right now. I'm going up there."

She didn't hear Sonia's reply. Jan dashed back to the Bronco. "Oh please, God, help Daddy," she prayed as she raced down the deserted road. She knew another dead sheep meant Fred had found Bucky Foster.

Hilda Bryant was waiting for the end. She felt drugged, beyond fear, beyond pain. She was going to die. A blazing light shone in her face.

"Are you all right, Hilda?"

"Of course," she replied languidly. What would he do to her?

"Hilda?"

"Please don't hurt me," she whispered, staring

into the light.

"Nobody's going to hurt you." He leaned close. It was Fred Elias. "Stay there and don't move."

There was a clatter behind him. He swung the light away. "Hold it," he said.

In the turning beam he caught the full profile of Bucky Foster, the Captain Terror suit ripped and splattered with mud. Bucky froze like an animal caught in a car headlight, then bolted out the door.

Fred Elias went after him at a slow lope, following the boy with his light. Bucky turned to see how close the old man was and fell in the tall grass. He climbed to his feet and started running toward the bluff, but caught his foot and fell again.

Fred kept his steady pace. As he closed in he could hear the boy gasping for breath, see his chest pumping hard as he lay in the meadow. The wind shrieked around them, coming from far out on the bay in a clockwise path from the storm center high in the icy mountain peaks.

Fred Elias felt winter in the wind penetrating his thin jacket. "It's me," Fred Elias told the boy, continuing to walk toward him.

"Get away," Bucky snarled, crabbing backward toward the edge of the bluff.

Fred held the flashlight in two hands like a pistol, and kept it on the boy's face as he advanced.

"It's me," Fred Elias repeated.

Bucky scrambled into a crouch, his face a mask of hate.

Fred stopped, his heart banging against his ribs. "I've come to stop you," Fred said.

They eyed each other, ten feet separating them. Bucky's eyes didn't waver or blink. "You—can't—

stop—me," he said slowly.

"I have to," Fred told him in a strong, clear voice. "You can't do these things anymore, Bucky."

The grass swirled around them, rippling with each gust of wind. Behind the boy and two hundred feet down, the surf beat rhythmically against the base of the cliff.

Bucky straightened up and put his hands on his hips, striking a pose. "Get—out—of—my—way, old—man," he ordered in sonorous tones.

"No," Fred said, continuing to hold the light on his face.

Bucky reached down carefully with one hand, never dropping his hard stare, and slipped the boning knife out of its scabbard along his right leg.

Fred could see that the blade was covered with fresh blood. "Put it down," he told him. "Put it down," he repeated, "and stop this."

Bucky Foster cocked the knife behind his right ear. "Let—me—go," he snarled.

"I can't do that," Fred said evenly. He braced his feet and waited.

"I'll—kill—you," Bucky threatened, pulling his arm back even farther so the elbow pointed directly at Fred Elias's heart."

"Let me help you."

"No!" the boy shouted. "I don't want your help."

"Bucky, please."

"You don't understand, Mr. Elias," Bucky told him, his voice jumping an octave. "Mrs. Bryant tried to hurt me." The knife dropped to his side. "She tried to hit me with that whip she carries. You know the one I mean?"

"I think so," Fred replied tersely. Carefully he

426

searched the meadow around him. Hilda Bryant's door was still standing open. They were alone in the pale windswept moonlight.

"She wouldn't stop hurting me, so I hit her. I had to. I didn't do it very hard, honest," he said with eager sincerity, as if seeking approval. The tears in Bucky Foster's eyes sparkled in Fred's flashlight beam.

Fred watched the transformation warily. He'd seen this act before. The pale face became animated, the thin lips pursed into a coy, childlike smile. Bucky Foster lowered his head in juvenile deference, his wet tangled hair whipping out in the breeze.

"I think maybe you hit her harder than you realized," Fred finally replied.

"I did not," Bucky insisted. Up came the head, the shoulders squared. "I was teaching her the truth." His voice dropped, the knife slowly rose from his side as if connected to an invisible string.

"Bucky, I want to help you," Fred said evenly, tensing his body so he could move quickly, "but first you have to give me that knife, please."

He had it cocked behind his ear now, quivering in his hand. Bucky swayed from side to side. "I don't need your help," he said mechanically. "People like you only understand one thing." Bucky Foster pulled himself up to Captain Terror's full height and charged, knife raised.

Fred didn't move until Bucky was close: then he stepped sideways quickly and brought the heavy flashlight down hard on Bucky's wrist, breaking the knife loose. The light went out.

The boy didn't even cry out. Before Fred could

get set again, Bucky slammed into his chest, knocking him backward and off his feet. Fred Elias hit the ground heavily, the breath knocked out of him.

He tried to get up, but Bucky was on him, clawing his face, spitting and snarling. The slippery rubber suit covered Fred's nose and mouth. He couldn't breathe. He was smothering. Gasping for breath, Fred got one arm free and wrapped it tightly around Bucky's head, holding on with all his strength. They twisted and writhed on the ground, rolling over and over.

Bucky was much stronger. He pulled and yanked and finally broke free, scrambling away in the darkness. Fred got to his knees, then forced himself to stand up. He knew he couldn't take much more.

The kick came out of nowhere, whacking into his groin. Fred's knees collapsed under him. In excruciating pain he fell forward, rolling into a ball. An irregular heartbeat hammered in his throat.

Painfully he forced himself to move. He got to his knees again and Bucky landed on him. It didn't matter; Fred knew he was dying. The paralysis had already started.

But there was one thing he had to do first. He felt for the face, the head of the monster. He found the eye and drove his thumb into it. Bucky howled in pain and fell off. Fred rolled over, pinning him down, and with his good hand grasped the boy's long hair and began rhythmically pounding his head on the ground.

A progressive numbness started on Fred's left side and crept over to the right. He must hurry. He slammed the head, harder and harder. Bucky was pleading, but Fred Elias couldn't hear him. The roar in his ears was intense, a waterfall of thick blood slowing as his body failed.

First the strength left his arm, and he stopped the up-and-down motion. Then his wrist went limp. He hung on to the twisted hair, but finally the fingers let go one by one. Bucky Foster's head dropped to the ground. Fred Elias fell over sideways into a fetal position, his knees drawn up to his chin.

"Sonia," he called. "Sonia?"

Bucky Foster started crawling. He dragged himself through the grass on his stomach, muttering as he went. Fred Elias raised one arm, just as the high-beam lights from Jan's Bronco swept the meadow. Bucky Foster came up out of the grass and into the glare, his head crushed, his face crisscrossed with dark ribbons of blood.

"Stop!" Jan shouted at him, as she jumped from the car.

He turned, dropping back on all fours, and began crawling toward the edge of the bluff. Bucky Foster was going away for good, just like his father went away. He was never coming back.

Jan Elias ran across the meadow to her father's side. "Daddy, what did he do to you?" she cried.

"Be careful," he croaked. A siren whooped in the distance.

Bucky was going back to the sea where Captain Terror lived, where it was safe. He could hear the waves calling him.

Jan stood up just as he lowered himself over the edge. "No!" she shouted.

He went anyway, finding a handhold and swing-

429

ing down. The surf pounded two hundred feet below, a long silvery line in the faint moonlight. He leaped across a vertical shaft to a tiny ledge. It was easy for Captain Terror.

"Bucky!" Jan screamed from above him.

He didn't pay any attention. It was just noise. Bucky calculated his next leap to an even smaller ledge. He was faster, braver and stronger than any of them. He jumped. Watch out! Watch out! Watch out! Here he comes! Here he comes! Here he comes! he screamed in his head as he flew through the air. She watched him fall, horrified, as he tumbled end over end, bounced once and landed on the breakwater.

A patrol car pulled up in front of the log cabin, its blue dome light flashing. Jan turned and waved at them as she ran back to Fred.

"Hold my hand," he whispered to her.

The hand was cold. "Where are your pills, Daddy?" she asked urgently.

"It doesn't matter. I tried to stop him but I wasn't strong enough."

"The pills?" she insisted.

"They're at home," he said weakly. "I just wasn't quite up to it."

"Where's Bucky?" Emulooth shouted, running up with Jim.

"He's dead," Jan told him. "He fell off the edge. He's on the rocks. You've got to help Daddy; it's his heart."

Jim Wentworth took Fred in his arms and ran to the patrol car. "You drive like hell," he told Emulooth as he propped up the old man in the back seat. Jan got in front.

Fred sucked in his breath sharply. "Tell Sonia I love her. Tell her. . . ."

Emulooth was speeding down the driveway, siren on. "Do something, oh God, do something, Jim," Jan pleaded.

Jim Wentworth crouched over Fred. "Get me a light," he told her.

Jan turned on the light while he pulled a syringe out of the medic bag on the floor.

"Did I hurt the boy?" Fred mumbled.

"You stopped him. You did what you had to do." Jim ripped Fred's shirt open.

"How we doin'?" Emulooth inquired over his shoulder, turning into Horsehead Point Road.

"Fine," Jim said. "Hold your dad's arm, honey." She reached back and held it tightly while Jim Wentworth jammed the needle into Fred's shoulder and pumped him full of Lidocaine. Fred moaned as the needle came out.

"Daddy, Daddy." Jan was crying.

"You're gonna be all right, Fred," Jim told him, bending close. "That's good medicine, and don't pull any funny stuff because I can breathe for both of us if I have to."

"We're almost there," Emulooth told them, not taking his eyes off the highway.

"You owe me a fishing trip," Jim said, "and you're not gonna get out of it."

"Okay," Fred replied faintly, closing his eyes.

Jim Wentworth reached across and took Jan's hand. "Your dad's gonna be okay, honey," he said.

HELL -O- WEEN
DAVID ROBBINS

On Halloween night, two buddies decide to play a cruel trick on the class brain...but the joke is on them.

They only want to scare their enemy to death...but their prank goes awry and one of their friends ends up dead, her body ripped to pieces.

Soon seven teenagers are frantically fighting to save themselves from unthinkably gruesome ends...but something born in the pits of hell is after them—and they have no hope of escape.

_3335-6 $4.50 US/$5.50 CAN